JUNGLE GAMES

A LINCOLN MONK ADVENTURE

TONY REED

BOOKS BY THIS AUTHOR

Lincoln Monk Adventures
Neptune Island
Jungle Games

Monk and Lee Adventures
Maclean's Kingdom
Desert Gold
Sonoran Fury

Short Stories
Mann's Best Friend

To the one and only Darby O'Shaughnessy.
Thank you for all the help, guidance, and patience.
You are indeed—a true saint.

PROLOGUE

Pittsburg County, Oklahoma
Six days before the events of Neptune Island

THE HOODED DRIVER fought to control the Mack prime mover with trailer as it slammed through the guardhouse, crushing the boom gate and obliterating the concrete façade. The spinning tires skidded over broken floorboards and mangled window frames caught below the wheels. The trailer bounced over a mound of shattered concrete and tilted off-center, teetering, before righting itself and rebounding back into line. Behind the demolished building, the guards stirred in their drug-induced stupor, unaware of the unfolding destruction.

In pelting rain the truck slewed across the waterlogged blacktop narrowly avoiding a drainage ditch running the length of the side road. Lit by occasional moonlight peeking through storm clouds, the truck thundered through the night, a cloud of water spraying from its eighteen wheels.

The balaclava-clad passenger focused on the side mirror for any vehicles from the McAlester Army Ammunitions Plant that was receding in the distance. He glanced at his watch with a conceited smirk. "Three... two... one—"

BOOM!

A giant fireball of churning flames and smoke hurtled the

charred debris of the munitions complex into the air. The passenger clutched his M-60 tighter, gaping at the billowing ball of fire rocketing skyward. The blast triggered more explosions throughout the facility, blasting roofs and concrete walls into smithereens. A set of strategically placed charges detonated in the carpark. The dozen cars driven by the nightshift exploded one after the other, somersaulting through the air in a fiery domino effect and then crashing back to earth as flaming wrecks of twisted metal.

The driver glanced at the carnage in his side mirror. He then refocused on getting the damned truck out of the county as fast as possible in the torrential rain without attracting attention or having an accident. The high-pitched whine of police sirens and the wailing of emergency services echoed across the landscape as fire and rescue trucks roared past and disappeared around the bend.

The passenger turned to the driver. "I can't believe it was that easy."

"Everyone can be bought, especially disgruntled low-paid staff. Our mysterious benefactor has deep pockets and friends in low places." With his million dollars for services rendered deposited in his Cayman account, the driver had no regrets for his role in the attack. His fee would allow him to retire to sunny Miami, a fitting goal for such an audacious and risky theft.

The passenger considered his next words. "Do you ever wonder who we're really working for?"

The driver shrugged "Don't know, don't care. He pays well, and he pays on time. That's all I need to know." He alternated his attention between the slippery road and the speedometer. With the tracking codes wiped clean, determining their route would be difficult. Nevertheless, glancing up at the sky, he considered the satellite surveillance over the military installation and the closed-camera locations around the county and prayed those pockets were deep enough.

As the early morning downpour continued, the truck turned onto Route 69 and headed south along the black stretch of highway.

The driver sighed. The assignment was nearly over. *A few hours from now I'll have a cold beer in hand and the cargo safely on the next transport to the island.* He pulled the balaclava from his head and welcomed the cool air over his sweat-covered face. "Call the number," he ordered the passenger. "Tell him we have the package."

Pacific Ocean; Northern Mariana Islands - Four days before the events of Neptune Island

HAMMERED BY DRIVING rain, the helicopter touched down on the waterlogged helipad. As the two guests disembarked, a bolt of lightning lit up the horizon, illuminating the night and surrounding jungle.

The driver of the Toyota Landcruiser parked beside the helipad opened an umbrella and ran toward the new arrivals. He held the umbrella over Tom Merrick who acknowledged him with a nod. The driver glanced at Peter Van Sant's Hawaiian shirt draped over his black military garb and figured he wasn't the type to use umbrellas, but he offered the cover anyway. Van Sant waved him off, preferring to feel the cool rain wash over his face.

The Landcruiser bounced along the dirt track, skidding on the wet soil. The driver corrected for the rough terrain and swerved back onto the trail, spraying mud and leaves behind. He adjusted the windshield wipers to full speed, but the torrential downpour, pummeling the vehicle, failed to drown out the squeal of rubber against the grime-covered windshield, and visibility was reduced to a few yards. The oppressive humidity of the tropics carried into the air-conditioned jeep. A large tree trunk, rotten with age and disease, appeared in front of the Toyota. The men braced themselves as the front tire caught its upper branch and launched the truck into the air before it crashed back down on the trail in an explosion of leaves. The driver gave an apologetic grin. "Sorry, gentlemen."

Van Sant leaned toward his side window. Beside him, Tom

Merrick dabbed the sweat from his face and turned up the backseat air-conditioning. He loosened his tie, brushed his hair back, and followed Van Sant's gaze through the water-blurred window to the tropical greenery rushing by. Van Sant turned to Merrick. "Boss," he said, indicating out the window. Merrick squinted through the rain and made out the warehouse-sized structure in the rainforest.

"Nearly there, folks," the driver announced, circumventing another fallen log. The tires continued to skid on the wet leaves carpeting the trail, but the driver managed to pull into the porte-cochere at the northern end of the building. Merrick and Van Sant climbed out of the Landcruiser and approached the giant closed doors where two men stood waiting.

Jonathan Kane greeted Merrick and Van Sant with a firm hand-shake. He waited while his security chief Leon Maxwell did the same. "Good to see you again, Tom, Peter." Kane's smile revealed pearly whites that contrasted with his dark complexion. "You're probably wondering why I asked you here today, considering that the legalities and paperwork have been agreed upon and our deal has been signed and sealed, as they say."

"Your request did pique my curiosity," Merrick said. "It's not every day that one of the world's richest men asks me to appear at a top-secret location."

"I apologize for the secrecy, but in the next few minutes, you'll understand why."

Maxwell, with his uncanny eye for deception, had been studying the men's movements and facial expressions, for anything that would give them away as industrial spies, or worse—the media. Besides being chief of security for the Neptune Corporation, Maxwell was Kane's long-time friend and confidant whose sadistic practices were legendary within the company. "Gentlemen," Maxwell said, discerning the bulge beneath Van Sant's loose-fitting Hawaiian shirt, "for safety and security, we must insist on no personal firearms in the complex."

Van Sant reluctantly handed over his Beretta 92FS.

With genuine admiration, Maxwell examined the grip's custom-made wooden insert. "Nice." He casually nodded to Kane who thanked him with a wink before entering his code into the keypad to the right of the doors.

"No sustenance is available inside, so, before we enter, may I interest either of you in a refreshing drink? The trip here is quite arduous, as you now know."

"No, thank you, Jonathan," Merrick answered.

"None for me, thanks, Mr. Kane."

"Okay, then. Let's proceed."

As they entered the enormous structure, cool air flowed over the men causing Van Sant to sigh with relief. His tours of the Middle East and expeditions into the jungles of Peru had accustomed him to heat, but the oppressive humidity of these tropical islands in the middle of the Pacific had taken its toll, and he longed for the balmy weather of Los Angeles.

Above their heads along the corridor, florescent lights flashed intermittently. Jonathan Kane glanced toward the ceiling. "Lightning struck our main generator," he explained. "This storm is playing havoc with our power supply." They made their way around a series of partitioned cubicles before the space opened to reveal a raised platform the size of a helipad. A set of steps led to a shipping container resting center stage on the platform's deck. Several armed men and a technician wearing a lab coat stood beside the container, awaiting Kane's instructions.

A smaller platform was connected to the first by a short walkway bordered by a handrail. A metal table, with multiple restraints hanging loosely from its sides, rested in its center. Several monitors and computer banks sat beside the table. Next to the steps, a pool of water had formed. Van Sant looked up to see that the retractable roof above the platform had not sealed properly.

Kane climbed the steps and turned to face his visitors. "Tom,

Peter, as you know, I have several research and development facilities around the globe, all of which are striving to create a better world and are generating a lot of excitement. As you are also aware, the Mariana government has leased Agrihan Island to me—or, as the world has affectionately dubbed it—Neptune Island. What most do not know is that the government has also leased me the top end of Northern Mariana Islands, which includes this island—Pagan Island. I have, in turn, sub-leased a portion of neighboring Alamagan Island to you.

"I have brought you here today so you could see with your own eyes my reasons for total secrecy. Gentlemen, when I say you are absolutely forbidden from landing on this island or entering the air space above, I am deadly serious. As per our contract, you are free to do as you wish with the northern end of Alamagan Island, including the beachfront below the plateau. That land is yours for the taking. However, southern Alamagan Island is strictly off limits. You are both aware of the requirements in the contract, so I don't need to go into detail. Until now you have abided by these rules, and I thank you. For the last six months your entrepreneurial funds and insight have created an exciting business opportunity, one that I hope will bring success to us both. When Leon first informed me of the proposal, I'll admit I was skeptical, but he assured me that the venture's unique concept will attract a select clientele—a clientele willing to pay handsomely for this type of entertainment. Therefore, I wish you all the best, since these locations are dangerous, deadly, and unforgiving. Do you understand these instructions?"

Both men read the contract's terms and conditions. They nodded, fully in accord with Kane's stipulation for privacy.

"I have good reason for these conditions, as I will now show you." Kane waved to a technician who tapped the keypad on the shipping container's rear doors before backing away as fast as he could. In preparation for the next phase of the demonstration, the guards pulled out electric cattle rods and stepped back, ready for action.

Merrick and Van Sant cast sideways glances at each other, unsure what to expect. Their curiosity turned to horror. With twenty feet from claw to claw and a body the size of a dinner table, a giant decapod emerged from the shipping container shackled with thick chains and screeching with rage as the chains, attached to the inside of the container, tightened around all ten legs, restricting its movement beyond the open doors.

Van Sant involuntarily jumped back. Shivers ran down his spine as he wished he still had his confiscated sidearm. Merrick gazed in disbelief at the creature before them, convinced he was having a nightmare.

Kane faced Merrick and Van Sant. Seeking their complete attention, he stared first in one's eyes and then in the other's. "Gentlemen, you see why you must and will not venture onto Pagan Island or Alamagan's southern end. My people are involved in these and other locations with many types of experiments. Do you understand?"

Maxwell approached the technician and reached for the electrical device in his hand. Aware of Maxwell's thirst for inflicting pain, the technician handed him the cattle prod and quickly stepped away from the creature. Maxwell extended the cattle prod and jabbed at the creature's unprotected flesh below the bulbous head. A bloodcurdling roar echoed throughout the building as the decapod stumbled and crashed to the metal floor. The overhead lights played along its carapace, highlighting its terrifying serrated shell. With a degenerate smile in keeping with his reputation, Maxwell gave the giant crab several hits with the cattle prod and watched it thrash about, moaning in agony. "You gotta show these crabs who's boss," he announced.

Merrick and Van Sant stared, mesmerized by the creature before them. "Are—are there any more like that thing?" Van Sant whispered.

Kane winked. "Many indeed."

"I didn't know crabs had heads."

"Ours do."

"I'll ask the obvious question," Merrick said, enthralled by the creature. "How do you raise them to be so big?" Van Sant turned to Kane, eager to hear the answer.

"Unfortunately, I don't have the time to explain the intricacies of the process. Let's just say hard research, money, and cutting-edge hybrid technology work well together," Kane said while the chains creaked in protest as the creature struggled to free itself. "Little Boy here was tranquilized a few hours ago, and he's about to wake up with one splitting headache." Merrick followed Kane's gaze and beheld the giant decapod grappling on the platform.

"This is the creature when it's *sedated*?" Van Sant stared, incredulous.

"Yes," Kane answered, keeping an eye on the platform and the technicians surrounding the creature.

"Little Boy. Fitting." Van Sant chuckled at the reference to the first atomic bomb dropped on Hiroshima in 1945. He could only imagine the damage this Little Boy could do if he ever managed to get free.

"Gentlemen, considering the work done here—and I don't exaggerate—this island is *the* most dangerous place in the world."

While Merrick continued to marvel at the creature, Van Sant looked on with deep concern. As a soldier, experiencing the world's most dangerous places was not new to him, but something was different here, something was unnatural. He shivered again. "Dangerous for sure. No doubt about it."

"Stay off this island, gentlemen, and everything will be fine. Understood?"

Merrick gazed in admiration. "Agreed."

Mariana Islands Chain - Alamagan Island
Yesterday 1:55 a.m.

As the drone of the trailbike's engine grew louder, Lockwood stumbled through the thick of the jungle fleeing the approaching whine. He clambered over fallen tree trunks, ignoring the thorny barbs of cat's claw as he frantically pushed through the vegetation. Caked with grime and dirt, Lockwood's shredded blue jumpsuit offered little protection from the underbrush. Blood seeped from his lacerated skin. He wiped the sweat from his eyes and tried not to think of the man pursuing him. The river was his last chance, his only way out of this nightmare. They had been warned repeatedly to stay away from the island's south, but he didn't care. He was willing to risk anything rather than the living hell he would otherwise face in the next few days.

Lockwood shrieked in pain as his leg collapsed under him. Blinking the sweat from his eyes, he peered at his bloodied foot, trying to inspect the wound in the poor light below the jungle canopy. A shard of broken wood, hidden beneath a clump of fronds, spiked his shoeless arch and protruded from the top of his foot. Fresh blood covered the wood and oozed from the wound. He knew what he had to do. He dragged himself to the closest tree and braced his back against the trunk. He took several deep breaths to steel himself against the pain. With clenched teeth, Lockwood gripped the bottom of the shard and closed his eyes, imagining a better time, a better place. He summoned all his weakening strength and, in one swift move—*Our Father, Who art in Heaven, hallowed be Thy Name*—yanked the shard from his foot.

Pain electrified his battered body. He clamped his mouth to stifle the cry. Tears rolled down his cheeks as he endured the agony of the wound and his hopeless circumstances. He slowed his breathing as much as his adrenaline-charged body would allow, and tearing a strip of fabric from his jumpsuit, wrapped it around the bloody wound. After taking another deep breath to regulate the pain, he grasped a tree branch for support and pulled himself up, careful not to apply pressure to the open wound.

He broke a bamboo stalk and, using it as a cane, continued into the jungle. Making headway through the thick foliage was slow with his wounded foot. The constant change of direction through the mangled undergrowth in the night confused his bearings, but he forged onward with the persistent whining from the assailant's trailbike ringing in his ears. Within minutes his enemies would find him.

The throbbing pain and loss of blood began to take its toll on his already exhausted body. Only the adrenaline coursing through his veins kept Lockwood from collapsing. He struggled through more undergrowth, and to his relief, the tangled mess of vegetation thinned.

Thy Kingdom come. Thy Will be done, on earth as it is in Heaven.

From behind a wall of trees came a thunderous roar—the river and the waterfall! For the first time since his escape, Lockwood smiled. With renewed vigor and an unrelenting drive to survive, he staggered through the foliage.

The greenery disappeared as he pushed aside the last of the fronds and paused to behold the most beautiful sight he had ever imagined. He stood on the edge of a mud embankment five feet above a rushing river. His eyes followed the flow of the river to where the white water faded into the distant black of night. The crashing cascade was louder now—just a few hundred feet down river by his estimation.

Despite the thunder of the falls and the racket of the approaching motorbike, another sound filled him with dread. The familiar low hum grew louder with every second. He hobbled back toward the jungle, trying to pinpoint the drone's direction. He looked up in time to see the unmanned aircraft fly overhead. He followed its course as it banked above the river before passing by again.

In a small, darkened office, surrounded by several monitors and keyboards, a young drone operator pushed his black-rimmed glasses back onto the bridge of his nose. Simon studied the laptop monitor while maneuvering the joystick and tapping commands into the computer. The image rotated before zooming in. The aerial view revealed a human figure standing beside a fast-flowing river. "He's standing on the bank of the river about one hundred and fifty feet north of your current position," Simon reported into his headset. He paused to check his readings and status before answering the second voice on the other end of the com-line. "Yes, sir. The digital feed is operational. We're still streaming live."

Lockwood stared at the drone, hovering just a few feet above the jungle treetop. His chance of surviving the swift waters was slim, but it was his only hope. He leaped off the muddy bank and into the river's churning rapids.

The rushing river enveloped him. Its chilled water was a welcomed comfort from the heat and humidity of the jungle, and, for this first time in days, his body relaxed. Yet he knew he couldn't allow himself the luxury of even a moment's pleasure. To evade the overhead drone and the gun-wielding biker, he ducked below the surface and swam as far as he could for as long as his lungs would allow. A short distance downstream, he surfaced and gulped in a lungful of air with the surrounding current threatening to drag him under. As the speeding river carried his hapless body closer to the watery precipice, he lost control.

Small geysers erupted in the water. Again, Lockwood ducked below the surface to evade the volley from the biker's deadly aim. Bullets sliced through the water inches from him, leaving small trail of bubbles. He felt a sudden sting to his shoulder as blood stained the water around his chest. Another bullet caught him in the neck. He clutched his throbbing throat and tried to stem the flow of blood. Because of the significant blood loss, he could no longer think clearly. His lungs burned from lack of oxygen. He had to surface.

Give us this day our daily bread—

Another bullet hit him in the torso. He gasped and began swallowing mouthfuls of river water.

—and forgive us our trespasses, as we forgive those who trespass against us. He could no longer breathe. He pushed aside the pain and clawed his way to the surface.

And lead us not into temptation.

Through the water, he could make out the full moon, high in the night sky. That beautiful white orb surrounded by the black of night gave him a glimmer of hope. He was an arm's distance from breaking the surface, from breathing in precious, life-giving air—

But deliver us from evil.

As if a giant hand had grabbed him, the water yanked his body down, down toward the riverbed. He felt himself free falling through the water, his oxygen-starved body shutting down, his vision narrowing to black. For his last seconds of consciousness, the calming cold of indifference replaced the fear of death. He was at peace with the world.

Amen.

Van Sant stood beside his KTM 690 Enduro on a rocky outcrop overlooking the falls. He removed his helmet and pushed his sweat-soaked blond hair from his face and neck. Two in the morning in the middle of the jungle with its overwhelming humidity and constant insect attacks was enough to break the soul of a lesser man, but Van Sant was not a lesser man. His former life as a Navy Seal had hardened him to the unspeakable horrors of war and death. The government did not pay well, but Tom Merrick did. Tom Merrick paid extremely well. Van Sant worked hard for his money, and orders were orders. So, although he understood the warning Kane had given them and dreaded traveling this far south having seen the potential danger first hand, he had carried out the mission.

He watched the current carry the body over the edge, where it tumbled end over end until it disappeared into the white veil of cascading water. He had to confirm that the runner was no longer a threat, so for several minutes his gaze never left the falls and the surrounding banks and river. After surveying the area and not seeing any sign of a body, he felt confident that Lockwood was dead. The bloodstained water leading up to the fall's edge guaranteed at least one bullet hit, and that Lockwood hadn't surfaced before or after he went over could mean only one thing. Besides, no one could survive that drop onto the jagged rocks beneath the foam at the base of the falls.

From his office, Simon stared at the image transmitted from the airborne drone. White water rushed over the falls and disappeared into the black of night. "Yes, sir," he replied into his headset. "I'll let him know." Simon tapped a key. "Van Sant, Mr. Merrick says the Germans want proof that he's dead."

Van Sant flung his rifle over his shoulder and mounted his bike. "He's dead." He spoke with confidence into his headset, his Southern drawl making two syllables out of *dey-id*. Van Sant waited while the voice on the other end of the communication aired its grievance. "If those boys want to come here and search downriver in the dark for a bullet-riddled corpse, they can be my guest. Otherwise, you can tell those Germans to kiss my ass."

He gunned the motor. The rear wheel spun on loose dirt as the bike roared off into the jungle and disappeared into the night.

DAY 1

CHAPTER 1

**Pacific Ocean; somewhere over the Marianas Islands Chain
Now**

THE C-47 CARGO plane lumbered across the darkening sky, a trail of black smoke billowing from the battle-scarred port engine. Hours earlier, after sustaining heavy damage from gunfire, the port engine's cowling had torn off, its flying metal shards shredding the tail fin. The aircraft, with its green-and-brown camouflage paintwork and elongated pontoons mounted to its underbelly, was a unique sight as it cut through the sunset, scattering a flock of frightened gulls in its flightpath.

"Ve are going down, but not in a good way, you know!" Roland Pom's droll German accent boomed through the cabin speakers as he wrestled the yoke, struggling to keep her steady, but the plane undulated through the sky on a path of uncertainty, her future unknown. Roland banked hard, and the aircraft dropped altitude.

Lincoln Monk tumbled across the cabin and landed in a seat against the port side. Roland ducked his head through the open cockpit and saw Lincoln staggering back to his seat where he tried to refasten his seatbelt, but the frayed material connecting the belt to the buckle had ripped apart. "Ve've had complaints about that seatbelt. You might want to change seats, you know."

"Now you tell me," Lincoln replied with a hint of sarcasm, nursing his bruised arm. "It's all good." He knotted the remaining strap ends together. Then he straightened his black baseball cap with the Neptune logo emblazoned across the brim and adjusted the T-shirt borrowed from the ill-fated observatory on Neptune Island. His black military-style trousers, acquired from a heavyset security guard who likely was now dead, were a loose fit, so he had shoved the pant legs into his boots.

"I could do with a cold Fosters right now," Mich said with a shaky smile. Long-time friend Mich Lee was scratching his wounds, courtesy of a lethal inhabitant of Neptune Island, but his eyes were fixed on the cabin window and the shattered engine beyond the streaming black smoke.

"I know what you mean." Lincoln glanced over the plane's wing and gripped the armrests tighter. "A six-pack of Coronas would go down well."

Even over the engine's drone, Marcus Enheim's gruff Cockney accent carried all the way from the plane's midsection to the cockpit. "What the 'ell's 'appenin' up there?" he grumbled, causing Napoleon to whimper from the safety of his harness strapped to Enheim's chest. While he stroked Napoleon under the snout to relax the small pug, Enhiem's gorgeous wife Katya cozied up to them and reassured Napoleon with a gentle pat on the head.

"What's your idiot half-brother up too? We should have landed hours ago."

Katya took Enheim's face in her hands and directed his view toward the window on her left. "My darlink husband, do you see any land down there?" she asked. The blue seascape that was the Pacific Ocean stretched from horizon to horizon with no sign of land.

"If he was a half-decent pilot, he would have found land—any land—by now," Enheim fumed. He soothed Napoleon by stroking the little dog's head and cooing in his baby voice, "Uncle Roland, the little wanker, and his sidekick the French Hulk are gonna get us all killed, aren't they?" Napoleon yawned.

From the back of the cabin where she sat sedated from a gunshot wound to the abdomen, Christina rested in a delirious semi-conscious state, mumbling lyrics to her favorite 70s tunes. "Mamma Mia, here I go again, my, my…"

Mich craned toward the muffled singing from the back of the cabin. "Is that—ABBA?"

Lincoln glanced at the others and marveled that this motley group had earned his trust and respect—but then, each of them *had* saved his life over the last two days. Yet, somehow, he had become the defacto team leader, the one to whom everybody looked for direction. He understood that leading these people out of danger was not only his duty but a responsibility and an honor he accepted with humility. He tipped his hat and quietly wished them luck. *We're going to need it.*

Michel Rousseau, Roland's co-pilot and chief mechanical engineer, studied the empty horizon beyond the windshield. He shook his head, his expression grim. "Mr. Pom, this is not good," he whispered, wiping the sweat from his face and across his overalls. Michel's gravelly voice struck Roland as out of place coming from one with such boyish good looks.

"I know," Roland replied, his eyes fixed on the windshield as he tugged on the collar of his turtleneck to allow his skin to breathe. He inhaled deeply on his cigarette while considering his options.

Michel, too, lit up again, and the cockpit filled with the aromas of Gitanes and cigarette smoke. He peered out the starboard side, searching for any sign of land, but the blue Pacific stretched without end in all directions. In the distance, a fog bank crept over the horizon—its misty shroud engulfing a speck of land. Michel squinted at their salvation.

"Mr. Pom, land at four o'clock!"

"Well done, Michel!" Roland checked the gauges before him.

After having dumped what little fuel they had left after the port engine explosion, they were running on fumes. In addition, the explosion had torn away the hydraulic feed lines to the wing, so oil pressure was low.

Roland spoke into his headset, "Okay, people. Good news. Michel has found an island. It's going to be a rough landing, so hold on tight." As an afterthought, Roland decided to lighten the tension that had built over the last few hours. "Ve vill be landing soon, so please place your seats in the upright position and fold back your trays. Thank you."

"Good one," Lincoln called, chuckling.

Christina moaned. Lincoln turned to see her shifting in her seat, the seat belt dangling in the aisle. He undid his makeshift belt, and, steadying himself between the headrests, made his way toward her.

Roland blew a kiss to the four-by-six of Marlene Dietrich in a seductive pose taped to his side window. "Wish me luck, my lovely." He sighed, took a long drag on his cigarette, and whispered, "Here ve go." With nerves of steel, he wrestled with the yoke and banked the plane toward the fog-shrouded horizon.

The C-47 dropped from the sky and leveled off just above the ocean waves. Roland and Michel watched as the contours of the island jungle swelled larger through the cracked windshield. A green canopy covered the island except for a narrow stretch of beach at the south end. Apart from the beach, Roland could see no place to make an emergency landing, especially with a jagged cliff looming where the sand ended. To land on the ocean wasn't an option. The pontoons were riddled with gunfire holes from the day's events, and a water landing would flood them and drag the plane down to a watery grave. The only chance was to line up the craft with the beach, land on the sand, and use the drag from the sand to slow the plane before it hit that rocky outcrop at the end.

Roland struggled but managed to bank *Ava* and maneuver her into a parallel course with the shoreline. The plane dipped lower, skimming the treetops at the beach's southern end. Palm fronds and chunks of splintered wood crashed over the wings and into the one working engine, slowing the plane's forward momentum. The starboard wing sliced into the bordering trees and foliage as the plane shot down the shorefront out of control. She slammed onto the sandy beach, kicking up a plume of fine white sand below the pontoons' floats. The rocky outcrop was fast approaching. Although the plane had slowed considerably, Roland calculated that their speed was enough to hurl them into the rocks. He had only one option. "Hang on," he yelled into his headset, "It's going to get bumpy, you know." He yanked on the yoke. The plane lurched right, then nosed headlong into the undergrowth of the jungle interior. Michel crossed himself and prayed.

Branches crashed over the wings and slammed into the cockpit's windshield, cracking the already damaged plexiglass. The plane continued into the jungle, leaving a wake of broken trees and a cloud of dust and leaves, but its momentum was slowing. The C-47 Dakota slid over a small hill and launched one final time into the air. A gnarled tree trunk filled the entire view of the windshield, and they braced for impact. The plane crashed into the oversized trunk, crumbling the nose cone. Roland and Michel flung forward as a large branch tore through the windshield between them, missing them by inches. The starboard engine still roared with life, its rotating blades slicing the ferns and vines. A cloud of dirt and shredded leaves whirled into the air before fluttering to the ground around the plane.

Roland regained his senses and throttled down on the one remaining engine. The blades slowed, then ebbed to a stop. He unbuckled his seatbelt and stood. In a friendly gesture, he put his arm around Michel. "Are you okay, my beautiful Frenchman?" Roland appeared calm, as if nothing had happened.

"Mr. Pom, how can you be so relaxed?"

Roland shrugged. He lit another Gitanes and slotted it into his favorite cigarette holder. "Vell, this is the third time I've crashed a plane, and, in this line of work, it probably von't be the last. You get used to it, you know." Roland reached behind his pilot seat and retrieved a bottle of sauvignon blanc. He passed it to Michel. "This will help with the nerves. But not too much. We need you sober, you know." Roland left Michel to gather his composure and made his way back to the cabin, cigarette holder in hand.

Enheim and Katya were still seated together, clutching Napoleon. Mich was strapped in directly behind the cockpit firewall. In the aisle at the end of the cabin, Lincoln had landed on his back with Christina lying on top of him, her crotch firmly positioned over his face, prompting Roland to reconsider the advantages of wearing safety belts.

"You two okay down there?" he asked with a cheeky smile, the smoke from his cigarette wafting lazily through the cabin.

"I'm fine," Christina mumbled as she managed to pull herself up before collapsing into her seat. The painkillers still affected her senses, making her oblivious to her awkward stumbling and surroundings. She felt light-headed and tried to shake the drowsiness from her brain and body. She glanced down at Lincoln lying in the aisle. "Sorry."

"No problem," Lincoln said, grabbing the armrests on either side and pulling himself up. He gave Roland a sheepish grin. "I know, I know, we should have been wearing our seat belts. Mea culpa." He unlatched the cargo handle and opened the hatch. "I don't know about the rest of you, but I'm ready to get out of this plane."

A wall of green plant life surrounded the C-47. The fog bank was settling in and creeping through the vines toward them. Soon visibility would be reduced to zero. He searched the jungle vista, hoping to see signs of human habitation. Nothing. The fog bank was shrouding everything in its path, transforming the landscape into a hazy, gray cloud. He was about to give up when he glimpsed a communication tower rising from the jungle canopy. Before the mist enveloped it, he calculated the tower to be about two miles away.

Before they lost their light, Lincoln assessed the damage to the pontoons. "Roland?" he murmured.

Roland's head appeared in the hatchway. "Mmm?"

Lincoln pointed at the pontoons. Roland's eyebrow raised in surprise. "Oh, my. I vasn't expecting that."

"Wasn't expecting what?" Enheim appeared and followed their line of vision. He shook his head. "Typical," he said to Roland with a curled lip.

Roland stiffened. "I flew a badly damaged plane with only one engine to safety. I landed the plane without killing us. Ve are all in one piece thanks to me. If it vasn't for my flying skills, ve would all be dead now. You should show me some respect, you know. You should be thanking me."

"Tell you what, Rolly baby, I'll thank you and show you some respect when you finish the job, okay?"

"I have no idea vy my sister married you, you know. Your ignorance towards other human beings shows no bounds. Even Napoleon respects me." Roland leant over toward Napoleon, secure in Enheim's chest harness. The little pug licked Roland on the cheek in appreciation. "You should take lessons from the dog, you know."

"You're sadly mistaken if you think I'm gonna kiss your ass."

Katya appeared next to Roland. "What's the problem, my darlink brother?"

"Your husband does not appreciate my flying skills."

Katya glared at Enheim. "Marcus, apologize to Roland. My brother just saved our lives."

"Not yet he hasn't." Enheim smirked, indicating the pontoons.

"Oh, my!" Katya clasped her hand to her mouth.

Christina nudged Enheim and Katya aside. "What's all the fuss about?" she asked groggily. She peeked out through the hatchway and giggled, indifferent to the view.

Lincoln smiled. He hadn't heard Christina laugh until now. Her chuckle had an almost schoolgirl quality that humanized her, made her more than just the assassin he suspected she was. "The painkillers will wear off soon," Lincoln said, "so, until then, could someone get Christina seated before she hurts herself, please?" Katya guided Christina back to her seat.

"What is happening back there?" Michel called from the cockpit.

Hoping to come up with a plan of action, Lincoln analyzed the situation. "It appears we haven't landed yet," he announced.

The C-47 had crashed into a copse of trees jutting from the crest of a steep ridge. The force of the impact had severed the treetops so that the plane rested on what was left of the shattered trunks. The wings, cabin, and tail were sitting fifteen feet above the ground, while the cockpit and nose hung over the edge of the high embankment. The only support for the plane's front was the gnarled trunk that had crushed the nose cone. From a different vantage, Lincoln thought, the sight would have made an irresistible photo op: a camouflaged WWII cargo plane teetering over the edge of a two-hundred-foot cliff dropping to a mist-shrouded jungle below.

CHAPTER 2

Marianas Islands Chain

An Airbus Eurocopter EC145 with the logo KSPN emblazoned down its sides flew, just above the jungle canopy, skimming the band of fog that engulfed the island. As the chopper thundered over the landscape, the rotor downwash created a vortex of mist beneath the craft that allowed the occupants quick glimpses of the exotic terrain below.

Marie "Becca" Perry slipped her dark hair behind her ear and peered through the dirty window. Her three-piece business suit conveyed an assertive, never-give-up attitude, that of a confidant and self-assured woman—and a woman reporting the biggest story of her life. Her attire, however, was a charade calculated to hide the pressure and anxiety she felt at this moment.

Shortly after the carnage and destruction of Jonathan Kane's flagship super dome, Becca witnessed a camouflaged WWII plane escaping from the doomed island. Chasing the plane was one of Kane's personal fleet of Osprey tilt-rotor aircraft. And the pilot? None other than Jonathan Kane himself! Becca watched in disbelief as Kane's aircraft crashed into the ocean. She had stumbled upon a blockbuster story—possibly the biggest of the decade. But her journalistic instincts told her that something was wrong. How could she reveal the truth about these recent events after the old plane they'd been following had disappeared somewhere in the jungle below—along with her story?

Becca turned to Roy, her KSPN cameraman. She had to give Roy credit. To keep these old-school cameras at shoulder height for a prolonged period took skill. However, as a result, he reeked of sweat and nachos, and more than a few times she had had to turn away from his distasteful body odor. "Did you see where they landed?" she asked via the headset.

Roy indicated the mist-shrouded sea of green. "Over there. The smoke trail from the plane's damaged engine disappeared behind the tree line."

She turned to the pilot. "That way," she shouted into her headset, pointing toward the island's south end.

The pilot studied the gauges before him and searched the vegetation below for a suitable landing site. At this low altitude, the fog bank rolling across the island was thickening fast, concealing the unknown topography. The dangers of flying into the cloud with zero visibility triggered his survival instincts. "I'm sorry, Ms. Perry, but we can't fly into the fog. It's just too dangerous."

"What?"

"Once I find a clearing with enough headway for the rotor blades, I'll land. Then we'll wait until the fog clears."

She leaned back in her seat, drumming her fingers in frustration as she imagined that Pulitzer prize. *So near and yet so far—*

Becca slammed against the wall as the helicopter jolted sideways to the shriek of twisting metal. A sliver of rotor-blade sliced through the cockpit, shattering the windshield. The pilot's head exploded, leaving his body jerking spasmodically in its seat.

Covered in blood and bone, Becca and Roy stared at each other in horror, unable to comprehend what had happened. The chopper lurched violently, and Roy dropped his camera. Completely out of control, the helicopter rotated laterally, spiraling earthward at an incredible speed. The turbine roared in protest as the chopper banked and dropped from the sky.

Through the cabin window, sky and jungle flashed by in a blur of color. The screech of the tormented engine sounded throughout the cabin causing Becca and Roy to cover their ears in terror. As the helicopter plunged toward the unknown, they braced themselves for the impending impact.

The chopper crashed through the forest's upper canopy and tumbled through the foliage where its tail rotor slammed into a large branch and snapped away. Becca took one last glance through the window at the ground rushing toward her when the scream of torn metal filled her ears. Her body broke away from its safety harness and catapulted across the cabin.

Becca Perry's world went black.

CHAPTER 3

"So, Monk, what's the plan?" Enheim asked in his gruff Cockney way. He was happy to put the American in charge since he trusted Lincoln to see them through this setback. Any man who would put his life in danger to rescue a small dog—his dog—was all right with him. Enheim's bald head, muscular arms, unshaven face, and bullet-riddled smiley-face shirt gave him the appearance of a middle-aged English soccer hooligan. No one would guess that he was a professor of quantum physics who had taught at the most prestigious universities in the United States and worked with top industry heavyweights in the field.

Flanked by Roland and Michel smoking Gitanes, Lincoln stood in the cabin's aisle facing the others. Christina remained at the back of the cabin, still light-headed from the medication.

Lincoln popped a piece of nicotine gum in his mouth, a gift from Mich. Ten years of smoking was too long. With all that had occurred in the last three days, he concluded life was short. He was determined to give up the habit this time, even if the circumstances were not ideal. "Okay. We'll start with the good news. The guys," he indicated to Roland and Michel, "have checked out our predicament with the plane and have informed me that all is okay."

Roland took a puff of his cigarette and cleared his throat. "Yes. *Ava* has landed on a dozen very sturdy trees. Ve got lucky, you know. The tree trunks are supporting all the major critical load points of the aircraft. The plane has no chance of slipping or falling. Her stability should be fine. However, ve can't take off with only one engine."

"Where on earth have we landed?" Mich asked.

"Our flight plan called for flying south toward Saipan, so my best guess, after looking at the map, is that ve have landed on Alamagan Island."

"Meaning?" Enheim asked suspiciously.

"Saipan is about two hundred and fifty nautical miles south of here."

"Any closer islands, inhabited or otherwise?" Mich asked.

"Pagan Island is sixty nautical miles away, but it's uninhabited. Michel is the only one with a cell phone, which is charged by the way, but we have no reception, and that means no connectivity."

Michel grudgingly held up his cell phone. The reception bar was empty.

Roland held up another phone with a thick antenna protruding from the side. "And *this* was my sat phone." A bullet had torn through its center, leaving a gaping hole.

"In addition," Lincoln continued, "a tree is now in the cockpit where the radio-set used to be." They all leaned toward the aisle and glanced down to the open cockpit door. The front end of the cockpit was crushed, and a large tree branch protruded through the windshield. Below the gnarled branch, a series of broken gauges and loose wires hung from the damaged console. "Roland tells me we weren't sending out a transponder signal when we crashed."

"What!" Enheim controlled his anger, but his tone was unmistakable. "We must have been transmitting. It's the law, isn't it?"

"Sometimes, in my line of business, I have to break a few rules. I switched the transponder to standby a while ago, and in all the chaos of the last few days, I forgot to turn it back on. I apologize, you know."

Enheim scowled at his brother-in-law.

"Even if the transponder *vas* activated, it vouldn't have made any difference," Roland said.

Enheim's eyes narrowed. "Why is that?"

"Michel didn't register a flight plan with the aviation authority when he left Saipan." Roland shrugged and looked around the group with upturned hands and a sheepish grin. "He vas instructed not to. My bad. Sorry. Old habits die hard, you know."

"Great," Enheim groaned. "So no one has any reason to look for us." Katya comforted her husband with a gentle pat on the hand.

"Sorry, people, but we're stuck here, you know, with no communication to the outside world."

"Okay," Lincoln said, considering all the facts. "This is the plan. To go out in that fog tonight would be suicidal. We don't know this island, so we don't know the terrain. One wrong step in the dark is inviting injury and possible death."

They all agreed.

"Before the fog bank set in, I spotted a tower about two miles north of here. Tomorrow morning I'll check it out."

"I'm going with you," Christina chimed from the back.

"You're not going anywhere with that—"

Lincoln paused at Christina's icy glare, the one he'd seen on Neptune Island when he'd questioned her abilities. Rather than lose the argument, he swallowed the rest of his comment.

Christina acknowledged Lincoln's change in attitude with a tilt of her head.

Before Mich could protest, Lincoln faced him. "As far as I know, you're the most capable of us all when it comes to these kinds of situations," he said, recalling the life experiences they'd shared. "But you know as well as I that you're in no shape to go trekking through the unknown. I'm sorry, but we don't know what's out there, and if the shit hits the fan, I can't have you slowing me down. Besides, I need your electronic skills to help Roland and Michel with the plane's communication system. Maybe you can get the radio working again."

Mich understood and patted the flash drive tucked in his pocket.

Lincoln turned to the Enheims. From experience he knew that Marcus could act impetuously. He had witnessed Marcus's impulsive behavior back on Neptune Island when he head-butted Jonathan Kane, one of the wealthiest men on the planet. Lincoln respected a man who stood up for his ideals and beliefs, but in the jungle, that type of behavior could get everyone killed. He needed Marcus to stay focused. "Katya, I need you to get Marcus up to speed with using guns." She nodded, understanding what had to be done. Enheim stroked Napoleon under his chin and grudgingly agreed. "You did good work back on the island, Marcus, but I think we all got lucky," Lincoln said. "Both of you will be on guard duty, so to speak, until Christina and I get back."

"Everyone needs to stay put," Lincoln continued. "Don't stray too far from the plane, and if you do explore, make sure you do so in pairs. I don't want anyone wandering alone out there. Jungle environments can be disorienting. This plane offers protection from the elements and from whatever lives on this island. Roland has checked the inventory, and we have plenty of water, food, and medical supplies—everything we need to stay alive for the next few days until we can figure something out."

He turned to Mich. "What are Christina and I looking for when we get to the tower?"

Mich frowned. "Look for a maintenance shed, or some sort of small box at the base of the structure. Whoever set up the tower would have built in a closed-link communication device that connects directly with the people involved."

"Look for a shed or a box. Got it."

"Disable it. Whoever built the tower will come looking."

"Sounds good."

Roland disappeared into the cargo compartment. He returned

with two Glock 19 handguns that he passed to Lincoln. "One for you and one for Christina, just in case. Fifteen rounds in each magazine." He glanced through the window at the jungle outside. "A gun might come in handy, you know. Think like a boy scout. Be prepared."

Lincoln thanked Roland and lay the guns beside his belt. "I figure it'll take a few hours to get to the tower and back. If we're not back by the end of the day, whatever you do, don't come looking for us. Just wait. We'll find our way back somehow. The last thing we need is for more of us to go missing in this jungle. Any questions?"

They shook their heads, satisfied with Lincoln's logic and rescue plan.

Michel cleared his throat. "I have something to say." Standing behind Roland, his hulking form dwarfing Roland's smallish frame, he took a drag on his cigarette. "I am Michel Rousseau, and my friends call me Mich. But we already have a Mich"—he tilted his head in Mich's direction—"so call me Rousseau. It will be less confusing for everyone, yes?"

"You got that right, Frenchy," Enheim said.

Lincoln surveyed the group and was met with nods of agreement. He shrugged.

"Rousseau it is. Roland, break out the food, and after dinner we'll all pretend to get a good night's sleep. Big day tomorrow."

CHAPTER 4

LEANING AGAINST KATYA'S soft shoulder with Napoleon asleep on his lap, Enheim tried to adjust the safety blade built into the trigger of the Glock that Roland had given him. "Damn these guns," Enheim grumbled as the trigger refused to pull back. He rubbed his shaved head in frustration.

Katya had found one of Roland's adventure magazines tucked in the seat pouch in front of her and was reading an article about alpine skiing in Austria. Her athletic and tanned body made her the envy of many women and the desire of all men. The tight shorts and tank top that she'd worn on the previous day's adventure, when her firearm skills had saved them all several times, accentuated her athletic form. Now her long blonde hair was pulled back in a ponytail, more conducive to her mellow mood.

Enheim glanced up and caught a look of sadness in Katya's eyes. "What's wrong, luv?"

"Nothing," she answered hastily. Too hastily.

"What do you mean, nothing? I may be a lot of things: ignorant, shallow, a pig on farm"—he smiled and softly nudged her in reference to her comment about him back on Saipan—"but I know when my wife is upset."

Her eyes welled up as she showed Enheim a picture of two skiers racing down a mountain. At first, he didn't grasp the connection between his wife and the picture. Then he recognized what the image meant to her. "The Olympic trials?"

"They're being held this week. I'm missing the trials, Marcus," she whispered, her Georgian accent more evident in her distressed emotional state. She resented the nickname her once revered peers had given her—The Catwalk Diva. She was better than that. Their taunts and vacuous attitude had driven her to be more than just a pretty face. With hard work and discipline, her dream of Olympic success—the pinnacle of human endurance—had been within reach.

Enheim appreciated the pain and effort Katya had undergone to reach the trials. The continuous training in preparation for the biathlon had consumed her life. To have competed in the winter Olympics would be a glorious achievement. He took her hand firmly between his. "How about when we get off this island and back to Saipan, I get your idiot brother to fly us to the qualifying events?"

"When we get back to Saipan it will be too late, Marcus. Qualifying trials begin today."

Enheim didn't know what to say. He would do anything, even die for her. He wanted his wife to be happy, but this situation was out of their control. If luck was on their side, they could get back to the mainland in a few hours—or they might be stuck in this jungle hellhole for some time. He preferred not to think about the latter. He looked Katya in the eye and kissed her cheek. "Luv, regardless of what happens, you'll always be a gold medal winner in my books. Always."

Katya smiled for the first time in hours. She squeezed his hand and thanked him with a return kiss.

At that moment Napoleon woke up and scurried onto Katya's lap. She picked him up, and he licked her cheek. She smiled at her big man beside her and her little man in her arms.

Christina's groan caught Lincoln's attention. The adrenaline shot she had given herself earlier had worn off, and the pain was setting in. She sat alone at the back of the plane, blood seeping through the bandage around her midriff. The pressure she applied to the wound did little to alleviate the throbbing. Lincoln wanted to help her any way he could. This stunning woman had saved his life, yet he knew hardly anything about her. After shooting her, Kane had left her for dead. Why a man of his wealth and power would harm a woman like her was beyond Lincoln, but he knew that if he didn't help her, she would die.

He unfastened his seatbelt, grabbed the medical kit from the seat next to Mich, and made his way to the back of the cabin. He noted the sweat glistening on her pale skin, while her furrowed brow and pained expression hinted at her life-threatening condition.

"What can I do to help?" Lincoln asked, opening the medical kit.

Christina peered into the kit. "Another shot of analgesic would go down well right now."

Lincoln injected the painkiller and another dose of antibiotics. He studied her abdominal wound. The bloodstain on the dressing was growing. He craned his head and maneuvered her gently so he could see her back. "Is there an exit wound?"

Her breathing was more labored. "No."

Lincoln realized that if the bullet wasn't removed soon, the wound could become infected. Christina's blood pressure would drop, and she could go into septic shock. He knew what had to be done. He looked her directly in the eye, hoping his expression would voice his thoughts.

She didn't hesitate. "Just do it."

Lincoln scanned the back of the cabin for the drinks bar Roland had mentioned earlier. He spotted the alcohol behind the open doorway to the cargo hold. "Back in a second. The analgesics will take a few minutes to kick in anyway." He reappeared with a bottle of whiskey and held it to her lips.

Christina didn't need prompting. She took a large gulp, then waited while the alcohol warmed her body. She took another swig and offered the bottle to Lincoln. "You're going need this as much as I am."

Lincoln hesitated. His police and medical emergency training that had taught him how to deal with life-threatening circumstances—stay calm and evaluate the situation—was many years ago. She was right. He took the bottle and drank, then passed it back to her. Slowly he undressed the wound. Blood was seeping from the small bullet hole in her side. Lincoln knew that opening the wound could cause enough blood loss to put her over the edge, but he had no choice. Under the circumstances, a safer time and place was unlikely; it was now or never.

Enheim watched from across the cabin as Lincoln searched the medical kit. "What's he going to do?" he whispered to Katya, keeping his eyes on Lincoln.

Katya gave Enheim a steadfast gaze. "What do you think he is going to do?" she replied.

He watched Lincoln remove the set of pincers from the medical kit and pour a sterilizing splash of whiskey over the instrument. "You gotta be kidding me," he said, as Lincoln's intentions dawned on him. He placed his hand in front of Napoleon's snout to block the little dog's view.

Katya sidestepped past Enheim and clambered to the back of the cabin where she sat opposite Christina and clasped her hand. Christina thanked her with a half-smile through the pain and held on tightly.

Lincoln wiped the sweat from his brow and handed her back the bottle. "Have a double on me," he urged.

Christina gulped another swig. She took a deep breath and looked Lincoln in the eye. "Do it."

Lincoln stared at Christina's open wound and then inserted the pincers. She flinched as the cold metal grazed raw nerves. She squeezed Katya's hand and struggled to control her erratic breathing.

"Did you ever see *First Blood*, the first Rambo movie?" Lincoln asked Christina.

She looked at him as if he was crazy. "What?"

"The first Rambo movie."

She sighed, her body shuddering from the constant pain. "Years ago," she managed through clenched teeth.

"About halfway through the film, John Rambo gets injured and has to tend to an open wound. He gets a handful of gunpowder, pours it into the wound, and lights it on fire. The wound cauterizes and seals itself. No more bleeding."

Christina stared at Lincoln, not wanting to believe the implications of his last statement.

"Personally," Lincoln continued, "I think it was Stallone's best film. He looked lean, more like a real person. He hadn't bulked up like he did for the sequels."

Katya looked at Lincoln through narrowed eyes, unsure of what he was getting at.

Focused on the weeping hole in Christina's side, Lincoln announced, "I've got good news and bad news." Without taking his eyes from the pincers, he asked, "Which do you want first?"

"Just tell me," Christina panted.

"Well, the bad news is you'll probably have a scar on your abdomen for the rest of your life."

Christina shrugged. "Emotional scares run deeper. And the good news?"

Lincoln grinned. Held tightly between the ends of the pincers was a small pellet of metal. He held it up to Christina's tormented face so she could see that the ordeal was over. "A little bit of distraction goes a long way, don't you think?"

As the tension disappeared, Christina smiled. She wiped the sweat from her face and took the pellet from the pincers. After cleaning off the blood, she placed the small piece of metal in her pocket. "A reminder," she said.

Lincoln pulled a needle and thread from the medical kit. In minutes he had sutured the wound. "It's not pretty, but you'll survive."

In the cockpit, Roland studied the branch protruding through the windshield one last time. Aided by Rousseau's natural brute strength, he and the Frenchman pushed the remaining branch back through the broken glass. Roland dabbed the sweat from his face. "Job well done Michel, I mean, Rousseau. You know, you will always be Michel to me, but for the people back there in the cabin I have to get use to the name change, you know."

"I understand," Rousseau said.

Roland retrieved two wine glasses and another bottle of sauvignon blanc from the cooler behind the pilot's chair. As he poured the wine, Rousseau murmured an appreciative *merci*. Roland tugged at his turtleneck. The small wall-mounted fan behind them circulated the warm air but offered little relief from the humidity. The wine went down well, and Roland was on his second glass when he saw Rousseau reach into his pocket for the third time in fifteen minutes. From experience, Roland knew that some of the biggest and toughest men were gentle by nature and that Rousseau was one of these men. "Maurice is getting a workout, I see," Roland said, perceiving Rousseau's nervous reaction to their predicament and seeking to console the big Frenchmen.

Embarrassed by his failure to hide his weakness, Rousseau reluctantly pulled the porcelain unicorn from his overall pocket and rested the small talisman in his upturned hand. "Sorry, Mr. Pom. Maurice calms me when I feel…" His voice trailed off, unable to finish the sentence.

Roland was mindful not to use the word *afraid*. A show of strength and compassion was needed to get them through this challenging time. "It's all right, Rousseau. I feel uncertain now, too, you know."

"My father gave me Maurice when I was a child. 'Rousseau,' he said, 'Maurice will comfort you in the bad times, but it is your head that will get you through.' At first, I did not know what he meant, but as I got older, I understood. Maurice is here to guide my soul; my brain is for everything else."

Roland leaned across the cockpit and caressed the statue in Rousseau's hand, then sat back in his seat and sipped the wine. "Vill Maurice help a gay pilot and a bunch of stranded passengers out of this mess?"

"He will. Maurice doesn't discriminate."

"That's good to hear, you know. The more help the better."

For the first time in hours Roland sensed that Rousseau had transformed from jittery to more relaxed.

Rousseau glanced down the aisle at Enheim gently stroking Napoleon's head. "Mr. Pom?"

"Yes?"

"Your brother-in-law, Marcus. He always seems"—Rousseau searched for the right English word—"grumpy."

Roland took a sip of wine. "A better word is *asshole*. That's just Marcus," he answered nonchalantly. "He's always been like that. He is good with mathematics but little else. He understands nothing of people and the needs of others, you know. He is what the French would call a buffoon."

"Yes, a buffoon. This is a good word."

Roland glanced down the aisle at his sister seated beside Enheim. He shook his head and took a gulp of wine. "She could have married better, but... You can't choose family, you know."

Lincoln appeared through the cockpit doorway. "Sorry, guys. Roland, quick question. Mich and I are thirsty. Would you by any chance have beer on board?"

"The refrigerator bar is in the cargo compartment behind the cabin, but I've rerouted the power to the avionics and the cabin, so the beer won't be chilled. But it will be cold, you know."

Lincoln gave Roland two thumbs up. "Always prepared. I like it." He noticed the figurine in Rousseau's hand. "Unicorn—cool. If you ever get the chance, check out Ridley Scott's films *Blade Runner and Legend*. Lots of his movies have unicorns." He went down the aisle and disappeared into the cargo compartment.

Rousseau carefully pocketed Maurice. Roland noticed that Rousseau was squirming in his seat. "What's wrong, Rousseau?" The hulking Frenchman averted his gaze to the lush greenery through the windscreen, unable to look Roland in the eye. "Rousseau, you have been my chief engineer and part of my business operation for three years. I trust you and your opinion. Please, vat is on your mind?"

Rousseau knew he would regret sharing what he had to say, but he understood that if he was to continue with Roland Pom, he had to reveal his true nature. He swung around in the co-pilot's chair and looked his boss in the eye. "Mr. Pom—"

"You know you can call me Roland."

"Yes, I know, but it would be unprofessional—disrespectful to our employer-employee relationship."

"As you wish."

"Mr. Pom—"

"Yes, Rousseau?"

"Earlier you said *my beautiful Frenchman.*"

"Yes. It was a term of endearment."

Rousseau hesitated before summoning the courage to speak. "Mr. Pom, I love this job. This job is the best I ever had. I did not mean to lead you on, so I must confess." In embarrassment he hung his head. "I'm not gay!" he blurted. "If you want to fire me, I understand."

The corner of Roland's mouth turned up as he eased Rousseau's worried frown with his reassuring tone. "You have no need for concern, Rousseau. I know you are not gay."

"You know?" Rousseau's jaw dropped. "How could you know?"

"You were working on the C-47 back on Saipan when the two tourists showed up in the hangar. You must have forgotten I was in my office. You invited those two buxom Austrian girls into the C-47's cockpit, and when you didn't come out for three hours, I knew you were not gay."

"You know of Sabine and Claudia?"

"Yes."

"And my preference for the ladies is okay with you?"

"Of course."

"This is good." A big grin spread over Rousseau's face. "Mr. Pom, let's have a toast."

Roland raised his glass.

Rousseau grinned. "To ladies with big bosoms."

"To big other things, you know."

Inside the cargo compartment, Lincoln found the refrigerator tucked away in the corner below several supply crates. He was grabbing two bottles when a familiar shape hidden under the tarpaulin caught his eye. Curious, he lifted the tarp. Beneath was a jet ski strapped down by several ratchet harnesses. Beside the jet ski was a crate stenciled: Life Raft—Caution Automatic Inflation. Lincoln laughed. *The man thinks of everything.* He envisioned Roland promoting his tourism business by providing clients with every imaginable option for adventure.

Lincoln slumped down next to Mich and passed him a beer. Aside from Mich's Japanese heritage, the two could have been brothers from different mothers, with both sharing the same height and athletic build. Their adventures since childhood had created a bond, a bond unbroken by time or circumstance.

Mich winced as he pulled his long black hair back and tied it with an elastic he'd found in the seat fold, no doubt left by a previous flyer. The morphine that had kept the pain at bay from his arm and leg injuries was beginning to wear off. His garish Hawaiian shirt hid the smaller bloodstains, but dried flecks marked his khaki cargo pants.

Mich moved over to the window seat and pointed to the seat he had just vacated. "No one's sitting there. It's empty."

"Yeah, I know." Lincoln ignored his offer the way old friends ignore each other. "So, what do you think?"

"Think about what?" Mich took a swig and allowed the refreshing brew to slide down his throat, sighing at this welcome distraction from the pain pulsating up his arm and leg.

Lincoln casually indicated Christina at the back of the cabin, her head resting against a pillow wedged between the headrest and the cabin wall. Despite what she'd just been through, Christina was stunning with her Asian features, tanned skin, and auburn waist-length hair, all perfectly complemented by her athletic physique. Even the bulky sweatshirt and baggy sweatpants couldn't hide her trim body. Lincoln couldn't resist the attraction he felt toward this breathtaking woman. He smiled as a faint snore of blissful sleep passed her lips.

"Don't look so obvious," Lincoln scolded as Mich craned to focus on her sleeping form.

Mich rolled his eyes. "She's asleep. I don't think she'll notice."

Wanting to keep their conversation private, Lincoln shifted close to Mich. Annoyed, Mich moved closer to the cabin's wall. "So?" Lincoln repeated.

"So *what*?" Mich took another gulp of beer.

"Well...she kissed me back at Neptune Island."

"Why the hell did she do that? Was she drunk?"

Lincoln ignored him. "I think she kissed me because I saved Napoleon from drowning."

Mich frowned as Lincoln edged closer, trapping him against the fuselage. Disregarding the grimace, Lincoln whispered, "I think she did Jonathan Kane's dirty work."

"What?" Mich took another mouthful of beer. "You think she did his laundry?"

Lincoln pointed at Mich's head and made a finger gun.

"Oh, *that* kind of dirty work." Mich glanced at Christina again, trying to assess Lincoln's apprehensions regarding the innocent-looking, petite female sleeping soundly in the back of the cabin. "Really?"

Lincoln took another quick peek at Christina.

"What makes you think so?"

"Well, for starters, she knows how to defend herself and use a gun."

"Tons of women know how to defend themselves and use a gun," Mich interrupted.

"—and a rocket launcher."

Mich's eyes widened. "Oh. I get your point."

"And those bullet wounds? Burn marks around them indicate that the gun was fired at close range. She said Jonathan Kane tried to kill her."

"She was seeing Kane?"

"In the Biblical sense."

"Wow." Mich finished the last of his beer. "And you want to know what I think about her?"

Lincoln's eyes reflected his eagerness for his best friend's approval.

"What the hell," Mich said, shrugging with indifference. "We'll probably be dead soon, anyway. Make your move, lover boy. Knock yourself out."

Lincoln smiled and leaned back in his seat. He downed some beer and was pondering his next move when he was distracted by the wall pocket. He pulled an information sheet from the pouch and studied its contents.

"Hey, Romeo." Mich tapped his empty beer bottle. "Any more where this came from?"

Lincoln ignored him. "This is cool," he said. "I remember first seeing Dakota planes in Hollywood adventure films when I was a kid. The C-47 was on my list of all-time favorite planes. Even now I enjoy reading articles about the *old bird*."

"Enlighten me," Mich said with his predictable sarcasm, holding the bottle upside down above his head and catching the last drops of beer with his tongue.

"Listen to this:

'*The Douglas Dakota C-47 is known by millions around the world for its durability and classic design. Seen in television and countless action films, the aircraft has lasted the test of time from its humble beginnings during the 1940s to the final days of the Vietnam War. Used as a troop carrier during World War II, the plane was praised for its workhorse longevity and soon became the favorite mode of cargo transport for many logistic companies the world over. To this day, the Douglas Dakota C-47 carries around the globe fun-loving passengers seeking the nostalgic charm of an era long past.'*"

Lincoln paused, considering their predicament. "Too bad today's not one of those days."

CHAPTER 5

Marianas Islands Chain: 7:35 p.m.

SAMANTHA MERRICK WAS a beautiful woman, but her looks were fading. The Botox injections and plastic surgery could hold back time for only so long, and she understood that her options were narrowing. Her relationship with Merrick, who was fifteen years younger, would not last. He would become disillusioned with her and look for a younger woman, one with beauty and the energy to fulfil her duties toward him. She did love him, Samantha told herself, but love comes in many forms. She understood his drive, and he understood her motivation. What they had together was a business partnership built on mutual respect, a relationship where both sides had a significant stake.

As the cabin cruiser rolled gently under her, Samantha examined her reflection one last time and applied the final touches in her make-up regime. She stood and turned toward the cheval mirror in the corner of the bedroom. Her black evening dress hugged her slim body, reminding her that she had once been compared to a young Audrey Hepburn. She loved that comparison. Even now, years later, she still had control over that Hepburn body, a body all men crave. She slid on her diamond earrings and adjusted her short blonde bob one last time.

The incessant chatter of insects and the sounds of nocturnal crea-tures filled the air as Tom Merrick stood watching the current rush past from the railing of his wife's hundred-foot luxury cabin cruiser that was anchored to a wooden jetty jutting from the riverbank. The full moon reflected off the tranquil water as he gazed beyond the deck's spotlights to where the river stretched into darkness, its banks lined with jungle vegetation. Behind him, tied to the stern, their his-and-her speedboats rocked with the rolling flow. He turned his attention to the waterfall three hundred yards downriver. If the anchor line were to break, his wife's beloved luxury cruiser and their home would be smashed beyond all recognition at the base of the falls, two hundred feet below the precipice. He smiled. To live is to live dangerously. He pushed his childhood of poverty on the crime-ridden streets of East London to the back of his mind, along with his years of working in an office in a nondescript building for a nondescript company. Tom Merrick controlled his life and his destiny, and that's the way he liked it—*absolute control*—no matter what the cost.

He focused on the once abandoned hotel, now reconstructed and overlooking the crest of the falls. He raked his fingers through his short black hair, meticulously trimmed, and basked in the glory of his magnificent achievement. The site was fully operational and ready for visitors.

A different kind of visitor.

"Tom." Merrick turned to behold a vision of beauty gracing the doorway. His face lit up as only a proud husband's could at the sight of his stunning wife.

Samantha glided across the deck to stand beside her husband. "I've had Chef Fabienne prepare your favorite dish, crab tourteau."

Merrick smiled and returned to the vista before them. "What do you see?" She followed his line of sight over the landscape as he indicated their surroundings.

"You mean, apart from the two-hundred-foot waterfall just a few yards away?" she teased.

Merrick laughed and gave her a warm hug. "Fear is good. Fear keeps us alive. It makes us *feel* alive."

"I know," she replied as the tingling sensation of danger and sexual arousal warmed her from within. She caressed the railing, admiring the boat's sleek design and contours. Her deceased father's boat was now her boat—not her greedy siblings', but hers. "Just keep my baby safe," she warned Merrick with a smile.

"Of course I will." He turned his attention to the view. "What else do you see?"

By his admiring gaze at the panorama before him, Samantha knew that her husband was fishing for compliments. She had seen that expression on his face years before with another business plan before it failed. This venture was different—unique—a sure-fire winner. "I see clients eager for a front-row seat," she said, watching the evening fog roll in across the island, obscuring the hotel's visibility.

"Yes, in six months we've achieved the unimaginable." Merrick beamed, marveling at their accomplishment. Situated beside the waterfall and perched majestically on the plateau's edge, the ten-story hotel commanded a spectacular view. Rooftop floodlights swept the sky, while below, the five-story glass atrium reflected the moonlight across the manicured lawns, casting the grounds and the hotel's façade in a glowing night light. Lights from the guestrooms silhouetted those on their balconies. Merrick cursed as the mist enveloped the cabin cruiser, obstructing the breathtaking scene.

From the shoulder holster beneath his Armani jacket, Tom Merrick pulled a Baikal MP-71 pistol, a favorite from his days of petty crime. "This is why we're here. We live in exciting times, Samantha, very exciting times." He took aim at the river below. "The world is changing every day. Every day technology is changing." He allowed for the refraction of the water, adjusted his sight, and fired. Seconds later, a giant barracuda floated to the surface, a large hole in its head. Carried by the running river, the dead carcass disappeared into the night and over the falls. "But humans never change," Merrick added, gazing toward the human silhouettes on the balconies. "Do you know how to succeed in this world?"

Samantha had heard Merrick's motto a hundred times. She knew she would hear it a hundred times more. "Tell me again," she said, reaffirming his abilities and his ego.

"Always one-up," he whispered.

"Always one-up."

Samantha hesitated, knowing her husband's sales pitch could have gone either way. "And the Russians?"

"They pulled out of the presentation."

"Why?"

Merrick clenched his fists but held back the anger that had built over the lost opportunity. "Uri said they preferred to focus on their business in the United States."

"Their loss," she assured him with a kiss on the cheek.

"That's right, their loss."

"It's a shame we had Chef Fabienne stock every guest room with that expensive Russian champagne. What a waste."

"I'm sure some of the other guests will appreciate Sovetskoye Igristoye."

"I'm sure they will. Rumor has it the English woman enjoys her alcohol."

Merrick pushed the disappointment to the back of his mind. "My franchise will make us billionaires. Our time is now. Like shooting fish in a barrel."

Merrick hugged Samantha tighter and smiled, enjoying the analogy for his business venture. He tucked the gun back into the shoulder holster as the deep thumping of rotor blades, growing steadily louder, filled the night air.

Samantha grinned. "Last but not least. Our English guests have arrived."

Merrick returned her smile. "Our lives are about to change."

"Are you ready?"

"Am I ready?" he asked in mock amusement. "Are *you* ready for wealth beyond your wildest dreams?"

The thumping reached a crescendo as the chopper swept overhead and prepared to land on one of the helipads behind the hotel. The helicopter banked across the river, disappeared behind the hotel, and touched down out of sight.

"We're both overdue for success." Samantha grinned a wicked smile. She straightened Merrick's jacket and wiped away flecks of dust from the lapel. Locking her arm through his, she gazed into her husband's storm blue eyes. "Mr. Merrick, I believe our future awaits."

Merrick took one last look at the hotel. "Yes, our future awaits." They stepped onto the jetty and made their way to the idling helicopter.

DAY 2

CHAPTER 6

SEDUCED BY ITS beauty and charm, Lincoln associated the jungle with adventure and mystery. He recalled the films of his childhood that he still loved watching—those with Tarzan swinging through the trees and outwitting the evil ivory traders, or with archaeologist Indiana Jones searching for ancient temples and lost cities. Seeing the jungle through rose-colored glasses, he was oblivious to its reality: life-sucking insects, deadly creatures, and unbearable steaminess.

As Christina powered ahead with her sweatshirt tied tightly around her trim waist, Lincoln couldn't help noticing her auburn hair swaying from side to side across the small of her back. "How's the wound?" he asked, trying to ignore the seductive vision before him, combined with the overwhelming humidity and sweat flowing from his every pore.

"Fine."

"So, you're an ABBA fan."

"What?"

"You're an ABBA fan."

"What gives you that idea?"

"I heard you singing before the crash landing."

"You need your hearing checked."

"We all heard you singing."

"Yeah, right."

"It's true."

"I'm telling you for the last time, I don't sing."

"Look, you can deny it all you like, but we all heard you singing "Mamma Mia." You *were* on some pretty heavy medication."

Christina shot Lincoln a glare that Medusa would have envied. *"I—don't—sing."*

Lincoln held up his hands in surrender at the finality in her tone. "I'm sorry. My bad. I'll inform the crew that we all need to visit an otolaryngologist."

Exasperated, Christina shook her head and focused on the trail.

"So," Lincoln continued, "are we going to talk about it?"

"Talk about what?"

"The kiss."

"Kiss? What kiss?"

"You kissed me back in the Duck, when we were escaping Neptune Island."

The corners of her lips curled up. How could she forget that kiss in the small boat? Lincoln had not only saved Napoleon from drowning, but he then put himself in danger by convincing her to leave the doomed craft before he did. Nevertheless, she rolled her eyes and shrugged. "Oh, that. Saving the little dog was very gallant of you."

"So what your saying is—you kissed me because I saved Napoleon?"

I've got to give him credit; he's persistent. "Yes." She hesitated. "Who could refuse a man who saves small dogs and rescues damsels in distress? You," she added with a touch of sarcasm, "are my knight in shining armor."

Lincoln sensed that Christina wasn't telling the complete truth. He had heard that sarcasm was the response of a dull mind, but he didn't believe it for a second. He'd always found satiric wit entertaining; Joan Rivers was proof of that. Christina's hesitation prompted his suspicions. He understood that she would have a wall around her emotions—possibly an impenetrable wall. Her ex-lover, Jonathan

Kane, had tried to kill her and had left her for dead. Under those circumstances, Lincoln would have felt guarded, too. Maybe some spark existed between them, maybe not. He couldn't be sure, but he hoped they had a connection. "Still," he pressed on, "the fact is you kissed me. I can't help thinking that kiss was more than an impetuous reaction to chivalry."

Christina continued down the trail, then paused to call back, "Tell you what, handsome. Next time I kiss you, you can consider it our first date."

Lincoln grinned. *She called me handsome.*

They followed the trail around a small hillock and halted. Before them, beneath a crumpled communications tower, lay the wreckage of an inverted helicopter. Black smoke drifted from the cabin, crushed beneath the steel girders. Lincoln concluded that the chopper's impact had toppled the tower, burying its top in a gaping hole in the ground.

Lincoln and Christina levered away a sheet of bent fuselage covering the side. The unoccupied cockpit, sliced down the center, was a jumble of tangled wires and shattered avionic instruments. Blood covered the empty cabin and dripped from the floor lining that now served as the roof. Lincoln tried to distinguish the letter markings on the tail, but the fuselage had crumpled back on itself making identification impossible. He spotted the rotors that had been torn from their turbine mounts, and were embedded in the surrounding tree trunks.

Hoping to find the occupants, Lincoln surveyed the immediate vegetation. Beneath a nearby palm and atop a fresh mound of damp dirt, he found a makeshift cross, its two sticks fastened with duct tape. Impaled on the cross was a card, flapping in the breeze. "It's the pilot's license," he called to Christina. "He worked for KSPN back on Saipan. Looks like the fog claimed another victim."

Christina emerged from the cabin. "From the way the front of the chopper is damaged, it seems that the pilot flew into the tower.

The rotor blades would have killed him instantly. A passenger or passengers must have buried his body and left."

"Sounds logical. They're probably out looking for help"—he indicated the dense foliage—"and we missed them. Not that missing them would be difficult in this place."

They both heard twigs snap down the trail. Christina darted behind a palm tree to the right of the track while Lincoln dove behind a tamarind to the left.

The sharp crack of gunfire echoed through the air. Chunks of bark tore away from the side of the trunk inches above Lincoln's head. Another barrage of bullets ripped into the tree tearing apart the lower branches that fell to the ground, creating a cloud of splinters and falling leaves. With short bursts of gunfire erupting about her, Christina struggled to pinpoint the shooter on the trail ahead.

Alerting the gunman that his targets were also armed, Lincoln drew his weapon and shot toward the gunfire, a ploy that sometimes worked in the city with inexperienced and nervous shooters. Lincoln knew that the chances of this ruse working here were slim, but he had to try.

A volley of bullets tore into the trunk behind him. *So much for that idea.*

As another bullet whizzed by, Lincoln peeked around the tree and saw a Willys jeep and a flatbed truck a hundred yards down the track. A jerry can strapped to the roll bar caught his attention. He ducked back to safety and ejected the magazine. Half a dozen rounds. He slammed the magazine back into place as a bullet tore into the tree inches from his head. Christina, still sheltered behind the smaller tree, glanced at him, bewildered.

Lincoln took a deep breath and rolled out from behind the tree's cover. As bullets tore up the earth around him, he took aim at the jeep and fired. The jerry can exploded, hurtling the driver through the windscreen and enveloping the jeep in a fireball of flame and smoke. The blast catapulted the second gunman across the track and into the foliage.

Lincoln took advantage of the lull to scramble over to Christina. "You okay?"

Christina checked her magazine. "Three left."

"I've got five." He glanced around the trunk. Another bullet ripped into the tree inches above his head.

Lincoln scanned the trail and surrounding jungle for any way of escape. The trail led back to the plane, but the dense undergrowth would hamper a quick getaway. They would be sitting ducks before they could get a hundred yards—

Behind them leaves rustled. Lincoln spun around. He winced from a sting on the back of his neck, stumbled, and fell to his knees. The deep blue sky and green of the jungle merged into a kaleidoscope of shape and sound. With his blurred vision fading and motor skills disappearing, he watched, helpless, as Christina fell beside him, stricken by the same plight.

The flatbed truck rumbled along the trail toward the northern end of the island, its all-terrain tires kicking up clouds of dust as the vehicle skidded across the dirt road.

Lincoln opened his eyes, but the glare of the sun burning bright into his retinas caused him to close them again. His throbbing head sent bolts of pain coursing down his spine and through his body. He took a deep breath to allow fresh air into his lungs. His hands were locked behind his back, restrained with zip ties. The rocking motion under his supine body told him that he was in a moving vehicle. Through the open window to the cab, Lincoln heard a voice with a Southern drawl carrying on what sounded like a one-sided conversation.

"We found them both near the communications tower," the voice was saying. "Their chopper really did a job on the tower. It's totaled... One male, one female. They're both unconscious. Phillipe had an itchy trigger finger and opened fire on them... Yeah, both were armed... He's dead and so is George... Well, that's what happens when a jerry can full of gas explodes next to you... We're on our way back now... He looks fit and healthy... Oh, yeah, she's a real hottie, definitely a keeper. I'll set them up at the hotel and keep guard until we know more. They each took a shot—just a small dose, nothing a good sleep won't fix. They'll be out for the next few hours, so I'll get answers in the morning... All right. Back soon."

Whatever they had given him had numbed his senses, but Lincoln struggled to stay conscious. *Relax. If they wanted you dead, you'd be dead by now.* His thoughts turned to Christina. He maneuvered his tied hands until he felt her body. She was lying on her side to his right with her back to him. He fumbled about until he found her hands and felt for a pulse. She was alive.

He exhaled and tried to forget his throbbing headache by focusing on the heavily armed unknown aggressors on this tropical island in the middle of nowhere. *Pirates? Drug traffickers?* He tried to open his eyes again, this time careful not to allow in too much light. It worked. Squinting, he looked to his left. The dead man's eyes stared back at him, inches from his nose. Slivers of glass and metal were embedded in his charred head. Next to him lay another victim of the blast, his head at an awkward angle to his neck.

So, we're in the back of a flatbed truck with two dead men travelling along a weather-worn trail. He figured the driver was busy controlling the vehicle over the rough terrain while his crony was cradling the tranquilizer gun. Moving only his eyes so as not to alert their assailants of his intentions, he scanned the metal tray for anything to cut the zip—

"Well, look who's awake!" the voice boomed from the cab over the flatbed's rattling chassis. Lincoln looked up to see an assailant with shoulder length blond hair wielding a gun. "Don't get any ideas. Ideas can be bad for you," he warned. "No, don't even think about it." The man took aim. Before Lincoln could struggle or protect Christina, he fired.

Lincoln's eyes rolled to the back of his head.

CHAPTER 7

Rousseau's upper torso was hidden in the left wing's engine bay as he repaired the bullet-riddled manifold on the Pratt and Whitney engine. Only the towel he had wrapped around his head for protection from the sun was visible. As he worked, he hummed the words to the latest techno-beat from France's top-ten music chart.

The afternoon light radiated through the plane's cabin where the heat and humidity were draining the energy from all inside. Katya fanned herself with the plane's safety manual and snacked on dried apricots while keeping an eye on a resting Napoleon. Enheim's soft snoring reverberated throughout the cabin. Mich rested against the wall dividing the cabin from the cockpit. Roland lounged comfortably in his custom-made recliner scooping spoonfuls of barbequed beans from a can and savoring their smooth flavor. He looked up to see Katya frowning in distaste. "Call me uncouth," he said, grinning, "but I don't care. Baked beans are delicious anyvere, you know."

Napoleon's ears pricked up, and he growled softly.

Roland was the first to hear the clunk against the rear hatch. Another clunk resounded throughout the cabin, alerting the others. Roland put a finger to his lips—*shhh*—then placed his beans on the seat next to him. He grabbed his Sig Sauer P229 from the cockpit. With no time to get the stash of weapons from the cargo to arm the others, he made his way to the closed hatchway. Careful not to make a sound, he examined the terrain through the window.

With no weapon, Katya grabbed the knife and fork from her snack, ready to wield them in self-defense. Mich, having skipped the lunch menu of dried apricots and sauvignon blanc, did the best he could. He yanked at the curtain rail attached to the window and snapped it in half, creating a makeshift spear.

Startled by another clunk, this time against the window beside him, Roland again peeked through the window, hoping to get a visual on the unknown perpetrator. The others brandished their makeshift weapons ready for whatever lurked outside.

"What's happening?" Enheim yawned, breaking the tense silence inside the cabin as he awakened from his nap.

"Shhhh." Roland indicated the hatchway. Footsteps up the ladder to the hatch sounded in the cabin. They braced themselves.

"Hello! Anyone home?" a friendly female voice called, followed by knocking. The hatch opened and folded back against the fuselage, revealing a young woman cautiously peeking inside the plane.

Roland emerged from the darkened cabin, pistol ready. Startled, Becca lost her balance and stumbled backward, grabbing for the doorframe. Roland caught her by the blouse and pulled her forward.

"Thanks." She stepped into the cabin and wiped the sweat from her face. "It's like a sauna out there." Mich sat upright at the sight of the green-eyed brunette standing in the hatchway. Even with her white blouse drenched in sweat and her pants rolled up around her knees, his heart skipped a beat.

"Who the hell are you?" Enheim demanded.

"Becca—Becca Perry. I'm a reporter for KSPN Saipan. Our helicopter crashed a few miles from here. By the look of it, you guys didn't fare much better."

Roland pulled a bottle of water from a small cooler in the cockpit. "Lemon scented with a touch of lime. Most invigorating, you know."

"Thank you," she said, and gulped the cool water.

"So," Enheim continued, "what is a reporter doing out here in the middle of nowhere?"

"Are you kidding me? The whole world watched that little boat speed away from the collapsing island with Jonathan Kane in hot pursuit. Then Kane dies in the helicopter crash, and the two from the boat make a death-defying leap into this old bird. That's a story that has to be told."

"So you were following us when you crashed," Enheim said.

"Yes." She looked around the cabin. "Where are they, the two from the boat?"

"They vent looking for help," Roland answered. "I believe introductions are in order. I'm Roland, the pilot of *this old bird*—her name is *Ava*, by the way—and that's my co-pilot Rousseau." He cocked his head toward the big Frenchman on the wing.

"I'm Marcus, and my wife Katya."

"Hello, darlink," Katya called, stroking Napoleon under the chin. "This is our baby Napoleon."

Mich forgot his injured arm for the moment and gazed into her green eyes. "I'm Mich."

"Pleased to meet all of you."

"Vere did you crash?"

"Our pilot must be the unluckiest bastard in the world. He flew into a communications tower. It's currently in two pieces, and one of those pieces is lying across our wrecked chopper."

"And your pilot?" Roland's eyes searched the clearing behind her.

"We buried him beside the helicopter. Wouldn't have been right to leave the poor guy to rot in the heat."

"We?"

"Roy, my cameraman. He's hiding in the jungle," she said, thumbing toward the tree line beyond the plane. Roland turned to the others with a look of concern.

Becca noted the somber reaction. "Something I should know about?" she probed.

"Lincoln and Christina were heading for the tower," Katya blurted.

"The two from the little boat?"

"Yes."

"I'm sorry to tell you, but they never made it there."

A head appeared in the doorway. "Everything okay, Becca?"

"Everybody, meet Roy," Becca announced.

Roland gently pushed him aside, his face drawn, and peered into the jungle. "No, everything is not okay."

The double dose of antibiotics that Mich downed earlier were eradicating the infection from within, but the antiseptic cream for the wounds did little to stop the itch. To take his mind off the insatiable urge to scratch his arm and leg, he turned his thoughts to Becca, seated opposite. Her blouse, still drenched in sweat, clung to her trim body, and Mich couldn't help noticing the outline of her perfect breasts rising and falling. "Something has been nagging me subconsciously that just now became clear. How did you plan to get the story to your news station?"

Becca downed the last of her bottled water. "I was going to email the story direct to the newsroom. We have a sat phone back in the chopper."

"You have a sat phone?' Roland blurted.

Everyone in the cabin sat upright and stared at Becca, while Roy, resting on the other side of the aisle, continued cleaning his camera lens.

"Vy didn't you tell us earlier, you know? So ve could have called for help by now?"

Becca dismissed his excitement with a wave. "Relax. I should have said we *had* a sat phone back in the chopper. It was damaged in the crash. Don't you think we would have used it by now if it still worked?" They all returned to their comfort zones, deflated by hope and dejection in the same moment.

Mich was annoyed that his idea hadn't panned out. Still, his fascination with all types of technology spurred him on. Besides, this topic was perfect for getting his mind off his constant need to scratch. "What type of sat phone was it? The old-school phones the size of a brick?"

"No," Roy answered, laughing at the memory of those old phones. "The station just spent a shit ton of money updating their technology. But I know what you're talking about. I once saw an elderly journo with a sat phone the size of a suitcase. The old boy carried it with him everywhere."

Becca smiled. "You mean Old George from the weekend weather?"

"Yeah, that's him. Great old guy. Boy, did he have some stories. Did he ever tell you about the time his plane was shot down over the mountains in Afghanistan?" Becca nodded, smiling at the memory. "All they had to drink was a dozen cases of bourbon earmarked for the local American airbase. As George tells it, he and his crew got so drunk, he tore the coat sleeve right off his arm trying to fight off his cameraman to prevent him from taking the last bottle." He laughed. "Those flyboys sure can drink."

"Sleeve," Mich repeated.

"Yeah," Roy replied. "He ripped his sleeve clean off the jacket. According to Old George, the cameraman was so drunk he didn't even remember the fight." Roy laughed again at the story that had been retold dozens of times around the station's water cooler.

"Your sat phone," Mich said. "Is it the new sleeve type?" He had read about the latest sat phones that were engineered such that any type of modern phone could slip into the wraparound cradle and connect instantly.

"Yeah, it is."

"So how do you know the sleeve is damaged?"

Roy stopped cleaning the lens and considered the question. Enheim and Katya turned from Napoleon and looked across the aisle at the cameraman with his feet on the chair. Becca took another swig of bottled water, waiting for his answer. Roland, with a spoonful of baked beans to his mouth, paused and looked expectantly at Roy.

"Well, the phone didn't work, so I assumed the SatSleeve was damaged, too."

"Assumed?" Roland grimaced.

"The sleeve connects wirelessly to the phone," Mich said, "but did the LED indicator on the sleeve light up when you fitted the phone back into the slot?" He waited, eager for the answer.

Roy tried to picture the phone's position in the sleeve and the small LED light that indicated a connection and realized that he hadn't checked the phone's connectivity with the SatSleeve. The phone could have been disconnected. He groaned.

"So, it's possible the SatSleeve is still functioning?'

"It's possible, yeah," he said, embarrassed.

"You're kidding me," Enheim sputtered. "We've been wasting away in this shitty plane, and we could have been gone by now?"

"It doesn't matter," Roy said, defending himself. "You told me your communications equipment is shot to hell."

"The avionics and satellite phone, yes. But we still have a cell phone, you know." Roland scrambled to the cockpit and searched for Rousseau's phone. He reappeared a moment later, empty-handed. "Has anybody seen Rousseau's phone?" he asked. "It was sitting right here on the co-pilot's seat."

The deep warble of Rousseau singing to the latest techno beat echoed from outside the plane. Roland peered through the cockpit window. Rousseau was working on the portside engine while swaying to the thumping beat coursing through his earpiece. The headset connected to the phone tucked into his overalls.

"*Scheisse!*" Roland yelled. "Rousseau, the phone! Turn it off!"

Rousseau looked up. Roland was shouting something unintelligible and making the shaka sign next to his cheek. Rousseau removed the headset and pulled out the phone. Seeing the red low-battery bar, he pressed *off,* then climbed up from the engine bay and hurried into the cabin.

"I—I'm sorry," he stammered. "I didn't know I wasn't to use it."

"It's okay," Roland said, patting him on the back. "You didn't know. *We* didn't know until a few minutes ago."

"We need to find them," Mich interjected, trying not to scratch the agonizing itching.

"I vant to find Lincoln and Christina, too," Roland said, "but Lincoln told us to stay here and vait. The last thing he vants is for us to split up and go vandering around in this damned jungle. He knows about these things. Trust his judgement, you know."

"If he'd known about the satphone," Mich added, "he would have gone after it. That much I know. And they haven't returned yet, which means something is wrong. They're out there, possibly injured or God knows what, and we need to find them."

Roland considered the options. "You're right, Mich, but if ve have any chance of getting off this island, ve first need to find that satphone."

"Yes," Mich agreed, "that's what Lincoln would do. Then, after we find the satphone, we look for Lincoln and Christina."

The crew agreed that Roland's plan was the best course of action. "Okay, who goes on the hike?" Enheim asked.

"I do," Roland declared. He glanced at Becca. "I know how to use a gun."

"I'm going." Mich stood, but grabbed the seat's headrest, still unsteady from his leg wound.

"Nice try, but you're not going anyvhere." Roland helped Mich back into his seat where he slumped against the side of the plane, dejected and annoyed with himself.

"I'll go," Enheim announced, passing Napoleon to Katya.

Roland stared at him with a weary expression. "But you can't shoot."

"Hey," Enheim growled, "I did all right back there on that friggin' island."

"You got lucky, you know. Next time you might not be so

fortunate." Roland's mind raced searching for an excuse to keep Enheim on the plane. He couldn't face trekking through a dangerous jungle with an inexperienced shooter complaining about everything. "My darling sister Katya vould never forgive me if I allowed her husband to get himself killed." Enheim considered his statement, but before he could answer, Roland added the final touch. "Besides, if something happened to you, how would Napoleon react?"

Enheim smiled at Napoleon in Katya's arms the way a father smiles at his newborn child. Napoleon licked his muzzle and stared back at Enheim with his innocent big brown eyes. Enheim's heart melted. "Fine," he muttered.

"You need to go with them," Becca said to Roy.

"Why me?" Roy asked, frowning.

"Because you couldn't stop bragging all the way from Saipan about how you love to shoot guns. Well, we need an experienced shooter."

Roy looked away, disturbed by Becca's last statement. New sweat glistened on his forehead. Preferring not to go back into the unknown, he stammered, "Well, I… I *can* shoot, but… I haven't had much practice in a while." He hoped he'd convinced the others, adding, "Sorry. I'm-I'm not your man."

Becca shook her head, disgusted at her camerman's cowardice.

Roy indicated the open hatchway. "Hey, I'm not going back into that jungle. I heard some weird strange-ass noises out there."

"So did I. Jungles make weird noises," Becca snapped.

Roy crossed his arms, not relinquishing his position.

Becca couldn't bear to look at the man she had respected hours earlier on the chopper. "I'll go," she announced.

Roland's eyes narrowed. "Do you know how to shoot a gun?"

"Sure." Becca shrugged. "You point the gun and pull the trigger. Simple."

At the group's collective groan, Becca conceded defeat. "Fine. But I'm a fast learner."

Katya stood. "I go. I know how to shoot better than all of you.

And, my darlink brother, along with Rousseau's skills fixing that damned engine, your piloting skills are needed here so that you can fly us out of this jungle."

Roland was about to protest when Enheim spoke up with a slight quaver in his voice. "You're not going anywhere, Katya." He knew Katya *was* the best shooter among them, but he wasn't going to have the love of his life risking death out in that green hell beyond the plane.

Katya put her arms around Enheim's neck and kissed his unshaven cheek, then looked lovingly at Napoleon beside her on the seat. "Marcus, my darlink, I do this for us—for our family."

"But, Katya—" Enheim groaned, trying to find another way around the problem.

"Lincoln saved Napoleon. It is our turn to help him."

Enheim grudgingly agreed, but he still wanted her with him in the safety of the plane's cabin. "Please?" he begged, even though he knew her mind was made up.

"For our family," she repeated. Looking around the cabin at the faces staring back at her, she added, "and for our new family."

Enheim could never say no to the woman he loved. Pulling away from Katya, he confronted Roy, a stern look etched across his face. He clenched Roy's shirt and lifted the cameraman from the floor.

"My wife is not going out there by herself. You're going with her because you can shoot, and you will do everything humanly possible to protect her." Presented with the threat of imminent violence and with fear in his eyes, Roy reluctantly agreed. Enheim continued, "I'm gonna tell you a story—"

Roland leaned across the aisle to Mich. "This should be educational," he murmured, his tone dripping with sarcasm.

Enheim ignored Roland's remark. "—This story is, I think, pertinent to our situation here. As most of you know, I'm a physics professor. At one of my lectures, a student's cell phone rang. Now that wasn't too bad. Sometimes a student would forget to turn off his phone, so I let that ring pass. However, the student decided in all his wisdom to *answer* his damned phone. Can you believe it? In the middle of *my* lecture? I was furious."

"So what did you do?" Roy asked, not wanting to hear the answer.

"I grabbed him and shoved that phone up his arse."

Mich laughed and coughed simultaneously. "For months afterwards, no one even brought a cell phone to Professor Enheim's class."

"Exactly. Now, how do you think I'm going to react if find out something has happened to my *wife*?" Enheim's steely gaze burnt a hole in Roy's brain. Roy feebly dipped his head.

"It vill be dark soon, you know," Roland observed. "Ve vill have to set out tomorrow."

Enheim glanced out the window to see the sun setting on the horizon. He turned back to Roy. "Tomorrow morning, you and my wife are going to go back into that jungle, and you're going to protect her like you're protecting the Queen Mum from an assassin's bullet. You're gonna find that helicopter, get that sat phone thing, and bring it back here so we can call for help. Then we're all going to find our lost friends. Because if you don't, I'm going to shove anything I can find up your arse, and whatever I find is gonna be a lot bigger than a damned cell phone. Understand?"

Roy nodded weakly.

Roland leaned toward Mich again. "Do you think my brother-in-law understands the meaning of *subtle*?"

"This is a bad idea Katya," Enheim muttered, stroking Napoleon nervously under the chin. "I should be the one going tomorrow, not you." He paced the aisle, trying to relieve the pent-up tension from Katya's decision.

Katya indicated for Enheim to sit beside her. Reluctantly he slumped into the seat. She cupped her hands around his unshaven face and whispered, "My darlink husband, everything will be all right."

Enheim shook his head. "I couldn't live with myself if anything happened to you. Let me go. I'll learn to use a gun properly on the way. I'm a fast learner—just ask Napums here."

"Marcus, you know that I am better with weapons than you. It is fact that I have a natural talent and you do not. I have trained for many months to qualify for the Olympics. Let me do what I was born to do. My skill will help everybody in this plane—including our baby." She patted Napoleon's head.

"But Napums needs his mum," Enheim protested, shrugging away her logic.

Katya smiled at Enheim's attempt to cover his own feelings by using Napoleon as an excuse to keep her close within the safety of the plane. She glanced lovingly at Napoleon and then at Enheim. "I need you to be strong for our family. Understand?"

"You know I'm not good with this emotional stuff," he complained in frustration. "I can't lose you, Katya. You're the best thing that's ever happened to this grumpy physicist, and if anything happens to you, I won't know what to do."

"Nothing will happen," she said calmly. "Roy and I will find the phone thingy, and then we'll all find Lincoln and Christina and get off this island."

The incessant chirping of insects filtered through the plane's fuselage and into the cabin. Fear of the unknown and the darkness beyond the plane exacerbated Enheim's anxiety. He looked Katya in the eye. "For our family," he agreed, coming to terms with the situation.

"For our family," Katya repeated, kissing Enheim's cheek and Napoleon's head. Napoleon reached up and licked Katya on the cheek.

CHAPTER 8

THE LAB TECHNICIAN woke to electricity buzzing and a light flashing intermittently. His eyes focused on the broken equipment scattered about the laboratory and on the crumpled metal girder protruding through the roof down to the polished tiled floor. Several lamps clung to life and dangled precariously from broken roof mounts, their fluorescent tubes strobing with the interrupted current coursing through the underground building.

Before the roof had collapsed and rendered him unconscious, the technician heard helicopter blades thumping above the lab followed by a thunderous roar mixed with the echo of tearing metal. He glanced at his watch—*shit!* That was hours ago. *Why hadn't the backup generator kick in?*

He stumbled to his feet, then winced from shooting pain in his left foot. He rolled up his pant leg to discover a swollen ankle. "Damn it," he muttered, and grabbed his computer notebook from the desk. He lowered himself to the floor and leaned against the side of the desk, relieved to take the pressure off his foot. Resting his head against the cool stainless steel, he took a deep breath to regain his composure. His head ached. Gently he searched his blond hair for the cause. Glancing at the trickle of blood staining his hand, he concluded that the cut was minor.

He tapped some keys, and a topographical map of the island

filled the screen followed by a digital overlay of the laboratory complex hidden below ground. His superiors would want to know why the system collapsed, and so would Jonathan Kane.

Several flashing icons across the image warned him that the power was out to all the labs. *How the hell did that happen?* He tapped more keys to access the system's log files, then scrolled down the screen to read all the power failures and their causes—*surge protection failure* appeared on every line followed by *power loss failure.* "That's impossible. The systems were operational during the storm four days ago, so why would they fail now?"

He searched the display for answers.

He ran an integrated system check of the power supply and backup generator, and after a few seconds, the information rolled down the screen. He read in dismay as the circumstances of the events took place. The lightning storm four days ago had knocked out the main power source, so the backup generator had kicked in. However, the surge protectors failed when the main power source rebooted, so the power transferred to the backup generators. *Oh, no! We've been running on backup for four days.* Annoyed by the system failure, the technician scanned the files for repair and maintenance orders. He found a file marked Urgent Repair Order. According to the report, Kane's people had known about issues regarding the faulty surge protectors but had failed to do anything. He slammed his hand against the desk. *Cheap bastards!*

The technician froze. *The cages!* The consequences of interrupted power sent shivers down his spine. He tapped more keys, and the image zoomed in on a detailed schematic of his laboratory and a list of interrupted power failure errors. The cages were open.

This isn't happening—this can't be happening. He tried to close the cage doors, but the system was down. He eased himself up from the floor, keeping a watchful eye for any movement through the wire mesh windows in the door to the hallway beyond. Using the table's edge as a crutch, he began hoisting himself up when a menacing hiss made his blood run cold. He swung around to face the creature from the Main Lab—the room where the experiments took place.

The alpha rat reared up and stood on its muscled hind legs. As tall as a man, he gazed around the room, hissing anger and vengeance toward the technician who had caused him and his fellow rodents pain. The rat's tight muscles flexed and rippled as it rested on its hind legs, its skeletal torso and lean muscular body appearing like a creature straight from hell. Black and yellow streaks of matted fur ran down the rat's spine, glistening in the fluorescent light, while his twitching snout sensed odors and vibrations in the air.

The technician's scream of terror was cut short as the alpha's jaws clamped around his neck, crunching bone. Arterial blood spurted into the rat's face as the assistant went limp in its jaws. The rat gnawed at the skin, bone, and muscle until the assistant's head separated from his body and fell to the floor. The oversized rodent observed the lifeless body jerking spasmodically and flung the corpse to the side. Next, he studied the severed head, whose face was contorted in a grimace of terror. The rat nudged the object with its muzzle, leaving a smear as it rolled the blood-soaked head across the polished floor until the rat was satisfied that its tormentor was dead. Blood and saliva dripped from its mouth as the rat unhinged its lower jaw and clinched the head tightly between its teeth. Then—it bit down, crushing the head to a pulp. It consumed the bone, brain, and flesh until only a few tufts of blond hair remained between its rotted teeth.

When the alpha had finished its meal, it thumped his tail signaling the others to enter the laboratory. Dozens of rats the size of rottweilers emerged from the dark folds of the complex and swarmed into the lab where they quickly devoured the technician's decapitated body.

With its nose twitching, the alpha's lips parted to reveal its blood-soaked teeth. The scent of other humans permeated the room. Its blood-shot eyes fixed on the darkened sky visible through the tangled girder. The wreckage of the communication tower lay at an angle, the tip of the tower at ground level, while the body of the structure formed an incline to the jungle above.

DAY 3

CHAPTER 9

LINCOLN WOKE TO the distant drumming of cascading water. He was naked in a four-poster king size bed with mosquito netting attached to each side. Disoriented and suffering from a throbbing headache, he pulled back the netting to better take in his surroundings.

The room, tastefully decorated with chic furniture, appeared to be in a luxurious hotel. Silk curtains that bordered the open balcony slider undulated in the breeze wafting through the room. Lincoln reminisced about a five-star hotel room where, many years ago, he and a female companion had fortuitously stayed.

The splash of running water caught his attention. He climbed out of bed and grabbed a pillow that he held in front of his groin before approaching the bathroom. The door was ajar, so he knocked. No answer. He knocked again, this time with more force. Still no answer. Slowly, he pushed back the door. The bathroom was filled with steam, limiting visibility.

Through the haze under the showerhead, he could make out Christina—naked. The water running down her body followed the curves of her tanned and slim physique. Her natural beauty, her allure, transfixed him—not as a voyeur, but as one mesmerized by a great work of art, like seeing Botticelli's the "Birth of Venus" for the first time.

Without warning, she turned.

Lincoln averted his eyes and blushed. "I'm sorry. I didn't know you were behind this door."

"Relax. I'm not shy." Christina continued rinsing her hair as if nothing had happened, completely comfortable with her nakedness.

"Maybe you're not, but I am," Lincoln mumbled, closing the door behind him. Inside the dresser, he found his clothes freshly cleaned and pressed. He got dressed and was putting on his Neptune cap when a knock sounded at the door. Still unsure of what was happening and not knowing who was behind the door, Lincoln peered through the peephole. A man wearing a waiter's uniform stood beside a food trolley, waiting patiently. Lincoln opened the door.

"Hello, sir," the waiter said as he pushed the trolley into the room.

"Excuse me," Lincoln said, "but where are we?"

"Sir, I am forbidden from having discussions with the guests. All will be explained soon." He removed the covers from the dinner plates. A burger and fries—Lincoln's favorite.

The other dish consisted of freshly steamed vegetables and a side serving of French fries. The waiter opened a bottle of Pinot Noir. He poured a little, stepped back, and waited for Lincoln to taste the wine.

With a friendly wave, Lincoln passed on the wine tasting. "Sorry, I'm not a big wine guy. Do you stock Coronas?"

"Of course, sir. I'll be right back with your beer." The waiter bowed and disappeared.

As the door shut, Lincoln heard the click of a lock. He crossed the room and peered through the peephole again. The waiter had disappeared and been replaced by two surly-looking men wearing army fatigues and armed with M60 machine guns.

What the hell is this?

Christina emerged from the bathroom in a black spandex jumpsuit. *Wow.* Lincoln couldn't help but notice how the one-piece hugged her curves perfectly.

"My clothes were gone when I woke up, and this outfit was

in their place," she said matter-of-factly. Spotting the veggies and fries, she added, "Someone came around while you were asleep, so I ordered for both of us. You look like a burger-kind of guy."

Surprised, Lincoln grinned at her perfect choice. "You got that right. A Whopper with cheese will do me any day."

"Well, I don't know about you, but I'm starving. Let's eat on the balcony."

The view from their balcony, several floors up, overlooked a fast-flowing river that bordered the hotel grounds. The river ended at a waterfall that emptied over an escarpment and into a narrow strip of jungle below. Beyond that stretch of lush greenery, a delta opened into the ocean two miles away.

Lincoln lifted the cover from a small dish tucked to the side of his burger. Two pills sat on a decorated bed of silk. He picked up the card beside the dish. *For the headache.*

The hotel door flung open. Van Sant and the two armed guards strode into the room. By his side, Van Sant held his Beretta, his trigger finger poised. "Please," he said, joining them at the table, "continue."

The guards took their positions behind Van Sant, who was reaching over and picking a fry from Lincoln's dish. "I'm Van Sant. Mmmm—Belgian fries. Chef Fabienne has outdone herself."

"I just lost my appetite," Lincoln said, recognizing the shoulder length blond hair and crooked smile as those of the assailant with the tranquilizer gun in the pick-up truck.

"You're gonna need it." Van Sant chomped on another Belgian fry and casually rested the Beretta on the table, the barrel directed toward Lincoln. He brushed his hair behind his ears and studied the two captives. "You've got no IDs and a whole lot of explaining to do. I want names, and I want to know why you're here."

Lincoln thought fast. *They found Christina and me at the helicopter, which means that they probably didn't know about the crashed plane. The crew back on the plane have a chance if I can distract and divert these men away from that area. Misdirection is the crew's only hope.* "This is a little embarrassing," Lincoln said, trying to sound sheepish. "But we're not who you think we are."

Van Sant bit into another Belgian fry. "Enlighten me."

"I'm Lincoln, and this is Christina." *Keep the story simple. Less chance of slipping up later.* "We were just joyriding in her boss's helicopter across the islands. The Neptune Island incident sparked our interest in privacy." He turned to Christina and gave her an embarrassed shrug, hoping she would catch on. "We thought maybe Kane had more surprise destinations along the island chain. You know, being a rich guy and all, he might have a secluded beach somewhere where a couple could be free to... enjoy nature, so to speak."

Van Sant took another fry and stared at the two, unconvinced. "We found you both at a crashed KSPN News helicopter, yet you're telling me you're not journalists?" He shifted the Beretta's barrel towards Lincoln's midriff. "You know, sometimes Chef Fabienne uses a tad too much salt. These fries are really hard to swallow." Van Sant helped himself to Lincoln's wine.

Taking her cue from Lincoln, Christina piped up, "When a trained helicopter pilot finds out that her station manager lover is banging the twenty-one-year-old production assistant... Well, helicopters tend to go missing."

Van Sant chuckled. He signaled to the guard beside him who spoke quietly into his earpiece.

"Payback's a real bitch," Christina sneered, warming to the roll of jilted lover.

"I bet you are." Van Sant looked towards Lincoln and smiled. He leaned across the table and whispered into Lincoln's ear. "Revenge sex. Ain't it grand?"

Lincoln gave him a wry smile.

The guard turned his back to Lincoln while he spoke quietly with Van Sant.

Van Sant's eyes narrowed as he assessed the couple before him.

"It appears that your story holds true. The AS350 Eurocopter belonging to KSPN Saipan was reported missing a few hours ago." He couldn't take his eyes away from Christina who oozed sex appeal with her flowing red hair and black spandex jumpsuit. "And you're the pilot?" he asked, surprised that a stunning woman could also have a helicopter license.

"I am," she replied, ignoring his sexist remark and munching on one of her fries.

Van Sant rubbed his stubbled chin as he admired her curvaceous body under the tight spandex. "A woman of many talents."

Laying on the fake charm, Christina toyed with a lock of hair that had fallen over her face and gave him a seductive grin. "More than you know."

"I'll bet you are indeed," he said, leering at her trim figure and alluring suggestion. "Pretty lousy pilot, though, flying into a hundred-foot tower. You're lucky to be alive."

"What can I say? Not my finest hour. I'm never flying in fog again, that's for sure."

Lincoln took his opportunity to seal the story. "We'd really appreciate it if this conversation stayed between us. KSPN is partially funded by a government grant, and the authorities don't look kindly on civilians stealing helicopters from government-sponsored projects. As they say, it's bad for business."

Van Sant wasn't convinced by the story, but he had no option. Time was short, and Merrick needed another player. He sized Lincoln up again, then motioned to the guards who moved quickly toward Christina. Lincoln bolted upright and half-rose to defend her when Van Sant leveled the pistol at Lincoln's head.

"Uh—uh—uh," Van Sant warned. Within seconds the two guards zip-tied Christina's hands. Her struggling proved futile as the first guard escorted her from the balcony and out of the room. The second guard positioned himself behind Lincoln, his sidearm pushed hard into the nape of Lincoln's neck.

"What the hell is this?" Lincoln demanded.

Van Sant ate the last Belgian fry and finished Lincoln's wine. "Don't worry, I'll get you another," he said, indicating the drink. "You know what? I think you would look great in blue. I definitely think blue would contrast well with those green puppy-dog eyes."

Lincoln shook his head, bewildered by the sudden turn of events. "What are you talking about?"

"Your girlfriend would have been perfect for our needs. She would have really upped the price, but it would have been such a waste of a beautiful woman. You, on the other hand, are exactly what they're expecting. You'll do nicely." He glanced at Lincoln's burger, still untouched on the plate. "You sure you don't want that? Chef Fabienne went to a lot of trouble to make that burger for you."

"Where are you taking Christina?"

"I assure you she'll be safe—for now." Van Sant continued to gaze at the perfect steak burger. "Last chance?"

"If you hurt one hair on her head—"

"Relax. She's fine. If I were you, I'd be concerned with my own welfare." Keeping the barrel at Lincoln's head, Van Sant lifted the plate over the table and rested it in front of himself. "Mmm... ooh la la," he grinned. He chomped down on the burger. "Once again, Fabienne has out done herself," he mumbled through a mouthful of steak.

The guard slammed Lincoln's head onto the table, then zip-tied his hands behind his back.

"You had your chance, Blue. I hope you've eaten recently, because you're going to need all the energy and stamina you can get."

CHAPTER 10

THE HOTEL ATRIUM towered above Tom Merrick as he stood before the group of potential business partners. The understated sheen from his bespoke Saville Row suit gleamed in the morning light. His dazzling white shirt, with the top button carefully undone to convey a sense of relaxed ease, accentuated his dark short-cropped hair and deep blue eyes. Samantha Merrick was by his side, wearing a casual and revealing low-cut blouse. Her trim waist and tanned body enhanced her natural beauty—assets she and Merrick knew would dispose clients favorably to their venture.

Sunlight streaming through the glass façade cast rays across the lobby and bathed the space in a warm glow. The walls, covered with meticulously trimmed vines, rose five stories above them. At ground level, rectangular pots sprouting the local flora were interspersed among custom-designed sofas and tables. The five-star opulence Merrick demanded had achieved the desired effect. Guests stood in awe of the hotel's elegance and beauty.

The Nigerian client from Lagos, Adedowale, and his assistant Abeo stood admiring the lobby while gulping their champagne. Adedowale beamed with approval, taking in the splendor and ambience.

Klaus accepted an apfelstrudel from Chef Fabienne's tray and stood studying the magnificent architecture. He loosened his tie and removed his jacket, preferring to relax in the tropical surrounds, while Wolfgang scooped a handful of strudel from the tray. Klaus looked away with distaste as a strudel slipped from Wolfgang's hand and rolled over his bulbous belly.

The late comers, Joanna and Baxter, kept a discreet watch on the others while mingling politely. Joanna was dressed in a smart business suit. She wore her silver blonde hair gathered into a spiral ponytail that cascaded over her shoulder. She sipped at her champagne as Baxter—her assistant, manservant, and helicopter pilot—stood loyally at the ready, hands clasped behind his back. "Baxter, you're allowed to have champagne," Joanna reminded him in her sophisticated British accent.

"I prefer not, mum," Baxter replied, straightening his tie. "It wouldn't be proper."

Joanna cringed at the word *mum*. The English used the word as a sign of respect for female employers and matrons, but she feared that those from other countries might take the meaning literally.

Merrick tapped his champagne flute. "Good morning, everybody. Some of you have been here for the last few days enjoying the amenities and hospitality of my private Shangri-La"—he glanced at the German and the Nigerian clients—"and our last guests have just now arrived." He gestured toward Joanna and Baxter. "Because Wolfgang's English is limited, his assistant Klaus will interpret for him.

"Let me start by saying that I trust you all had a pleasant trip to my beautiful island home. The journey is long, but the business opportunity that exists within this small island paradise—an opportunity that will bring fortune to each of you—will eclipse the travel time. Whether you represent venture capital or wish to personally fund the enterprise, you will be eager to participate once you experience my proposal. I assure you that the next few days will not only compensate for your long journey, but they will render that journey insignificant. Now, without further ado, let's, as they say, get this party started."

"Mr. Merrick," Joanna said, "I would like to convey my employer's thanks for this invitation to your beautiful island to see your business venture firsthand. I'm sure I speak for everyone here," she glanced around at the other clients, "when I say the setting is spectacular."

Everyone concurred with nods of approval.

"Nevertheless, my employer wants assurances that the proposal on the table is sound and risk-free. The businessman I represent has no interest in high-risk ventures."

Merrick smiled, having prepared for such a question for the last six months. "I understand completely. If you will, indulge me for a moment."

"Of course." Joanna leaned back in her chair and sipped some champagne.

"I sent my invitation to a select group of investors:

investors trusted by our mutual business associates to have the foresight to recognize a burgeoning business with limitless potential; investors who understand the primal needs of those who have the vision to see the prospects for my business opportunity; investors with a proclivity for ultimate alternative forms of entertainment, entertainment considered too extreme for the general population. This exclusive opportunity, an investment potentially worth billions, is offered to these chosen few.

Merrick paced before his clients like a general addressing his men. "Today, you will have the chance to witness a new era in entertainment. My concept is so revolutionary—yet so simple—that if you choose to proceed with the contract, the rewards of this business synergy will, if marketed correctly, exceed all expectations. If you wish, you may avail yourselves of my unique services for a share of the proceeds, or you may buy the concept outright to do with as you wish. If you opt to accept my services, I shall manage all logistics, location, and staffing, including shipping and setting up at the destination of your choosing.

"However, as you all know, my concept requires absolute privacy and seclusion, which is why I am offering the services and isolation of this island if you so decide. My business connections in the local districts and principalities and with the Mariana Islands government assure me of complete privacy. The locals avoid the island, and key government and law enforcement officials have been compensated handsomely to guarantee our seclusion. What we do here is completely off the radar from any bureaucratic body. Our privacy on this island is one hundred percent assured. This location is ideal for this business venture, although the choice is yours should you wish to take the concept abroad."

Joanna nodded. Merrick had done his homework. He had secured a remote location and structured a sound business model.

"So let's get down to business. I have been informed that my long-time friend and colleague Jonathan Kane has died under tragic circumstances. While this news is unfortunate, I am confident that if Jonathan were alive, he would personally be here presenting this unique investment opportunity."

Wolfgang murmured into Klaus's ear and nudged him with his phone. Klaus raised Wolfgang's cell phone in the air. *NO RECEPTION.* "Mr. Merrick, you have poor reception on the island," he announced, looking about the group with concern.

"We have no reception for a reason, Klaus. We are dead serious about security on the island. Our scrambling system blocks all incoming and outgoing signals so that nothing gets in or out without my express consent. This added precaution is necessary for our isolation from the outside world."

Klaus turned to Wolfgang and in hushed tones relayed the

response in German. Wolfgang stuffed another apfelstrudel into his mouth and agreed.

"During your stay, you will have opportunities to contact family, friends, and business associates and, if you wish, inform them of the day's events. Each evening, at a predetermined time of your choosing, we will disable the scrambler for such contact.

"So let's get down to why you have all been invited here, shall we? You are here to witness the birth of a new sporting event. Most contests will be held here on the hotel grounds so that you may watch from your hotel balconies. Or you may choose to view the contests in complete privacy from the comfort of your hotel room. Multiple cameras and drones will record every second of the action that will be streamed live to your televisions. You can choose to watch from one camera angle or from several angles displayed simultaneously on the monitor. The choice is yours. If you desire a more personal, close-up view, we will gladly provide comfortable seating at the events."

Joanna cleared her throat. "Mr. Merrick, again I expect that I speak for everyone here when I thank you for your kind hospitality. I am sure our stay on this beautiful island will be memorable. However, my employer is a busy man—as, no doubt, are these fine gentlemen. Time is money, as they say."

"Of course, forgive me. I get carried away with the excitement and grandeur of it all, and I ramble. Allow me to summarize the proposal. The schedule is simple: four events, four days. The rules are straightforward: You lose, you die. If no one dies during the contest, the last contestant to finish the event dies by execution. Either way, one man will die by the end of each event."

"A most brutal game, Mr. Merrick," Joanna observed with distaste.

"Perhaps your companion can watch the contests and relay the results to you."

"Mr. Merrick, I wasn't always a consultant for the wealthy business sector. During my life I've witnessed too many acts of brutality—the deaths of men, women, and children—so don't assume that my gender or my empathy will compromise my ability to make informed decisions."

"I meant no disrespect, Joanna. I sincerely apologize."

"Apology accepted."

"Do you have a name for these events?" Adedowale's booming voice echoed throughout the foyer.

Merrick cleared his throat and waited until all eyes turned to him. Samantha Merrick noted the predetermined sign. She gestured toward Chef Fabienne, standing discreetly behind the clients. After filling the guests' flutes with champagne, Chef Fabienne retreated to the kitchen.

The cost and perseverance of sitting in a dentist's chair for all those uncomfortable hours was about to pay off. Tom Merrick's smile revealed perfect, dazzling white teeth. The sweat and sheer will to create their destiny was about to pay off. The Merricks raised their glasses. "Gentlemen and lady, welcome to Jungle Games."

CHAPTER 11

KATYA AND ROY made their way through the thick undergrowth with Katya leading and Roy close behind. The morning sun, piercing through gaps in the canopy, cast its rays over the vegetation. Dust particles caught within the light beams reflected in the warm air, giving a magical aura to the tropical forest enveloping them.

Roy, his pistol constantly at eye level, scanned the jungle for any sign of danger, mindful of Enheim's promise of bodily violence if anything happened to his beloved Katya. "Just stay close, okay?"

"Sure, darlink." Katya relished the exercise the trek offered. Relieved to be free of the confines of the cabin, she pushed her body to its limits, eager to regain what she'd lost since she'd been unable to perform her daily workout. With an AK-47 slung over her shoulder, courtesy of her brother's stash on the plane, she surged through the foliage, sweating, stretching her leg and arm muscles whenever she could, paying little attention to the nervous man behind her.

Roy's physical ability was second-rate compared with Katya's Olympic prowess. Before long he lagged several yards behind. Weary from the strenuous pace, he paused to wipe his brow. Leaves crunched behind him. He swung around, gun poised, shouting, "Katya!" At Roy's urgent tone, Katya stopped midstride and raised her rifle.

With the pistol swaying in his trembling hands, Roy surveyed the surrounding vegetation. The rustling continued, this time adjacent to the path. Fear of the unknown surged through his body, and terror set in. His heart raced as he aimed the rifle toward the sound, hoping the sight of the barrel would ward off any unwelcome visitors. His voice trembled as he tried to take control of the situation. "We're armed," he announced without conviction toward the wall of green foliage.

Katya's gaze fixed on the moving rustling that circled around them. Calm and disciplined, she readied herself for action. With total control of her emotions and weapon, she raised her gun and lined up the sights. Gently, she released the safety.

The rustling stopped, but Katya held her aim.

Roy joined her. "What do you think it is?" His voice quavered, as back to back they covered their surrounds.

"Quiet." Katya focused on the shadows in the greenery.

The rustling returned behind them. As they swung toward the hidden visitor, Roy's anxiety took control, and his entire body trembled. He pulled the trigger. The round tore into the bark of a nearby tree, the shot ringing in the air around them.

"What are you doing?" Katya shook her head, unimpressed by Roy's cowardice.

Roy took aim at the vegetation just a few yards away. "Something's there." A clump of leaves parted at ground level.

"Don't shoot until I say so," Katya commanded. Roy's eyes widened as more leaves moved aside. Katya carefully trained her gun on the movement and took aim.

The largest rat Katya and Roy had ever seen scurried from the bush. The rodent, the size of a rottweiler, stopped midstride to study them while its tail, twice the length of its body, thumped the ground. The rat reared up on its hind legs and sniffed the air, contemplating the threat posed by these humans. Then it hissed and bared its fanged teeth before disappearing into the ground cover.

Katya lowered her gun and wiped the sweat from her brow.

Roy tried to track the creature, but the greenery obscured the path. With deliberate hesitation, *he—lowered—his gun*. "That's the biggest damned rat I've ever seen."

Katya shrugged off his statement. "Clearly you've never been to Chicago."

Katya wrenched back the helicopter's crumpled door. "I'll wait outside," she said, her gun trained on the jungle while Roy climbed into the wreckage of the cabin.

Roy tried to forget the sight of the dead pilot's eviscerated body after impact. He wanted to erase from his mind how he and Becca had pulled the remains away from the wreckage and buried the poor fellow in the woods. That ad hoc funeral was the best they could do under the circumstances. Roy figured that when they got back to the mainland, the pilot's family would arrange a proper burial.

Roy searched the cabin. He found his carry-on bag wedged behind the crushed bench seat. He yanked at the bag until it tore free, its contents spilling onto the floor. He picked up his phone with the SatSleeve still attached and turned it over, inspecting it for damage. The screen was shattered. The upper section was smashed, and electronics spilled from the casing. Roy noticed a dim green light on the back of the SatSleeve. Mich was right. Roy cursed himself for missing such an obvious sign but convinced himself that the pressured circumstances had clouded his judgement. "The SatSleeve still works," he called to Katya.

Katya didn't respond.

"Katya, I found it," Roy repeated. Ubiquitous bird calls and incessant insect buzzing filled the air. Alarmed by the thought that Katya had abandoned him, Roy froze. All the horrors of being left alone in the jungle filled with creatures wanting to kill him flashed through his mind. "Katya?"

He placed the phone and sleeve in his vest pocket. His heart pounded as he climbed without a sound toward the open doorway. He rested his head on the door's metal frame, prepared for the worst. His hand trembled as he lifted his pistol. He stole a look through the doorway and ducked back inside. The clearing outside the wreckage was empty. Katya was nowhere to be seen. "Bitch," he whimpered.

Roy took a deep breath, braced himself, and edged through the doorway. Climbing down from the open hatch he kept an eye on the vegetation. *Katya left me to fend for myself. I hate her for leaving me alone.*

The overbearing humidity of the midday sun bore down causing sweat to trickle from every pore in his body. He felt a scratching on his neck and brushed the area with his hand to relieve the itch. "Shit!" he screamed. The largest spider he had ever seen clung to his hand. Frantically, he tried to shake the spider off.

Katya appeared from the bush and swiped the spider from his hand. The spider, more afraid of Roy than he was of it, scurried into the jungle. "Back inside," Katya commanded, indicating the cabin. Roy was still frozen with terror, so she pulled him to the plane and shoved him through the hatch. Inside the safety of the helicopter, she raised her pistol at the doorway. "Get ready," she whispered.

"Get ready?" Roy repeated blankly, still in shock from the encounter with the spider. An unknown force slammed into the side of the chopper. "What the hell?" Katya kept focused on the doorway, ignoring the frightened man beside her.

Another shudder rocked the chopper. Katya edged toward the open doorway and braced herself against the inside of the airframe, daring a peek through the door.

Dozens of giant rats the size of large dogs were emerging from the jungle and scurrying around the chopper. Some waited near the jungle's edge and kept watch while others made their way to the wreckage. Katya had never seen such behavior. The rats' movements appeared coordinated, akin to that of soldiers carrying out orders.

A head baring a row of fangs and its snout covered in slime

and dirt appeared in the open doorway. An overpowering stench from the brown fur matted in grime and excrement filled the cabin, causing Roy to heave. The creature's red eyes scanned the interior of the chopper, searching for prey. The rat snarled at Roy who was backing into the cabin. The rodent began thumping its tail against the chopper's cowling to alert the others that it had found the prey. The creature hissed with menace.

Katya's rifle appeared next to the rat's head. She fired.

Chunks of gray matter sprayed through the air as the rat's body fell away from the doorway. Two more terrifying heads appeared, their fangs dripping with slime.

Katya fired again. Their heads erupted in a shower of brain and bone, spraying a fine mist of blood over her and Roy. Roy wiped the blood from his eyes, his body and mind unable to comprehend the lethal situation. "I can't stand this," he whimpered, skulking further back into the cabin behind Katya.

"Just shoot them," she barked, focusing her attention on another head in the doorway. She pulled the trigger and the rat fell away, only to be replaced by more heads filling the doorway with a wall of snarling death. Katya fired her last round. The magazine was empty.

"This isn't happening, this isn't happening," Roy muttered, closing his eyes as he curled into a ball.

"You call yourself a man!" Katya grabbed Roy's pistol and continued to shoot at the rats flooding the doorway. "When my husband finds out about this, he's going to kill you."

A smaller rodent, the size of a Bull Terrier, gnawed its way through the broken windscreen and into the cabin. It jumped onto the pilot's seat and dug its claws into the soft vinyl—ready to strike. Roy froze. The creature's fangs were inches from his face. Urine stained his sweat-soaked crotch.

Hearing snarling behind her, Katya whirled around and fired. The rat's head burst apart, covering Roy's face with more brain and blood. Katya grabbed the remains and threw it at the rats in the doorway. The carcass bounced off their heads and tumbled to the cabin floor. In unison, they bared their rotted teeth and hissed as if enraged at the sight of their dead comrade. As their snarling grew louder, Roy whimpered in the corner, tears coursing down his cheeks, while Katya braced herself. Her thoughts turned to her loving Marcus, her loyal Roland, and of course, little Napoleon— the joy of her life. As thoughts of her family filled her mind with happiness and well-being, she understood what had to be done. She raised her pistol at the horrors in the doorway, knowing she didn't have enough ammunition to defend herself from the onslaught. But she wouldn't have had it any other way—*never give up, never surrender*. Katya took careful aim at the nearest rat and, blowing a lock of hair from her eyes, prepared to fire. "Come on, darlinks. If I'm going to hell, you're coming with me!"

The hoard of rats edged closer, fangs bared. Their ears twitched as they turned to each other, unsure what to do. Without warning they disappeared from the doorway, their tails thumping and heads darting from side to side. Katya heard leaves crunching as the creatures retreated from the helicopter and into the jungle. With her gaze fixed on the doorway, she raised her gun and approached the opening. Cautiously she peered into the clearing. Carcasses lay strewn across the groundcover, but the rats had disappeared—why, she didn't know. She turned to Roy, still cowering in the corner. "They're gone."

Roy opened his eyes. He forced a half-smile as he saw the open sky through the doorway, and pulled himself from the corner. He stumbled to join her and peered outside, breathing in the clear air free from the creatures' stench. The chirping and buzzing of the jungle filled his ears, and for the first time that morning, a feeling of hope and optimism returned. He started to leave when Katya gripped his shoulder.

"Wait. We don't know why they left. They could still out there."

"I don't give a shit. We have a chance to leave, and I'm taking it." He climbed through the doorway.

Katya seethed with loathing. "You stupid man. Think! They are not dumb creatures. They were coordinated. Didn't you see the way they worked together?"

"I don't care. I'm getting out of here. I'm not gonna die stuck in some wrecked helicopter. No way!"

"Listen to me. I just saved your life, and I'm trying to save it again. Those creatures are intelligent. They—"

"Screw you, bitch," Roy sneered. "I'll do what I have to do to survive." He climbed down the wreckage and stumbled into the rainforest.

Katya watched Roy disappear into the foliage. She glanced at the dead creatures on the ground and the encompassing undergrowth around the helicopter. She had a sinking feeling that the rats were close by, watching, waiting for a chance to attack. She checked her gun for ammunition. The magazine had a dozen rounds. She wrenched the pilot's chair away from its broken mounts and positioned the seat over the hole in the windscreen, jamming it into the shattered screen to make sure it held tight. She peered out through the broken doorway one last time, then rested her head against the interior wall to regulate her breathing and calm her body. If the rats returned, she was ready for them.

With nose twitching and tail swaying, the Alpha fixed his red eyes on Roy as he stumbled through the forest. The rat sensed fear as the human crashed through the jungle, oblivious to his surroundings. Lesser rats understood their place in the hoard and kept their distance from the leader, but a small rat scurried close to the Alpha. Still transfixed by the human, but annoyed by the lesser creature beside him, the Alpha snarled to reveal black, rotted fangs. The Alpha whipped its steel-like tail through the air and struck the small rat across the torso, sending it flying into the bushes. Unperturbed, the Alpha thumped its tail, signaling the others to join him as he sniffed the air for the trail and followed Roy into the rain forest.

CHAPTER 12

Joanna opened the sliding door and stepped onto the balcony. "Oh, dear," she sighed. "It's only 9:30, and already the day's humidity has settled in." She sat on one of two sage wicker chairs and placed her hot tea on the small table between them.

Baxter, in an immaculate three-piece suit and with hair meticulously combed, followed Joanna onto the balcony and stood behind her. His electronic pad in hand and holstered pistol at his side, he was prepared to serve at a moment's notice.

Joanna reached into her handbag and pulled out a monogrammed handkerchief to dab the beads of sweat from her forehead. Sadly, she gazed at her cup of hot tea. "Baxter, darling, would you be a dear and see if you can find me a cold beer, please? I'm afraid hot tea just won't cut it today."

"Of course, mum." He stepped back into the hotel room.

Joanna lit a cigarette and stood by the railing studying the hotel property. The lobby and atrium, directly below, opened onto perfectly landscaped gardens that surrounded the building. Lush palms encompassed the hotel complex. The Olympic-sized pool sparkled in the morning light. A shade-sail protecting the tennis court and alfresco dining zone flapped in the sultry breeze. The hotel grounds ended at the river's edge a stone's throw from where the fast-flowing water disappeared over a picturesque waterfall that emptied into a lagoon at the base of the cliff. Enclosed on three sides by dense rain forest, the lagoon glistened in the morning sun. The hotel and the waterfall overlooked the lagoon and a strip of flourishing jungle vegetation that ran the length of the cliff's base and stretched two miles beyond to the Pacific Ocean.

A narrow tributary snaked from the lagoon and through the green landscape to a delta opening on the beachfront. As the sun rose, the humidity from the basin dimmed the morning light, creating a soft orange radiance across the island. "Very nice," she murmured, lowering her sunglasses to get a better look at the magnificent vista.

Baxter stepped into a cloud of drifting cigarette smoke and brushed aside the rancid odor. He placed a cold glass of unpasteurized and unfiltered Pilsner Urquell on the table and resumed his position behind his employer. "If I may be so bold, mum, those cigarettes are doing you harm. Would you care for some nicotine gum, or possibly a vapor-pen? I hear the watermelon flavoring has an agreeable fragrance. I have both for such an occasion."

"No, thank you, Baxter. As you know, I like to live dangerously. Please, sit down." She offered Baxter the spare chair beside her. "You're making me nervous back there."

"We've had this discussion before, mum. With all due respect, my position requires knowledge of place and decorum. Thank you for the offer, but I shall refrain from acting on the invitation."

Joanna took a drink of the cold beer and sighed with satisfaction. "I respect your dedication, Baxter—I really do—but the offer will always be there."

"Thank you, mum," he replied with genuine sincerity.

Joanna took another drink of the beer and allowed the cool refreshing beverage to wash down. "Good choice, Baxter."

"Thank you, mum."

"And, please, stop calling me mum. The Merricks and their clients will think I'm your mother, for God's sake."

"Yes, mum."

On the balcony above Joanna and Baxter's, Klaus was dusting a chair for Wolfgang who was waiting patiently to be seated. With the business of the morning over, Wolfgang now wore sweatpants and a loose-fitting shirt. He gazed toward the pool where the contestants gathered, surrounded by several armed guards.

On the adjoining balcony, Adedowale and Abeo rested against the railing, waiting for the first event to begin.

CHAPTER 13

The First Event

THE GUESTS WATCHED from their hotel balconies as the six contestants in different colored jumpsuits assembled beside the Olympic-sized pool. The contestants cast tentative glances at one another as Merrick, his Baikal pistol tucked behind his belt, positioned himself before them. Less than waist-deep yellow river water, the source of the pool's water supply, filled the lower section of the pool whose exposed concrete walls glared in the morning sun.

Merrick tapped his headphone to confirm that the system was working. Simon's youthful voice sounded through the earpiece. "The cameras are in position, and your voice is being transmitted directly to the guests' earphones, Mr. Merrick. On your command, I can have your voice broadcast through the speakers set up around the hotel. Everything is working one hundred percent from my end; all systems are go. Ready when you are, sir."

"Thanks, Simon." Merrick cleared his throat. The time had come to launch the franchise that would change his life forever. He could smell the millions, all his, ready for the taking.

Merrick stood before the six contestants like a general addressing his troops. He encompassed all those before him, his arms wide. "Let's get the show started!"

Several men in black tactical garb positioned themselves around the group. They kept a watchful eye for any breakaways with suicidal thoughts of escape. Beside Merrick, Van Sant fixed his gaze on the contestants, his Beretta tucked into his shoulder holster for all to see.

"Screw you," an Australian voice called from the contestant line-up. He flipped Merrick the bird.

Merrick grinned at the Aussie in the yellow jumpsuit. "I like Australians. I honestly do. The Gallipoli campaign was an unmitigated disaster, yet you Aussies made it your finest hour with that spirit of true comradeship coupled with your never-give-up attitude against overwhelming odds. You can't help it. It's in your nature. It's in your blood. You have that fighting spirit—much like we Brits."

The Australian folded his arms in a gesture of non-compliance. Merrick shook his head. This defiance could not go unpunished. The time had come for him to assure the clients and contestants that he was a man to be reckoned with.

"You see"—Merrick scanned his iPad for the contestant's name—"Trevor, I need to show everyone what is at stake and, in no uncertain terms, the consequences of non-compliance." *What a waste, but I must make an example of the contestant in yellow to show the world who is in control.* Merrick leveled his pistol at Trevor and fired.

As the bullets tore into his flesh, the Aussie's body jerked like a macabre marionette, splattering blood over the other contestants before falling backward into the pool. In seconds, blood stained the surrounding water.

Below the water's surface, a sleek shadow undulated toward the floating corpse. In horror the contestants watched its dim form pass beneath the body before disappearing into the murky depths.

The contestants turned to each other, their expressions grim.

The shadow reappeared. As it circled the body, the water erupted beside the dead man. When the water settled, the contestants jumped back, terrified.

A thirty-foot python was wrapping itself around the dead Aussie and squeezing his lifeless body. As the snake's grip tightened, blood and bodily matter spewed from the corpse's mouth. The snake's head rose from the water. For a moment, its yellow reptilian eyes studied the men beside the pool while it decided whether they were a threat.

The snake turned to the dead body within its grasp. In preparation for its meal, its mouth widened. Slowly its jaws descended over the head leaving only the Australian's body visible. Then the body disappeared inside the reptile. The contestants stared in horror at the outline of the human inching down the length of the giant snake, until the reptile disappeared beneath the water.

"Leaves you speechless, doesn't it?" Merrick addressed the contestants mimicking a shiver. "No matter how many times I've seen this, it still sends shivers down my spine." Lincoln and the other contestants exchanged grave looks while Van Sant averted his gaze from the pool, preferring not to see a man consumed by a giant snake.

Merrick turned his attention to his clients watching from the safety of their balconies. "The reticulated python, native to Asia, is one of the lesser understood snakes. Its muscle structure allows it to constrict around its prey, crushing its prey's body. Many of us have been led to believe that a snake can unhinge its jaws to feed on larger prey. This is not true. In pythons, ligaments rather than bone connect the jawbone to the skull, thus allowing the creature to widen its jaws up to one hundred and fifty degrees. With its widened mouth, the snake can feed on anything from small rodents to"—Merrick paused for effect—"larger animals. Once his prey is immobile, the snake swallows its victim whole and begins to digest the meat and bone. The python is indeed a remarkable creature.

"The python you see before you is indeed larger than most found in the wild where they can grow up to twenty-five feet. Thanks to our state-of-the-art breeding program, our snakes weigh three hundred and thirty pounds and are a minimum of thirty feet with a belly diameter of no less than six feet. A creature of this size can be reproduced, but, because of the time required to breed and nurture the creatures, a fully mature specimen can only be guaranteed in six months. If time is a consideration, I can supply smaller specimens up to twenty feet long. The contract includes shipping, and I personally guarantee transport of said creatures—should you prefer not to take advantage of this island's facilities and location."

Merrick turned back to the contestants. "The rules are simple. The game is over when one of you dies in the pool. If everybody survives—and I doubt that very much—" he shrugged and indicated his weapon, "then the last man out of the pool never leaves the island. Okay, boys, in you go."

Red leaped into the water with a maniacal laugh, but fear and apprehension gripped the others. With caution, they descended into the murky yellow pool.

The waist-high water made mobility difficult, so Lincoln knew that to outrun anything would be next to impossible. Green, who was balding and middle-aged, whispered, "They've screwed up." His tone held a hint of arrogance.

"How?" Lincoln asked, keeping his eyes on the water around him.

"A human body is more than enough food for a python. That snake won't feed again for days, maybe weeks."

"You sure about that?" Gray asked from behind, facing the opposite direction in preparation for the python's return. The eldest of the contestants, he understood that his small physique and mild manner would be no match for the coming event.

"One hundred percent," Green replied.

"Why so sure?" Lincoln was still not convinced of Green's assumption.

"Think about it. It will take hours, if not days, for the snake's internal digestive system to process that amount of meat and flesh. Merrick and his gang of thugs screwed up big time. Believe me when I say this: We're safe for now."

Lincoln shrugged. Green made sense. The snake would probably feed on the dead body for some time. He continued to scan the water for movement beneath the surface, but for the first time since entering the pool, the tension in his mind and body toned down a notch.

With a thumbs up from Merrick, several guards positioned themselves around the edge of the pool and lifted the large metal grates built into the sides. The grates had been flush with the concrete edge, unnoticed by the contestants.

The contestants peered into the gaping holes behind the lifting grates. The three-foot-wide concrete aqueducts were covered in algae and moss. Water stained the front of the ducts while darkness shrouded the rear. The faint humming of a compressor reverberated about them. As one, the contestants felt the deep rumbling throughout the pool and surrounding area. They glanced at one another and braced themselves, dreading the unknown.

Horizontal torrents of water burst from the aqueducts and into the pool smashing the contestants with the force of a freight train. Green and Gray lost their footing and slammed over in the waist high water.

Lincoln managed to keep upright, but the force of the water gushing around him pushed him off balance. He struggled to stay above the water until another aqueduct opened, and the geyser slammed him full on. Like the others, he fell into the roiling water.

Lincoln searched under water for moving shadows or unwanted visitors. He surfaced and took in a lungful of air.

Stay alert. Stay focused.

Moments later, the others surfaced.

The guards lifted a set of metal screens adjacent to the grates. Long shadows deep inside the water torrents flowed into the pool. Lincoln and the other contestants turned to Green with narrowed eyes.

Green shrugged *sorry* as several thirty-foot pythons glided beneath the water searching for their next meal.

Shit.

Long narrow shadows shot through the water and surrounded the five men.

Merrick picked up the knapsack beside him and pulled out five knifes. "The rules are simple. Kill one, and you get to live." He threw the knives into the center of the pool yelling, "May the best man win!"

Lincoln was the first to react. He dove into the murky water and found a knife. He gripped the handle with all his strength as the first shadow passed by. A snake's head emerged from the silty water, its yellow eyes focused on its next meal—*Lincoln Monk*. Lincoln waved the knife before him in preparation for the strike. He followed the snake as it glided through the water with ease, circling him. Because the bottom of the pool was covered in slime, getting a foothold was difficult. Lincoln slipped several times as he maneuvered about trying to keep eye contact with the deadly predator. With his oxygen running low, Lincoln had no choice but to break surface. He sucked in as much precious air as he could without taking his eyes off the snake.

Lincoln shot a glance at the other contestants in the pool. Red was slicing a deep gash down the belly of a python writhing around him. Green, grinning from ear to ear, searched the water, beckoning a snake for a fight. "Come on, my little princess, let's see want you have for daddy." He passed the knife from one hand to the other, readying himself for the fight. Gray stood his ground, waiting for his snake to strike. With fear in his eyes, he held his knife out before him, his hand shaking with fright.

Lincoln recognized that the older man would be no match for a jungle predator like a python. The other contestants, younger and leaner, stood a better chance of survival. Gray would be the first to die. Lincoln twisted in the water, keeping constant eye contact with the python closing in on him. He felt empathy for the older man who seemed doomed to die a horrible death.

Wolfgang took a mouthful of Heineken and leaned forward over the balcony's rail to watch the outcome, grinning with satisfaction at the first event. He paid particular attention to Red, already slicing another gash down the snake's spine. The writhing snake thrashed about, its long tail whipping through the water. Wolfgang leaned over to Klaus. The assistant tapped his earpiece. "Mr. Merrick, my employer would like to enter a wager. Would that be out of the question?"

Merrick turned his attention from the spectacle in the pool to the clients watching from their balconies. He grinned and waved to them. "Of course not. You may bet as much as you like on whomever you think will win or lose the coming events. Once the wager is completed, my people will either pay cash to the winner or transfer the dollar amount into an account of his or her choosing." The conditions met with Wolfgang's approval. He opened the briefcase beside him, pulled out a stack of hundred Euro notes, and passed them to Klaus.

"However," Merrick continued, "I believe it would be unfair to bet on an event that has already begun. But feel free to gamble on the upcoming events." The assistant whispered to Wolfgang who glared at Merrick, clearly unimpressed. He snatched the stack of hundred Euro notes and threw them into the briefcase and slammed the lid.

Merrick smiled back at the overweight German on the balcony. "Take that, you asshole," he murmured, with a friendly wave toward the Germans. "No one tells me my chef serves dog food. No one."

The python moved into position and began wrapping itself around Gray. He screamed in terror as the reptile pinned his arms to his sides, making movement impossible. Gray gasped as the snake's body tightened around him, constricting his breathing. The snake's head whipped around and focused on the terrified man, its yellow eyes level with Gray's eyes. As it moved closer, its jaws widened. Hissing resonated throughout the pool and bounced off the concrete walls. The snake's jaws opened wider and it struck out at Gray, its fangs biting into his flesh. Gray managed to free his arm and hold it up in defense but screamed in agony as the snake's mouth clamp around his forearm. Lincoln couldn't let the older man die like this.

With his pulse racing and his heart drumming in his chest, Lincoln struggled to get a foothold on the slime-covered floor. As the python closed in, wrapping itself around his body, and constricting his movements, he had little time to think let alone save the older man. A National Geographic documentary flashed through his mind, and Lincoln did the only crazy thing that might work. "This is insane," he murmured biting down hard on the snake's spine. As the snake hissed in pain, Lincoln felt the monster release him.

Holy shit, it works. His survival instincts had delivered.

With no time to spare, Lincoln crouched down and braced himself as best he could on the mucky bottom then sprang from the water onto the snake's body. Using the snake as leverage, he launched himself over to Gray and fell upon Gray's snake. Taking the creature by surprise, he slammed his knife hard into its flat head. The knife pierced the soft skull and penetrated down through the upper jaw. As the snake released its hold on Gray's arm, its tail whipped through the air, striking Lincoln on the shoulder and driving him into the water. Stunned, Lincoln took several seconds to regain his senses. With the knife embedded in its skull, the snake withdrew beneath the water, leaving a trail of blood as it disappeared into the murky water away from the two men.

Lincoln felt Gray shaking from the ordeal as he supported him to keep him above the bloodstained water. "Thanks," Gray heaved in relief, not caring that the knife had punctured his arm.

The snake that preyed on Lincoln undulated toward them, maneuvering into position around him and Gray. The long body glided through the water, its scales glistening in the sunlight. "It's not over yet," Lincoln noted. "Mine's still hungry."

The creature's head swayed almost rhythmically as it closed in for the kill. Lincoln grabbed Gray's knife and brandished it before them while ushering Gray back to keep as much distance as possible between him and the deadly reptile. The old man stumbled in the water, lost his balance, and fell. As Lincoln helped him to his feet, the snake was around them. Lincoln felt the muscles beneath the snake's skin contract and heard Gray gasp for breath as the creature tightened around his torso, cutting off the blood supply to the brain.

Lincoln lost his footing just as he caught sight of the snake with the knife impaled in its head. The lifeless python's body had sunk to the bottom of the pool, but its head lolled above water, its dead eyes staring at Lincoln. Lincoln yanked the knife from the creature's skull.

With a knife in each hand, Lincoln stabbed the snake constricting them, ripping upward and out as far as he could with both arms. The python's innards spilled from the gaping gash, filling Lincoln's nostrils with the stench of raw snake meat mixed with bile. The snake loosened its grip on the two men, thrashed about, and uncoiled itself before slithering into the murky water, leaving a trail of blood and innards in its wake.

Lincoln and Gray exhaled in relief.

The older man leaned on his haunches and gulped in a lungful of air. "I don't know how to repay you. I owe you my life, Blue. Thank you."

Lincoln gave him a thumbs up and took a deep breath to calm his nerves. "It's Lincoln. If we ever get off this shitty island, you can buy me a beer."

"If we get away from this godforsaken place, I'll buy you a brewery." Gray smiled, still gasping to catch his breath. "I'm Lucius. Lucius Gray. And, yes, I'm aware of the color code and my name. I think Mr. Merrick thought it would be easy to recognize the contestants this way."

The guard fired a round between Lincoln and Lucius. "You two—out," he commanded, waving the assault rifle's barrel toward the ladder mounted along the pool's side. Lincoln and Gray climbed out and stood poolside. The guard stationed himself behind them, his rifle poised, ready for any attempt to run.

Red emerged from the pool and joined them as two more guards closed in from both sides. Red laughed at them and smirked with contempt as Purple clawed his way from the pool.

Gray searched the water. "Where's Green?"

"Looks like Green is lunch." Lincoln pointed to a python with a leg in a green jump-suit protruding from its widened jaw.

From the penthouse balcony, Samantha Merrick gasped with pleasure. The fire in her loins burnt from within as she fixed her gaze on the dying men in the pool. This quirk, this sickness in her genetic makeup, had to be quelled. She was the one who had recognized this inherent lust for others' suffering and death, and together, she and Tom were a formidable duo striving to better their places in the world with their insatiable appetites.

Watching her husband give orders to the men by the pool, Samantha sighed with pleasure. The corners of her lips turned up at the thought of what he would do to her that night when she offered herself to him wearing nothing but a smile and her new diamond necklace. Taking one last look at the death scene below, she retreated to the penthouse to prepare for the evening's bedroom entertainment.

CHAPTER 14

As he stumbled through the jungle, Roy felt like his blood was pounding through his veins at a hundred miles an hour. Not wanting to be caught in the open, he stayed parallel to the dusty trail, keeping a close eye on the meandering path so as not to get lost. What drove him was not the lesser creatures inhabiting the jungle, but fear of the unknown. He didn't care what was in front of him; running into thorn bushes and fronds infested with spiders and whip scorpions didn't bother him. What was behind him was what terrified him. Fearful that the giant rodents lay in wait close by, Roy surged into the green wall of foliage, hoping to make it to the safety of the plane before the rats discovered his flight from the helicopter wreckage.

The deep rumble of a motor caught his attention. A Willys jeep bounced along the forgotten track hitting every pothole that pockmarked the trail as the driver fought to keep the jeep on the dirt path. Two men in black military garb with M16 assault rifles strapped to their sides clung to the panels in the cargo bay. Resting between them an M134 Minigun glistened in the sunlight.

Something is wrong. Gunmen with that type of firepower are not friendly. Roy hid behind a clump of palm leaves and watched as the Willys jeep flew by heading toward the chopper. Satisfied that the threat had passed, he congratulated himself on having left the helicopter, then glanced around one more time before continuing into the jungle.

Katya woke to the sound of sniffing outside the helicopter. She wiped the sweat from her face and realized she must have dozed off for a few minutes. The short rest had relaxed her tense muscles and allowed her to unwind and collect herself from the earlier horrors. For the first time in hours, she felt invigorated. She checked the magazine and readied herself against the inner wall of the cabin, then peeked through the doorway. Her blood ran cold. Dread and despair filled her as she realized she didn't have enough bullets for what waited outside the helicopter.

Dozens of rats surrounded the wreckage, sniffing the air in search of prey. A dozen more creatures emerged from the vegetation to converge on the helicopter.

Katya checked to ensure that the chamber was loaded. She shifted the slide one more time then locked it in place. She took a deep breath and readied herself. "I love you Napoleon... and Marcus."

The roar of machine gun fire reverberated through the cabin as guttural squeals and screeches filled the air. The Minigun continued sounding, its strafing killing every creature in sight. Within moments, the squealing was replaced by the stench of cordite and death. Katya flattened herself against the wall as a dying creature managed a solitary squeal that was quickly followed by another round of machine gun fire. Silence.

Footsteps approached then halted outside the open doorway. The barrel of an M16 glided through the opening, followed by a bald head and an unshaven face. Her savior glanced around and spotted Katya. "Howdy, darlin'," he said with a Texas drawl. "Y'all need some help?"

Behind him, two men in black military garb wandered about the clearing, kicking then shooting any rodents clinging to life.

Katya's initial joy at seeing the newcomer faded as he leveled his rifle in her direction. Sensing that these heavily-armed men were not the saviors she thought, she vowed not to give them any information that could jeopardize her companions at the crash site. *Lead them in the opposite direction, away from the plane.* Her ploy had worked well on strangers and in other threatening situations, so why not on this island?

The bald-headed guard zip-tied Katya's hands and helped her into the Willys Jeep beside the M134 Minigun mounted in the back. He wiped the sweat from his face and was ogling her tanned legs and trim form when a second guard, sporting a buzz cut and handlebar moustache, interrupted his thoughts.

"I've contacted the control room. That kid Simon said the faulty up-link appeared on his malfunction report, but the tower was useless anyway. Apparently, they don't use that tower anymore because they communicate directly with the satellite back at the hotel—or somethin' like that. He said thanks for checkin' it out."

"Whatever," the bald guard answered, annoyed at the distraction. He tore his eyes away from Katya's athletic allure and surveyed the carnage around him. As the sun's heat warmed the dead carcasses, a putrid odor wafted across the crash site.

"I've never seen rats this big before," the second guard said with apprehension, clutching his rifle and nervously fingering the trigger. "These are biguns."

The bald guard took one last look at the massacred rodents. "Me neither. This end of the island gives me the creeps. Van Sant said not to spend any more time down here than necessary. We did what we came here to do, so let's get the hell out."

"You got that right." The second guard looked toward Katya. "So, who's the stunner?"

"I have no idea. She doesn't speak English. I think she's Russian or somethin'."

"Where the hell did she come from?"

"Your guess is as good as mine. She keeps pointin' north. Maybe she's new hotel staff and got lost. Who knows? Mr. Merrick has new people arrivin' all the time."

"She had a gun. You don't find that a bit odd?"

"Everybody on this island has a gun. Even that ugly chef woman carries a gun."

The second guard conceded with a shrug. His partner was right—everybody on this hellhole had a gun.

"Van Sant said to bring her back, and that's what we're goin' to do."

With Katya secured in the back, the guards climbed into the Jeep. The engine roared to life, its spinning back wheels kicking up a cloud of dust and dirt as it sped off down the dirt track heading north toward the hotel.

CHAPTER 15

VAN SANT AND two guards escorted the remaining contestants to the hotel's recreation room. Cots rested along the far wall, and gym equipment lined the adjacent walls. A table laid with prepared dishes ran down the center of the room. The exhausted contestants shuffled inside.

"This, gentlemen, will be your new home for the next few days," Van Sant announced. "Through that door behind you, you'll find a shower and toilet facilities. Take advantage of the food provided; you're going to need all the energy you can get. If I were you, I'd be lifting weights and getting in shape for the upcoming events. You all know what's at stake—and what the consequences are for not towing the line. If you're thinking about escaping, think again. Guards are stationed non-stop outside this door, and cameras are on you twenty-four seven. Well, gentlemen, make the most of it," he said, indicating the food and gym equipment, "and I'll see you all bright and early tomorrow morning."

Van Sant closed the door behind him. The bolt locking into place clanged throughout the room.

Lincoln stood beside the table surveying the remaining contestants. Purple huddled in a corner, his arms wrapped around his shins, fear etched in his eyes. Gray sat on the edge of a bunk and nursed his injured arm. Red headed toward the food.

"Out of my way, Blue," Red snarled, shoving Lincoln aside to get to the roast chicken.

Lincoln stumbled but regained his footing. He glared at the towering cretin as Red tore a leg from the chicken, but he knew when to stand his ground and when to back off, so he allowed Red the chance to eat what could be his last meal. "We need to help each other," Lincoln explained, watching Red gorge on the white meat.

"Piss off. I'll take my chances without your help."

"If we work together, maybe we can all survive and get out of this death-trap."

Red grabbed Lincoln by the neck and clamped down. The man had incredible strength. Lincoln protested, but to no avail.

"Listen to him, Red," Gray said, rising from the bunk. "Blue makes sense."

"Shut up, old man," Red snapped. He turned to Lincoln. "I plan on winning. You and the others are dead to me; you just don't know it yet." He released Lincoln and turned back to his meal. Lincoln rubbed the soreness from his neck, grabbed a quick selection of food, and backed away.

The thump-thumping of rotor blades echoed from above. Lincoln peeked between the vertical blinds on the floor-to-ceiling glass wall. A Chinook CH-47 tandem rotor chopper carrying an underslung shipping container kicked up a cloud of leaves as it descended from the night. The helicopter hovered at the base of a concrete ramp at the rear of the hotel where armed men were positioned around the landing zone. As the container thudded to the ground, the men released the three ventral cargo hooks. Then, directed by Merrick's men, the helicopter lifted into the darkness where its tail swung around before the craft lowered to a helipad beside the hotel.

Lincoln spotted four more helicopters sitting behind the hotel—two Sikorski Skycranes, a Bell Jet Ranger, and a Hughes MD500E. He smiled at the MD500E, immediately recognizing the Cayuse/Loach version from his favorite film *Capricorn One*.

As the Chinook's rotors slowed to a lazy spin, Merrick's men opened the shipping container's metal doors and wheeled a thirty-foot crate into the shadows at the base of the loading ramp. The darkness hid their movements, but beyond the Sikorsky Skycranes, Lincoln caught a glimpse of more men scurrying about the base of a construction crane, its dimly lit boom swiveling through the air. The darkness and jungle vegetation made a clear view impossible. Reluctantly Lincoln turned and joined Gray on the adjacent cot.

"Anything interesting?" Gray asked, trying to take his mind off the deadly situation.

Lincoln considered what little he had seen from his obstructed vantage point. "Maybe." He picked at his food, distracted by the day's brutal events. Nevertheless, Van Sant was right. He needed to keep his energy up if he was to survive the week. He took a bite of chicken and washed it down with a glass of water while observing the others in the room.

"How did you get into all of this?" Gray asked with genuine sincerity.

Lincoln wanted to trust Lucius Gray, but sticking to the helicopter story was safer for his and Christina's sake, so he decided not to tell the older man about the others back at the plane. He had saved the man's life, but given the choice, he knew Gray could give him up for a chance to live. "I was sightseeing across the islands and my helicopter crashed not far from here. Merrick's men found me. I was pretty much in the wrong place at the wrong time. Just my luck."

"That is quite bad luck. To survive a helicopter crash and then be forced into this sick, twisted game."

Lincoln nodded. "Mind if I ask how you came to be here? No offense, but you don't appear to be the sort of guy who would be involved in this type of situation, either.

"No offense taken." Lucius paused, recalling a better time, a better place. He smiled ruefully. "An associate and I were declared no longer viable."

"Meaning?"

Lucius glanced about the room, careful not to attract any undue attention. "My colleague Dr. Lockwood and I were hired by Merrick's people to tend to the staff's medical requirements. Nothing too over the top—just sprains, cuts, minor injuries, akin to a ship's doctor." The old joke about ships' doctors sprang to mind, causing Lincoln to smile. Gray noticed and smiled, too. "We doctors are all aware of the joke. *Ships' doctors are only one step away from a malpractice suit—which is why they're on the ship in the first place.*" Lincoln and Gray chuckled at the poor attempt at humor, appreciating that the light-hearted joke distracted them from their dire circumstances, if only for a moment.

Lincoln was tempted to seek Gray's medical opinion on Mich's injuries but decided against giving away the crew's existence. "Sounds like you're a handy guy to have around. So what happened?"

"When Merrick's people came to us with unusual wounds and symptoms of diseases uncommon to this geographical region, Lockwood and I asked too many questions. When we threatened to notify the Philippine Department of Health, we sealed our fates. Merrick's people forced us into this sick game."

"Where's Lockwood?"

"He escaped from the hotel."

"How?" Lincoln probed, hoping for some useful information.

"Dr. Lockwood was a small man. He slipped through a window in the bathroom that has since been boarded up."

"*Was* a small man? Isn't it possible he's still alive?" Lincoln asked, wanting to believe there was hope.

Gray looked at Lincoln's jumpsuit with sadness. "My boy, my friend and colleague Dr. Lockwood was designated Blue."

"Sorry." Lincoln could think of nothing else to say knowing that Lockwood must certainly be dead. If the jungle hadn't killed the man, Merrick's men would have finished the job.

Gray glanced around the gym and paused at Red's steadfast

glare from across the room. Red stood and strode toward their cots. "Looks like we're about to have company," Gray whispered.

Lincoln spotted Red closing in.

"I apologize. I looked in his direction," Gray confessed, overwhelmed by Red's bulk and muscle. "I'm not much of a fighter."

"Let me handle this."

Red stopped between the cots and thrust his chest out. "What are you two whispering about?" he demanded.

"Just trying to decide what to have for dessert. Gray here has a hankering for tiramisu, but I've always been an apple pie and coffee man," Lincoln admitted.

Red grabbed Lincoln by the vest and lifted him from the cot. "Maybe I should kill you both now."

Lincoln turned his head as Red's foul breath wafted over his face. "Any chance you could brush your teeth first?"

Red's face contorted in anger. He threw Lincoln across the floor where Lincoln slid into the buffet table, knocking it over. Table settings and food crashed to the ground as Red charged toward him.

Merrick and Van Sant sat in the control room watching Simon tap multiple keyboards.

"Tell me the bugs are working," Merrick said.

"The microphones are working well. They pick up almost every sound in the hotel rooms."

"Good," Merrick said with relief. "What are the Germans saying?"

Simon opened another window, and guest transcripts rolled down the screen. "I have no idea," he admitted. "The translation program doesn't recognize Wolfgang's dialect—but I keep hearing the word *strudel*."

Merrick shook his head in disgust. "Still complaining about the food. What an asshole."

"What about the Nigerians?" Van Sant asked.

"They're watching the repeats of the day's events on the television. I hear lots of laughter coming from their room."

"Sick bastards," Van Sant whispered.

"And Joanna and her manservant?"

"Apparently, he saw a spider, and she enjoys her alcohol."

Merrick eased back into his chair and relaxed. "Good. The first day went without a hitch. I want complete transcripts of all the conversations coming out of those hotel rooms."

"Yes, Mr. Merrick."

"And the contestants?"

Simon turned to the footage from the security camera mounted in the top left corner of the recreation room that recorded every second of the contestant's movements and whereabouts.

"Give Blue back his Neptune cap," Merrick instructed Van Sant.

"Why?" Van Sant lit a cigarette.

Simon waved away the foul-smelling smoke from the monitor. "Must you? Dammit!" he cursed. "This is expensive equipment."

Van Sant ignored the skinny operator and inhaled, then taunted Simon by blowing smoke over the LCD screen.

"Dickhead." Simon carefully wiped the screen with a lint free cloth while Van Sant laughed.

"Any advertising is good advertising," Merrick continued, irritated by the interruption. "I want to let the clients know, in a subtle way, that this venture is associated with the Neptune Corporation."

Van Sant gave Merrick a curious glance, not understanding the connection.

"Advertisers see the Neptune cap, and subconsciously they associate the games with Neptune, which adds credibility. That little cap is a visual reminder of the power and influence backing this venture."

Van Sant shrugged, knowing nothing of sales. "Okay, boss, if you say so, but the cap is probably at the bottom of the pool."

"Get one of your guys to find it. And make sure it's clean. I don't want any blood on the Neptune logo." Merrick looked at Red and frowned. "Make sure he doesn't get too aggressive with the others. The last thing we need is to have to find more contestants. Besides, the Germans just placed a million euro bet on Red to win, so I don't want him getting killed unless he's the second-to-last man standing."

Van Sant chuckled as he watched the fight on the control room monitor. "Blue sure knows how to get Red fired up."

Merrick's steady gaze never left the screen as Red pulled Lincoln from under the table and threw him into the gym equipment. Lincoln fell over the barbells and landed heavily on the concrete floor. The big Russian leaned in, fist raised, and was about to strike when Lincoln positioned his feet under the barbells and drove his legs up. The metal bar struck Red hard across the nose. Red roared in agony and staggered backward, clutching his bloodied nose. His eyes watered from the pain, blinding him. Lincoln grabbed the barbell. He scrambled to safety and released the weight discs from the bar. Grabbing the bar with both fists, he wielded it like a weapon, prepared for the next attack.

"Quick thinking. I like that." Merrick grinned as he observed the fight in the recreation room. "But keep an eye on Blue. We can't have him messing things up."

"Will do."

"Where did you find this Red character?"

"He works for you."

Merrick turned to face Van Sant. "He *what?*'

"Correction. He *worked* for you. When he discovered what we had in mind, he volunteered for the games—said it would be an honor and a privilege to win the first-ever Jungle Games."

Merrick stared. "You're kidding me, right?"

"Nope."

"Is he...?" Merrick circled his finger beside his temple.

"Good question." Van Sant shrugged. "Probably."

"Well," Merrick said, contemplating Red's actions, "I suppose if the man has a death-wish, who are we to deprive him of his chosen destiny?" He turned back to the monitor.

Red was snatching the bar from Lincoln's hands. In a show of brute strength, he gripped both ends of the metal rod and, with abs bulging, slowly bent them together. Lincoln gulped. *Oh, shit.*

Red laughed and threw the bar aside. He swooped up Lincoln from the floor and wrapped his bulging biceps around Lincoln's torso. With his arms trapped at his sides, Lincoln's options were limited. Red roared with laughter as Lincoln struggled to break free from his deadly hold. "Your ass is mine," Red bragged with satisfaction, tightening his grip.

Pain shot through Lincoln's ribcage. He gasped for air while his spine ached from the extreme pressure. He kicked down on Red's knee, digging his heel deep into the soft tissue above the joint. Red yelped and released Lincoln. He rocked on the floor clutching his bruised knee while Lincoln took a deep breath.

"This ends here," Merrick commanded.

"Come on, boss. It's just getting interesting." Van Sant was enjoying every movement of the entertainment on the monitor.

"I can't have them killing each other now. If they die tonight, we won't have enough contestants for the tomorrow's event, now will we?"

Merrick was right. Van Sant knew that finding Blue at the last minute to replace Lockwood had been a stroke of luck. He didn't care to push his good fortune twice.

"I want them fit and ready for the sinkhole tomorrow. They can do what they like to each other then, but tonight I need them both alive."

Lincoln swung his fist hard across Red's jaw.

Red's head snapped back. Blood flowed from where his teeth had been.

Lincoln was preparing for another hit when he fell to the floor. His vision blurred and refused to focus. He lay on his back, the fluorescent lights dancing before his eyes. *Not again.* As he pulled the tranquilizer dart from his neck, for the third time in two days he lost all sensation in his hand. Despite his eyes growing heavy with colors swirling before them, his last vision of two guards lifting the bloodied Red from the floor made him smile.

CHAPTER 16

ENHEIM SHUFFLED UNEASILY by the bottom of the Dakota's makeshift rope ladder while he waited for Napoleon to do his business in the nearby undergrowth. He held a garbage bag over his head against the torrential rain as he stared into the surrounding jungle, hoping that Napoleon would return sooner rather than later. "Don't go far, Napums," Enheim called, peering into the foliage and keeping a watchful eye for any dangers lurking in the green folds. He sighed. Katya should have been back by now.

Napoleon barked.

Enheim bolted to attention. "What's up, boy?"

Napoleon barked again, this time with deeper resonance.

"Napums?" Silence. Something was wrong. "Napums, where are you?" Enheim clawed his way through the underbrush and followed the muffled barking, regretting his decision to allow Napoleon to wander unsupervised for a change of scene from the plane's cabin. He searched frantically, palms sweating and stomach churning, desperate to catch a glimpse of his beloved dog. "Come on, boy. Where are you?"

Fronds crunched. Twigs snapped. Branches cracked. The heaving breathing and crashing grew louder on a path straight toward him. "Come on, boy! Daddy's right here." Enheim knelt, arms outstretched, ready to catch Napoleon.

A figure leapt from the foliage and slammed head-on into Enheim's waiting arms, knocking Enheim from his feet as they both tumbled to the ground. Enheim cleared a frond to see Roy's face, clouded with fear, inches from his own. "What the hell?" Ignoring Enheim, Roy scrambled to his feet, and raced to the plane's makeshift ladder.

Enheim was brushing a few leaves from his shirt when Napoleon scampered through the low-lying bushes. Enheim knelt and Napoleon leaped into his arms. He stroked the little dog's head and picked small twigs from his fur. "Good boy." Enheim smiled for the first time in hours at having one of the loves of his life back in his arms. "Good boy. Who's a good boy?"

Roy stumbled through the hatchway. Once inside he collapsed on the floor, panting in relief.

Mich and Roland looked at Roy lying on the floor, then turned to each other and shrugged.

"Did you find the SatSleeve?" Mich asked.

Roy retrieved the SatSleeve from his pocket and tossed it to Mich who caught it but found the cameraman's nervous behavior unsettling. "What's wrong?"

"And where's Katya?" Roland asked, scanning the outside jungle with concern.

Enheim appeared in the hatchway. He rested Napoleon on a nearby seat and picked Roy up by the collar. The cameraman squirmed, but Enheim held tight. "I don't see my wife out there. Where is she?"

Delirious from fear and exhaustion, Roy could only mumble.

Enheim's tone turned to a menacing whisper. *"Where—is—my—wife?"* Roy barely heard as the adrenaline coursed through his veins, his ears pounding and his heart racing. Enheim slapped Roy hard across the face to snap him from his fear-fueled stupor. "I'll ask nicely one more time, and then I won't ask nicely. You understand?"

Roy's eyes darted from Enheim's glare to the open hatchway. "Close the door! Close the door!"

"What?" Enheim and the others stared at the hatchway. Through a break in the clouds, the setting sun streamed through the jungle canopy, basking the plane in a warm orange glow.

Becca knelt beside Roy. Putting her arm around his shoulder, she spoke calmly. "Roy, where's Katya?"

Roy took in several deep breaths to relax his frayed nerves. He glanced around at the expectant faces waiting to hear what he had to say. He focused on the open hatch. "Sh-she's b-back at the helicopter," he stammered.

Anger boiled up within Enheim. He gripped Roy's collar tighter and jerked him closer. "Explain!"

Roy instinctively shook his head, unable to tell the people around him the events at the crash site. Enheim's steely-eyed gaze bore through him like a laser. Roy averted his eyes, unable to confront this man threating him with violence.

Roland decided on a different tact. He offered a bottle of water that Roy half-heartedly accepted. As he lifted the cold refreshing water to his lips, Enheim slapped the bottle away. Roland groaned.

"Mate," Enheim shouted, pulling his arm back to punch Roy, "you answer our questions, or I start hitting! Your choice!"

Roy gulped in more air. His pounding heart began to slow, his nerves became less tense. "I told her to follow me, but she wouldn't leave the site."

"Why would she stay at the site?" Roland asked.

"The rats. Giant rats. All over the helicopter. They took us by surprise. We didn't stand a chance."

"Giant rats?" Becca asked. "What are talking about?"

Roy, wide-eyed, stared at the open doorway. "We need to close that door. Now."

Roland could see Roy was on the verge of a nervous breakdown. Mich glanced out the window. The jungle appeared still.

Mich shrugged. Nevertheless, Roland closed the door and locked the handle in place. "See? We're safe," he said, his voice reassuring.

For the first time in hours, Roy's body relaxed. He wiped the sweat from his face and struggled to keep his emotions in check. He peered around the anxious group and realized that he needed to justify his actions. "We were attacked. Rats. Giant rats, the size of dogs. Hundreds of them. They overwhelmed us. When they retreated, we had a chance to escape, but she chose to stay behind. I tried to convince her, but she wouldn't listen."

"You left my wife to fend for herself?" Enheim clenched his fists tighter, ready to strike.

Roland frowned, confused by Roy's explanation. "Vhy vould she stay behind if she had a chance to leave?"

"I don't know." Roy's eyes darted about the group. "Ask her." His tone held a hint of arrogance. At the sight of Enheim's fist, he blurted, "There were men."

"What men?" Roland probed.

"Men, armed men, heading toward the crash site—maybe the same people who took your friends. They've probably taken her, too."

Enheim slammed his fist into the headrest, an inch from Roy's face. Roy gulped.

Napoleon's ears pricked up. He turned to the door and growled.

Outside on the wing, Rousseau preferred rain to being cooped up in the stuffy cabin. He was working on the Pratt and Whitney engine when he caught sight of movement in his peripheral vision. He peered down at the trees lining the clearing below. Over the drumming rain, the air was filled with the constant drone of insects and birds calling. He was about to turn back when he spotted several large rats peering at him, their noses twitching. Rousseau glanced around and saw more rats—large rats—scurrying along the jungle floor toward the plane. Within seconds, hundreds of rodents filled the clearing, all staring intently at Rousseau and the damaged plane.

Leaves tearing and branches breaking echoed throughout the clearing as the alpha rat made his way to the front of the rat horde.

Rousseau started at the sight of the human-sized rat resting on its haunches, its red eyes staring back at him, poised to strike. Rousseau kept his hands by his sides and tried not to make any sudden movements. "Mr. Pom?" he called into the cabin.

"Yes, Rousseau, I'll be there in a moment, you know."

Mich slipped the cell phone into the SatSleeve. He sighed with pleasure as the dim green light flashed. He tapped the screen and watched connection data roll down the page. The phone's wireless system linked with the SatSleeve connection. The turning hourglass *Please wait* icon filled the screen. "Come on," he prayed as the phone communicated with the satellite sleeve, "please make this work."

A message window appeared center screen: *Device connected. Waiting for signal.*

Tears welled up in his eyes. "It works," he called to the group in the cabin. "Now all we need is a clear sky so the SatSleeve can link with a satellite." He peered through the window at the cloud covering and the pelting rain. "Yep. Just our luck."

Rousseau cleared his throat. "Mr. Pom. We have company."

CHAPTER 17

"They're the biggest rats I've ever seen—even bigger than the buggers in Chicago." Enheim stared at the giant rodents swarming into the clearing surrounding the plane.

Roland grabbed Enheim's head and angled his line of sight toward the jungle's edge where the alpha rat's blood red eyes stared back at them, its nose twitching. "I stand corrected," Enheim murmured.

Roland raced into the cargo compartment and returned with a handful of Sig Sauer P229s. He passed one with a magazine to Mich who was still attempting to get a better signal now that the sat phone was working. "Lincoln said you can shoot," Roland said, concerned about Mich's capabilities, given his injury.

"I won't let you down," Mich assured him. He quickly adjusted the phone and passed it to Becca. "Here—the phone's set to receive and the GPS transponder is on, but the weather is playing havoc with the satellite link. You need direct line of sight with the satellite for the phone to make a connection. When you get the LINK CONFIRMED prompt, tap the hash key." Mich indicated the roof hatch in the cockpit. "But you already knew that, right?"

Becca accepted the phone as well as a pistol from Roland. "All too well," she sneered, glancing at Roy huddled in the corner. "He may have the stamina to hold a camera, but he's lousy with technology."

Roland made his way to Enheim. "Marcus, my brother-in-law,

ve have our differences, but you haf to be honest with me. Ve need all the help ve can get right now. You need to tell me if you can handle the veapon, you know."

In a show of confidence, Enheim slammed the magazine into the Glock and pulled back the slide. "How's that for assurance?" he said, keeping a watchful eye on the jungle's edge.

Roland raised an eyebrow in admiration. "Good enough."

Enheim's hand shook as he rubbed Napoleon under the jaw. His lack of weapons training played on his mind. With Roland turned away, he casually stole a glance at the safety latch built into the trigger. "You can do this," he whispered.

Roland peered through the cabin door's window. Dozens of giant rats were scurrying toward the plane. "How many on your side?" he asked Enheim.

Enheim peeked out the window. "I count a dozen." After ensuring that Napoleon was secure in his harness, he positioned himself beside the doorway to wait for Roland's instructions.

"Me, too." Mich watched the rats disappear into the trees below the plane. He joined the others at the closed door, racked the slide, and prepared for battle.

Rousseau climbed down through the cockpit's roof hatch, vacating the confined space of the flight deck to allow Becca to settle into the co-pilot's chair and hold the phone against the windscreen to get a better signal. She glanced nervously at the men positioned at the cabin doorway and discreetly made the sign of the cross.

Roland passed a pistol to Rousseau who stood beside him at the door. "Mr. Pom?"

Roland never took his eyes from the rats converging on the plane. "Rousseau, you have vorked for me for three years, you know. Please, call me Roland."

"Yes, Mr. Pom. I have a request."

At the nervous quaver in Rousseau's voice, Roland turned. "Vat is it?"

Rousseau looked at the hoard of rats swarming the base of the plane. Several had clawed their way onto the fuselage and were scampering over the wings. Claws scratching against metal echoed from overhead as more rats scurried over the cabin.

"Mr. Pom, it occurs to me that since I have known you, I have been shot at, escaped a tsunami, survived a plane crash, and will now probably be killed by very big rats."

Roland couldn't dispute Rousseau's statement.

"And all in the last four days."

"Well…" Roland sought to put a positive spin on the events but was at a loss for words.

'Mr. Pom, if we survive these rats, I think I deserve a raise."

The alpha edged closer to the plane and peered through the cabin door's plexiglass window. With lips pulled back, teeth bared, and saliva flowing from his gasping mouth, he locked eyes with Roland.

"If ve get out of this, I'll give you vatever you vant, you know."

Rousseau smile at his boss's promise faded when he confronted the terrifying view outside the plane. "Won't be enough," he murmured.

"Get ready, everyone," Roland said. "Ven I open the door, shoot anything that moves."

"You got that right," Enheim muttered. Roy remained huddled in the cabin's corner.

Preparing to be exposed to the hoard of creatures outside, Mich and Rousseau positioned themselves for clean shots and leveled their weapons. Roland turned the handle to the unlock position. He took a deep breath and pushed the cabin door open.

A snout with blood-matted fur appeared above the opening. The rat sniffed the air, bared its fangs, and leaped into the cabin. Mich fired point blank. The rat's head blew apart as its body fell to the floor, spraying the men with blood. Another rat leaped through the opening and met the same fate, this time from Roland's pistol. The carcass landed in Roy's lap.

As the dead body jerked spasmodically on his groin, Roy

whimpered, his nerves at breaking point as gunfire reverberated throughout the cabin. Claws scratching against the fuselage worsened his condition. Unable to control his fear of the horror around him, Roy banged his head repeatedly against the interior paneling, hoping to rid his mind of the terrifying sights and sounds.

Enheim fired at a rat scurrying across the port wing and missed. The bullet left a hole in the metal skin as the creature scampered out of sight.

"Enheim, you asshole, watch the plane, you know," Roland said, putting a round into the torso of the nearest rat heading their way.

Enheim avoided eye contact and zeroed in on the next target.

"Where did the big bastard go?" Mich asked, his tone worried as he searched the clearing.

Becca shifted to the captain's side of the cockpit and maneuvered the phone in another direction against the windshield. Still no signal. Startled by thumping above her, she leaned against the side window to look up and discover its source. Splat! A blood-soaked rat's torso slammed against the windshield. The carcass slid down the glass leaving streaks of blood and chunks of flesh before its lifeless body fell into the foliage below. Another body hit the windscreen—bam!—this time with more force. The glass spider-webbed as the rat slid out of sight.

Becca peered through the cracked glass. Poised on the aircraft's nose, the alpha bared its teeth and stared back through blood-shot eyes. A smaller rat scurried between him and the windshield. The alpha snapped the rat's neck and hurled it at the glass. More cracks spread across the windshield as the dead rat slid to the jungle below. Becca's eyes widened as the alpha clawed over the nose cone. Reaching out, it gripped both sides of the windshield, then slammed its skull into the glass hole left after the removal of the protruding branch. The crunch of weakening glass filled Becca's ears as the creature repeatedly banged its head into the hole. She covered her face for protection from the splintered glass spraying from above and fired through the shards. "Guys," she called, "if we ever get out of this alive, it's gonna make a helluva story."

"You got that right," Mich yelled from the doorway where he was still firing at the horde in the clearing. He left the trio to cover the doorway and hurried down the aisle to respond to Becca's SOS.

The windshield was all but shattered, its glass frame ready to collapse into the cockpit. The alpha saw Mich and snarled, focusing with hate-filled eyes first on the gun in Mich's hand, then on his face.

Mich hesitated, sensing intelligence behind the piercing gaze. "It knows," he mumbled, taken aback by the creature's acumen. The alpha slammed its bloodied head into the windscreen again. The glass shifted in its sealed frame but held. "Sweet Home Al-a-bama, where the skies are so blue, Sweet Home Al-a-bama, Lord I'm com-ing home to you. Sweet Home Al-a-bama—"

"Are you from Alabama?"

"Do I look like I'm from Alabama?" Mich said with a touch a sarcasm, indicating his Asian features.

Becca frowned. "I guess not, but then what the hell are you doing?"

"When I get anxious, I sing. Helps calm the nerves."

She shrugged at Mich's quirky behavior, and then decided to give it a shot. "Sweet Home Al-a-bama, where the skies are so blue, Sweet Home Al-a-bama, Lord I'm com-ing home to you. Sweet Home Al-a-bama," she belted out, firing at the alpha through the windshield. "Hey, it works!" She gave a short laugh, her stress level reduced ever so slightly.

Over the gunfire, Enheim's gruff voice called to Rousseau, "What the hell are they singing about?"

Rousseau targeted a rodent venturing close to the hatchway and opened fire. "Maybe the singing helps." Enheim moaned as the big Frenchmen began humming the Lynyrd Skynyrd tune.

Roy's eyes darted from the rodents and shooters to the cramped walls of the plane. He weighed the terror outside with being trapped in the cabin as the creatures made their final assault. *Out in the open, I stand a chance of survival, but I'm as good as dead inside the cabin with the rest of the them.* He leaped to his feet and stumbled toward the open door. Fear clouded his judgement, causing him to trip on the doorway's metal frame and tumble face-first to the jungle floor. He lifted himself from the mud puddle and froze. Less than a yard away dozens of red eyes glared at him. Roy soiled himself as he sobbed.

The crew turned from the open door, unable to stomach the horde of giant rats tearing Roy's screaming body from limb to limb. Napoleon yelped and ducked his head into the harness.

Becca slipped the sat phone into her pocket and held the windscreen in place with both hands. "Oh, Roy," she whispered, averting her thoughts from the garbled cries outside the plane.

Mich edged open the pilot's side window and fired three times at the alpha. The rat squealed in pain as three fountains of blood erupted from its torso. Its claws lost traction on the nose cone's metal surface, and the rat slipped from view.

Becca heaved a sigh of relief. "We really need to get out of here," she said, wiping the sweat from her brow.

"If only it were that simple," Mich said.

Roland ducked his head into the cockpit, pistol ready. "Everything okay?"

Becca kept an eye on the terrain below. "For now."

Gun shots rang throughout the cabin as the crew continued to defend the plane. Through the broken windshield, Roland scanned the tropical forest surrounding the aircraft. A sparkle of light through the greenery caught his attention, and he recalled Rousseau mentioning a river at the base of the cliff. He raced down the aisle where he lifted the carpet to reveal a small lid.

Enheim's pistol locked open. "I'm out."

Roland threw him a magazine, but Enheim fumbled and dropped it out the open door. "Sorry," he said in his gruff voice.

"Sweaty hands." Roland tossed him another magazine, then lifted the lid to reveal a hidden compartment.

Mich peeked from the cockpit and grinned for the first time in what seemed like weeks. "Just like the Millennium Falcon."

"Vich falcon?" Roland asked.

"You gotta be kidding me." Mich regarded Roland as if he were from another planet, but he welcomed the distraction from the horrors around them, even if it was temporary. "You don't know the Millennium Falcon?"

"Enlighten me."

"Han Solo? Chewbacca?" Enheim chimed in, equally incredulous. "These names ring a bell?"

"The only ship to do the Kessel Run in less than twelve parsecs?" Mich added.

Roland shrugged the names away and climbed down into the compartment.

"Surely you've heard of a film called *Star Wars*?" Mich called after him.

Roland dug around inside the small chamber. "Never seen it, you know."

"You've never seen *Star Wars*? The greatest film of all time?" Mich and Enheim stared at each other, stunned.

Enheim recovered first and grinned. "If we're comparing our situation to *Star Wars*, well then—I'm Han Solo."

"You're Han?" Mich repeated with skepticism.

"Yeah. I'm the cool, handsome, rogue type."

"Right. The cool, handsome, rogue type with a pug strapped to your chest. Okay, then. Who am I?"

"It's obvious. With the long hair, you're Chewbacca."

Mich shook his head in disbelief but decided to play along. "Okay, I'm Chewbacca. And everybody else here—who are they?"

The crew continued to fire at the rats scurrying over the plane, grateful for the momentary distraction.

"We have Princess Leia in the cockpit there," Enheim said, pointing to Becca, "and my annoying brother-in-law is obviously C3PO."

"And Rousseau?"

"Rousseau's like Wedge. Handy guy to have in a fight, but in the background."

"How about Roy?"

"I'm mixing my science fiction here, but he was definitely a red shirt."

"Unfortunately, you got that right." Mich was well aware of the *red shirts* who died in astonishing numbers on the original Star Trek TV series.

Roland shook his head, ignoring Enheim's comparison, and found the metallic suitcase. He reached up and placed it on the aisle floor then hoisted himself up. He opened the suitcase to reveal a thin block wrapped in black Mylar plastic.

"What the hell is that?" Enheim asked, studying the 11" x 2" x 1.5" block.

Roland quickly opened two small containers, one with the detonator and the other with the trigger. "Cyclotrimethylenetrinitramine."

"What?"

"Otherwise known as C-4," Mich called from the cockpit.

Enheim's eyes widened in disbelief. "You mean I've been sitting next to explosives the whole time, and you didn't bother to let me know?"

"It's for emergencies, you know."

"What type of emergency requires a friggin' block of C friggin' 4!"

Roland sighed, weary of Enheim's constant droning. With arms akimbo, his eyes followed scuttling claws across the fuselage above them. "Satisfied?"

"You got me there," Enheim conceded, "but Napums is still nervous." Napoleon growled as the claws scraped across the wing's metal paneling.

"Relax. It's safe. Only a pressure wave can set off C-4."

Enheim backed away from Roland. "What do you propose to do with that?"

"Rousseau, I need the tool kit," Roland called, ignoring Enheim and disappearing into the compartment again. He lifted a metal grate to reveal an outer panel of the undercarriage.

Rousseau ran to the cargo bay and reappeared seconds later with a knapsack of tools. He lowered the tool collection to Roland who withdrew a battery-powered electric drill and a Philips screwdriver bit. He locked the bit into place in the drill and went to work removing the outer panel from inside the plane.

"Hey, Rolly, what're you doing?" Enheim said, rubbing his chin in frustration.

"Roland?" Mich asked, also curious for an explanation.

Roland unscrewed the bolts locking the outer cover in place. "Rousseau said there's a river at the base of the cliff."

"And?" Enheim asked.

Mich peered out at the sea of greenery below the base of the cliff, two hundred yards below. He groaned.

"Ve stay here, ve die." Roland removed the last bolt and emerged from the compartment. "But down there"—he indicated the cliff and jungle below—"ve have a chance."

"And just how do you propose we get down there?" Enheim asked.

For the first time, Rousseau spoke up. "Mr. Pom's idea might work. The plane is structurally sound. Only the engine is damaged. These old planes were built to last. Ava can take the stresses and strain. She can do it."

"Do *what*? Frenchy, what are you talking about?" Enheim dreaded the answer, but he needed to hear the insane idea spoken aloud.

"Rousseau, vere do I place the charge?" Roland asked.

Rousseau considered the aircraft's weight and balance. "The tree trunk below the cockpit. That and the laws of physics should do the rest."

Roland nodded, pocketing the trigger. He emptied the tools

from the knapsack and placed the C-4 and the remote detonator into the bag. Then he zipped the bag shut and slung it over his shoulder.

"Mr. Pom, the explosive has to be facing the tree trunk for maximum effect. Once the tree's support is gone, the plane's weight will do the rest."

Roland took the cigarette from Rousseau's mouth, inhaled one last time, and returned the cigarette. "I need cover fire, people."

They nodded.

"I speak for all of us when I say good luck, Mr. Pom."

"Thank you, Rousseau." Roland ducked into the compartment.

Mich glanced at Enheim. "Looks like we're going for a ride professor. Do you like rollercoasters?"

Enheim finally had confirmation for what his brother-in-law had in mind. He watched as Roland disappeared into the floor compartment. "I hate rollercoasters."

While the others created a diversion spraying a barrage of bullets into the clearing, Roland carefully lifted the cover away from the fuselage for direct access to the outside of the plane. The gap in the outer skin revealed the foliage and ground cover below the fuselage. He peeked through the opening, careful not to be seen by the creatures surrounding the craft. Without a sound, he climbed down from the open compartment. Near the nose cone, he grabbed hold of the adjacent tree trunk supporting the plane's fuselage. Slowly he climbed to the tree's base where, resting on his haunches, he unzipped the bag and removed the C-4.

The thick vegetation below the plane offered perfect cover. Roland moulded the soft plastic material for maximum adhesion to the trunk's rough bark. The explosive held in position. Carefully, he inserted the detonator. A yard from the tree's base, a rat turned his snout upward and sniffed. Hissing, he locked his red eyes on Roland as he struggled to get a grip on the flaking bark. Another rat appeared from the scrub and they hissed in unison. Roland carefully drew his pistol and took aim at the closest rodent. Two more rats scurried into view ready for the kill, saliva dripping from their open jaws.

"I have a full magazine, you ugly bastards," Roland whispered, knowing he still had the upper hand.

The alpha emerged from the greenery and climbed atop a boulder jutting up through the fronds. Despite the blood seeping from his torso, his tail thumped the rock, signaling the other rodents. His muscular hind legs rippled like coiled springs as he prepared to strike. Roland looked around and saw a dozen rodents scurrying at him. He glanced at the pistol in his hand—not enough bullets. He calculated the time it would take to climb the tree and crawl back into the compartment. The realization that the rats could overpower him in seconds and that he didn't stand a chance shot through his mind.

Roland leveled the pistol's barrel at the alpha rat. "If I go, you're coming with me."

The end of a coil of rope dangled before him. Roland needed no further encouragement. He gripped the rope as Enheim and Rousseau hauled him back to the safety of the plane. Roland grabbed the outer panel and slammed it across the open compartment, but the alpha's head knocked the cover from his hands, its jaw snapping inches from Roland's face. Enheim's fist smashed into the rat's snout. The rat squealed in pain and fell from sight as, from his pocket, Roland pulled the trigger and flipped the switch.

The blast obliterated the main tree trunk supporting the plane. Splintered wood erupted in all directions, killing any rodents within the impact zone. The shockwave pulsed through the plane knocking everyone to the floor. The crack of shattered wood below the fuselage echoed through the cabin as the plane leaned over the cliff-face.

Becca covered her open mouth in terror as the sky that had filled the windscreen was replaced by the jungle canopy below. "Hang on!" she yelled, gripping her armrests as the plane's forward section dipped over the cliff's edge.

Roland and the others barely had time to strap themselves in before the aircraft slipped from the shattered jungle and over the precipice, its forward momentum snapping its anchor and mooring ropes. *Ava* hurtled down the cliff's forty-five-degree face, an unstoppable juggernaut leaving a path of crushed jungle in her wake. The crash of metal smashing into wood resounded as the plane's fuselage and pontoons crushed the tropical forest below. Roland and the crew braced themselves as the aircraft jolted on impact with each hidden furrow and fold in the sloping terrain. *Ava's* wings slammed into palms branches and jungle flora, scattering leaves and fronds everywhere. Becca peeked through the shattered windshield and made the sign of the cross. *Please, God, save us.*

The plane emerged from the jungle, rocketed over a smaller precipice, soared through the air, and slammed into the river's rushing water at a forward angle. Its nose dipped into the river, causing a surge of cool water to wash into the cockpit. The tail lifted high, hung in mid-air for what seemed an eternity to the crew, then crashed into the river. Water streamed over the wings and cabin as the plane corrected for balance, while the pontoons kept the craft upright, confirming that any question of damage was unfounded.

Mich and Becca staggered from the cockpit towards the mini-bar. Roland and Rousseau lit cigarettes and checked the cabin for signs of permanent damage. Enheim felt the relief that washed through the cabin. Even Napoleon poked his head from his harness and yapped contentedly. "You got that bloody right, Napums," Enheim said with a sigh, rubbing Napoleon under the chin.

The alpha leaped into a nearby tree and licked the wounds under his charred fur. Below, the horde surrounded the trunk's base, awaiting further commands. From his higher vantage point, through the destruction left in the aircraft's wake, the alpha watched the plane drifting away on the river's current. He sniffed the air and snarled, his serrated teeth dripping blood. With his face contorted in anger, the giant rodent's charred tail thumped the ground.

DAY 4

CHAPTER 18

The Second Event

DARK CLOUDS CHURNED across the sky, shrouding the morning rays and casting a dim and dreary light over the terrain. After playing havoc with the Pacific region for a week, the tropical storm swung around from the Philippine Sea and hit the Mariana Islands chain with full force. Lighting flashed on the horizon as high winds and torrential rains lashed the island.

Behind the hotel complex a vast sinkhole, the product of erosion and natural decay over a millennium, spanned two hundred feet in diameter and two hundred feet in depth. Surrounded by dense jungle and with an ever-growing green canopy closing over its rim, the natural formation remained hidden from the outside world.

A construction crane rested beside the edge of the giant sinkhole in a clearing created by Merrick's team for this event. Merrick's office, at the back of the clearing adjacent to the machine, offered a perfect view for the day's deadly game. The two Sikorski Skycrane helicopters that had lifted the construction crane to the location rested opposite the crane and Merrick's office.

The downpour continued, forming pools of thick mud and water on the saturated ground. Manufactured thunder echoed throughout the clearing as Merrick's men pounded the crane's giant metal legs deep into the earth to anchor the machine in place. The crane's boom, a hundred feet of strengthened metal girder, extended over the sinkhole like a giant fishing rod awaiting a catch. Suspended from the boom by several chains was a large tree trunk the length of a school bus swaying over the gaping abyss. The drone of jungle life returned as cackling and buzzing filled the rain-drenched forest.

Merrick's men had assembled a viewing stage with a shade sail and buffet breakfast for the clients. However, caught in the gale force winds, the shade sail had torn apart and disappeared into the jungle. The deck chairs and buffet table, shipped directly from the French Riviera, had rolled across the staging ground and into the sinkhole.

Standing beside the sinkhole, Merrick seethed as he watched the clients retreat to the comfort and safety of their hotel rooms. "Shit!" He stormed into the temporary office erected at the jungle's edge and grabbed a towel to wipe the rain from his face. The storm had washed out the next event and, if it continued, could seriously damage his reputation and the viability of his franchise. He picked up the nearest object he could find, an office chair, and hurled it against the wall.

The door swung open. Van Sant entered and quickly closed the door to prevent the wind and rain from making a mess with the office interior. "Uh, sorry, boss." He hesitated. "You won't want to hear th—"

"Then don't tell me!" Merrick snapped. Still livid from the clients' response to the morning's non-event, Merrick retrieved his office chair and plunked down. He closed his eyes and breathed in slowly and deeply, then exhaled, and repeated the process.

Van Sant opened his mouth to continue when Merrick gestured *don't*. "Give me a minute," he growled.

Van Sant retreated to the sofa. He preferred not to upset his employer by relaying further bad news, but he knew that Merrick would demand all the facts before making his final decision regarding the morning's washed out event. He lit a cigarette and waited for Merrick to gain control.

Merrick reached into the drinks cabinet and poured himself a double bourbon. He gulped it down and poured another. "Okay, you have my attention."

"The engineering supervisor warned that the soil under the crane could liquefy from the constant rain. In addition, the boom can't be operated in high winds because the crane could become unstable. So if the downpour continues, he won't be able to guarantee his men's safety."

"Oh, is that all?" Merrick hissed.

"Just relaying the message, boss."

Merrick gazed through the rain-streaked window at the crane sitting beside the giant crater. The jungle foliage surrounding the sinkhole swayed violently as wind and driving rain rolled across the clearing. Palm fronds and loose vegetation swirled and tumbled through the air. *The investors' enthusiasm can't wane with my personal fortune at stake. The cost of renovating the hotel and setting up the events has stretched my bank account to the limit. If I don't see a return on this investment soon, I'll have to declare bankruptcy and forget my Cannes and New York properties. To guarantee my financial stability, I must persuade the investors to sign now. Any delay will ruin my chances of raising funds for future ventures. It's now or never.* He turned to Van Sant. "Bad weather and that little whining pissant will not stop this event from proceeding. Tell the engineering supervisor that he and his men get triple pay plus advance bonuses. That'll shut him up. And get the drones ready. I want them operational and streaming direct to the hotel rooms in five minutes."

Van Sant started toward the door.

"Wait," Merrick said. "Will the drones fly in these winds?"

Van Sant glanced at the tropical storm raging outside. "I doubt it."

"We've got three drones. I need at least one for the later events. We can risk two. They're cheap, and they might get some good footage."

"Simon's good, but he's not that good. He can't operate two drones simultaneously—let alone is this weather."

"True." Merrick paused. "I saw Clive messing around with a drone last week. Station him in the control room to help Simon." Van Sant gave Merrick a thumbs up and left, the wind and rain whipping around the office before he could slam the door shut.

In preparation for the next event, Merrick straightened his coat and tie. He tapped his phone and plugged in his earpiece. As soon as all the clients responded to his request for an audience, Merrick cleared his throat. "I apologize for this morning's most unexpected and inclement weather. However, we will not allow a bit of rain to spoil the day's events. If you would please turn on your television sets, you will be able to view the morning's action streamed live to your rooms. Feel free to order whatever you wish from room service. My personal chef will prepare your heart's desire, and our selection of imported wines and spirits is world-class. The second event will begin shortly, so, please, sit back and enjoy the games."

Soaking and miserable, Lincoln and the other contestants stood by the rim of the sinkhole and watched the last deckchair disappear into the gaping depths of the cavity. With the wind blowing at him, Lincoln cautiously peered over the edge and into the abyss, unable to see the bottom of the giant hole in the darkness below. "Shit. This is high," he whispered, clutching his freshly-cleaned Neptune cap. He felt lightheaded and began to sweat. *Relax. Deep breaths, in and out, in and out. Feel the solid ground underfoot.*

Armed guards in full wet-weather gear surrounded the rim, their coats flapping in the winds. A makeshift rope bridge, constructed by Merrick's team of engineers, spanned the sinkhole. Two lengths of rope held together by three feet wide wooden slats functioned as the bridge's walkway. At each end, two wooden posts driven into the soil anchored the rope bridge in place. Lincoln groaned. *No handrails.*

To make a good impression on the clients, Merrick posed before the contestants with his hands clasped behind his back and his head upright like a general about to lead his men into battle. After a casual glance at the multiple cameras positioned in the trees around the sinkhole, he addressed the contestants. "The rules of this event are simple, gentlemen. Cross the bridge to the other side. Last man through the end anchor posts loses." He looked to Van Sant who raised his rifle—the alternative for non-compliance—and shouted, "May the best man win!" Merrick retreated to the porch fronting his office as Van Sant ushered the men to the bridge entrance. Above, two drones swayed in the whipping winds. Simon and Clive, Merrick's employee who flew drones as a hobby, watched the monitors from the control room as they struggled to keep the drones airborne.

The rain hammered the contestants as they eased their way onto the bridge. Getting a foothold on the slippery wooden slats was difficult. Van Sant signaled the crane operator. The machine's engine spluttered to life. Moments later, the boom pivoted above the sinkhole. The operator was cautious to swivel the boom back and forth, back and forth, until the log, dangling at the ends of the chains, arced through the air like a giant pendulum over the hole. The log's course passed over the bridge and half-turned in mid-air. The contestants watched as the log swung back around and sailed past on its trajectory to the opposite side.

The crane operator lowered the trunk by several inches so that it swung a foot above the bridge. On its way, a small branch caught the wooden slats. As the branch held tight, the trunk dragged the bridge until it reached the zenith of its arc. The branch snapped and the rope bridge sprang back, lurching wildly before returning to its position. The contestants gripped the anchor posts as the wooden floor beneath them swung back and forth.

Van Sant fired a round into the air, signaling the contestants to move further out onto the bridge. Reluctantly they edged away from the anchor posts.

"Out of my way!" Red barked, pushing through the others and charging down the makeshift bridge. "You're all dead men!" Halfway across, he flattened himself against the wooden slats as the log swooped past, inches above his head. He scrambled to his feet and dashed across the remaining portion of the bridge, knowing that the log would return in seconds. In his eagerness to make it to the other side, he slipped on the wet slats and slid over the side of the bridge. He grabbed a slat and hung, suspended, his legs splayed in the air above the sinkhole.

Red kept an eye on the returning log as he clawed his way back onto the bridge. He ducked as the log swept past just above his head. He crawled the last few yards across the swaying bridge until he reached hard ground. He pulled himself up and passed through the anchor posts, his arms raised in triumph. He turned and sneered at the other contestants on the opposite end of the rope bridge.

One of Merrick's men, standing guard beside the anchor posts, guided Red to a small shelter for the surviving contestants. Red grabbed a towel and grinned as he watched to see who would attempt the crossing in the torrential downpour.

Shivering from the cold and wracked with fear, Purple snapped. "Screw this! I ain't coming last!" He pushed past Lincoln and Gray and bolted across the bridge. He had calculated the time it took for the log to make a pass and return. The safety window was a few seconds. He didn't have much time, but it could be done. With the fear of death clouding his judgement, Purple stumbled across the bridge. His heart raced and his blood pumped through his body as he staggered past the mid-point. He saw the log barreling toward him and dove to the slats as the tree trunk thundered overhead.

A sudden gust mixed with the updraught from the sinkhole created a whirlwind above the hole. The airstream caught the first drone and drove it into the air where it smashed against the extended boom, its pieces cast to the wind. "Shit!" Clive threw down his joystick as the image on his monitor was replaced by static.

The rope bridge swayed violently in the gale force wind, knocking Purple off balance. He tried to regain his footing but slipped to his knees, blinded by the lashing rain. He clutched the slats and pulled himself up, wiping the water from his eyes. Through the whipping rain and howling wind, he could make out faint cries behind him. Struggling to keep his balance on the swaying bridge, he turned toward the voices.

Lincoln averted his eyes as the tree trunk slammed Purple. The sickening crack of shattering bone filled the air as his body snagged on the tree's rough bark. The log, with Purple splayed across the trunk, swung through the air and continued over the sinkhole. "Oh, yes!" The crane operator, a balding unshaven slob, laughed at the sight. "The fun has begun."

Adedowale and Abeo watched the event as it played out on their hotel room's giant television. Adedowale clapped with glee at the sight of Purple hanging from the log. "Most impressive," he cheered, not taking his eyes from the screen. "Remind me to congratulate Mr. Merrick on such a creative game." Abeo tapped keys on his notebook.

At the sight of Purple's lifeless body caught on the swinging tree trunk, his legs swaying in the wind, Joanna cringed and turned from the television.

"A man is dead," Lincoln yelled to Van Sant through the roaring wind and rain. "The game is over."

Van Sant listened to Merrick in his earpiece and raised his rifle again. "Not yet," he shouted. "You still have to cross. We have a show to put on for our customers." He took aim and fired into the ground at Lincoln's feet. Bullets tore into the bridge's slats, exploding splinters of wood into the air.

Joanna glanced at Baxter.

"Yes, mum?"

"Could you get me another drink, please?"

"Of course, mum."

"This time, Baxter, could you please make it something a little stronger than beer?"

"Of course, mum." *A good valet always understands his employer's needs.* "Would you prefer a double or triple?"

"Two contestants still remain. Better make it a triple."

Lincoln and Gray backed away from the gunfire, with continuing down the path their only option. "Do what I do," Lincoln shouted. Gray looked into the deep hole and at the swinging tree trunk and nodded vigorously.

Baxter glanced at the television, then returned to making the perfect triple scotch on ice. "It appears the rules are not concrete, mum."

Joanna sighed as the last two contestants made their way onto the bridge. "They never are."

CHAPTER 19

WITH AN EYE on the tree-trunk—passing, rotating, and swinging back—and with Gray close behind, Lincoln edged down the slippery slats. The slats offered no secure foothold, so trying to maintain balance on the slick surface in the strong winds seemed impossible. A sudden gust tore the Neptune cap from his head. Lincoln watched as the cap spiraled into the abyss below. He gulped.

The log roared past then rotated. The gale force wind hitting the side of the trunk slowed its trajectory. The log continued to oscillate like a pendulum, but at a thirty-degree angle to the bridge, with its zenith closer and closer to the crane. A crazy idea formed in Lincoln's mind. *It just might work.* He got down on his hands and knees and lay on the bridge with his back against the slats. With his legs in the air, he wrapped his arms as best he could around the slats under him. Gripping with all his might, he indicated to Gray to do the same. Both men lay on their backs like crazed upside-down turtles in the rain.

Wolfgang pointed out the unusual move to Klaus who shrugged.

"What the hell are they doing?" Merrick asked Van Sant through his earpiece.

"No idea, boss."

Joanna sipped her scotch. "I didn't see this coming."

Lincoln shouted to Gray. "When the log swings by again, watch me, okay?"

"Okay."

Lincoln looked heavenward. *Please, God, if this works, I promise I'll give up Dr. Pepper.* He steadied himself and, with split second timing, pushed his feet against the side of the tree trunk as it swooped by. The log adjusted its trajectory and turned laterally. On the return arc, Gray lifted his legs. With all his might he pushed against the tree trunk as it swept across the bridge.

The gale caught the trunk's mass. The log spun wildly over the sinkhole and back toward the crane where the operator was frantically working the boom's joystick. He watched, helpless, as the trunk swung toward him.

The trunk sailed past the control cabin, its forward momentum creating downward pressure over the rim of the sinkhole. The crane's gearbox tore apart and the cab swiveled out of control. Swinging behind the cab, the log continued its course back toward the hole. The waterlogged soil beneath the crane gave way, and the front section of the machine lurched downward, sinking into the soft soil. The screech of tortured metal pierced the air as the boom, now level with the rim of the sinkhole, strained to lift and control the added pressure of momentum.

The trunk swiveled through the air as it swung back past Lincoln and Gray on a direct course toward the crane. The tree's butt slammed into the sinkhole's rim, shaking the ground and sending a shower of mud and dirt into the air. The waterlogged soil shimmied as the earth reverberated beneath the crane. Finally, the crane's anchored legs tore free from the soft soil.

Lincoln and Gray looked on with terror as the trunk, now at bridge height, thundered back toward them. They scrambled over the side of the bridge and clung to the slats as the out-of-control log sailed overhead and slammed into the anchor posts, ripping them from the earth. As the log careened toward them again, the flimsy rope caught around the log's bough, tearing the southern end of the bridge away from the rim.

"Hang on," Lincoln yelled as the rope bridge arced down through the air and slammed into the northern face of the rim. On impact, Gray lost his grip on the rope. He clawed for a handhold, for anything that would save his life. His fingers slipped off the wet rope.

Lincoln grabbed Gray's flaying arm. "That was close," he said with a smile. "I'm going to swing you over to the wall where you'll be safe on a ledge that goes around the sinkhole." Speechless from shock and fright, Gray nodded, his eyes bulging. He forced a half-hearted grin as Lincoln swung him toward the rock face where he landed on the narrow ledge and held tight to the jagged rocks jutting from the crag. Moments later Lincoln joined him. They leaned against the wall relieved that the ordeal was over. The bridge's torn rope and broken slats dangled over them, hiding them on the cliff.

Transfixed by the events on the screen, Joanna lowered her empty glass to the side table without turning from the television. "Really, mum," Baxter said with disdain. He stepped beside her and placed a coaster on the ornate antique table beneath her glass.

"Clever boy." Joanna smiled, her eyes glued to the spectacle before her.

The ground beneath the crane's rear legs succumbed to the torrential rain. The crane tilted backward and to the left, lifting the boom and the giant log high into the air above the sinkhole. The laws of motion took control: *For every action, there is an equal and opposite reaction.* The log continued its forward momentum until it swung around over the hole and back toward the left of the crane.

Merrick leaped from the porch and dove into the mud-soaked ground as the log barreled through his office, splintering the walls and roof into thousands of pieces. The force of the impact released Purple's body from the trunk and catapulted it across the clearing toward the crane.

"Oh, fu—" The crane operator's final word was cut short as Purple smashed through the cab's windscreen, crushing his larynx.

Merrick wiped the mud from his eyes and watched, helpless, as the giant tree trunk swung toward the two Sikorsky Skycranes. The log slammed into the first craft, shattering its metal body. The log and the wreckage from the first chopper smashed into the second, crushing it beyond recognition. As one of the fuel tanks ignited, what was left of the helicopters exploded in a red-hot fireball of flaming debris.

Standing beside the rim, Van Sant was caught in the shockwave and thrown backward across the clearing. The trunk continued its circular trajectory, pushing the remains of the two wrecks to the rim of the sinkhole where the blazing wreckage toppled over the edge. The crane operator babbled through his crushed larynx as the trunk, caught in the burning helicopters, dragged him and the crane over the edge.

Lincoln looked up in time to see the fiery wrecks tumble down the wall. The other fuel tank exploded, engulfing the sinkhole's upper level in a fireball of splintering metal.

Oh, shit.

Lincoln and Gray flattened themselves against the ledge as slivers of smoking metal embedded themselves in the nearby rock wall. A rotor blade snagged on the rope bridge and ripped its remaining anchor posts from the earth.

Simon watched the anchor posts fly over the rim and hurtle toward the scr—*static.* "Oh, boy. The posts must have slammed into the last drone. Merrick is gonna be pissed."

Lincoln and Gray gripped the jagged rocks protruding from the rock wall and held tight as the tangled bridge rocketed past. Black ash and smoke trailed the shattered crane, burning choppers, and remnants of the rope bridge as they disappeared into the abyss.

Lincoln and Gray breathed deeply, happy to be alive. Gray managed a smile and said, "Looks like your plan worked."

"I wasn't expecting it to work to this extent," Lincoln conceded, surprised at the astounding success of his simple idea as evidenced by all the carnage. He peeked into the blackness below as the echo of crunching metal rose around them. "Yes, it looks like the plan worked really well."

Lincoln scanned the sinkhole wall for any grooves or jutting rock to use as handholds. The ledge extended around the smooth rock-face but provided little else to cling to. He estimated that they were less than twenty yards below the rim of the sinkhole, but the torrential rain rolling down the smooth rock face made it impossible to climb to safety.

A faint glow of light emanating from a fissure in the rock wall caught Lincoln's attention. He searched the rim for signs of Merrick's men. With no one in sight, Lincoln ushered Gray along the ledge toward the narrow opening.

Van Sant lifted himself from the mud and wiped the sludge from his eyes. Having had the wind knocked out of him, he rested on his haunches, gulping in mouthfuls of air and trying to steady his nerves. Merrick arrived at Van Sant's side, his face contorted in pure rage. "Where the hell are they?"

With his ears still ringing from the explosion and his equilibrium off kilter, Van Sant fumbled for an answer. "I have no idea. The last time I saw them they were behind the bridge. They're probably dead."

Merrick trudged across the thick mud to the sinkhole's edge and peered down through the black smoke. The rock walls gleamed as the rain washed over their craggy surface and disappeared into the void. Blue and Gray were nowhere to be seen. He tapped his earpiece. "Simon."

"Yes, Mr. Merrick," the voice replied through the ear microphone.

"Check the drone footage. I want to know exactly what happened to the last two contestants."

"Yes, Mr. Merrick. I'll get on it right away."

Merrick returned to Van Sant. "If by some chance Monk is still alive, I want his head on a fucking platter. You understand?"

Still trying to catch his breath, Van Sant panted, "You got it, boss."

CHAPTER 20

"WELL," JOANNA SAID, sighing in relief and unable to keep from smiling at the outcome of the event, "that was certainly unexpected."

"Yes, mum," Baxter replied in his usual tone.

Joanna took a sip of her freshly filled drink, this time a double. "Are you a betting man, Baxter?"

"No, mum."

"Really! You've never made a bet?"

Baxter reconsidered the question. "Just the one-armed bandits, mum."

"Hmmm. I'd have never pegged you for a slots player. Humor me, Baxter. If you *were* a betting man, on whom would you bet to win Merrick's games?"

Baxter considered the grainy image of carnage and destruction on the television screen streamed from what appeared to be a backup camera mounted on the hotel's roof. Merrick's men were dashing around in the mud and rain. His office was a pile of splintered wood. Two helicopters, a crane, and the rope bridge had disappeared into the abyss. Thick black smoke gushed from the sinkhole. "We-e-ll, it appears the very large gentleman wearing the red trunks is quite proficient at this type of activity."

Joanna continued to watch the screen. "Yes, Red does seem the obvious choice to win," she said, but her thoughts had turned to Lincoln.

Baxter knew his employer well. Often in the past, he had observed Joanna in deep contemplation. He cleared his throat. "However, mum, I believe you wish the young man Blue to win."

Joanna smiled. "You know me well, Baxter."

"A good butler-slash-assistant-slash-servant pays attention, mum. I'll get Mr. Merrick on the line. How much would you like to wager?"

After Lincoln and Gray had crawled through a tight tunnel for what seemed an eternity, the fissure opened to reveal a cavern the size of a warehouse. A string of florescent tubes mounted to the ceiling ran the length of the cavern illuminating the upper section in a soft white glow. The dew-covered ground glistened, while the limestone walls on either side disappeared into the darkness.

Lincoln and Gray felt their way down into the cave, carefully stepping around the jagged rocks and small crevices peppering the ground. The uneven surface and dim light made progress difficult, but eventually they reached the far end of the cave.

"Dammit!" Lincoln said as he stubbed his toe against a flat box hidden by the darkness. As he tried to rub the soreness away, he slipped on the wet surface and fell onto another box. Squinting, he could make out the label: Parachute. "Watch out. The ground is covered with crates."

Gray edged his way forward, feeling for ground obstructions. As his hands glided across a corrugated surface in front of him, he stopped and probed the facade. Through the dim light, he could make out a metallic wall. "Looks like this is as far as we go."

Lincoln tapped the barrier. He raised an eyebrow as the surface flexed and the tapping echoed softly. He felt along the wall and disappeared into the darkness.

"Wh-where are you going?" Gray strained to see where Lincoln had gone.

Lincoln found the switch for another row of overhead lights. Brightness flooded the cave, revealing wooden crates of all shapes and sizes stacked to the roof and covered with tarpaulins. He spotted several tarpaulins draped over a bus-sized object resting behind the stockpile. *Well, well, what have we here? Now why would anyone lock assorted items in an underground warehouse?* He pointed at the metal wall. "It's my guess that that isn't a wall. I think it's a door." Lincoln searched the rock face and found the control panel, but before he could identify the switch, the wall lifted, grinding on metal rails as it rolled back along the ceiling.

Van Sant stood before them, Beretta in hand. Behind him were several guards with drawn guns who rushed into the room and surrounded them. Lincoln glanced behind Van Sant and spotted the concrete ramp glistening from the rain.

"We didn't know the cave opened to the sinkhole," Van Sant said. "Looks like you found the reason there's so much moisture down here. I always thought it was the constant rain." He tapped his ear and looked at Lincoln. "Because of your little stunt out there, my ears are still ringing." He shook his head to relieve the buzzing. "I'm not your biggest problem, though—not by a long shot. Now Merrick, he really wants you dead. His exact words were, 'I want his head on a fucking platter.' Boy, is he pissed at you. Now I'm the guy who gets things done, the guy who cleans up the mess." He leveled his Beretta at Lincoln. "And you and Gray here are a big friggin' mess."

Gray glanced at Lincoln, trembling with fear.

"However," Van Sant continued, lowering his gun, "today is your lucky day. Both of you will live for at least another few hours. You see, a large bet has been placed on you to win the games. Now how will it look if two of the winners of the event turn up dead? The clients would lose all faith and trust in Mr. Merrick, wouldn't you say? So, livid as he is, Merrick needs you alive for the next event." He grinned and moved closer so that his face was inches from Lincoln's.

"If I were you," he said, pressing the Beretta's barrel against Lincoln's chest, "I'd make peace with God now, because as of tomorrow, you're all Merrick's. And, boy, does he have plans for you." He motioned two of the guards. They rushed Lincoln and Gray and bound their hands behind their backs, while two others whipped out sacks and slipped them over their heads.

"Can't have you seeing where the front door is, now can we?"

Lincoln recognized Van Sant's muffled voice through the burlap sack. He knew what was coming and braced himself. A lightning bolt of pain shot through his skull as the rifle butt hit him squarely on the temple.

CHAPTER 21

IN THE CORNER of the hotel room, Christina was squatting on her haunches and keeping vigil on the entrance when the clunky metal lock slid back. She bolted upright, ready for action as the door flung open. Two armed guards escorted Katya into the room and threw her onto the bed. They ogled her and Christina, their eyes wandering over their taut bodies.

"What a waste," one of the guards said, shaking his head in disappointment. "Enjoy what little time you have left, ladies." With his gun barrel he gestured toward the alcohol in the mini-bar. "Make the most of it. If you believe in a Higher Being, you'd better start praying now 'cause soon you'll wish you were dead." The two guards stared up and down at the stunning women one more time before leaving the room and sliding the bolt back into place.

Katya leaped from the bed and hugged Christina. "How are you, darlink?"

"I'm fine," Christina said. Unaccustomed to displaying emotion, she awkwardly returned the hug.

"Have they *done* anything to you?"

"No," Christina replied, suffocating from Katya's bear hug.

"This is good," Katya said, continuing to squeeze Christina. Without warning, she released her grip and searched the room. "Where's Lincoln?"

"I don't know. They separated us, and I've been in this room the whole time. The owner forced Lincoln and several others into a series of deadly games. The bastard is televising the games for the hotel guests, and that's how I found out." She nodded toward the television screen. "Lincoln's still alive, but I don't know how much longer he can last."

"Lincoln, the poor darlink." From her perch on the edge of the bed, Katya spotted an armed guard leering at them from the balcony. As Christina pulled the blackout drapes together, the guard sneered and returned to gawking at Samantha Merrick who was sunbathing naked on the deck of the cabin cruiser anchored beside the hotel.

"Tell me, Katya, how did *you* end up here?"

Katya finished pouring some champagne into a tulip glass. "This guy can't be all bad if he stocks Sovetskoye Igristoye." She sniffed the champagne as she swirled it in her glass, then took a sip and savored its aftertaste. "Roy left me to die with the giant rats, but these men saved me."

"What?" Christina frowned as she failed to process the information.

"Sorry, darlink, I'm a little, how you say it—" she searched for the right word—"frazzled. Yes, frazzled." Christina waited for Katya to relax and collect her thoughts. Katya gulped the last of the champagne and took a deep breath. "After you left with Lincoln to find the tower, a helicopter carrying a news crew that followed us from Saipan also crash-landed on the island. The reporter and cameraman found their way to our plane. They said they might have a working satphone in the helicopter wreckage, so I went with cameraman, Roy, to look for phone, but he left me to die when big rats show up." When she was nervous, her Georgian accent shone. "Christine, darlink, they were terrible creatures… creatures with beady eyes, big long claws… rotted teeth. It was horrible."

Christina had a vague notion of Jonathan Kane's genetic experiments. Through Leon Maxwell, Kane's right-hand man, she'd learned about the existence of the crab-creature they called Big John, but she understood little about how they had created him. She had been privy to many of Kane's bedroom cell-phone discussions that referenced secluded laboratories and genetic experiments, but not the details.

Christina wanted to comfort the poor woman shivering on the bed, but she didn't know how. Life experience had taught her to be independent, that getting involved with others and their problems led to weakness and vulnerability. In her line of work, she couldn't afford to expose herself to emotions that would only lead to death. Still, she wanted to repay Katya for her kindness. She poured her another Sovetskoye Igristoye and sat beside her on the bed, hoping her feeble display of compassion would compensate for her silence.

"Thank you, darlink," Katya said, accepting the drink. She contemplated what the future held for them and the others, and decided she wasn't going to allow circumstances to get the better of her. Instead, she steered the subject in a more womanly direction. "If you don't mind my asking, are you and Lincoln in a relationship?"

Christina drew back at Katya's direct question. "Lincoln and me?"

Katya waited.

"What makes you ask that?"

"Darlink, I am many things, but blind is not one of them. I see the way the he looks at you when you are not watching, and—"

"There's nothing between us."

"—and the way you look at him when he's not looking."

Christina blushed and turned away. "Th-there's nothing going on between Lincoln and me." She busied herself with pouring a scotch to distract Katya from her line of questioning, then gulped the drink.

Needing a diversion from the horrors of the jungle, Katya persisted. "Your eyes say differently," she probed.

Christina refused to allow her emotions to cloud her thinking. She had let her guard down with Jonathan Kane by succumbing to the weakness of her heart, and she had paid dearly for that mistake. Never again would she allow that to happen. "I appreciate Lincoln's skills. He's a good man to have in a fight—nothing more." She averted her eyes while Katya waited for an honest answer.

Katya shrugged. "Like I said, he looks at you, too, when you are not looking."

"That doesn't concern me," Christina replied, her tone detached, but her curiosity was piqued. With casual indifference she added, "However—if Monk *did* concern me—how does he look at me?"

Christina's answer stirred Katya's passion for talking about life and relationships. She grinned for the first time in hours. "When Lincoln was treating you on the plane, he was admiring your hair and neck."

Unconsciously Christina brushed her auburn hair back and ran her hand down her slender neck.

"You have beautiful features—but of course, you know this," Katya said. As she waited for Christina to respond, the television screensaver caught her eye. *Jungle Games.* "What's this?" she asked, pointing to the screen.

CHAPTER 22

LINCOLN SAT ON the edge of his bunk and picked at the chicken on his plate. Gray shifted restlessly on the opposite bunk, shooting glances around the gym. "Doc," Lincoln said, sensing that the older man wanted to share his thoughts, "you want to say something?"

Gray scanned the room again. Satisfied that Red, who was lifting weights, was out of earshot, he leaned toward Lincoln, averting his faced from the watching corner camera. "I must thank you again wholeheartedly for saving my life in the pool and at the sinkhole. I will never forget that."

"No worries."

"I should have trusted you when you saved me at the pool, but I had to be sure that you weren't working for Merrick."

"I understand. In this place, you need to watch your back twenty-four seven. I get that."

Gray looked away, embarrassed at not having confided sooner in this man who had now saved his live twice. "Please forgive me."

"Come on, Doc." Lincoln said, overcome with curiosity. "What's on your mind?"

Gray cleared his throat, took one last glance around the gym, and whispered, "I'm sorry for not having told you earlier, but—I know a way off this godforsaken island."

Lincoln choked on his chicken.

At the sudden outburst, Red's eyes locked on Lincoln and Gray. He sneered at the interruption, but after a dirty look in their direction, returned to his muscle building.

"How?" Lincoln whispered.

"A supply ship arrives twice a week from Saipan."

"Where?"

"Behind the hotel. There's a loading dock in the lagoon at the base of the plateau. Lockwood was headed there, but..." Gray shrugged. "With an army of men chasing him, he must have become disoriented."

"Fear does that to a man." Lincoln eyed Red, who was still lifting weights. "How do we get to the dock?"

"Mounted to the plateau's escarpment is a heavy-duty elevator for hotel supplies that connects the hotel to the dock. If we can get to that elevator, we're home free. We can hitch a ride on the ship and be back in Saipan in two days."

"Sounds like a plan." Since Gray was being upright with him, Lincoln decided that now was the time to repay that honesty. "I haven't been totally up front with you, either. I, too, apologize." He glanced at the camera mounted high in the corner and casually turned his back from the constant monitoring. "I'm here with a group of people. We crash-landed on this island. Merrick's people found Christina—the woman I told you about—and me, but as far as I can tell, they don't know about the others yet. Most likely my people are out looking for us."

"What happens now?"

"We survive the games, find my friends, and get off this damned island."

"Unfortunately, my boy, that is easier said than done."

Lincoln sighed. "You got that right."

CHAPTER 23

THE MERRICKS WERE on the cabin cruiser's deck enjoying their crabe tourteau when Van Sant appeared through the living room doors. He knew that Merrick hated interruptions during dinner, that he considered dining and enjoying his wife's company sacrosanct, so he waited as Merrick ate and sipped his wine. Merrick placed his goblet on the damask tablecloth and turned. "What is it?" he asked with disdain.

"Sorry for the interruption, boss. I know you cherish your private time, but it's important. It's the Germans."

"What is it this time?" he grumbled, taking another bite of the tender, juicy filet.

Van Sant carefully considered his next sentence. "They have a special request."

Merrick sighed. If they hadn't had the capital investment he so desperately needed, he'd have thrown them off the island long ago. "First, they complain about the accommodation. Then they complain that the food is…" Merrick searched for the word.

"Not fit for a dog," Van Sant supplied, adding hastily, "Their words, not mine."

"This food is fit for a king." Merrick took another bite of steak, anger swelling within him. "I poached Chef Fabienne from *Le Cinq* in Paris, and the Germans say the food is garbage. So I fly in another chef—specially requested by them—and they still have the audacity to protest the time it took to transport him here from Japan."

"What can I say?" Van Sant shrugged. "They're Germans."

Merrick licked a dot of sauce from his lips. "What do they want now?"

Van Sant hesitated.

"Well?"

Van Sant waited. When Merrick looked up, Van Sant discreetly tilted his head toward Samantha who was enjoying her salad.

"Samantha, would you mind getting us another bottle of wine, please?"

Samantha looked up from her mixed greens. From their somber mood, she sensed that Van Sant wanted privacy. She dabbed her lips with her napkin, sashayed across the deck, and disappeared into the cabin cruiser.

"Okay, what is it they want this time? Women? Animals? What?"

Van Sant couldn't believe what he was about to say. He had trouble at the mere thought of the words. His hands shook as he lit a cigarette.

"What? Just say it!"

Van Sant took a deep breath and slowly exhaled. "In the next event, they want a kid."

Fine china clattered as Merrick dropped his cutlery onto the plate. He stared at Van Sant, his resentment for the Germans turning to repugnance. "They want to use a boy—as canon-fodder—in a game like this?" He shook his head in revulsion. "I want nothing more to do with the Germans and their sadistic demands."

"They're willing to pay."

Merrick paused. He had invested in these games to secure himself and Samantha for life. The Germans' money, along with that of the other contributors, would allow them to live in a style for which he desperately hungered. He gulped the last of the wine, disgusted by his own words. "How much?"

"A million euros for a boy under ten."

Samantha appeared with a bottle of merlot just as Merrick picked up the corner of the table and flung it, scattering its contents about the deck. She understood her husband's temper and backed away, keeping a watchful eye on the proceedings while allowing him the space to make tough decisions. Merrick wiped his hand over his face, contemplating his answer, wrestling with his conscience. He leaned over the rail and stared at the jungle beyond. "Make sure the boy is from another island," he murmured.

"What? You're not serious! You really want me to kidnap a kid?" Van Sant spluttered as Merrick washed down a glassful of wine, trying to get the taste of his last command from his mouth. "Tom, you know that if you bring a child into this nightmare, you're signing the kid's death warrant."

Merrick gazed into the jungle, hoping the picturesque view and the thought of over a million euros would ease his qualms. "On the west side of Guguan Island you'll find a fishing village."

"Please, Tom. Don't ask me to do this."

"I sign your paycheck. Just do it."

Van Sant stared at Merrick. *Bringing an adult into the games is bad enough. Most adults have lived full lives. But a child? Merrick has crossed the line—like they all do in their search for glory and riches. He's no longer a businessman with a brutal idea. He's a monster, just like the other evil bastards I've worked for.*

Van Sant turned to leave and nearly bumped into Samantha who stood behind him, a satisfied smirk on her face. *She agrees with this atrocity.* He glanced at the merlot she held and flicked his cigarette butt into the river. "Red wine with king crab? I don't think so." He exited the deck, snickering.

CHAPTER 24

Guguan Island, fifty-six nautical miles south of Alamagan Island

VAN SANT PEERED through the acrylic windshield of the MD500E chopper. He watched the western beachfront of Guguan Island disappear to be replaced with a sea of palms and mangroves. The pilot flew low over the rolling terrain in search of the next contestant in Merrick's deadly game.

The lush rain forest canopy vanished to reveal a sports field with a small concrete building at the north end. Children from the local villages were competing on the soccer ground. A dozen adults, resting on coolers and other makeshift chairs, milled about outside the change-rooms, drinking beer while watching their children play their favorite sport.

Several boys in their early teens passed the ball from one to the other, laughing, oblivious to what was about to happen—an event that would change their young lives forever. Van Sant readied the tranquiller gun and indicated to the pilot that he wanted to land.

The young boys stopped their game and watched the chopper as it alighted on the southern end of the field. The boys moved further from their parents and closer to the helicopter, eager to see the craft close up. A cloud of dust swirled as the chopper touched down. The boys backed up and covered their faces from the blowing particles and grass.

The parents turned to one another, wondering what was happening. They stared as Van Sant emerged from the dust cloud, his gun by his side. At the sight of the weapon, the boys froze.

Van Sant took aim and fired at the nearest youngster. The boy dropped to the ground, motionless, as the tranquilizer reacted instantly with his metabolism.

Like stunned deer caught in the headlights, the parents and boys watched, helpless, at the horror playing out before their eyes. A woman screamed as Van Sant strode to the child and flung his unresisting body over his shoulder. The screaming boys on the field scattered as fast as they could in any direction, afraid to meet a similar fate.

Spurred by protective instincts and without regard for their own safety, parents rushed across the grounds. They charged toward the chopper without weapons and with little hope of survival.

Van Sant lifted the boy's limp body into the chopper and turned toward the frantic mothers and fathers. Pulling out his Beretta, he fired several times at the grass just ahead of them. Dirt and grass sprayed into the air. Most of the parents stopped, but one athletic man in his early thirties continued running toward the chopper. "Please," he pleaded over the roar of the idling Rolls-Royce turbine, "he's my only son."

As the distraught father neared, Van Sant climbed into the chopper and took aim. The bullets tore into the earth around the approaching man.

Just stop, Van Sant whispered without conviction, wishing the hysterical father would abandon his child and allow him to do his horrific job. He had carried out many orders and witnessed many atrocities in his life, atrocities that would haunt him forever, but knowing now that he was the monster played with his conscience.

The father rushed forward, oblivious to the deadly onslaught. Van Sant lined up the sights on the Beretta. "So be it," he said with empathy, and fired at the charging man.

The 9mm bullet tore into his shoulder, spinning the man backward through the air. He landed heavily, crying out in anguish—not from the pain pulsating through his body, but from his inability to save his child.

Van Sant slammed the door shut, and the pilot pulled back on the cyclic stick. The helicopter rose in a flurry of leaves and dust, swept low across the field, and disappeared over the treetops.

CHAPTER 25

THE MERRICKS AND their clients lounged in the living room of Merrick's penthouse suite that opened onto the balcony. The torrential rain had eased to a constant drizzle, but the high wind continued to blow from the north. The evening warmth was a welcome change from the incessant downpour and lashing winds of that morning. He understood his clients' need for comfort and satisfaction and glanced around as they relaxed with drinks and hors d'oeuvres, allowing them the opportunity to voice any unanswered questions from the day's disastrous outcome. With the clients at ease the better the chance of his business venture's success.

Chef Fabienne was personally clearing the table. As she reached over to collect the dishes, her skirt rose to reveal a Sig Sauer P238 strapped to her thigh. Merrick spotted the pistol and coughed lightly in her direction. She glanced over to see Merrick looking at her leg. Realizing that the gun was exposed, she casually lowered her skirt and left the balcony, balancing the plates.

Merrick leaned against the glass rail that had been custom-made so as not to interrupt the magnificent view from the penthouse. He admired the subtle glowing lights running along both sides of the riverbank that the outdoor designer had installed to enhance the beauty of the landscape. Docked at the jetty beside the hotel, his one-hundred-foot cabin cruiser gently rocked with the current, her interior lights illuminating the glistening rear deck and surrounding quay. Behind the cabin cruiser, Merrick's personal speed boats bobbed with the flowing water, their varnished brightwork gleaming in the soft light. The deep rumbling of the waterfall beside the hotel permeated the night as distant lighting strikes lit up the ocean landscape beyond the plateau.

Klaus and Wolfgang joined Merrick who greeted them with a warm smile. "Mr. Merrick, may we ask a favor?" Klaus said with an awkward smile.

"Of course, and, please, call me Tom."

"Tom. My employer feels the communication restrictions are becoming quite cumbersome." Wolfgang nudged the younger assistant to continue.

Merrick tilted his head. "How do you mean?"

"Well, it's just that having to ask permission every time we wish to communicate with the outside world is annoying. Lifting the ban to allow us to contact our partners and associates when we wish would be much easier." Other clients, overhearing the conversation, strode over to hear Merrick's reply.

"The restrictions are in place for a reason, gentlemen. They allow our activities to go unnoticed by outside influences."

"Tom, being able to contact our people directly would be a major influence on our decisions regarding your enterprise."

Merrick weighed the risk involved in lifting the electronic ban against the maxim *the customer is always right*. Against his better judgement, he said, "Of course. I'll have my people get on it right away."

"Thank you so much." Klaus and Wolfgang smiled with satisfaction.

"Today has been quite eventful, Tom, wouldn't you say?" Adedowale smirked, sipping his champagne.

Merrick smiled. Getting close to independent wealth meant getting close to clients, and that first step was establishing a first-name basis—even if that client was a brutal warlord.

"It appears that the today's game has not gone as planned," Adedowale continued.

Merrick could see where this was leading. Any doubt about his ability to run such a complicated enterprise could kill the franchise before it had a chance to succeed. He needed to steer the clients from the day's events. "All businesses incur setbacks at some point, but challenges inspire us to achieve greater goals. Don't you agree?"

The Nigerian sipped his champagne. "Yes, businesses *do* incur setbacks, and on this tiny island, you can do as you wish with little regard for outside influences. However, a major setback like the one we witnessed today will have consequences in the real world."

Merrick understood Adedowale's concern for cost and workforce expenses. "I assure you, Jungle Games will be totally managed by myself and my people. Any concerns you may have are unfounded. To run the operation to its fullest potential is my responsibility and mine alone. If challenges arise, financial or otherwise, they *will be overcome,* I assure you. I absolutely guarantee entertainment for every event at any location of your choosing."

The Nigerian solemnly accepted the reassurance but kept an eye on Merrick's face for any tell-tale signs of dishonesty. Merrick grinned back and drank the last of his champagne. Adedowale turned to the breathtaking view below them. "A most stunning location. Quite impressive, Mr. Merrick—Tom."

"Thank you," Merrick replied, glancing at the bartender for more drinks. After refilling their champagne glasses, the bartender retreated into the shadows.

"So, Tom," Abeo began, unconvinced by Merrick's charm, "may I ask what you have in store for us tomorrow?"

Merrick had planned the third event months earlier. His research into human nature and the brutality of man had repeatedly brought up references to sport and battles involving few men. This third event, an unforgiving and brutal game, had played at the hearts of men for thousands of years: hand-to-hand combat. Loser dies. So simple, yet so effective. "Do you enjoy gladiator sports?" he asked.

The Nigerians agreed with broad grins, while Klaus, after relaying to Wolfgang, gave a non-committal shrug. Joanna, however, looked away, sipping her drink. Merrick caught her subconscious act of disapproval. "Something wrong, Joanna?"

She shook her head and tried to wave off the disappointment in her voice. "Of course not. The day will be wonderful."

Merrick smiled at the others and then at her. "Somehow I don't believe you."

"No-o-o... really, I think the idea is wonderful."

Merrick heard the lack of enthusiasm behind her positive response and irritation rose within him. Trying to conceal his annoyance from the crowd, he said, "Please. I appreciate honesty. Honesty gives us a better understanding of each other, don't you think?"

Joanna had the group's attention. "Well, it's that the whole gladiator thing is just so, so..." She searched for a kind word to describe Merrick's uninspired choice. "Cliché. The gladiator bit has been done a hundred times before."

Merrick grinned at Joanna through clenched teeth to hide his anger. The other clients turned to each other with similar expressions of disappointment.

Samantha Merrick, her hair twisted in a relaxed updo, stood beside her husband looking very much the supportive wife in a low-cut black crepe evening dress accessorized with a double-strand white pearl necklace. Seeing the clients' dissatisfaction with her husband's event choice, she seethed at the Englishwoman with her snobbish British accent and superior attitude. Samantha would have liked nothing better than to have seen Joanna on the rope bridge, falling to her death with the Purple contestant.

Samantha turned to the jungle below for inspiration, for anything that would trigger an idea for an original game the clients would appreciate. Her man was floundering, and to rescue the situation was her duty. Never again would she allow herself to suffer the embarrassment of poverty. She had worked too hard and too long to get here, and no one was getting in the way of her dream and destiny. She glanced toward the river where the waves lapped against the moored speedboats glistening beside the cabin cruiser. The sight of the two pleasure crafts sparked an idea.

Still trying to ease the situation between Merrick and herself, Joanna said, "Please, I'm sure it will be a spectacular day. Forgive my insolence. I'm afraid I'm still on UK time and a bit jet lag—"

"No apologies necessary," Samantha interrupted. "From the United Kingdom to the Marianas *is* a long journey, and, naturally, someone of your—" she raised her voice so everybody could hear— "someone of your *maturity* would require more time to adjust. I'm sure the other clients won't mind if you sleep-in for a few hours tomorrow." She looked to the others with curled lips before she turned back to Joanna with a patronizing smile.

"Thank you for the kind offer, but it's unnecessary." Joanna leaned in toward Samantha and studied her pearls. "That necklace truly catches my eye. Is it real?"

Samantha's smile faded. "Of course it is," she snapped.

Joanna decided to have one last jab at Samantha Merrick. "It looks so… When this is all over, you must give me the name of the establishment responsible for such, such an eye-catching piece of jewelry." Joanna smiled, knowing her backhanded insult did not go unnoticed among the clients. The Germans turned away and chuckled while the Nigerians waited, eager for more.

Samantha swallowed her rising anger and forced another smile. "Of course." She gulped the last of her champagne and indicated to the bartender for another. She glared in Joanna's direction, then turned to those assembled. "My husband is eager to get to the fourth and last event. Yes, it *is* a gladiatorial game, but one so visionary and so revolutionary that it will astound you."

Joanna raised her eyebrow. "Sounds very exciting."

"It is." Samantha raised her voice to ensure that all the clients could hear. "The third event will prove to be most entertaining. Indeed, we have quite a day in store for everybody tomorrow—a day you will never forget."

Merrick smiled at his wife and casually slipped his arm around her while giving her a peck on the cheek. "What are you doing?" he whispered. "You know that the third event is the fight in the field and the fourth is to have the last two contestants battle it out on the waterfall's edge."

Samantha smiled and returned his kiss so the guests could see their love for one another. "Things change. I have two better ideas." She gazed first at the speedboats moored behind her beloved cabin cruiser and then across the island to the northern horizon. "As you say, darling—always one up."

DAY 5

CHAPTER 26

The Third Event

MERRICK LEANED CLOSER to the four monitors at Simon's workstation, stilled impressed by the kid operating four keyboards simultaneously. The bottom screen displayed the two boats preparing for the race while the top three repeated the boat images.

Merrick indicated the multiple images. "What's this?"

Simon continued to tap keys. The top three images dissolved to the clients in their hotel rooms. Merrick watched as the Nigerians argued over some minor issue while the other screens displayed either the Germans or Joanna with her butler casually waiting for the event to begin. All parties appeared to be staring directly at the camera lens.

"Can they see us?" Merrick asked.

"Not a chance," Simon replied.

"Where did you hide the cameras?"

"In plain sight. They're pinhole cameras that I mounted in the fake power sockets behind the televisions."

"Ingenious. When I give the go-ahead, I'll need you to cut the feed to the clients' televisions. Understood?"

"Sure."

"Will we lose the feed, too?"

"Not a chance. The raw data from the last drone is fed into this room only. We control the stream to the clients' rooms."

"Good." Merrick gazed at the monitor as the drone's camera recorded in high definition. "Crystal clear image, by the way. Well done."

"Thank you, Mr. Merrick."

"I'm going down to my cabin cruiser. Wait for my call."

Simon gave him a thumbs up.

Anchored to the southern side of the jetty opposite the cabin cruiser, two classic runabouts rocked with the current that passed beneath their hulls. The nineteen-foot Chris-Craft Barrel Back replicas, made famous circa 1940, were Merrick's pride and joy. Seeking to exude a sense of wealth and refinement, Merrick had had the two custom-made, one for himself and one for Samantha. The mahogany veneer and polished steel railings, an addition at Merrick's request, glistened in the morning light. Completing the design, each craft's stern hull tapered to a rounded transom to give the boat its barrel name.

Merrick sat on the cabin cruiser's back deck with Van Sant beside him. He watched as one of his men, a boating enthusiast, instructed the contestants on the speedboat's control system. Samantha, wearing a chic one-piece swimsuit and sun hat, lay nearby on a deck chair. Peeking over her Ray-Bans, she was eager for the event to begin, certain that her idea would thrill the clients.

"Everything ready?" Merrick asked, keeping his eyes on the boat with Lincoln and Gray in the cockpit. "Those two are not to make it back, do you understand?"

Van Sant heard Merrick's deadly tone and understood what was at stake. The clients' wagers on this event were substantial; any mishap would cost Merrick dearly. Van Sant knew that Merrick would blame him for any mistakes, so he chose his words carefully. "I have *your* guys positioned all along the river." Van Sant hoped to impress on Merrick that it was his personnel, not Van Sant, who would be responsible if anything went wrong. "At your command, we'll interrupt the drone feed. We'll call it static interference from the storm. When the cameras are off, we'll make our move. They won't be coming back."

Merrick contemplated Van Sant's response. After a few moments, he turned his gaze back to the speedboats moored to the quay. "Just get it done."

"You got it, boss."

Merrick tapped his earpiece to apprise the clients watching the televisions in their rooms of the rules. "The contestants, two per boat, must follow the course of the waterway around the island. First boat back wins." He glanced over at Samantha who gave him a cheeky smile, now sunbathing topless beside him. Sex sells, too.

Wolfgang rubbed his groin at the sight of the helpless child being lifted into Red's craft. Adedowale and Abeo couldn't take their eyes off the semi-naked Samantha Merrick on the cabin cruiser's deck. At the sight of the child, Joanna shook her head in disgust and averted her eyes. *Merrick has gone too far.*

"Let the game begin!" Merrick shouted in his best show-man's voice.

Red smirked at Lincoln as Merrick's men dropped the small boy into his runabout. Eyes wide with terror, the boy cowered on the seat and huddled in the far corner, keeping his distance from the hulking Red. The engine spluttered to life and Red's runabout accelerated away from the riverbank.

"Poor kid," Lincoln fumed, enraged that Merrick had brought a child into the games. His plan to run into Red's boat and smash the hull were gone. With Gray by his side, Lincoln throttled up and the runabout roared away from the riverbank. The 350MAG engine churned the muddy bank at the shoreline and a rooster tail of water sprayed the jetty.

"Son of a bitch!" The bald-headed guard closest to the river cursed as he wiped the slime and mud from his clothes and face.

The second guard caught most of the unfiltered green water. He removed chunks of mud from his face and cleared the globules of gunk from his eyes. "Goddamn, this shit stinks!" He grabbed a water bottle from his side and quickly washed away the residue.

"Relax," Van Sant said, leaning against the cruiser's railing and picking the last dollop of mud from his utility vest. He watched Lincoln's speedboat disappear around the bend.Merrick contemplated Van Sant's response. "Best of luck, guy. You're going to need it," he whispered.

CHAPTER 27

MANGROVES CLUNG TO the riverbank, their gnarled and insect-infested branches extending far into the waterway. Sinewy vines reached down from the branches to the water's surface, creating a veil of wooden strands that stretched half-way across the river. Red veered around the hanging vines and continued down the waterway with Lincoln close behind. Through the spray of water sent up by his engine, Red could see that Lincoln's boat was closing fast.

Swerving around mangrove roots and water plants spilling from the riverside, Lincoln banked the speedboat toward the center of the waterway and followed Red who led by a full hundred yards. Above them, the drone buzzed through the sky like a giant mosquito chasing its prey. The camera swiveled and focused on both boats as they roared through the tributary with mud banks and jungle greenery flashing by.

Lincoln glanced at the drone. "Dammit," he murmured, realizing that a quick getaway into the narrow waterways adjoining the river was out of the question.

Watching the race from the privacy of their rooms on wall-mounted television screens with full HD 1080p picture with 5-1 surround digital sound, the clients were immersed in the contest's sights and sounds. Although the previous day's driving rains had subsided, the churning clouds cast dark shadows along the river.

Prevailing high wind gusts caught under the hulls and lifted the speeding crafts from the water before they crashed back again.

In addition to Red's erratic steering, Lincoln now had to deal with gale force winds slamming the bow head-on. Struggling with the controls, he pulled up alongside Red, careful to keep a distance. As the heaving water and wind played havoc with the navigation, Lincoln saw that Red, too, was straining to keep his boat upright and steady.

Red looked back at Lincoln and grinned. He banked hard right, causing the starboard side of his runabout to slam into Lincoln's hull. Scraping wood and the screech of tortured metal echoed across the water as the side rail from Lincoln's boat folded then crumpled around the railing on Red's boat. The two boats locked together, pummeling the waves. Red swerved left, and Lincoln's port side railing tore away. The railing caught on Red's boat and dangled along the hull, bouncing through the water.

Merrick and Van Sant watched the drone's direct feed on a laptop resting on a glass coffee table on the cabin cruiser's deck. Van Sant tapped his earpiece. "Simon. Are you ready to interrupt the feed?"

"Ready when you are."

Merrick studied the drone's aerial view of Red's boat racing downriver and marveled at the crystal-clear image relayed from the drone. "The picture is remarkable, don't you think?"

"These new generation drones capture a full 1880-pixel rate—state of the art. Just what you asked for, boss."

"Yes." Merrick smiled, congratulating himself with a sip of scotch, and waited for Red to make his move.

"Simon, zoom in on Red for me," Van Sant said. The image closed in on Red behind the wheel, struggling to control his craft as it skipped across the water. "That wind could be a problem. He may have trouble driving and shooting at the same time."

"He'll manage because he knows what's at stake. My bonus will see to that."

Red turned toward the drone buzzing behind the boat and waved, signaling that he was ready.

"Okay, Simon, cut the feed—now!" Van Sant ordered.

The Nigerians cursed as the television picture turned to static.

Klaus looked away with disapproval as Wolfgang slammed his fist onto the coffee table.

Joanna shifted on the couch, annoyed that white static had replaced the image of the boats racing down the river. "Baxter?"

"Yes, mum." Baxter glanced at the screen. He rolled up his sleeves and proceeded to examine the telly. He angled the device from the wall and peered behind, careful not to damage the mount. "All the connections appear to be in place, mum. However, a very large—enormous, actually—spider is lying behind here. I do believe it's the same one I spotted earlier. If it's all the same to you, I prefer not to be so close to arachnids, even if they are dead."

"That's right, you don't like spiders. Well, stop fussing and put the television back in place. And call housekeeping."

"Yes, mum. Thank you." Baxter placed the television back against the wall, wiped his brow, and sighed. Even a dead spider made him sweat.

Joanna took a sip of beer. "It appears Mr. Merrick doesn't want anyone to see the outcome of the race. Most interesting."

"Yes, mum, it is." Baxter gulped a bottle of water with shaking hands, his encounter with the albeit dead spider still preying on his mind.

Joanna tapped her earpiece. "Mr. Merrick, the race was quite exciting, but it seems we've lost reception. All we're seeing is static."

"Please accept my sincere apologies, Joanna." Merrick's voice came over the piece. "We appear to have a technical difficulty. The wind is interfering with the feed from the drone—something to do with the static electricity in the atmosphere. My people are looking into the problem as we speak. We will resume coverage as soon as possible. Meanwhile, please enjoy the beverages provided. I'll get back to you the moment the feed is operational."

"I understand," Joanna replied, tapping her earpiece to end the conversation. She turned to Baxter. "What do you think?"

"His explanation sounds plausible."

Joanna took another sip. "Yes, plausible," she murmured, her eyes narrowing.

Baxter took a deep breath to calm his nerves. "Mum, your wager."

Joanna gazed at the static on the screen and contemplated the large sum she had placed on Blue to win the games. "I get the impression that Mr. Merrick doesn't wish for Blue and Gray to succeed. Nevertheless, Blue seems to be very good at getting out of tough situations." She smiled. "Let's see how he handles this one."

Baxter turned up his nose and sniffed the air. "Mum, may I be so bold as to offer my opinion on the subject?"

"Of course, Baxter."

"I believe I smell, as the Americans say, bullshit."

"Yes," Joanna said, sipping her scotch, "I smell it too. Let's retire to the balcony, shall we?"

CHAPTER 28

LINCOLN FOCUSED ON the river ahead, careful not to get too close to the unpredictable Red. "Keep an eye out for anything floating," he yelled to Gray, pointing to the rotted wood bobbing near the riverbank. Gray gave him a thumbs up and scanned the tree-covered ba—*Ratatatat!* Machine gun fire filled their ears as sparks flew from the bullet impacts along the bow. Lincoln and Gray ducked behind the control board for safety.

"What the hell?" Gray's eyes widened at the puncture holes that riddled the polished mahogany.

Lincoln groaned. "Augh—that's not fair!"

Red took aim with a Heckler & Koch HK21 machine gun and fired again.

This time his aim was off, and the bullets strafed the river along the speedboat's port side sending geysers of white water into the air.

Gray turned to Lincoln, bewildered. "I don't understand. Where did he get the gun?"

"Looks like Merrick doesn't want us to live."

Another strafing line tore into the deck and the dual wind-shields, sending Lincoln and Gray deeper into the cockpit. Through the spider-webbed glass, Lincoln could make out Red, the gun by his side, focusing on the left riverbank. Red swerved hard left and disappeared around the bend in the river.

Something is wrong. Why would Red stop firing? He had true line of sight, and we're easily within range... Lincoln kept an alert watch for any more surprises.

He didn't have to wait long. Two men wearing black security garb emerged from the greenery on the left bank. The first gunman pointed toward Lincoln's runabout as it roared past while the other leveled his RPG-7 rocket launcher at the racing vessel.

"Hang on!" Lincoln shouted. He banked the speedboat hard right, away from the men on the shore. Gray gripped the rail beside the cockpit as the piercing shrill of the rocket-propelled grenade approached the boat.

A stream of white smoke trailed the grenade's flightpath across the river. The high wind caught its tailfins, and the grenade passed over the runabout and continued into the jungle on the river's right bank. The explosion ripped the shoreline mushrooming shards of wood and shredded palm leaves into the sky. Lincoln sped away from the carnage as the remnants of the jungle fluttered down to the river's edge. The runabout was fifty yards further from the riverbank when the gunman finished reloading his RPG-7, took aim, and fired again.

Lincoln headed for a rotted abandoned jetty a hundred yards in front of them. Beside the jetty an upturned dinghy floated idly in the water, its beam sloping skyward at a thirty-degree angle. Approaching the jetty at top speed, Lincoln lined up the runabout with the dinghy.

Gray guessed what Lincoln was about to attempt. He turned to him, wide-eyed. "You've got to be kidding."

"Hang on."

The runabout hit the dinghy at full speed, launched over the water, and arced through the air over the jetty. Meanwhile, the rocket continued its trajectory and slammed into the derelict pier, blasting the rotted supports and wooden walkway high into the sky.

The runabout slammed back down onto the river, kicking up a spray as the jetty blasted apart behind it. Lincoln and Gray ducked below deck as a plank of shredded wood the length of a railway sleeper flew over their heads and into the river. They emerged to see heavy smoke drifting in the air where the jetty had stood, and small eruptions pockmarking the river as debris splashed down around the fleeing runabout.

Before Lincoln could catch his breath from the rocket attack, three jet skis with armed riders emerged from the mangroves lining the river's left bank. Bullets ripped into the stern, puncturing holes in the transom's hand-polished mahogany. Lincoln swerved across the waterway to avoid the new threat. The bullet-riddled mounts securing the speedboat's backseat had come loose from the boat's frame, allowing the seat to lurch toward Gray and Lincoln. Gray propped his legs against the leather bench to hold it in place. The jet ski riders held back, cautious at the speedboat's erratic maneuvering as Lincoln snaked down the tributary. The undulating wake rolled away from the boat, crashed against the riverbank, and cut back into the jet skiers' path, hampering their stability and forcing them to repeatedly slow to regain control.

The crack of gunfire rang in Lincoln's ears as another volley of bullets zipped over the speed boat from behind. Lincoln scanned the river for cover, for anything to shield them from the assault. Apart from the tall reeds and mangroves lining the banks, the river was bare of protection.

"Go into the reeds and follow the bank!" Gray shouted.

"Why?"

"I have an idea."

Lincoln changed course toward the reeds running parallel with the bank. The slime-covered reeds jutting from the green water slapped against the hull as the speedboat raced adjacent to the shore-line. The boat shuddered as the stalks slowed its forward momentum, so Lincoln adjusted the throttle to accelerate. The engine howled in protest as the wooden hull crashed through the vegetation, the tortured prow taking the full brunt of the brutal assault.

Gray twisted the last remaining plastic mount free from the boat frame. He lifted the bench seat from the deck and dropped it into the water behind the runabout. "There's always one guy," he called to Lincoln as they watched the seat splash into the water then resurface among the reeds. Lincoln shot Gray a curious glance, still not understanding the older man's intentions.

Sure enough, the more gung-ho of the jet skiers, looking for a quick kill to add to his belt, veered from the safety of the river and followed Lincoln and Gray into the reeds. With less weight and mass, and the path's having been cleared by the boat, the jet ski shot through the reeds, bearing down on the lumbering craft. The rider lifted his M-60 and took aim at the speedboat weaving through the stalks. At forty miles an hour the jet ski slammed into the bench seat, catapulting the craft and rider end over end through the air and into a tree overhanging the riverbank. The rider hit a rotted branch with a bone-snapping crack and crashed into the leafy ground cover where the jet ski's over-heated engine ignited the fuel tank, erupting in a shower of flame and smoking debris.

Lincoln held the boat true and continued alongside the bank. "Yep. There's always one macho asshole."

Gray grinned with the pride and satisfaction of a job well done.

The dense clumps of reeds running alongside the riverbank were slowing the runabout, allowing the two remaining jet skiers to adjust their speed and remain parallel with the boat. Taking advantage of the opportunity the slower speed provided, the riders steadied their jet skis and took careful and deliberate aim at the blurred speedboat plowing through the reeds, hoping to neutralize Lincoln and Gray and end the chase.

As the volley of bullets tore into the boat's starboard side, pressurized oil sprayed across the stern. Another round of bullets ignited the heated oil. Flames licked the transom with a rising cloud of black smoke trailing behind. Lincoln jerked on the throttle in frustration as the engine spluttered from a mortal wound.

Gray grabbed an extinguisher mounted beside the captain's chair and smothered the fire engulfing the stern. "What can I do to help?" Gray asked, ducking beside Lincoln as another barrage of bullets sealed the boat's fate. Deprived of oil and fuel and choking on air, the engine coughed its death throes.

Lincoln glanced around the hobbled speedboat and considered the beating it had taken from the continuous onslaught. The old girl had stood up to Merrick's goons, and for that Lincoln blew her a kiss, but he knew in seconds another shower of bullets would destroy her. The riders followed just yards behind the reeds, and Lincoln could sense their satisfaction at a job well done. "Hang on," he shouted over the stuttering motor and banked hard right through the reeds.

The closer jet skier was taken by surprise as the speedboat's bow crushed his chest. As the craft crashed over the flailing jet ski, its rider disappeared below the boat's hull. His M-60 machine gun flew onto the speedboat's bow and slid toward the side railing.

Gray snatched the weapon before it went over the side and smiled at Lincoln. "Finally, we get a break." The stern of the speedboat lifted as the jet ski exploded under her, throwing Lincoln and Gray against the dashboard and driving the bow below the water's surface. Lincoln sighed with relief when the boat's buoyancy corrected for the sudden shift in weight. A wave of water washed over the bow swamping Lincoln and Gray in green algae and muddy water.

The last jet skier, now yards away, couldn't miss his targets. He leveled his weapon at Lincoln and Gray and pulled the trigger. Nothing. The magazine was empty. A hail of bullets ripped into the rider's body. The jet ski roared uncontrollably across the river and slammed into a gnarled stump above the surface, its rider dead before he hit the water.

Surprised, Lincoln stared at Gray. The older man held the M-60 at arm's length, his eyes wide with shock. "Well done," Lincoln said, smiling.

"I didn't know I had it in me to kill another man."

"We never do, until we're in a life or death situation," Lincoln said, steering the boat toward the center of the river to keep away from any gunmen lurking in the reeds. "You passed—with flying colors."

Gray studied the weapon in his hand, now empty of ammunition, slowly realizing that, if necessary, he could hold his own. He smiled.

CHAPTER 29

As RED ROARED toward the hotel, Merrick signaled to Simon who rapidly tapped keys. The image of Red racing down the river appeared on the clients' television screens. "Thanks to the hard-working staff in my technology department, we again have reception," Merrick's jubilant voice announced through the client's headsets. "Please enjoy the remainder of the race."

"How convenient," Joanna murmured.

Not far behind Red, Lincoln and Gray followed the meandering waterway through the jungle terrain. The runabout's engine was dying. Lincoln estimated that they had minutes before the over-heated motor seized. He banked the speedboat around a bend in the river and groaned.

Despite all the confusion and gun battles, they had survived the watercourse and were on the homeward stretch. Downriver, beside the hotel's jetty, Red sat in his boat, arms crossed, smiling with the knowledge that he had finished the course first and that Lincoln and Gray would soon be dead. As the young boy scampered off the runabout, Red lifted his hand, made a gun gesture at them, and pulled the imaginary trigger.

Merrick and Van Sant stood gazing at Lincoln and Gray from the rear deck of Merrick's cabin cruiser that was anchored to the other side of the jetty. Three guards, wearing Merrick's standard tactical garb for the cameras, stood on the jetty, armed and ready for Lincoln and Gray's final approach. The drone buzzed overhead, its camera prepared to capture every moment of the losing contestants' last moments of life. The guards cocked their weapons and waited for Merrick's word.

With Baxter by her side, Joanna leaned over the balcony railing, preferring to witness the event with her own eyes rather than the skewed video supplied by Merrick's team. She watched as Merrick, Red, Van Sant, and the guards waited for Lincoln and Gray to make their move. From her vantage point on the balcony, the speedboat was hidden behind the riverbank's foliage, but the black smoke drifting up from the jungle gave away their position on the river.

With broad smiles the Nigerians also appeared on their balcony, certain that in the next few minutes, the outcome would favor the wager they'd placed on Red. They slapped each other on the back at a bet well-placed and eagerly watched for the boat to come into view of the hotel.

The Germans, too, stepped out from their suite and slipped on sunglasses against the sunshine. With drinks in hand they leaned against the balcony's safety railing as if the deadly proceedings were a party. They saluted themselves, drank top-shelf spirits with gusto, and called for the room attendant to fetch another round.

As Lincoln studied the downriver scene, Gray watched the three guards position themselves for the best firing lines while Red looked on with satisfaction. "They really don't want us to win, do they?" Gray said.

Lincoln caught sight of a possible avenue of survival. "No, they don't, but—" He made the calculations and decided it was their only chance against the waiting gunmen. "Have you ever seen a Tarzan film?"

Gray gave Lincoln a questioning look. "Of course, everyone has. But maybe now isn't the best time to discuss old films." He pointed his chin toward the waiting men, guns ready to fire, beside the hotel grounds.

"Humor me."

Gray recognized the glimmer of hope in Lincoln's eyes, having been saved by this young man beside him on more than one occasion these last three days. Lincoln steered the speedboat on a parallel course with the riverbank. He braced his legs against the captain's chair, as if poised to leap from the boat. "Did you ever see the Tarzan movies of the thirties and forties—the ones with Johnny Weissmuller playing Tarzan?"

Gray smiled at the memory of the old films from his youth. "Absolutely. Johnny was by far the best Tarzan—period."

Lincoln focused on the riverbank upstream from the jetty and maneuvered the speedboat toward the giant tree overhanging the shoreline. "In addition, he had Boy and Cheetah to keep him company."

"That's right. Cheetah was the chimp and Boy was his son."

"And don't forget Jane."

"Who could ever forget Jane. Loved those loin cloths."

"Do you know what I like best about those old Tarzan films?"

Gray didn't need the answer. As Lincoln aimed for the overhanging vines they had avoided at the beginning of the race, he understood what Lincoln had in mind.

Lincoln spotted two guards holding the young boy on the lawn beside the jetty. *Good. He's safe and away from the boat. Maybe Merrick has a shred of decency after all.*

"Let me guess. Tarzan swinging from the vines?"

Lincoln smiled. "Ready?"

"Do I have a choice?" Knowing the answer, Gray's features strained with dread and apprehension.

"We can do this this. Just grab a vine as we pass under and hang on tight." Gray took in a slow deep breath and exhaled, trying to relax his nerves as best he could. Lincoln patted him lightly on the shoulder and smiled. "You're okay, Lucius." Gray braced himself against the decking.

Joanna turned to Baxter. "What do you suppose Blue is doing now?"

"No idea, mum."

Joanna shielded her eyes from the glaring sun and leaned further over the balcony, trying to get a view of what Lincoln and Gray were doing.

Tom and Samantha Merrick watched with Van Sant as the speedboat entered the clump of vines hanging from the branches extending over the river.

"Now," Lincoln yelled, as he leaped from the deck and gripped a passing vine.

Gray followed.

The forward motion propelled the two men like a pendulum toward the riverbank as the boat passed by beneath them. The temporary momentum dissipated as Lincoln and Gray completed the zenith of the arc. They swung back out over the water as the speedboat emerged from the last of the vines heading toward Red's runabout.

The unexpected turn caught Red completely off-guard. He scrambled out of the boat but slipped and fell back onto the deck. Lincoln's speedboat T-boned Red's craft at thirty knots, ploughing through the wooden frame and crushing Red below her hull. The battered frame drove the fuel tank back into the flaming motor, causing both crafts to shatter in a fiery explosion below the jetty. The wooden slats making up the jetty's walkway blew apart, blasting the three gunmen through the air and into the river.

The Merricks and Van Sant dove to the safety of the inner cabin as flaming fragments of wood and metal rained down around them. Spot fires broke out across the cabin cruiser's deck until the stern was teeming with smoke and flames.

Lincoln held tight to the sinewy vine, his feet barely above the water's surface as he and Gray swung through the air. As the swaying slowed, Lincoln glanced at the hotel. The guests peered back at him, some smiling and others with looks of disbelief. When he saw a guard herd Katya and Christina back into a room several floors up, Lincoln exhaled audibly, relieved that the girls were unharmed. He made a mental note of the room's location.

Joanna couldn't help grinning broadly. *Yes, Blue was a very resourceful young man.* Beside her, Baxter peered over the balcony watching the events with curiosity and satisfaction. He straightened his tie and suit. "Mum, it appears your instincts were correct—again."

Joanna winked at Baxter. She was considering hiring a clever quick-thinker like young Blue to work for her organization.

"Mum, when do you think is the right time to collect your winnings?"

She glanced down at the burning jetty, the smoking wreckage of two speedboats, and the cabin cruiser's burning deck. "Let's give Mr. Merrick time to put out those fires—shall we?"

"Yes, mum."

CHAPTER 30

MANGROVE SHRUBS, COCOA trees, and coconut palms lined both sides of the river dwarfing the C-47 aircraft as it rested among the reeds and water pads lining the shoreline. Rousseau held onto the strut connecting the port pontoon to the undercarriage and inspected the bullet holes beneath the water just below the float's hull. The tell-tale sign of small bubbles streaming from the holes meant only one thing. He released his grip on the strut and lay flat on the pontoon to get a better view of the damage. The cool water was a refreshing change from the heat as he plunged his arm into the flowing river. Rousseau ran his hand over the pontoon's surface below the water. The bullet holes were too deep for his outstretched arm to reach.

Lifting his hand from the water, he spotted a leech clinging to the underside of his arm. Anxiety at the creature's presence built within him. He grabbed a cigarette lighter from his overalls' pocket and in so doing, dislodged Maurice from the safety of the fold. He gasped as the porcelain unicorn dropped onto the pontoon and slid into the water. He quickly passed the flame over the blood-sucking parasite, keeping an eye on the black disgusting worm as it fell into the water and, along with Maurice, disappeared from sight.

Beside his pilot's chair, Roland adjusted the tiller controlling the small rudder at the back of each pontoon. From the plane's lackluster response, Roland sighed in defeat, realizing that only one of the rudders was still operational. He was about to turn back to the area charts in his lap when Enheim appeared and made himself comfortable in the co-pilot's seat.

"We need to talk," Enheim said in his arrogant way, rubbing Napoleon under the chin.

"Marcus, I'm busy trying to steer Ava. This old girl needs my undivided attention, you know."

"This will only take a minute."

Roland sighed. He folded the map and waited, knowing that Marcus would not give up until he had finished what he had come to say.

Enheim cleared his throat. "Napoleon here wants to thank you for getting us out of that mess back at the cliff."

Roland patted Napoleon on the head and smiled. "Any time, my little man." He turned to Enheim and waited for *his* thank you. Enheim tapped his knee and debated. Finally he said, "That's it." He stood and returned to the cabin.

Roland watched Enheim sit down and peer out the cabin window to the jungle beyond. *That's the best I'm going to get from him.* He shook his head in disbelief.

Rousseau appeared in the cockpit. "Mr. Pom, we have a problem."

"Of course ve do." *The last few days have been the toughest of my life; vy should today be any different?* "Vat is the problem, Rousseau?" He lit another cigarette and inhaled. The shot of nicotine allowed his body and brain to relax, even if only for a few moments.

"When we first landed, I didn't get a chance to inspect any possible damage to the pontoons. We focused on the mechanical repairs to the port engine."

Roland took another puff. "Let me guess. One of the pontoons has a leak."

Rousseau turned away, his look of despair giving Roland the answer he dreaded. "Bullet holes have punctured the aluminum casing, Mr. Pom. It's only a matter of time before Ava begins listing to port. Even if we get the engine working, the extra weight of the water inside the pontoon will strain her thrust capabilities. If we tried taking off, the plane would tear itself apart."

"Can you repair the leak?"

"Oui."

Roland noted that Rousseau was jiggling his foot and licking his lips. "And?" he probed.

"Mr. Pom, to repair the leaks I have to go into the river."

"Yes. The holes are below the vaterline."

Rousseau did not reply. His uncomfortable silence worried Roland. "Please, Rousseau—I need to understand vat is troubling you, you know."

"The water is filled with leeches!" Rousseau blurted. "Disgusting, black, slimy, horrible little creatures that stick like glue and suck blood." His gestures emphasized the appalling nature of the leeches.

Roland took a deep drag on his cigarette. He understood the fear in Rousseau's quavering voice. "It's okay, Rousseau." He sighed and lifted his tired body from the pilot's seat. "Looks like I'm going for a swim."

"And there is one more thing, Mr. Pom. It's Maurice."

Roland combined the aluminum and reactant putty and placed the doughy substance over the first bullet hole in the pontoon. Impervious to water, the putty would harden after several hours and bond with the existing aluminum, becoming one. Waist deep in the muddy water and with his feet sunk in riverbed slime, he moulded more of the concoction and plugged the second hole.

As Rousseau swiped away a swarm of hovering mosquitos, Roland lost his footing on a slime-covered rock and disappeared below the surface. Rousseau held his breath until Roland reappeared, coughing brown, murky water.

"*Scheisse!*" Roland spat. "That is nasty vater, you know."

"Mr. Pom, I'm sorry to rush you… but there's one more hole."

"Give me a minute, Rousseau." Roland paused to catch his breath. Rousseau brushed away more mosquitoes as his employer and friend leaned against the pontoon and glanced at the mangroves surrounding them. The constant whining reminded them of the dangers from waterways like this one. All types of disease could be contracted from mosquitos: malaria, yellow fever, dengue, encephalitis, West Nile virus, Zika. Roland made a mental note to give himself a shot of antibiotics back onboard the plane.

After plugging the final hole, Roland ducked below the water and resurfaced moments later. With Rousseau's help, he climbed back onto the pontoon and passed the porcelain doll to the big Frenchman. "Maurice is safe and sound, you know."

Rousseau cupped the doll in his hand, happy to have his good luck charm back. As Roland steadied himself, Rousseau's expression transformed from pure delight to total terror.

"Rousseau, what's wrong?"

Unable to stomach the sight before him, Rousseau turned away, trying to remove the terrifying image from his mind. He covered his eyes and pointed at Roland's back as he vomited into the water.

A dozen slimy black creatures, writhing with parasitic intent, clung to Roland's body. "Vell, that sucks!" Unphased by the leeches, Roland stepped toward the big Frenchman who flinched as Roland removed the cigarette lighter from his overalls' pocket. As Roland went to work on the disgusting creatures, Rousseau could only shiver at the thought and looked away, rubbing Maurice for comfort. With the setting sun casting a warm orange glow across the island, the sizzle of burning leeches reached his ears. He tried to concentrate on the lush beauty of the riverbank as Roland burned the parasites away.

Positioning the lighter over his pasty upper arm, Roland set the flame to a leech attached to his tattoo of Marlene Dietrich in a sultry pose. "Sorry, Marlene, you know."

CHAPTER 31

LEANING AGAINST THE penthouse's railing, Merrick took a gulp of his fifteen-year-old scotch. He peered down at the smoking deck of his cabin cruiser and awaited the inevitable confrontation with the Nigerians. He didn't have to wait long. They barged through his living room and onto the penthouse's deck, pushing past Chef Fabienne who was holding a tray of hors d'oeuvres.

"Out of my way woman," Adedowale commanded, ignoring her as the tray tumbled to the ground, spilling its contents across the floor.

Chef Fabienne glared with contempt at the two men striding across the deck toward Merrick. She glanced at Merrick and discreetly reached for the hidden gun tucked in her thigh holster. Merrick considered the situation, decided his safety was not a concern, and subtly shook his head. Nevertheless, she picked up her tray with unhurried purpose, keeping an eye on the hostile Nigerians as she moved toward the penthouse kitchen.

Merrick smiled broadly at the men. "Gentlemen, how can I help you?"

Adedowale dismissed Merrick's false charm and stabbed his chest with his finger. Merrick was taken aback by this invasion of his space, but quickly regained his composer, this time without the smile. "Can I get you a drink? We have the finest Scotch in the islands."

"We do not care about your Scotch," the Nigerian hissed. "We are down by a large sum of money, Mr. Merrick."

"I agree. Yours is a substantial loss."

"What are you going to do about that?"

"A bet is a bet, gentlemen."

The Nigerian's eyes bore into Merrick, the glaring white around the pupil contrasting with the deep black of his skin. His anger at the lost wager boiled within him, his rage barely under control. "You guaranteed your man would win. He failed."

"Gentlemen, let me assure you, the outcome of that race was not planned. We had no idea Blue and Gray were such resourceful men."

"And where does that leave us, Mr. Merrick? How am I to leave here knowing I have lost a considerable sum because of your inadequate screening process? How do you think this makes you and your company look? Hmmm?"

Merrick conceded that the Nigerian made a good point. Future contestants would have to be thoroughly screened and checked out before being conscripted for the games. Blue's last-minute entry had cost him dearly. The Nigerian and German delegates were doubtful about his ability to maintain control of his company. So as not to incur bad publicity, Merrick understood that he must fulfil the desires of the Nigerians before they left the island. But he couldn't return their money. That would set a precedent that would destroy future betting. His thoughts turned to the two captured women locked in a guest room. He had hoped to use these stunning women for the final event, but he appreciated that he had to appease the Nigerians if they were to supply repeat business. What a shame. The women were indeed beautiful. Such a waste. "What type of host would I be if I didn't offer some form of remuneration to my special guests?"

The Nigerians eyed him suspiciously but calmed at the thought of a new deal. "What type of remuneration are we talking about, Mr. Merrick?"

Merrick smiled, knowing he had the upper hand. "Gentlemen, I'm sure we can come to an agreement over your lost wager." He snapped his fingers, and Chef Fabienne appeared with another glass of Scotch on the rocks. Merrick took a sip of his drink, secretly enjoying keeping the Nigerians waiting. "Gentlemen," Merrick announced, "in addition to my services at a heavily discounted package, courtesy of Merrick Enterprises, it is my honor to offer you a treat you are sure to enjoy."

Adedowale gazed at Merrick with curiosity. "What do you mean—*treat*?"

Merrick flashed his gleaming white teeth. "Gentlemen, do you enjoy the company of beautiful white women?"

CHAPTER 32

WITH VAN SANT by his side, Merrick and the clients strolled down the loading ramp toward the metal door at the base of the slope. Brick walls towered on either side of the concrete ramp.

A pungent smell clung to the air surrounding the concrete ramp. Baxter sniffed and glanced at Adedowale who was devouring a Nigerian meat pie, a mutton and onion concoction wrapped in pastry. He turned away, trying to ignore the foul odor. Abeo laughed as Baxter attempted to hide his retching. Adedowale grinned at the manservant's discomfort and took an exaggerated bite.

Merrick straightened his suit and prepared for the oncoming show. He smiled in the knowledge that the next few minutes inside the cave would change his clients' view on his ability to supply them with all their needs and desires. The last three days had not gone according to plan. The outcome of the events had placed serious doubt on his management skills, and he was about to replace those reservations with confidence.

Armed guards stood on either side of the giant metallic door at the base of the ramp and came to attention as Merrick and the guests approached. "In a few moments, you will see the added bonus my company has to offer." Merrick faced the Nigerians. "I am positive, Adedowale, that my merchandise is in demand in your country. As you know, civil wars are not cheap, and any support from willing backers will help in your comrades' struggle for independence."

Merrick turned to the Germans. "Klaus, a tidy return could be made from reselling products to willing buyers. I'm sure your connections would guarantee sales in the Eastern European arena." Klaus translated for Wolfgang who responded with a puzzled look.

Merrick ended his well-rehearsed speech by addressing Joanna. "My research tells me your employer profits considerably from the European stock market. An influx of stability in certain regions where he has stakes would only increase his revenue, don't you think?"

The group glanced at one another, their interest piqued.

Showman that he was, Merrick widened his arms in a gesture of invitation and motioned to the guard by the door's control box. "Gentlemen—and Joanna—welcome to the main show!"

The metallic doors slid aside.

Before them, arranged at ground level, were the pine crates that had been stacked along the walls of the cavern, their lids carefully placed beside the open crates. Inside was a multitude of weaponry, from small personal firearms to military-grade explosives: pistols, AT4 rocket launchers, M60s, good old AK47s—all laid out for Merrick's clients to peruse and inspect.

Another guard handed Merrick three binders that he passed to his clients. "Thanks to careless management practices in Saint-Étienne, we have a shipment of French FAMAS assault rifles, Heckler & Koch G36Vs, HK416s—and even a parachute if needed courtesy of *Le Commandement des opérations spéciales*."

Adedowale flipped through the pages of his binder. The thought of such weaponry in his control sent his mind racing with endless scenarios. He salivated over the weapons, grinning from ear to ear. His eyes fixed on a weapon he had not used since childhood. "May I?" His eyes gleamed as he indicated the open crate.

Merrick sensed Adedowale's enthusiasm. "By all means. Be my guest."

Adedowale lifted the Excalibur Matrix 405 crossbow from the crate. His eyes feasted on its elegant design and the craftsmanship needed to create such a weapon. "Magnificent," he murmured, transfixed by its simplicity and beauty.

Merrick indicated a crate near Adedowale that contained a supply of arrows. "A tad more sophisticated than the crossbows of your youth, yes?"

The Nigerian's eyes lit up at the carbon fiber shafts glistening in the overhead light. "Tom, you have outdone yourself."

Merrick knew that the big Nigerian had a penchant for traditional weapons. "It's yours. A gift from the Merricks."

Klaus murmured to Wolfgang who was studying the inventory list with appreciation.

Joanna considered the catalogue to the last page where her eyebrow raised. An item sent shivers down her spine. She showed the page to Baxter who returned a grave look. "Mr. Merrick?"

"Please—Tom."

"Tom," Joanna corrected herself and turned the binder toward Merrick.

"Is this accurate?"

"Of course." Merrick beamed with pride. "Every item in the catalogue is on display before you right now, available to ship anywhere in the world at your request." He indicated the back of the cavern. "Please, after you."

Prompted by Merrick, Joanna and the other clients made their way around the open crates to the back of the display where, glimmering beneath the florescent lights, the rocket-shaped bomb rested on a launch slide. Thirty-feet in length, the device sported two electronic guidance stalks protruding from the nose cone and petal-styled tailfins at the rear. Merrick's broad smile and excitement betrayed the device's deadly capabilities. "Gentlemen and lady: the frosting on the cake. I give you the GBU-43/B Massive Ordinance Air Blast, affectionately known as the mother of all bombs. This little lady will send your enemies back to the Stone Age. With the destructive yield of eleven tons of TNT and the blast radius of one mile, the GBU has all the awesome power of a nuclear detonation but none of the after-effects of your conventional nuclear weapons." Merrick beheld the weapon of death, admiring the device the way a father would admire an overachieving son. "Magnificent, don't you think?"

"And the locator card?" Joanna probed.

Merrick pulled the electronic card from his inside suit pocket. "Wiped clean and rendered useless. Completely untraceable."

Joanna and Baxter glanced at one another with concern, but Adedowale clapped loudly. "Well done, Tom! Well done!"

Abeo studied the specifications for the device listed in the binder while appreciating the actual bomb before him. "A wonderful display indeed."

"Thank you," Merrick said humbly while congratulating himself with a smirk, knowing the Nigerians and Germans were back in the fold.

The Nigerian turned from the bomb to look Merrick straight in the eye. "Tell me, Tom, does it come in blue?"

"What shade of blue would you like, Adedowale?"

"Wonderful!" He clapped louder. "My American friends at the embassy are in for a big surprise," he added with a Cheshire cat grin.

This last statement shook Van Sant to the bone.

CHAPTER 33

MICH WAS RESISTING the urge to scratch his wounds when Becca sank into the opposite seat and offered him a beer. "Better make the most of it. This six-pack is all that's left." She placed the satphone on the seat beside her.

"Well, if you insist." Mich needed no encouragement and gladly took a mouthful of the amber liquid. With the power transferred to avionics, the refrigerator and all other non-essential devices had been left powerless, so the beer could barely be considered cold, but he didn't mind. He let out an audible sigh, grateful for the chance to have a beer one last time. "What about the others?"

"Roland and Rousseau are wine drinkers, and the professor seems happy sharing a bottle of water with the little dog."

Mich indicated the phone. "Any signal yet?"

"No, but occasionally a star will poke through the cloud cover, so fingers crossed we'll get a link sooner rather than later."

"Sorry about your friend Roy." Mich couldn't think of anything else to say. He did not know the man whose actions spoke distasteful volumes about his character.

"What can I say? Roy was... Roy." Becca's tone was nonchalant as she sipped her beer. She watched as Mich rubbed the bandage. "How's the injury?"

"Itches like hell, but it's a whole lot better than before."

"May I?" Becca indicated the bandage, haphazardly wrapped around Mich's lower arm.

"Be my guest." Mich leaned back in the seat and held out his arm, grateful for the assistance.

Becca removed the bandage and rewound it tighter and with symmetry, careful to have each layer overlap the edge of the previous layer. "When you have three brothers, you do this on a regular basis."

Mich grimaced as Becca stretched the bandage to breaking point as she continued wrapping the wound. He took another mouthful of beer to ease the pain.

"I'll ask the others about their part in this whole Neptune island story eventually, but I thought I'd start with you and Lincoln. I'd love to get your perspective. You two got the story started, right?"

Mich's eyes narrowed as he recalled the events of the last few days and the USB drive still in his pocket. Legally, many of the group's decisions were questionable, so he considered her request with caution. "On or off the record?"

"Which do you prefer?"

Mich took a swig of beer. "Well, I suppose it doesn't matter now. The whole world saw what happened. Kane died and his island destroyed itself."

"In a most peculiar fashion." Becca continued to apply the dressing tighter than Mich thought possible. "But I want to hear the human side of the story. The ragtag group of people on this plane isn't exactly a military elite strike team, is it? Let's start from the beginning."

"Sure."

"Your name is Mich Lee, right?"

"Yep."

"I'm no expert, but with those high cheek bones and your stature, well…" she wrinkled her nose and chewed her lip, "you look Japanese, but Lee is a common Chinese surname."

"I'm of Japanese heritage but my foster parents—the Lees—were Chinese."

"Aha. Now I get it. So, tell me about your relationship with Lincoln. How do you two know each another?"

"It's a long story."

"We've got time."

"Okay." Mich finished the can and reached for another. His open hand exposed the faint line of a faded scar running across his palm. "It all started with this scar."

"Lincoln did that to you?"

"No. This scar is why I met Lincoln Monk."

Becca finished the dressing and rested back against the seat, curious to hear the story.

"Thanks," Mich said, nodding toward the fresh bandage. "All right. You want me to start at the beginning? Here goes.

"I was the new kid in St Mark's middle school. I'd seen Lincoln around, but he kept mostly to himself. Some of the older kids decided they didn't like anyone from a different ethnic background. Five older kids came at me. I took two of them down. The biggest kid—Tommy Murphy—decided he was going to teach me a lesson with a knife he'd stolen from the kitchen." Mich held out his palm. "Self-defense reflex."

"Ouch."

"Ouch is right. Fourteen stitches."

"What happened next?"

"Tommy got his two remaining goons to hold me down, and I'll never forget his next words: *All chinks must die.*"

"This Tommy sounds like a disturbed child."

"Oh, he was a real prince," Mich replied, his tone edged with sarcasm. "So, there I was, being held down by the biggest kid in the school. Tommy was only in his early teens, but he towered over most of the Brothers. He held a knife to my throat and explained to me and everyone within earshot what parts he was going to slice off first."

"You must have been terrified."

"I honestly thought I was about to die."

"So what happened?"

Mich chuckled at the next memory, a memory he would hold forever. "A chair came out of nowhere. Not the cheap plastic kind you see today, but an old-fashioned, metal-framed kind of chair with a wooden backrest and seat. That chair hit Tommy square in the face. I never imagined that much blood could pour from someone's nose. Besides the broken nose, Tommy ended up with three missing teeth. Everyone was astounded to see Lincoln, the smallest kid in the school, take on the biggest bully and win. A true David and Goliath story."

"And?" Becca could hardly contain her excitement, imaging the story she could write.

"Brother Albertus saw the commotion and broke it up. He dragged Lincoln and me to the headmaster's office while the school nurse saw to Tommy. While we were waiting for our penance outside the office, we could hear Brother Albertus laughing with Brother Tobias about how Tommy finally got his comeuppance."

"Great story. And the penance?"

"We had to clean all the excess wax from the votive candles. Could have been worse; Tommy had to polish the pews—on his knees."

Becca smiled.

"I'll never forget what Lincoln said when I asked why he helped me."

"What did he say?"

Mich thought about the words spoken by his long-time friend so many years ago. "He said *It seemed like the right thing to do*. I guess that just about sums up Lincoln Monk."

"I wonder what motivated Monk."

"We didn't find out until later that we were both orphans. My foster parents were a wonderful Chinese couple eager to have a child of their own. Life was great for a while, but the foster care system doesn't always work for the best, so I was separated from them after a few years. They still send gifts." Mich recalled their last gift—the double doors to his bungalow—that had saved his life along with those of the others. "Lincoln never spoke about his parents, and I didn't pry. I figured he'd tell me sooner or later, but he never did. I guess that part of his life he wants to keep to himself."

Becca slumped back in her seat and sighed. "I suppose he does. Do you think he'll agree to an interview when this is all over?"

"If you pay for the Whopper with cheese, he's all yours," Mich joked. He reached for one of the remaining beers and glanced at the satphone. The illuminated screen said LINK CONFIRMED. "Shit! We have a connection!"

"Mich, this interview isn't over." Becca grabbed the phone and bolted toward the cockpit where she would have a direct line of sky perfect for the satellite link. "Hey, everyone!" she yelled to the group in the C-47's cabin. "We just got a satlink! We're gonna be rescued!"

CHAPTER 34

Emergency operations center – Saipan

THE DISPATCHER TURNED to her supervisor. "Sir, we've just received a distress call from the Department of Public Safety Boating Safety Division. A C-47 Dakota aircraft has crash-landed on one of the northern islands. Seven survivors need urgent Air Evac."

The supervisor looked up from the piles of paperwork on his desk. At sixty-five he was coming to the end of a thankless career, burnt out from the stress of dealing with bureaucracy and constant cutbacks. All day every day, all he dealt with were drunk, high, or worse—rich visitors to Saipan—who thought they could do whatever they wished whenever they wanted. He yawned and for what seemed the thousandth time asked, "Where are they?" envisioning yet another group of moronic tourists who had gotten themselves into trouble.

The dispatcher typed in the coordinates. The image on her computer screen zoomed to the northern end of the Mariana Islands chain. "Sir, the call originated from Alamagan island."

Crash! The supervisor dropped his cup of coffee. "I'll take it from here," he said, trying to sound casual.

The dispatcher stared, taken aback by her supervisor's sudden behavioral shift. "Sir, I can alert Joint Rescue Sub-Center Guam and USCG Sector Guam from my workstation, no problem."

"I said I'll take it from here. It's procedure."

"If need be, I can contact the U.S. Navy Helicopter Sea Combat Squadron 25 from Andersen Air Force Base."

"It's my job," he repeated, keeping up the performance and glad to have implemented a chain of command guideline for such an event.

The dispatcher gave him a questioning look but transferred the information to the supervisor's personal computer. She was about to ask the second dispatcher beside her about potential delays in the unusual procedure, but calls continued to flood in, and she had no choice but to take them.

The supervisor studied the information on his monitor. In one tap of a key, he erased its existence. Tonight, after the shift ended and only skeleton staff operated the phones, he would call for a diagnosis of the dispatcher's computer, and, thanks to his accomplice in IT, the call from Alamagan would be erased from his department. He sighed, relieved that he had been on duty when the call came in. He got himself another cup of coffee and smiled. Merrick's money would come in handy after his retirement.

CHAPTER 35

Squawks, screeches, shrieks, growls, and hoots filled the jungle as nocturnal creatures awakened. The cooler night air, mixed with the day's humidity, washed across the island. Joanna was reclining on her balcony and enjoying the tropical evening with a glass of wine and a cigarette when Baxter interrupted her reverie. "Is the world coming to an end?" she asked, irritated at the disturbance.

Baxter handed Joanna a satellite phone. "Mum. Mr. Mills is on the line."

"Thank you, Baxter." Joanna put down her drink and took the phone. "Mr. Mills, I wasn't expecting to hear from you so soon. Mr. Merrick still has one more event planned for tomorrow... He has an interesting concept with this Jungle Games enterprise. Yes, it could be a lucrative venture, and it does have potential, but too many variables make the project nonviable."

Baxter topped up Joanna's drink and waited dutifully beside her, his arms by his sides.

"Just give me another seventy-two hours and I'll have a full risk and evaluation report on your desk." Joanna listened as her employer stated his position, then said, "I believe we should not make any hasty decisions until the final event... Of course, the decision is yours, I apologize... Yes, Mr. Merrick's armament stockpile is thorough. His range of reliable weapons could be useful in our endeavors. Mr. Mills, Merrick has access to a GBU-43... Yes, the tracking codes have been removed, and the Nigerians seem eager for a sale. I believe our American friends should keep a watch on the Nigerians' movements... Thank you." Joanna paused while her employer explained the recent developments with another project. "Of course. I'll give Mr. Merrick your best wishes. Thank you, sir. Goodbye." She handed the phone to Baxter. "Has Mr. Merrick paid the winnings from the last three events yet?"

"Yes, minus a small transaction fee imposed by Merrick Enterprises, the remaining amount in British pounds has been transferred into your personal account, mum."

"Good, because I believe Mr. Merrick would renege on my bet once he receives the disappointing news."

"Mum?"

"We have to leave the island post-haste. Mr. Mills would like us to pay a visit to the British Antarctic Territory, in particular, Queen Elizabeth Land. It appears one of his business projects has gone awry, and he needs eyes on site as soon as possible."

"Yes, mum."

"Would you ready the helicopter, please?"

"Of course." Baxter paused. "Mum?"

"Yes?"

"You only packed for warm weather."

Joanna finished her drink. "Looks like we'll have to stop in Melbourne. I hear this year's fashions are quite adventurous."

"Yes, mum."

In the control room, Simon tapped keys and waited for Merrick to answer. "Mr. Merrick, I've just recorded the British woman on a satellite conversation with London. The microphone will only pick up this end of the conversation, but you'll want to hear this, sir. I'll transfer the audio file to you right away."

Floral aromas filled the night air as Merrick and Joanna strolled side by side along one of the many garden paths that crossed the hotel grounds. "You have created a unique sporting event," Joanna said as they passed manicured gardens and trimmed hedges. "It's all quite overwhelming."

"It should be. We all deal with death in different ways. Some find the Fever immoral and abhorrent and are sickened to their stomachs, while others find it exhilarating, hypnotic even. The Fever affects many like a drug. Once they taste it, they crave more. They will pay again and again to indulge in the forbidden."

"My employer found the initial concept exciting."

"It is. And it's an exciting time to be alive, don't you think?" Merrick beamed.

"Most exhilarating. My employer agrees that this investment opportunity is unique."

From the tone of Joanna's voice, Merrick sensed that the conversation was about to turn. "What a delightful fragrance!" She inhaled the frangipani lining the garden path. "These gardens remind me of my childhood in the British Virgin Islands," she lied. She wanted Merrick to know as little about her and her employer as possible.

Joanna turned to face Merrick. She preferred to look potential business partners in the eye when giving unwanted news. "Mr. Merrick. I shall be frank with you. My employer does not wish to proceed with the investment."

From Simon's recording, Merrick had known what to expect, but the finality of the news still came like a blow to the head. However, Merrick hid his disappointment well. Gracious to the last, he waited for Joanna's explanation while seething inwardly.

"I have informed him of the three days' events and have supplied him with an analysis of the proposal. My employer understands the financial requirements of such a project. He feels at this time a capital investment in a venture such as Jungle Games would be a substantial risk, a risk he is unwilling to take. At face value, your enterprise appears promising, but several glaring anomalies must be addressed before the concept can reach the next phase."

"Such as?"

"The first is contestants. In the third world, where life is cheap, finding contestants would not prove difficult, but in more developed countries, it would be problematic. Second: The scale of the enterprise commands large upfront costs—wages, the price of possible logistics, bribes. The risk of being exposed is significantly greater once you leave this tiny island chain. My employer values anonymity, Tom. He prides himself on being unknown and goes to great lengths to avoid the limelight. He cannot afford and will not tolerate media or government agencies interfering in or jeopardizing his business dealings. The list goes on. The concept is still in its early stages, but with the luxury of time and better vetting, the games could soon reach their full potential. Your unique model can work, Tom. It just needs... refinement."

As if having been told of a death in the family, Merrick's heart sank. To compensate for the crushing news, he reaffirmed his convictions that inside the hotel, two more investors awaited his skills and business savvy.

"Tom, my employer wishes you all the best with your enterprise, and he hopes to do business with you in the future."

"And the frosting on the cake?" he asked, referring to the stockpile of weapons, hoping to salvage some success by making an arms deal with the British client.

"My employer is well-supplied with all the necessities in our line of work. However, he thanks you for the offer. Possibly in the future he may choose to do business with you regarding weapons supply, but not at this juncture."

Merrick looked on, speechless.

Joanna turned to leave but paused. "Tom, may I ask a favor?"

To add insult to injury, she now wants a favor. Merrick struggled to keep his anger and disappointment at his client's sudden departure bottled within.

"May I have a quick word with the Blue contestant, please?"

Merrick numbly acquiesced.

Under the watchful eye of Merrick's men, Lincoln and Joanna stood on the lawn behind the hotel. Baxter was preparing the helicopter for take-off as Joanna took Lincoln by the arm and strolled across the manicured lawns. She passed Lincoln a cold Corona. "Drink up. You deserve it."

Lincoln took a swig.

Joanna carefully considered her words. "If I could take you and the older gentleman away from here now, I would. Unfortunately, Mr. Merrick would think otherwise. If I tried to remove you from this island, I fear Baxter and I would become part of the next contestant list.

"Lincoln, when you find your way off this island, and I know you will, I would like to offer you employment. I can use a man with your skills and expertise. Over the last three days, you've handled situations extraordinarily well under extreme circumstances. You're resourceful and resilient, you have a conscience, and, most important, you're good with people—a rare combination of skills in my business." Joanna passed Lincoln her business card. He flipped the plain white card over and read the one word printed in script—Joanna.

"Simple yet effective, don't you think?"

"I've got one question."

"Just one?"

"I figure if you're on this island, then you deal with the likes of Merrick on a regular basis. Thus, the job offered is high risk, to say the least, but likely lucrative."

"I'm hired by others to acquire either information or worthy items of interest."

Lincoln looked askance at her, took another gulp of beer and waited for a more definitive answer.

"I'm not a thief. Think of me as a middleman—a very expensive middleman. Like yourself, I do have a conscience, and, yes—my job pays well." She tapped her headset and indicated to Baxter in the pilot's seat. The rotor blades began to turn. "What's your question?"

Lincoln considered Joanna's proposal and toyed with the offer. "You don't have a number on the card. How do I contact you?"

"My darling boy. I have eyes and ears everywhere. When you need me, I contact you." As Lincoln slipped the card into his jumpsuit and pondered her cryptic answer, she put her arm around his shoulder and kissed him on the cheek.

"Try not to get yourself killed if you can help it. It would be such a shame for a buff young man like yourself to go to waste." She looked him over then winked. "If only I were twenty years younger."

"Why?" Lincoln shot back with a grin.

"Don't tease me, young man. Some day you just might get what you're asking for." Her lithe figure accented every movement of her body as she sauntered toward the idling chopper.

"Do I get fries with that shake?"

"Cheeky."

As Joanna disappeared into the helicopter, two guards converged on Lincoln and ushered him back to the gym.

CHAPTER 36

HEARING THE RESOUNDING close of their hotel room's door, the Merricks looked up from studying the weapons sales on Tom's notepad. Van Sant strode across the balcony toward them. "Boss, are you really going to let the Nigerians have that bomb?"

Taken aback, Merrick said, "Why wouldn't I?"

"Those assholes are gonna use it on the Americans."

"Those assholes are paying customers."

"It doesn't bother you that innocent Americans will die?"

"As they say, all's fair in love and war."

"Tom, please, don't sell it to them."

"The money's in the bank." Merrick winked at Samantha. "All Samantha and I have to do now is figure out which model G5 Gulfstream to buy. My stunning wife here favors the G500, but I have my eye on the G550 with the full upgrade." As a sign of support, Samantha kissed him lightly on the cheek and hugged him from behind. "Forget it, Van Sant. It's a done deal. I have another job I want you to do." Merrick took a gulp of his whiskey as Samantha scrutinized Van Sant. "I need you to go Pagan Island and get that thing."

Disheartened by his boss's uncaring attitude towards his countrymen, Van Sant gave a weary sigh. "Thing?"

"That thing in the shipping container. I want you to get it for me."

"You're kidding, right?"

Merrick's deep blue eyes, somber and humorless, stared at Van Sant.

Van Sant averted his gaze and glanced at Samantha, who stared at him with a thin smile. *Her idea.* He shifted uneasily at the request. "Jonathan Kane was specific about the experiments conducted on Pagan Island—that the facility is a no-go zone for everyone, including us."

"I'm sure he won't mind."

"I beg to differ."

"Oh? Well, Kane is dead, so he doesn't give a damn anymore!" Merrick snapped. He quickly regained his composer and smoothed his hair.

"My men won't go anywhere near there. I've seen the creature, and *I* don't want to go anywhere near those sites. You've seen the creature. That damned thing is lethal."

Merrick sighed in frustration. "Offer them all bonuses, and give yourself a ten percent raise." He turned back to his charts. "Just get it done."

"And how do you propose we get that thing here?" Van Sant was exasperated, but he knew his employer would have already worked the logistics.

"We still have the Chinook, right?"

DAY 6

CHAPTER 37

As the rotor blades turned lazily above Van Sant's head, the morning sun streamed across Pagan Island. He stepped down from the Chinook and took in the immensity of the laboratory complex before him. Two armed guards appeared with M4 assault rifles slung over their shoulders and their pistols ready. Before landing, Van Sant briefed his men about the dangers and the need to keep alert at all times. Fearful rumors about Pagan Island were well-known, so Merrick's people were determined to follow his orders to the letter.

Serrated black basalt peaks atop steep flanks layered with lush jungle circled the valley's floor, and dense greenery covered the rolling landscape. Van Sant, gazing at the magnificent vista, was lulled by its peacefulness, but his instincts told him to stay alert. Something was wrong. Then it dawned on him—the silence. They should have been bombarded with constant chatter and squawking from the jungle inhabitants, but only the whistling of the ocean winds and the groaning of the wooden walkway reached his ears. *Stay alert.*

The complex included several warehouse-sized buildings circling a central man-made lagoon of deep blue water. Jungle vines crept along and down the buildings' façades. More greenery was interspersed along the pathway, creating an image of a jungle paradise. *If only that were true.* The water rippled as a shadow passed below the surface, causing Van Sant to keep a cautious eye on the pool as he strode from the helicopter pad to the first building. Merrick's instructions were simple: Get the shipping container housed in Building 1. *Yeah, right.* Van Sant turned to the pilot and gestured to him to keep his communication open. Then he indicated to the guards to follow him as he proceeded to the complex.

As the wooden walkway around the lagoon creaked under his weight, Van Sant realized with trepidation that the lagoon flowed beneath him, too. He studied the meandering current as the waterway slinked between and around the base of the buildings like some tropical moat protecting the castle's secrets. A shadow undulated through the water and passed below. Van Sant grabbed his Beretta from his shoulder holster and followed the creature's path with the gun barrel. The shadow disappeared into the water's depths. With the threat temporarily over, Van Sant cautiously reholstered his gun. "This place gives me the creeps," he murmured.

"You got that right," Guard One said as he trained his SAINT AR-15 rifle on the man-made river and waited for another shadow to appear. "You know what else gives me creeps? The place seems so, so—"

"Deserted." Van Sant noted that no one had greeted them. Even for a secluded site like Pagan Island, arriving guests were always greeted by the spokesman or site manager.

Van Sant saw it first—a splattering across the path. He knelt to inspect the blood as the two guards raised their guns, ready for action.

"What the hell is this place?" Guard Two whispered, keeping his eyes on the surroundings.

"You didn't know? This entire island was owned by Jonathan Kane. Pagan Island is one of several research and development sites operated by the Neptune Corporation." Van Sant swiped his finger through the red pool and studied its molasses consistency. Even in this humidity, the blood would coagulate over time. Whatever happened here had happened within the last few days."

"Van Sant," Guard One whispered, training his rifle on the arched walkway ahead. Passing over a wider portion of the river, a vaulted causeway, lined with shrubs and flowers of all kinds, arced over the water leading into the depths of the complex. A headless body lay across the path, arms and legs splayed, its spine and serrated neck exposed for all to see.

Van Sant raised his pistol and scanned the surrounds for any movement.

"We need to tell Mr. Merrick about his," Guard Two insisted.

"We can't," Van Sant answered calmly but with apprehension building within. He passed his gunsight over the buildings and gardens. "We'd need to switch the electronic scramble system to standby, but we can't because the relay towers in the mountains surrounding the valley require a code that we don't have. So nothing gets in or out."

"That's just dandy," Guard One answered in a sardonic tone to hide his unease.

Van Sant took one last glance at the buildings and moved forward. "The sooner we're out of here the better."

Building One, the biggest structure, was the size of a depot with the height of a five-story apartment complex. The upper level veranda offered a clear view of the jungle canopy, while the portico overlooked the gardens and lagoon walkways. Made from giant concrete slabs, the outer facade loomed over Van Sant and the two guards as they approached. Guard One peered up at the colossal construction and frowned. "What the hell have they got in there—King Kong?"

With Van Sant leading the way, the guards moved through the sunlit atrium and entered the hallway beside the empty visitors' booth. Guard One noticed that Van Sant knew his way around the building. "You've been here before, Van Sant."

"Unfortunately."

The corridor led to a set of steel reinforced doors with a bolt-action slide locked from their side. Guard Two slung his rifle over his shoulder. He turned the bolt lever upright and slid the bolt aside. Van Sant and Guard Two steadied their weapons as Guard One pushed open the doors.

In a space the size of an aircraft hangar, desks and cabinets lined the upper floor overlooking an elevated platform at the back of the room. Enormous sliding doors remained locked together behind the platform. Overhead was a closed glass retractable roof. The forty-foot shipping container Van Sant had seen just days earlier remained in the center of the platform. The metallic table on the adjoining platform was covered with blood. A channel of metal mesh and barbed wire the size of a subway tunnel connected the side of the shipping container to the giant doors. Several DANGER! *Electric Fence* signs hung at eye-level. Guard One stepped away from the fencing. "New," Van Sant commented. They climbed the short flight onto the platform and took up positions around the shipping container. As if sensing intruders, a loud thump echoed from inside the container followed by another thump at the other end.

Guard Two turned to Guard One, his breathing quickened. "Whatever is in there can move damned fast," he whispered. Exchanging uneasy looks, both guards turned to Van Sant.

Van Sant took a deep breath and exhaled. "Okay. Open the roof," he ordered, pointing toward the ceiling. "Let's get this over with."

CHAPTER 38

Rousseau manned the cockpit while Becca dozed across two seats. Having taken all the antihistamine tablets and applied the last of the anti-itch cream, Mich tried not to scratch his healing wound through the bandage and glanced round the cabin to distract himself.

He found a cooler bag in the cargo compartment and removed its female USB port. After ten minutes of delicate electronic rewiring he had connected the cooler bag port to the end of the charge cable for the satphone. With the USB drive from Neptune Island slotted into the cooler bag port they could now access any data on the drive via the satphone's screen.

He passed the phone and USB drive to Enheim. "Professor, maybe there's something on the drive about this island."

Wracked with anxiety over Katya's disappearance, Enheim was grateful for the distraction. He glanced at the screen while stroking Napoleon who slept in his lap. Dozens of unopened files awaited his scrutiny. His interest piqued, he pored over the data.

Mich plunked down beside him and offered him a beer, courtesy of the cooler bag. They drank in silence, enjoying the refreshing beer, their first positive experience since crash-landing on the island.

"He may have been an asshole who owed me five hundred bucks," Enheim conceded, "but Eddie Ramirez was a thorough asshole—I'll give him that." After scrolling through pages of classified Neptune

Corporation information, Enheim suggested they start in alphabetical order. He stopped at a folder labeled ANNEX 17-36-2 N 145-50-0 E and murmured, "This could be interesting." Mich recognized the ordered numbers from his computer consultancy days on Saipan, but he couldn't recall the significance of the sequence.

Enheim studied the schematics on the screen. "That other asshole Jonathan Kane was into some heavy shit."

Mich took a sip of his beer. "What are you talking about?"

Enheim indicated to a 3-D image of the building complex on the screen. "Whatever this place is—this annex is massive. And look at the venting layout running through the structure; those rooms must be a series of connected laboratories." Curiosity got the better of him. He tapped the screen and delved into the classified information. "Of course!" He slapped his forehead for not having seen the pattern earlier.

"What are you talking about?"

"Can't you see it?" Wide-eyed, Enheim was rubbing his hands, unable to contain his excitement.

Mich struggled to conceptualize any of the diagrams on the cell-phone screen as having a structure or form. They appeared to be a jumble of shapes crisscrossed with dozens of lines and numbers. "See what?"

"The venting system is the key."

Mich squinted to make sense of the image.

"It's underground," Enheim explained, falling back into his rhythm of teaching and enjoying every moment, "which is why they need heavy-duty air recycling."

Mich took Enheim's word on the matter. If his old physics professor assured him the arrangement of lines depicted in the image were schematics for some laboratory, then that was fine with him.

Energized by the information on the USB drive, Enheim smiled for the first time in hours. He scanned multiple files. "If I could just find the friggin' inventory, we could see what he was up to."

Mich glanced at the phone's red power bars and pointed to the flashing low-charge indicator. "Sorry, Professor. I'd like to see the inventory, too, but we don't have much time. Where is this annex?"

Enheim groaned, annoyed that his train of thought had been interrupted, but zoomed out of the image. The underground structure shrank to be replaced by the topographical map of an island. "The annex appears to be in the middle of an island." He searched for a name or a location. "You'd think they'd have its identity and location handy. I can't find the info anywhere."

"Maybe they don't want anyone to find the island. May I?" Mich reached out, and Enheim reluctantly passed him the phone. Mich went to work until he recognized the number sequence. "They're latitude and longitude co-ordinates!"

"Of course. So where the hell is the annex?"

Mich tapped the info into the geo URI. "It's here. Alamagan Island."

"That explains those nasty rodents and those friggin' crab creatures on Neptune Island. If Kane was messing with crabs, why not rats, too?"

"Why would a billionaire want to create oversized creatures? And more importantly, how was he creating them?"

"Who knows? The guy was a billionaire nut job." Enheim looked lovingly at Napoleon. "He was a nut job, wasn't he, Napums?"

Outside the cabin, Roland rested his head against the left support strut connecting the pontoon to the fuselage. The ordeal with the rats and yesterday's leeches had unnerved him, and the warm sunlight soothed his taut mind and body.

Without mooring ropes, anchor, or proper rudder control, Roland had warned Rousseau to keep the plane close to the riverbank, preferring to run the craft aground if need be. From the cockpit, Rousseau watched the glistening water flow swiftly beneath the shadow of the wing. For the first time in days, he allowed himself the luxury of relaxing, if only for a few minutes.

Roland was glancing at the jungle greenery lining the riverbanks when Rousseau steered the plane around a bend. The mangrove trees and reeds running alongside the right bank ended as the hotel came into view. Roland bolted upright, startled by the first sign of civilization, then grinned from ear to ear.

"What are all these numbers?" Enheim asked, pointing to the random numbers spread across the island.

"This is a Landsat image. What we're looking at is the island's topographical elevation above sea level."

Simultaneously Enheim and Mich realized the topographical numbers abruptly descended toward the island's northern end.

"What does that mean?" Enheim asked, his tone cautious.

"Probably a cliff or something. The entire northern end of the island looks like a narrow basin of some kind. We must be on the plateau at the southern end." Mich had a sinking feeling in his stomach.

Enheim eyed the descending numbers and the direction of the river and paused mid-stroke above Napoleon's head. "So where are we on this map?"

Mich located the southern end of the island and pinpointed the beach where they had crash-landed. Enheim followed Mich's finger as he traced the river's meandering course until the elevation numbers abruptly dropped at the river's end. "Waterfall." They groaned in unison as the red charge bar flashed one last time before the phone shut down.

Roland basked in the sun's rays streaming over the landscape, their warm orange light reflected in the hotel's glass façade. The local fauna's croaking and whistling completed the picturesque Shangri-La landscape with its magnificent hotel and serene set—

He sat up, annoyed by the distant thunder of crashing water. He glanced in its direction past the hotel to where a fine layer of mist rose from the river. "Scheisse," he whispered.

In haste Roland climbed around the strut and clawed his way

over the makeshift rope ladder connecting the backend of the pontoon and the open hatchway. He leaped into the cabin and, to everyone's surprise, sprinted down the aisle shouting, "Everybody, get ready to jump!" He flung open the cockpit door. "Rousseau, run the plane aground—now!"

Startled, Rousseau paused. He has never seen his boss frantic. "Mr. Pom, what's wrong?"

"Run the plane aground, you know," Roland repeated. "Vaterfall, two hundred yards." The roar of the waterfall filled the plane. Rousseau stared in horror at the veil of mist now two hundred yards downriver. As he veered the plane starboard toward the hotel, Roland shouted, "Ve only have basic rudder control, and ve can't stop in this fast-flowing current. Evacuate the ship now, you know."

"What the hell…?" Enheim muttered, glancing down the aisle and through the cockpit windscreen. His blood ran cold at the sight of the river dropping away into nothingness, with only the sky over the island's north end filling his view.

Mich hobbled along, but the dull pain still throbbed through his arm and leg. Enheim fastened Napoleon in his chest harness, pocketed the satphone and the USB drive, and readied himself beside Mich. Becca met them at the hatch.

"Is Napoleon secure?" Mich asked.

Enheim rechecked the harness. "Yep."

As the Dakota C-47 glided through the water toward the riverbank, the hotel came into full view before them. The armed men who stood on the muddy embankment turned and stared in disbelief at the sight of the plane drifting toward them.

With the jetty destroyed and no way to attach the plane to the shoreline, Roland had no choice but to repeat his order to the crew. "Abandon ship! People! Into the vater!"

Enheim leapt from the cabin into the water followed by Mich and Becca. Roland entered the cockpit and tapped Rousseau on the shoulder. "Time to go, you know."

Rousseau checked that Maurice was safe in his pocket before climbing out of the cockpit. In seconds he was in the water. Roland sprinted down the aisle and paused to take one last adoring look around the cabin. "Sorry, my beautiful Ava." He blew her a kiss and leaped into the river.

Merrick straightened at the balcony's railing, dumbfounded by the sight below. At that moment, Van Sant appeared. "The shipping container was heavier than we estimated, so I had to send the chopper back to Pagan Island with extra slings. It should be arriving here shortly."

Merrick nodded.

"Boss, something's happened at Pagan Island."

"I don't care." Merrick's thoughts were on the intruders below.

"The island is void of human life, and dead bodies are lying around. I tell you something seriously bad happened there."

"Frankly, I'm with Clarke Gable on this one. I don't give a damn."

"We have to tell the Neptune people in case they don't know. They have a right to know."

"I have enough to deal with without getting involved in someone else's problems," Merrick snapped. "Let Kane's people deal with it."

Van Sant knew when to back off. He'd seen Merrick's indifference before, and he was seeing it now.

Roland's group made it to the shoreline where they dragged themselves from the water and watched the current whisk Ava toward the waterfall. The plane's pontoons slammed into the side of Merrick's cabin cruiser with a crunch and bounced away with the fast-moving water carrying the aircraft toward the falls. The cruiser listed to port as river water flooded her lower compartments.

Roland's shoulders slumped as he watched his beloved Ava, the pride of the Pom collection, make her final journey into the unknown. The floats slid over the waterfall's crest, the nose dipped, the tail lifted into the air, and the plane disappeared over the edge.

Wet and exhausted, Roland and the team huddled together as Merrick's men surrounded them and confiscated their weapons.

Van Sant followed Merrick's gaze over the penthouse railing and was transfixed by the sight of the camouflaged C-47 vanishing over the cliff face and down into the misty veil. Incredulous, he and Merrick stared first at the plane and then at the group of bedraggled survivors encircled by Merrick's men.

"Now we know where all these uninvited guests are coming from," Van Sant commented.

Belying his calm demeanor, Merrick's voice seethed with anger. "How the hell did that plane get on this island undetected?"

Van Sant thought through the events and the weather conditions of the last three days scratching his head in exasperation as he searched for an answer. "If they were flying low enough, they could have evaded our radar. And that fog bank three nights ago would have hidden their location."

Merrick watched the gathering crowd below as more of his black-garbed military men converged on the intruders at the riverbank. Like a single mass of unstoppable brute strength, they confronted the hapless group, guns ready.

The sight of his assembled men cemented Samantha's idea in his mind, an idea that he had dismissed as too crazy to work. But Samantha was right. The last event would be like none other—a true spectacle—one never before seen by his clients or himself. The corners of his mouth curled with the hint of a smile.

CHAPTER 39

The Fourth Event

UNDER THE SCORCHING morning sun, Lincoln and his crew marched through the barriers ushered by a guard who directed them toward the field's center. Concrete barriers ten feet high and ten feet long surrounded the football field. Initially used as flood breaks for the river, the barriers' current purpose was to keep a deadlier onslaught at bay. A dozen guards patrolled the barriers carrying M4 assault rifles and wearing sidearms. Some kept a close watch on the last two contestants and the new arrivals while others scrutinized the horizon beyond the plateau.

Lincoln studied the barriers surrounding them with dread. "What is it this time?" he asked the closest guard, referring to the next event.

With his weapon trained on the terrified group, the guard backed away, smirking. "You'll find out soon enough." He ducked behind a barrier before the metallic crunch of the closing gate sounded.

Lincoln gave his friends from the plane a half-hearted smile. "It's great to see you all again, but I wish it was under different circumstances."

"You're not going to believe vat ve've been through the last four days," Roland said.

"We had to battle giant rats and leeches," Rousseau explained, now comfortable addressing the newcomers in his life.

"And poor Ava took a nose-dive over that damned vaterfall," Roland said, with sadness.

"But we managed to contact emergency services back on Saipan. Help should be arriving any time now." Becca beamed with pride.

Lincoln nodded. "Good to hear." He could see that their nightmares in the jungle and his ordeal at the hotel had brought them closer as a team. He indicated Gray. "Everybody, this is Lucius."

They all greeted Lucius with a nod.

"Just call me Gray. It's easier."

"Where is Katya?" Enheim blurted, anxiously stroking Napoleon who was still strapped to his chest.

"Yes," Roland said, "vhere is my sister, and is Christina here?"

"As far as I can tell, they're being held captive in the hotel."

"Are they okay?" Enheim's grave tone conveyed his concern for his wife's well-being.

Having seen the women on the balcony being ushered away by armed guards after the boat race, Lincoln tried not to alarm Enheim. "I saw them yesterday," he said, trying to sound upbeat, but in his gut he knew that anything could have happened to them since then.

The child from the boat chase clung to Lincoln's leg, his eyes filled with fear. Lincoln knelt and took the boy's hands in his. "It's scary, but I'm here. You're safe." He wiped the tears filling the boy's eyes. "What's your name?" he asked softly.

The boy looked away, too embarrassed by his sniffling to make eye contact with Lincoln. "Leo," he managed through his tears.

"Well, Leo," Lincoln tore a strip of cloth from Mich's torn Hawaiian shirt, much to Mich's disapproval, and dabbed the tears away. "I'm going to take a deep breath. You can take one, too."

Leo refused to look Lincoln in the eye. Lincoln tenderly turned the boy's face toward him to show the child that he was calm and confident. "Okay?"

Leo nodded.

Lincoln extended his hand to the petite brunette standing beside Leo. "We haven't been introduced. I'm Lincoln—Lincoln Monk."

"I'm Becca Perry, a reporter for KSPN news. You're the guy in that Duck boat, the guy who rescued the little dog and killed Jonathan Kane. You're the reason I'm here."

"Well, Kane met his fate from his own hand, but I'm hoping the world has seen what Neptune Island represented."

"If we ever get out of this mess," she said, indicating the arena and the guards surrounding them, "I'd love to do an interview. The world needs to know what really happened on Neptune Island."

"Sure, why not? But the first round of Coronas is on you."

"Deal."

"Careful, you'll end up paying for the whole night," Mich warned.

Lincoln grinned at the sight of his old friend and slapped him on the back. Mich winced and grunted.

"Still?" Lincoln probed, concerned that the wound inflicted by that Neptune Island crab creature hadn't healed.

"Just a littler tender, that's all." Mich cradled his right arm and gently scratched the bandage. "Itches like hell, though."

Lincoln unwrapped the bandages and inspected the gash. The laceration was healing well, yet Mich continued to scratch the irritated skin. He gave no sign of false bravado, but Lincoln could tell that his friend was still in pain. "What about the medication on the plane?"

"All gone."

Leo sobbed beside Becca. She knelt and hugged him tightly. "Take some deep breaths with me. Everything is going to be all right." She glanced at Lincoln and recalled his feats of derring-do back at Neptune Island. She felt comforted knowing they were in capable hands with Lincoln leading them, despite the guards lining the concrete barriers.

"Lincoln, vat's happening, you know?" Roland asked, his eyes darting around the field.

Lincoln reapplied the bandages around Mich's arm. "Our host has one more game for us to play."

Enheim studied the arena and surrounding concrete walls. "Host? What host? And what type of friggin' game?"

From a distance came a thump-thumping that grew louder as it neared. "I think we're about to find out." Lincoln sensed that this arena was Tom Merrick's last chance to please his clients since his blueprint for hosting a series of games had not merely gone awry; nothing had gone according to plan. Lincoln sighed, certain that the next event would be the toughest.

The pulsing beat of rotor blades echoed across the island as the Chinook thundered above the northern beachfront, crossed over the green canopy and climbed toward the high plateau. The tremendous downwash from the blades flattened the vegetation below the chopper creating a path of crushed trees and foliage through the forest. The chopper swept low across the terrain then climbed over the gorge and waterfalls before banking toward the makeshift arena beside the hotel. Lincoln watched as the dual-rotor helicopter lifted the shipping container over the tree line and flew toward the hotel. The forty-foot container, suspended from thick cables beneath the helicopter, swayed with the craft's movement.

The pilot banked past the hotel, maneuvered into position over the concrete enclosure, and slowly descended. The shipping container thumped down on the wet soil in the middle of the arena. Inside the cabin, the rigging chief released the chain lock, and the four chain-links clattered from the chopper to the container's roof.

Without warning, the screech of tearing metal filled the air as the container's left corrugated wall bulged out. The guards patrolling the perimeter snapped to attention. Van Sant had tried to inform them of what was to come, but nothing could prepare these jaded military men for Merrick's final spectacle. As another blow from inside the container dented out the right wall, the guards readied themselves for action.

A briefed guard cautiously made his way to the front of the shipping container. He unlatched the door, threw it open, and hastily retreated, his M4 raised and ready.

Two claws, the size of compact cars, emerged from the darkness.

Shit, Lincoln groaned. *Not again.*

CHAPTER 40

VAN SANT HAD no option but to follow through with Merrick's instructions regarding the two women hostages. He collected the frightened women from the comfort of their hotel room and led the way down the corridor followed by Christina and Katya with two guards bringing up the rear. They stopped at the closed elevator while Van Sant tapped the up button.

Christina held Katya's trembling hand. "Where are you taking us?"

Van Sant ignored her question and waited impatiently for the elevator.

"I said, where are you taking us?" Christina demanded. From the guards' ominous expressions and bleak stares, Christina sensed that their situation was grim.

Katya squeezed Christina's hand and prepared for the worst.

The elevator doors opened, and Van Sant ushered them inside. The second guard tapped the keypad and the doors closed with a thud.

Van Sant eyed the stunning women beside him, wanting to prepare them for the worst. "If you want some advice…" He searched for the words but couldn't find any. "Just do as they say."

"What are you talking about?" Katya's fear was audible in her quavering voice.

The elevator doors opened to the pungent odor of mutton pie wafting down the corridor—Nigeria's trademark dish. Christina sneered at Van Sant as he led them to a hotel room, his eyes averted as he struggled with his conscience. He knocked on the door, aware that the women didn't stand a chance against the animals inside. He'd heard stories about the Nigerians' appetite for violence and white women. These women needed help—any help. A room service trolley sat beside the closed door. Van Sant scanned the tray and spotted what he was searching for.

Adedowale opened the door. From the hallway, Christina cast a discreet eye over the room. Adedowale grinned at the sight of the white women, his hungry eyes ogling first Christina's and then Katya's body with lust. "La-dies." He licked his lips and gestured for the women to enter.

Adebowale's assistant Abeo stood beside the balcony's slider, his AK-47 slung over his shoulder, the whites of his eyes in glaring contrast to his dark skin. A full quiver of arrows sat on the bed alongside a crossbow, and a gleaming machete rested against the bedside table.

Van Sant indicated the women. "Courtesy of Mr. Merrick," he said without conviction. "He hopes you enjoy your afternoon."

"We most definitely will. I shall thank Mr. Merrick personally." Adedowale leered with glowing approval, not taking his eyes from Katya's long blonde hair.

Van Sant did the only thing he could think of to give the women a chance of survival. "I'll get Chef Fabienne to arrange another one of her delicious aromatic dishes for you," Van Sant said wryly. He caught Christina's gaze. "And I'll make sure the room waiter brings a bottle of our finest wine along with the cutlery for the meal."

Christina shot Van Sant a curious glance. As he slipped a small meat knife against the back of her hand, she registered his intentions and tucked the knife into the small of her back, away from the grinning Nigerians. Van Sant's last image of the women was of Katya whimpering against Christina's shoulder as Adedowale slammed the door.

"Rumor has it the two Nigerians are brutal toward women," Guard One commented.

"You got that right." Guard Two shook his head. "What a waste."

"Then again, I heard those two chicks were tigresses for our guys to capture."

The elevator doors opened. "Yeah, sometimes women fight back," Van Sant replied with a hint of a grin.

CHAPTER 41

LINCOLN BRACED HIMSELF as the beast materialized from the shadows. The crab creature scuttled down the ramp and stood defiantly beside the shipping container, its long forefront arms swinging maliciously from side to side, its pincers snapping through the air.

The sun glistened off the decapod's yellow and black striped exoskeleton as it swayed back and forth. With its arms extended, its claws spanned twenty feet from tip to tip. Rows of jagged barbs ran the length of its shell. The ten legs, working in unison, cackled as the creature turned to study its new surroundings. The stalked eyes swung about on its bulbous head, gathering information on the terrain and nearby threats. The giant decapod found its prey and slammed its oversized pincers onto the ground. The earth shook from the impact, a sinister warning of the fate to follow.

Becca gasped at the sight of the crab creature, her eyes wide with fear. "What the hell?"

"Big John's brother." Lincoln sighed, recalling the crab creature he'd battled on Neptune Island. "Let's hope the second time's the charm." Roland and Mich groaned, recollecting the same nightmare. Rousseau wiped the sweat from his eyes, hoping the image of the terrifying beast would go away.

"One of these days we really have to have a serious discussion about these damned crustaceans on these friggin' islands," Enheim snorted.

"Vell then, ve'd better hurry," Roland said.

"You got that right," Lincoln scanned the arena, which was the size of a football field, searching for a way out. A plan formed in his mind. "Here's what we do. Becca and Rousseau, look after Mich and Leo. Get as far away from that thing as you can. Try to get into the gap between the barriers in the far corner. It'll offer some protection." They nodded.

"Gray, Roland, and Enheim, you run in opposite directions— space out—distract the creature any way you can. We need to confuse it so it can't corner us in one area."

"And what are you gonna do?" Enheim asked, keeping his eyes on the giant claws swaying through the air.

"I've got a plan," Lincoln said, grinning with self-satisfaction. He flipped his knife in the air to show off his skill and confidence but miscalculated the spin and fall rate, and the knife hit the ground. As Mich rolled his eyes at Lincoln's display of overconfidence, Lincoln picked up the knife and wiped his hands over his jumpsuit. "Sweaty palms," he apologized. "Okay, everyone, let's roll!"

Watching the arena from the penthouse balcony, Merrick tapped his earpiece. "Simon?"

"Yes, Mr. Merrick?"

"Cue the music."

"Yes, sir."

Merrick tapped his earpiece again, cutting the connection. With his gaze glued to the creature and the contestants below, the corners of his mouth curled into a depraved grin. "It's time to rock and roll."

Samantha gave Merrick a congratulatory kiss on the cheek and turned back to the spectacle below with fervor in anticipation of the event. "Claus and Wolfgang will love this. The Germans adored Freddy."

Gray, Enheim, and Roland were preparing to act on Lincoln's plan when the wireless speakers positioned around the concrete barriers came alive with a pulsing beat. Queen's *Another One Bites the Dust* echoed over the arena. Stunned, Lincoln looked to Gray, Enheim, and Roland who responded with equal surprise as the lyrics boomed. He glanced up to see Merrick beaming back at him from the penthouse.

> *Are you ready, hey, are you ready for this?*
> *Are you hanging on the edge of your seat?*
> *Out of the doorway the bullets rip*
> *To the sound of the beat*
> *Another one bites the dust*
> *And another one gone, and another one gone*
> *Another one bites the dust*
> *Hey, I'm gonna get you, too*
> *Another one bites the dust*

Lincoln sighed. "Sonofabitch."

"What a complete wanker," Enheim fumed.

"I use to like zat song, but now—" Roland kept his eyes on the terrifying creature—"not so much, you know."

Gray turned to the others with a hint of a smile. "This is probably not the best time to say this, but I saw Queen at Wembley Stadium for the Live Aid concert back in 1985."

"Great, Doc," Lincoln replied. "If we get out of this alive, remind me later to ask you what The Beach Boys were like live."

From his balcony, Wolfgang tapped his foot in time with the thumping beat as he watched the proceedings below. "This good, ya," he beamed to Claus in broken English. "Freddy still my favorite."

Claus nodded.

Wolfgang turned back to the show, pleased with the choice of music, and stuffed another flaky, sweet strudel into his mouth.

The men took off for opposite ends of the arena while Rousseau and Becca helped Mich and Leo to a far corner away from the creature. The decapod, confused and unable to hunt down the scattered prey simultaneously, tracked the movement of its closest quarry, Roland, who waved his arms to further distract and entice the creature. The giant crab shuffled around to focus its stalked eyes on Roland who was just yards away—an easy kill. As the creature started toward him, its sensory receptors picked up a ground vibration that caught it off-guard. Its stalk-eyes swiveled back to fix on Lincoln who was sliding through the mud under its exoskeleton.

Lincoln disappeared under the creature's carapace where he raised his arm, and, in one swift motion, sliced through the soft skin below the head. The crab's high-pitched screech reverberated across the arena. Its front arms flayed about as its pincers snapped the air. Blood sprayed across the arena as the disoriented creature struggled to comprehend its wound.

Lincoln scrambled from the ground, ready for another attack. The giant crab ignored him and lowered its body to the sandy ground where it rubbed the wound with dirt and mud until the mixture filled the gash and the bleeding stopped.

But I'm ready, yes, I'm ready for you
I'm standing on my own two feet
Out of the doorway the bullets rip
Repeating to the sound of the beat oh yeah

Lincoln calculated that he had seconds to make his next move before the crab retaliated. He flipped the knife in his hand and this time caught the handle. Grinning with satisfaction, he leaped onto the back of the creature's exoskeleton and lay flat against the shell, gripping its edge. The creature's head turned, trying to get eyes on Lincoln, but the carapace restricted its movement. The pincers swung to remove the intruder. They slammed down inches from Lincoln, weakening the exoskeleton and forming hairline cracks along the shell. Lincoln ducked as a serrated pincer snapped wildly where his head had been. He gripped the shell's edge tighter at the nearest leg joints.

"Try covering its eyes!" Mich hollered from the alcove between the far barriers.

"It doesn't work!" Enheim and Roland shouted back in unison.

"Why not?"

"I'll tell you later," Lincoln yelled over the loud music as he clung to the creature's back. Lincoln knew from experience that the old "throw the towel over the dog and the dog does nothing" trick didn't work.

Maybe this wasn't such a good idea after all.

Lincoln discovered small folds in the shell. He inched his way forward until he was an arm's length from the bulbous head. Taking a deep breath, he raised his knife and stabbed down as hard as he could. As the knife pierced the skull, the creature roared in pain. Without reflex memory, the creature stumbled about, unable to get a firm foothold. Blood flowed from its head, spilling over Lincoln and the exoskeleton.

Becca stared wide-eyed at the nightmarish spectacle. She covered her mouth in horror as the bloodied head, with the knife still protruding from its skull, pushed against the cracked shell around its neck. The shell shattered, and the creature's head twisted to face Lincoln.

Lincoln groaned. "You've gotta be friggin' kidding me."

The eyestalks swiveled and focused on the invader clinging to its shell. Its snapping jaws revealed thrashing mandibles. Emitting a cry of agony, the decapod staggered to the side but regained a moment of defiance, vomiting green bile over Lincoln. As the warm liquid splashed its foul odor across his face, Lincoln dry-heaved. His hands slipped from the slime- covered shell and he slid toward the raging head.

There are plenty of ways that you can hurt a man
And bring him to the ground
You can beat him, you can cheat him
You can treat him bad and leave him when he's down

Without a weapon, Lincoln could only swing around on the shell, legs first, and slam his foot into the creature's head. The head snapped back, but the creature roared in fury and refused to die. Lincoln kicked again. This time his foot smashed the creature's face, breaking the sharpened teeth surrounding the mouth. The mandibles closed around Lincoln's foot. Prepared for excruciating pain, he kicked as hard as he could with his free leg when two shadowy figures climbed past him. They thrust two more knives into the writhing skull. The creature's body went limp and collapsed to the ground. Its death throes reverberated in Lincoln's ears as its pincers clawed the air one last time before falling limp.

Lincoln grinned at Roland and Enheim with Napoleon whimpering inside the harness. Roland reached down and offered a hand that Lincoln gladly accepted. Roland glanced at the three knifes projecting from the dead creature's skull. "That was close, you know."

"Too damned close." Lincoln leaned on his haunches to catch his breath. The creature's left claw swayed in a final act of defiance as its life ebbed away. Panting to catch his breath, Gray appeared and gaped at the dying creature.

Another one bites the dust
Another one bites the dust
And another one gone, and another one gone

Another one bites the dust
Hey, I'm gonna get you, too
Another one bites the dust

"I hate that man," Merrick seethed, rubbing his face in frustration as the song came to its conclusion. He gulped the last of his scotch, trying to hide his contempt and anger over Blue's having yet again defied his attempts at eliminating him from the contest, then shattered the glass on the tile floor.

"Resilient bastard," Van Sant admitted with a tinge of respect.

Merrick glared at Van Sant. He was pouring himself another drink, this time a double, when the first shot echoed over the arena.

CHAPTER 42

LINCOLN, GRAY, ROLAND, and Enheim joined the others between
the barriers as more gunshots rang out. A guard stationed at the
southern barrier fell from the wall. More shots followed. Startled
by the unexpected turn of events, Lincoln and the others looked at
one another, unsure of what was happening.

Alarmed, Merrick turned to Van Sant. "Who the hell is this?"

Van Sant couldn't help but reveal a thin smile. "That popping
your hearing is the tell-tale sound of an AK47, and quite a few
islanders own AK47s. I don't know for sure, but I'd guess the
shooters are probably pissed off locals who don't like having their
kids kidnapped."

Merrick glared at Van Sant. He regained his composer and
turned back to the battle below. "My men can deal with this. Piece
of cake."

The guards poised on the northern barrier fired into the jungle
while the arena guards abandoned their watch over the contestants
and joined the guards on the northern barrier. Within moments,
staccato gunfire filled the air.

"Now what's happening?" Mich asked in disbelief.

"Sounds like the cavalry," Lincoln said as he scooping up the
small boy under his arm.

With the screech of torn metal, the shipping container's rear doors burst open. The twisted doors took another hit from within and bulged outward at crazy angles. At the other end of the shipping container a pair of pincers wavered about—a cautionary survival defense before revealing itself in full to the world.

From the dark confines of the container, another decapod emerged. The creature scampered down the ramp and into the arena. As a joke, someone, a twisted lab technician or security personnel, no doubt, had hastily painted BIG BEN across the creature's exoskeleton. This decapod had red and black stripes running down its shell and was the size of a school bus. It slammed its claws into the soft soil and prepared for battle.

Lincoln stared, incredulous. "Give me a break!"

Becca cringed, and Rousseau's jaw dropped at the sight of the second creature.

"Two this time," Enheim murmured.

"Looks like it, you know."

"You guys have seen these things before?" Becca asked in disbelief.

"Unfortunately, we have," Enheim said, without taking his eyes from the giant claws slashing and waving through the air. "But this one..." Enheim's voice trailed away as he took in the sheer size of the terrifying crustacean.

"Stephen King would piss in his pants if he saw this *thing*," Mich added.

From the penthouse balcony, Merrick's eyes lit up. He looked to Van Sant with a raised eyebrow. "Did you know about the second creature?"

"I had no idea," Van Sant replied with an honest shrug.

Merrick grinned with satisfaction. "Looks like we have ourselves an unexpected bonus round."

With gunshots continuing above, the creature's eyes scanned the arena. A guard fell from atop the wall to the ground, causing Big Ben to turn. His stalked eyes fixed on the wounded guard who, despite the pain pulsating through his body, was attempting to stand. He staggered a few steps, then dropped back to the turf, clutching the bleeding hole in his abdomen. Alerted to the easy prey, the creature ignored Lincoln's group and scuttled to the wounded guard. The guard looked up in horror as the decapod loomed over his failing body. His shaking hands attempted to aim his rifle at the creature, but the pain was too much. Big Ben raised his claws and snapped his barbed pincers in a show of might and superiority.

"I can't watch this," Becca croaked, burying her head against Mich's chest.

The guard's cry of terror ceased as the claw slammed through his skull. Pulverized brain and bone exploded as the guard's body went limp. Big Ben lifted the dead guard in one claw and sliced his body in half with the other. The creature's mandibles tore at the remains of the upper torso, and the bottom half he threw against the wall.

At the sight of the gruesome death, Samantha Merrick sighed with pleasure, her body reacting to the stimulation below. She caressed her firm breasts, her nipples hard, and squeezed Merrick's hand, licking her lips in anticipation of what would follow.

Distracted from the gun battle by the cries for help, a bearded guard stared agape as the flesh of his friend washed over the exoskeleton, coating the shiny shell with blood. A bullet whizzed past, and the bearded guard dropped below the top of the barrier, keeping his rifle trained on the jungle.

Screams of agony came from the western barrier as several bullets tore into the chest of a guard who fell head first onto the arena grounds. The sickening crack of shattered skull alerted Big Ben who looked up from his gorging on human flesh. Eager for more easy prey, he dropped the meat and scampered toward the fallen guard.

Several men leaped from the top of the barrier and charged across the arena, guns blazing, their tattered and disheveled appearance in stark contrast to their resolve. The men fired continuously at the creature, their bullets tearing into its exoskeleton.

Lincoln and the others backed further into the concrete alcove.

With two concrete barriers protecting them on the sides and the metal gate protecting the rear, all Lincoln had to do was protect the group from a frontal assault. Despite the safety the barriers afforded, with a rampaging creature from hell killing everything in its path and a gun battle raging around them, Lincoln preferred to be elsewhere.

Wolfgang and Claus ducked as stray bullets shattered the balcony's glass railing.

"Time to go?" Claus asked Wolfgang anxiously, hoping his boss would agree.

Wolfgang shot a nervous glance toward the balcony as more rounds thudded into the hotel's façade. "Ja," he said, scooping up the last of the strudel from the coffee table.

Rope ladders draped the western barriers. A dozen islanders hustled down the makeshift ladders and scattered across the arena firing at Big Ben and the remaining guards. A loan figure ran toward them despite the bullets ripping into the concrete at his feet. Ignoring the danger and shards of concrete flying through the air, the man fired at another guard running along the crest of the barrier above the alcove. The guard's chest exploded. He fell in front of the group, his neck breaking as he hit the ground.

Lincoln scooped up the guard's M4 assault rifle and sidearm. He threw the pistol to Gray, slung the rifle over his shoulder, and shouted to the group, "Grab whatever weapons you can!"

Leo's eyes lit up, and for the first time Lincoln saw the boy smile. He broke free from the safety of Lincoln's grip and sprinted toward the armed man with his AK-47. "Daddy!" Tears of happiness roll down the father's cheeks, overjoyed to have his son back in his arms.

As more bullets peppered the concrete wall and courtyard, another guard shrieked in pain. With blood spurting from his chest, he fell backward from atop the concrete barrier and into the surrounding jungle.

Leo's father waved over two heavily-armed islanders and

whispered instructions while pointing to his son. They nodded. After kissing the boy lightly on the cheek the father handed him over to the men who returned to the rope ladder and disappeared over the barrier with Leo.

Lincoln was relieved to see that Leo was being returned to the safety of his family. His father was shaking his hand in gratitude for protecting his son when movement on the penthouse balcony caught his attention. He shaded his eyes to find Merrick and Van Sant staring back at him. Lincoln saw the pure hatred burning in the father's eyes. He watched as the father fired blindly at the balcony but missed his targets.

A concrete barrier exploded in a cloud of dust and rock, allowing more islanders to sprint through the gap and into the arena. Merrick's remaining force did their best to defend the grounds, but the gunfight favored the islanders. Nevertheless, Merrick's men, outnumbered five-to-one, fought to defend the hotel from the invading islanders swarming across the arena and the hotel grounds. Lincoln predicted the fight would end soon.

"Is it over yet?" Becca asked, her face still deep in Mich's chest.

Several islanders continued to fire at the creature, but the bullets ricocheted off its hard shell. Annoyed by the distraction, Big Ben scuttled around to face the men. The creature snatched two islanders who were standing too close and swung them wildly through the air.

"Not yet," Mich said.

Their terrified screams lessened as the first islander was sliced in two. Big Ben raised the second islander in the air and hurtled him across the arena, slamming his body into a concrete barrier with a bone-crunching crack.

The carcass of the smaller decapod came into Big Ben's line of sight, and he hastened toward the creature. Clamping down hard on the dying beast, he sliced through two legs. Another swipe of his serrated claw severed the smaller decapod's left arm. Trapped below the larger crab, the decapod tried in vain to defend itself, its blood spraying over their exoskeletons as the larger crab came in for the kill. Big Ben lifted his claw high and slammed down without mercy, pulverizing the smaller decapod's skull. The decapod went limp, its head a bloodied mess of bone and gray matter. Big Ben continued to crush the remains until the exoskeleton and legs were a bloodied pile of crushed shell and bone.

"I feel sick." Becca said, trying to erase the terrifying sight from her mind. Mich held her hand.

Disgusted yet transfixed, Enheim couldn't take his eyes off the sight of the savage creature feeding. He covered Napoleon's head murmuring, "Don't look, Napums."

As the creature tore up more exoskeleton to gorge on the flesh, the trembling group gaped, knowing that their turn was next. The cracking of the hardened shell resonated about the arena before a second explosion rocked the earth beneath them.

Big Ben ignored the warfare and finished the smaller crustacean. Then he turned. Lincoln and the crew huddled beside the barriers—another easy kill.

With a smirk, Merrick slapped the balcony railing in excitement. Finally, after three days of anxiety and torment, he was about to be rid of that irksome Blue. His deep blue eyes glinted with delight. "Come on, you big ugly bastard. Do your damned job!"

Samantha slipped her arm around Merrick's waist and squeezed, a familiar indication to her husband of her insatiable hunger for death. The sex tonight would be good. She moaned. No, not good; exceptional.

Van Sant lit a cigarette, his eyes fixed on the showdown between man and beast. *Keep on doing your thing, Blue.*

With all eight legs working in unison, Big Ben reared up in a fearsome display of dominance before charging across the field at the helpless group. They opened fire on the stampeding creature, but their bullets bounced off Big Ben's shell. Without warning, Big Ben skidded to a halt, kicking up a cloud of dust. His antennae swayed from side to side picking up vibrations within the arena.

To everyone's surprise, the stalked eyes swiveled to focus on Enheim. Lincoln cast a *what the hell* look at Enheim before returning to the giant creature studying all of them, but in particular Marcus Enheim. Napoleon ducked into Enheim's harness and whimpered.

Big Ben dropped his mighty claws and edged back, apprehensive, when a barrier close by exploded in a cloud of concrete dust. A Willys Jeep shot through the opening with a bloodied rodent head impaled to the hood, on display like some macabre trophy.

"Yea-ha!" the bald guard from the helicopter wreckage shouted at the top of his lungs steering toward the giant crab.

Poised behind the M134 Minigun mounted on the rear tray, his off-sider with the buzz cut and handlebar moustache tightened his finger around the gun's trigger and continued firing into the jungle behind them. "Kiss my ass you ugly rat son'bitches!"

"Twelve o'clock!" the bald driver yelled over the rapid-fire droning, ignoring Lincoln and the others who watched, stunned at their sudden appearance.

The off-sider swung the deadly weapon around to face forward. "He's a biggin!" he said with a broad grin.

The Gatlin gun's six rotating barrels gave off a high-pitched whine as two thousand rounds a minute tore across the arena and into the decapod's shell. Big Ben stumbled from the barrage but recovered and with lightning speed charged the Jeep. Alarmed at the creature's resilience and now under the attack, the bald driver yanked hard on the steering wheel to avoid this unexpected turn of events, but the maneuver was too little, too late. The tires failed to grip, and the Jeep skidded sideways over the grassy area on a collision course with fate. Big Ben's left pincher sliced down through the hood and drove the shattered engine into the ground below, bringing the Jeep to a screeching halt. The right pincer closed around the cab, crushing the framework. The creature lifted the broken vehicle, with the two men still aboard screaming in terror, and tossed it like a child's toy across the arena.

Big Ben ignored the Jeep as it crashed back down to earth, silencing the screams. He swung around and fixed his eyes on Enheim for a moment longer before turning to the hole in the concrete wall. Comprehending that the greenery beyond represented freedom, Big Ben took one last look at the humans huddled in the corner, then shuffled through the hole onto the hotel acreage.

Gray watched in wonder as the creature barreled through the ground cover and disappeared into the hotel gardens. "Did you see that?"

"Yeah, I'm impressed. It's not every day you see a giant crab throw a Willys Jeep with two rednecks on board fifty feet through the air."

"I'm talking about the creature's reaction. The decapod recognized an escape route."

"So?" Lincoln shook his head, still amazed by the creature's brute strength.

"Crustaceans were always believed to have only rudimentary brains. Whatever that thing is out there, it has high cognitive abilities. Possibly it's even sentient."

"Meaning he can feel things?"

Gray nodded.

"That's great, Doc. I've got a question for you. Why the hell did he stop when he saw Enheim?" Lincoln waited, hoping for any plausible answer. The others, too, looked to Gray and waited.

"I have no idea." Gray shrugged. "It's possible the giant crustacean picked up the canine pheromones from Napoleon and they triggered a fight or flight response in the creature's brain. Decapods have been known to sense and react to danger from many land-based predators."

"Or, it sensed the islanders on the other side of the barrier," Mich suggested.

"Maybe the thing knew it vas no match for my brother-in-law's vitty charm," Roland offered. Enheim gave Roland a wry smile.

In his peripheral vision, Roland caught sight of a creature he had hoped he'd never see again. With a jerk of his head he alerted the rest of the crew. Poised atop the concrete barrier beside the cavity torn open by the latest explosion sat the alpha rat, glaring at them through red eyes, its bared teeth protruding from its bloodied jaws. "This isn't fair, you know."

Enheim leaned over to Lincoln. "We thought we'd tell you about Mickey here at a more convenient time, but..."

The rat studied the cluster of humans as the rodent hoard swarmed through the concrete rubble and onto the field. The rat-a-tat-tat of gunfire erupted as islanders and guards took on the new danger. Lincoln and the crew stood helpless, as this latest battle raged before them.

Intent on feeding their hunger, the giant rats attacked the nearest humans in sight. Islanders' screams filled the field as the rats struck without mercy. As the rats converged on the sentinels, more guards toppled from the barriers.

The anxiety of not knowing the whereabouts and well-being of his beloved Katya had taken its toll on Enheim. With fangs bared, a rat the size of a bull terrier leapt at Enheim through the dust haze. In one swift move, Enheim grabbed the rodent by the scruff of the neck, clenched his fist, and gave the rat a bone shattering upper cut to the snout. The creature dropped to the ground squealing and scuttled away with its tail between its legs.

"A gift from the Enheims," Enheim shouted at the retreating rat. Lincoln and Mich shot each other surprised looks, then shrugged away Enheim's unexpected defense, ascribing it to stress.

Becca screamed as a rodent jumped from the barrier and landed on Mich's shoulder, its beady red eyes and salivating open jaws inches from her face. "These things are ugly!" She clenched both hands around the thick neck of matted fur to keep the creature at bay when its head exploded across her face. Mich pumped another round into the rat and it fell to the ground.

The alpha thumped its tail, and the hoard paused its onslaught. Gazing toward the broken concrete barrier, the rats sniffed the air. The alpha let out a high-pitched squeal that sent the smaller rodents scampering into the dust cloud surrounding the hole in the nearby barrier. The alpha took one last look at the humans and leaped off the barrier toward the hotel.

"What the hell just happened?" Mich stared as the rats scurried off.

"I can't be sure, but I think Mickey just found bigger fish to fry," Lincoln answered.

They heard the metal latch slide through the guides and watched as the gate open with a screech. Prepared for the worst, Lincoln leveled his rifle at the opening. An islander with missing front teeth and an AK-47 smiled as he ushered Leo's father through the opening. Nodding farewell to Lincoln, Leo's father darted toward the hotel.

Lincoln faced the group. "That's our cue, people. It's time to get off this goddamned island."

CHAPTER 43

"AT THE EASTERN flank of the hotel is a loading elevator that goes to the lagoon at the plateau's base where you'll find a docked supply ship," Lincoln explained. "I'll meet you there."

"Why don't we just go back through the jungle?" Becca asked. "We know that way takes us to a beach. Maybe we can set a fire and alert passing ships and planes."

"We know what awaits in the jungle." Lincoln indicated the giant rat carcasses littering the arena. "Not to mention Big Ben. Our chance of survival is better if we get the hell off this island. The doc here assures me there's a supply ship docked at a quay at the base of the plateau. If we can reach the quay, we can get off this damned island."

The group agreed that Lincoln's logic was sound.

"What about you? Where are you going?" Enheim asked.

"Gray and I are going to get Christina and Katya and pick up medical supplies for Mich." Lincoln turned to Gray. "Right?"

Gray checked that the pistol was loaded with the trigger in the forward safety position. He was getting the hang of using weapons and smiled. "My office is just beyond these barriers, around the side of the hotel at ground level."

"We won't be long." Lincoln turned to Mich. "When I get back, you owe me a beer."

Mich rolled his eyes. "Yeah, yeah."

Roland and Rousseau lit cigarettes to calm their nerves. After inhaling deeply, they exhaled away the stress of the last few days.

Napoleon barked softly. "Napums says we're going with you," Enheim announced, rubbing the little dog's neck nonstop.

"*What?*"

Enheim gave Lincoln a steely-eyed glare. "My wife's in that hotel, and I'm going to get her."

"I know you want to rescue Katya—we all do—but you need to stay here with the others. It's safer. Gray and I can do this."

"My wife is up there somewhere, and I'm not leaving this hotel without her."

Lincoln didn't have time to argue. Every second counted. He grabbed a sidearm from a dead guard and tossed it to Enheim. "Time to go, people."

As the crew passed through the gate, Roland restrained Lincoln. "Seriously, Marcus is an emotional man. He does not think before he acts. I vant my sister back, too, but Enheim vill get you killed, you know."

Lincoln smiled. "With any luck, not today."

CHAPTER 44

MERRICK PEEKED OVER the balcony as bullets whizzed by. "I don't give a shit if the boat's sinking," he snapped, his phone glued to his ear to block out the background rat-a-tat-tat of machine gun fire. "I don't want to hear any excuses. You're the pilot of that goddamned Chinook, and I command you to hook up my wife's cabin cruiser. When my wife is safely aboard, you'll take her back to Saipan, and you'll arrange to have her damned boat fixed." Ignoring the pilot's plea for understanding, Merrick exploded. "*I don't care about the gunfight!* I pay your wage, and I pay you well, so just do it! Get the boat hooked up!" He shoved the phone into his pocket.

Samantha observed her husband as the pressure of the last four days took its toll. His concern with the repairs to her cabin cruiser over the safety of his employees and his island made Samantha realize that her husband's mind had cracked under the strain of the failed games and the loss of a key client. She had seen this behavior many years ago with another failed business venture. Merrick's mind had shut off to the dangers surrounding them, and he had focused on small concerns rather than the big picture.

Samantha crouched by his side, her face strained with fear. They ducked as more rounds tore into the elegant plate-glass railing, shattering the custom-made balustrade into thousands of pieces. "Sonovabitch islanders," he cursed, firing toward the grounds below as men scuttled about. Van Sant joined them, drawing his Beretta and returning fire.

In the atrium below, the glass façade blew apart, showering glass and wood over the immaculate lawns. Another muffled explosion shook the hotel. "Screw this." Merrick spat away his anger and stood.

"What are you doing, boss?" Van Sant said, pulling him down behind the safety of the support beams.

"What the hell does it look like I'm doing? I'm putting an end to this once and for all!"

Van Sant glanced over the balcony. Several islanders were running toward the Chinook that sat on the lawn beside the cabin cruiser at the river's edge. "Boss, you hired me to protect you, your wife, and this enterprise. Believe me when I tell you it's a no-win situation down there. We're outnumbered five-to-one. If we can, we should get to the chopper and cut our losses." He paused. "There's always next time."

Merrick stared at Van Sant, his blue eyes steely and his expression one of absolute control. His dream of wealth and power was over. All he could do now was salvage the remains of his empire. "There *is* no next time. It's now or never. You said it yourself, Van Sant. I'm the boss." Merrick took one last peek at the hoard of islanders swarming the hotel's grounds and pathways. "After I take the private elevator and confirm that no one is waiting for us downstairs, I'll send the elevator back up. Take Samantha to the chopper. I'll meet you there. I'm trusting you with my wife's life. Don't let me down."

"What are you gonna do?"

"Monk has been a pain in my ass for the last four days. It's time for retribution. It's time for him to feel my pain."

Samantha understood that her dreams of security and stability at Tom Merrick's side were over. "Honey, I want you beside me. Please don't go," she begged.

"Everything will be okay. Pack your bags, and I'll meet you both at the helicopter in fifteen minutes." Merrick kissed her lightly on the cheek.

Samantha Merrick grabbed her husband's face in both her hands for his fullest attention. For the first time in their relationship, Merrick was taken aback by the underlying anger in her demeanor. The fury in her eyes burned into his soul. "Lincoln Monk has destroyed our lives. Destroy his." A rush of sexual pleasure flowed through her at the thought of her husband killing another man. Moaning with pleasure, she kissed Merrick hard on the mouth. As the passionate kiss ended, she regained her composer and lightly flicked away invisible lint on Merrick's coat.

"I'll see you soon, Mrs. Merrick," Tom Merrick whispered, "with Monk's head on a platter." Samantha blew him a kiss as he crossed the deck and disappeared into the penthouse.

Once Merrick was out of sight, Samantha turned to Van Sant. "Go down to the safe and get my jewelry and the money."

"But Mrs. Merrick, Mr. Merrick asked me to stay by your side."

"You know as well as I that this business venture has failed. If we're lucky, we'll get out with our lives." Van Sant couldn't argue with her, but he remained hesitant to disobey his employer's commands. "Look around, Van Sant." She spoke quietly, appealing to his rational decision-making. Smoke billowed past the penthouse railing and gunfire echoed about them. "It's over. You know that Tom's judgement is clouded with anger and desperation."

Begrudgingly, Van Sant agreed.

"Good. Now get my jewelry and all the cash from the safe and meet me back here. We'll need every cent to get out of here and back to safety. Believe me, Tom will thank you for it later."

An explosion rocked the hotel, cementing the truth of her common-sense. Van Sant made his way through the debris to the safe.

CHAPTER 45

LINCOLN, ENHEIM, AND Gray kept low as they scampered along the garden rows toward the doctor's office. "Aren't the flora magnificent?" Gray marveled at the splendor of the manicured plants and floral arrangements that lined the pathways circling the hotel grounds. He indicated a row of blossoming white flowers. "*Bikkia tetrandra*. We know them as torchwood, but the locals have their own name—*gausali*. Once the flower has died, the people use the stems as candles. The plant life of these islands is fascinating, don't you think?"

"I'm sure it is, Doc," Lincoln said absently, studying the labels on the doorways along the ground level. "But right now, we need to focus on the job at hand."

"Of course. I apologize for the distraction. The endemic flora of Micronesia was the reason I took this job in the first place. You see, botany is my hobby—my passion, really."

Enheim sniffed the air and took in the sweet smell of the frangipani and beach hibiscus. "Katya loves flowers," he said, trying not to think of her abduction and what could be happening to her. "When we get off this friggin island, we're gonna buy Katya all the flowers she wants, aren't we, Napums?" Napoleon responded with a soft bark.

Lincoln pointed to a door labeled Doctor's Office. Gray nodded. Lincoln lifted his leg to kick in the door when Gray waved him away. The older man gently turned the knob. "I've never had to lock it."

He shrugged. "Surprisingly, these cutthroats running the island are reliable when it comes to following orders. Honor among thieves and all that."

"Great. I'll let the union know their boys are doing a good job," Lincoln said sarcastically. "Grab the medication. We don't have much time."

"Just as I left it," Gray murmured, referring to the clean and tidy condition of the office. "Looks like they haven't had time to replace us yet." Lincoln and Enheim stood guard by the door while Gray searched the cabinets for the medicine, grimly recalling the night he and Lockwood had been unceremoniously dragged from that very room and placed under guard in their bungalows. Fear of the unknown had sent his mind racing and shivers down his spine.

Within moments, Gray reappeared with a bag brimming with medicinal supplies. Without warning, Napoleon whimpered and ducked down into the harness. An enormous shadow passed the office window and slowed. Lincoln brought his finger to his lips as the scuttling of many legs working in unison reached their ears. Gray froze, wide-eyed, while Enheim covered Napoleon's head with his hand for protection. Lincoln peeked through a slat of the closed venetian blinds and gulped. Big Ben lurked outside the office. Lincoln and Gray quietly backed against the office wall, a single row of bricks the only barrier between them and death.

Hungry for prey, the creature's antennae searched the air for minute vibrations and honed in on movement near the hotel's western flank. The decapod shuffled along the veranda and disappeared into the darkness.

Lincoln snuck another peek through the blinds and confirmed that the creature was gone. "Okay, let's go."

Gray closed the bag, slung the strap over his shoulder, and gave Lincoln a thumbs up.

Enheim sighed and dabbed the sweat from his forehead. "Luckily I'm wearing brown underpants."

CHAPTER 46

CHEF FABIENNE WAS removing the crabe tourteau from the hot plate when the rat-a-tat-tat of sharp cracking gunfire reached the kitchen. As the dish clattered onto the counter, she drew her P238 from her thigh holster. She peeked out the kitchen's serving window that overlooked the five-star restaurant and lobby and spotted several men armed with AK-47s running through the atrium and via the glass wall door to the gardens. She glanced at the kitchen's open doorways that allowed the breeze to waft through the stuffy kitchen. *Dammit.*

Fabienne ducked below the counter where she ejected the magazine from her pistol to count the available rounds; two shy of a full magazine. Relieved, she recalled having fired only two rounds at the shooting range days earlier. She slapped the magazine back into the handle as the clacking of multiple feet hitting the concrete grew louder.

A shadow passed over her. Startled, she looked up. *Merde!* The giant decapod loomed above her with sous chef Ruth's severed head impaled on its jagged exoskeleton. As Fabienne fumbled with her pistol, Big Ben's right claw pinned her arms to her sides and lifted her to eye level. She shrieked in pain, writhing in agony with her legs dangling above the floor. Meanwhile, Big Ben's stalked eyes studied the cooked crab resting on the counter. He roared with rage and refocused on Chef Fabienne who was gasping between his saw-like claws. His open mouth revealed double rows of bloodied teeth. The decapod maneuvered its left pincer over Fabienne's head so that the serrated edges locked around her neck. "Go screw yourself, you—" She paused at the sight of the crabe tourteau, then sighed in resignation as the claw snapped shut.

Inside the walk-in vault, Van Sant removed the last of Samantha's necklaces from the deposit box and placed them in the backpack along with her other jewelry and stacks of cash. As he zipped the bag shut, the ground shuddered from an explosion close by. *Time to go.* He threw the bag over his shoulder and was about to leave when he spotted the envelope at the back of the deposit box. Knowing what it contained, he grabbed the letter and dashed out of the safe. *A Nigerian warlord killing Americans? Not on my watch.*

Van Sant left the heavy door wide open, allowing whomever to ravage the contents of the room—his gift to the locals.

CHAPTER 47

ENHEIM AND GRAY followed Lincoln up the hotel's emergency stairs. After making a quick calculation, Lincoln stopped on the fifth-floor landing and raised his finger to his lips. Seeing no security personnel, he confirmed that the heavy door was alarm-free and edged it open. Apart from a room-service trolley halfway down the corridor, the floor was empty. Lincoln led the way down the hallway to the floor's third room, the one he'd seen from the river. "Ready?"

Gray checked that his safety was off and gave Lincoln a thumbs up.

Anxiety and fear overcame Enheim. "We do this my way!" he blurted. Before Lincoln could stop him, he raised his foot and kicked open the door.

The room was empty. Enheim checked under the twin beds while Lincoln searched the bathroom. Gray slid open the balcony door and inspected the terrace. Sniffing the air, he recognized the distinctive odor of Nigerian meat pies wafting over the balcony. The smell reminded him of Mr. Merrick's distasteful reward tactics, and his heart sank. "Oh, no," he groaned.

Enheim glared at Gray. "Oh no? What does *oh no* mean?"

"The women are with the Nigerians."

Lincoln stopped. "What makes you think that?"

"Before I was conscripted for the games, one of my last duties as the island's general practitioner was to attend the aftermath of a Nigerian party."

"What the hell does that mean?" Enheim croaked, fearing the worst.

"Let's just say that poor island girl will never be the same."

Sensing his master's desperation, Napoleon whimpered. Enheim ran his hand over his shaved head, his breath coming in short gasps. "Where the hell are these friggin' Nigerians?"

"Just follow the smell."

From the safety of the balcony, Abeo watched with concern as the gun battle raged below. "Adedowale," he called.

With an overconfident swagger, Adedowale stepped onto the terrace and peered over the railing. "Well, now, hasn't this been an exciting afternoon. First, we get to see Merrick's two magnificent creatures, and now we get to see the natives put on a show." He placed a reassuring hand on Abeo's shoulder. "Yes, these events have turned bad. But Merrick can deal with the natives. We have more important matters to deal with." He turned back to the real show in the hotel room, his lust overshadowing the spectacle outside.

Adedowale lifted the loaded crossbow and the quiver of arrows from the bed with care and placed them on the couch. "Mustn't damage Mr. Merrick's wonderful gift," he said, grinning. Unbuttoning his silk shirt, he faced the girls who stood steadfastly in the room. "I see fear in your eyes, little ladies, but this fear is unjustified. You do not need to worry. If you allow yourselves the pleasure of our company, this experience can be enjoyable for all of us. Please, make yourselves a drink."

Christina and Katya stood rooted in defiance of Adedowale's request.

"So be it."

Abeo, his AK-47 slung over his shoulder, moved from the

balcony into the room, stopping to scrutinize Christina's lean body. As he removed his shoes and shirt, she looked away in disgust.

"Should you choose to resist our charms…" Adedowale's voice trailed off as he shot a lascivious smile at his associate.

Abeo tore his eyes from Christina's alluring body and picked up the machete. He moved toward the women with lust-filled eyes, but Adedowale restrained him with a hand on his shoulder. "In good time my friend, in good time." He eased the machete from Abeo's hand and, after brandishing it at the women, finished his vodka martini while perusing their trim bodies. Christina knew that his ostensibly pleasant attitude had given way to his desires. He unfastened the last button and threw the Armani shirt aside to reveal long scars down his heavy-set torso.

Katya and Christina froze at the sight of the old scars running from shoulders to midriff. The long, hastily-stitched wounds could only have been inflicted by a sword—or machete.

"The machete is a fascinating weapon," Adedowale explained, not taking his eyes off the women's horrified gaze. "It can be a blunt instrument, as you see before you, or it can be pointed or hooked, depending on its many uses. The possibilities are many."

Katya buried her head on Christina's shoulder. Adedowale's towering frame and penetrating eyes sent chills down Christina's spine.

"Do not be afraid, little ones. The choice is yours."

On cue, Abeo strolled across the room and jerked Katya away from Christina. With his AK-47 aimed at Christina's head, he dragged her toward the balcony, leaving Katya alone before Adedowale wielding his machete.

"Bastards!" Christina spat, struggling to free herself from the Nigerian's grip. Abeo lifted the rifle and cold-cocked Christina across the temple. She fell hard to the floor, her vision blurred.

Adedowale laughed. "A feisty woman. This I like. I prefer the ones that protest—heightens the anticipation, don't you think?" Christina struggled to stand, but with pain coursing through her skull, she could only manage to avoid the assistant's second swing. "Enough," Adedowale ordered. "I want them without bruising— for now."

Abeo sneered at Christina crawling on her hands and knees on the carpet and kicked her in the ribs. She moaned and crumpled to the floor, clasping her side. From the pain she felt every time she took a breath, she suspected that he had cracked a rib. From the corner of her eye, she spotted the loaded crossbow yards away on the couch. She could see Abeo hovering above her, watching her every move, and realized that she might never be this close to a weapon again. Running on adrenaline and instinct, she decided to go for the crossbow. The weapon was their last chance. The pain dulling her senses would slow her reaction time, but she had an idea that might give her a few precious seconds, an idea that depended on Katya.

"Katya," Christina reached toward her, flinching at the pain. "Just do it."

Katya stared at Christina in disbelief, horrified at what she was saying.

Christina edged closer to the crossbow. "It'll be okay. Show them what you're proud of."

Katya hesitated. Why was Christina encouraging her to let these animals ravage her? After they finished with her, they would turn their attention to Christina. It didn't make sense.

"Please, Katya," Christina pleaded.

Adedowale grinned, his pristine white teeth belying his darker self. He closed in on Katya. "Listen, little lady. Listen to your friend. She makes sense. I do not want to hurt you, but if I have to, I will."

Although her instincts told her otherwise, Katya trusted Christina. Slowly she lifted her tank top to reveal her naked breasts. She raised her arms higher and maneuvered the spandex top over her head. Standing before her, Adedowale's loins burned with desire for Katya's tanned athletic body and flowing blonde hair. He grabbed her arm. She pulled back, but his natural strength was too much for her.

Distracted by Katya's writhing semi-naked body, Abeo's thoughts turned to what he would do with her after Adedowale finished.

It's now or never. With her strength ebbing, Christina lunged for the crossbow and fired. Abeo spotted the movement, but too late. His eyes rolled back with the arrow's end protruding from his forehead and the tip from the back of his head. He stumbled, then fell, face first, to the floor, driving the arrow further through his skull. Adedowale spun to see Abeo's body jerking on the carpet. Enraged, he glared at Christina as she fumbled to reload the crossbow.

The door burst inward, slamming against the wall with the sharp crack of splintering wood. Marcus Enheim, with Napoleon strapped to his chest, stood in the doorway, his incensed gaze on the man brandishing a machete over his semi-naked wife. As Napoleon growled at Adedowale, Lincoln and Gray stormed into the room. Adedowale dropped the machete. Enheim leaned back and, with all the force and wrath he could muster, gave Adedowale the greatest head-butt in human history. Lincoln winced as a bone-crunching crack filled the room. The Nigerian crashed backward, clutching his broken nose and fractured forehead. As he staggered, unable to comprehend these unexpected developments, Enheim powered him across the room and charged on toward the balcony like a bull. The thought of this asshole violating his wife sent Enheim into a fury that Lincoln would never have imagined possible. With hate-filled eyes, Enheim lifted Adedowale above the railing and dropped him over the edge.

Adedowale screamed, arms flaying, as he tumbled down the hotel's façade. He crashed through the glass atrium ceiling before plummeting into the foyer and landing with a sickening crack on the polished marble.

Katya ran to Enheim who embraced her like a long-lost love. She clung to him, sobbing, and buried her head in his shoulder. Enheim stroked Katya's soft hair. "Nothing breaks up my family," he whispered. "Nothing." He reached on the floor for Katya's tank top. As soon as she slipped it on, he enfolded her in another bear hug. "The Enheim way wins every time."

Lincoln knelt by the couch where Christina had collapsed. He lifted the crossbow from beside her and placed it on the floor. Brushing her hair from her face, he murmured, "You okay?"

"Nothing—a good painkiller—won't fix." She tried to stand, but the agony from the cold cock and the kick in the ribs was too much. Lincoln raised Christina to her feet and eased her arm around his broad shoulders.

Crushed between Enheim and Katya, Napoleon whimpered. Katya smiled through her tears and gently lifted him from the harness. The little dog licked her face, releasing the stress of the ordeal she had faced and causing her to sob like a child. Enheim's smile as he wiped away her tears brought her back to reality. She turned to Christina and Lincoln. "Thank you, darlinks."

Shots rang out across the hotel's grounds, reminding them of the battle below.

"Sorry to interrupt this reunion, guys," Lincoln said, "but we have to go."

"Where?" Katya asked, sniffling away the tears.

CHAPTER 48

SURROUNDED BY JUNGLE, the lagoon opened to an inlet that flowed to the ocean a mere two miles north of their location. The *Tapochau Royal*, a one-hundred-fifty-foot supply ship out of Saipan, lay at anchor at the base of the cliff inside the lagoon beside a rotted jetty. Her rusted hull and peeling paintwork were reminders of her age and the unforgiving waters of the Pacific Ocean.

Standing on the bridge wing, Captain Sayoc knew his ship's limits all too well as he lowered his binoculars. Lesser captains would have failed where he excelled. His ship and his crew had survived wild weather and dangerous waters that even the most hardened seafaring adventurer would fear, but his contract with Tom Merrick had brought new dangers to his and his crew's lives. Stories of local islanders disappearing without a trace and rumors of giant ungodly creatures running amuck throughout the outer islands had kept his superstitious crew on edge. However, he was a man who was prepared, always prepared; working for Tom Merrick he had to be. Now, to add to the list of perils, a gun battle raged high above, out of sight.

He kept his concerned gaze on the cliff top as shots echoed across the sky from the hotel grounds, then turned his attention to the bedraggled group on the loading dock. He wiped his sweaty hand on the stained undershirt that stretched over his bulging belly, then nervously rubbed his unshaven jaw.

With an M4 from the arena slung behind his back, Roland was the last of the crew to step from the loading elevator to join Mich, Rousseau, and Becca on the loading dock. The roar of the waterfall emptying beside them from the river above filled their ears as a cloud of spray hovered over the lagoon.

"What happens now?" Becca shouted over the thundering falls.

"Now we get off this jetty," Mich replied, starting toward the ship.

Sayoc looked Mich up and down with curiosity and a coy smile. "Stay where you are," he warned. "Do not come closer to my ship."

Mich stopped, but he continued to smile at the unkempt man studying them from the bridge. "You speak English, and you're the captain—great. I'm Mich Lee, and this is Becca, Roland, and Rousseau." Becca smiled while Roland and Rosseau gave him a wave. Not wanting to concern the captain, Rousseau gently maneuvered his M4 behind his back. Becca caught a glimpse of Rousseau's subtle move and slipped her pistol between her skirt and the small of her back.

"I am Captain Sayoc," he said, his tone curt. "What's going on up there?"

"Payback."

Sayoc raised an eyebrow.

"The local islanders have taken control of Merrick's hotel," Mich explained.

Stunned by the news, Sayoc bit his lower lip and contemplated his next move. "What do you want?"

"Captain Sayoc, we crash landed on the far side of the island and have been looking for a way back to Saipan."

"So?"

"It would be much appreciated if we could journey with you back to Saipan." Mich lifted his arms in a show of compliance.

Sayoc spotted the sidearm tucked into Mich's belt and snatched his own pistol from his oversized pants. He rested the gun on the railing, its barrel leveled at the group. "Stay where you are!"

"Please," Mich said, seeing the captain's nervous reaction to his gun. "We mean you and your men no harm. This weapon is only for protection. This island is a dangerous place. You must understand that."

"Back away from my ship."

Roland could see this was going nowhere. He tried a different tact, a language all businessmen understood. "We have money, you know."

"How much?"

Mich turned to the group and whispered, "I've got nothing. How much *do* we have?"

Becca held up her empty hands and shrugged. Rousseau swallowed hard and gave everyone a sheepish grin after retrieving just three United States dollar bills from his pocket. From his waterlogged wallet, Roland pulled two hundred United States dollars, the official currency of the Marianas.

Mich groaned and reluctantly faced Captain Sayoc. "We don't have much on us now, but if you can get us back to Saipan, we can give you more."

"How much do you have now?"

"A little over two hundred US dollars—but we can get more."

"You are wasting my time."

"Please, Captain, we need your help," Mich said, taking a tentative step forward.

Sayoc lifted his pistol and waved it at Mich.

Rousseau turned to Becca and blushing, indicated to her breasts. "Rebecca, they are men. Men are easily distracted, you understand?" When it dawned on her what the big Frenchmen was implying, she gave a subtle nod. She unbuttoned the top of her tight blouse, hoping the sight of tanned cleavage would help sway the captain and his men. They were sailors, after all, men who spent long days at sea and, like all men, could be influenced by a tantalizing taste of heaving breasts.

Becca strutted her way to Mich's side, presenting what nature had given her for the captain to ogle.

"It won't work," Roland murmured to Mich.

"Why not?"

"Captain Sayoc is gay."

"How can you possibly tell from here?" he said to Roland with a disbelieving look.

"A gay man can tell."

"Aw, come on. I find that hard to believe."

"It's true."

"Okay, how? How can you tell he's gay?"

"Simple, you know. Didn't you see the vay he looked at you earlier? His eyes vere devouring your form."

Mich thought back to the captain's unusual expression when he first approached the ship. His jaw dropped. "I'll be damned. You're right."

"A gay man senses these things." Roland shrugged with a knowing grin.

Swaying her hips and pouting, Becca did her best to get the captain's attention, but to no avail. "It's not working," she said, as her efforts were met with a face of stone.

"We know," Mich and Roland chimed together.

Becca's journalistic instincts took over, and she came up with a new plan. She edged toward the ship and saw the captain clearly in all his glory for the first time. "What a slob," Becca murmured, disgusted by Sayoc's triple chin, greasy complexion, and sweat-stained undershirt. Forcing a smile, she said, "My name is Rebecca Perry. I'm a reporter for KSPN news out of Saipan. I can write a favorable story about how the brave captain and his crew of the—" she glanced at the ship's name in faded paint across the bow "—*Tapochau Royal* risked their lives to rescue stranded survivors of a plane crash in the Northern Mariana islands. I'm sure this publicity would favor your business."

With a menacing scowl, Sayoc focused his pistol's aim on Becca. Becca backed away. "Then again, maybe not."

Mich leaned over to Roland. "Looks like our good captain here is media shy."

"The good captain here vorks for a ruthless businessman on a private island in the Pacific who has access to creatures the vorld has never seen. Secrecy and confidentiality vould be his main concerns. Did you expect the captain vould velcome us with open arms, tell us his story, and vant a book deal?" Roland said in a matter-of-fact tone.

"Good point," said Becca with an awkward grin. "Obviously the whole reporter thing was a bad idea. What now, then?"

"Vell," Roland mused. "Unless Mich here vants to offer himself to Captain Sayoc—"

"—that ain't gonna happen," Mich was swift to reply.

"Then I suppose ve only have one option, you know."

"Which is?"

Roland stepped toward the ship, grabbed the M4 assault rifle strapped over his shoulder and presented the weapon to Sayoc for him to see. "Ve have guns!"

Mich, Rousseau, and Becca quickly followed suit, indicating their weapons.

Sayoc ducked into the bridge and returned moments later wearing a mocking smile. "So do we." From the ship's superstructure, a dozen heavily armed Filipino men stormed onto the deck and took up positions along the gunwale, their Uzi sub-machine guns targeting Roland and the crew on the loading dock.

This time Roland held up his hands in surrender, nodded to the others to do the same, and backed away from the supply ship. "So much for that idea," Roland said. "Vat now?"

Mich peered up at the plateau's precipice towering above them and took a deep breath. "Looks like we have no choice. Now we wait."

CHAPTER 49

SUPPORTING CHRISTINA WITH his arm, Lincoln sprinted behind Gray, Enheim, and Katya across the manicured lawn in the direction of the loading elevator with gunshots echoing through the air. Although the battle between Merrick's men and the islanders raged within the hotel grounds, with a little determination and a whole lot of luck, this nightmare would soon be over.

Gray spotted the elevator near the plateau's edge. As they stood on the platform ready to descend the rock face to the waiting supply ship, a bullet ricocheted off the handrail beside Lincoln. They turned to see Van Sant charging toward them, gun raised.

Lincoln reached for his rifle as Van Sant closed in less than ten yards away. "Try it, and you're dead," he said calmly, his gun's barrel leveled at Lincoln's forehead.

Lincoln grunted with dissatisfaction, annoyed at their allowing themselves to be captured at this stage. Slowly, he moved his hand away from the rifle, and Van Sant confiscated the weapon.

"You, too, old man," Van Sant said, pointing his chin at Gray. As Gray's hands shot in the air in surrender, Van Sant grabbed Gray's sidearm along with Christina's crossbow.

Van Sant studied the bedraggled group. He contemplated his actions and the repercussions of those actions. It was now or never. "My employer Tom Merrick plans to sell a high yield weapon to a couple of Nigerian warlords. Normally, I wouldn't care what animals like that do to each other in some shithole part of the world, but when they started talking about using it on Americans, well… I may be a bastard, but I'm also a patriot. I love my country."

The group glanced at one another, unsure of where this speech was leading.

Van Sant took a long last look at the group before returning their weapons. He lowered his rifle to his side. Speechless, Lincoln and Gray took back their guns, still confused by the unforeseen turn of events. "Merrick has gone off the rails," Van Sant said. "His lust for wealth has clouded his judgement. This—" he indicated the hotel and the surrounding jungle—"all this is one thing, but bombing Americans? Well, that's something else."

"What do you propose to do?" Lincoln asked with uncertainty.

"Over the last four days, you pissed off my employer to the limit. He threw everything he had at you, but you remained alive."

With an angry grimace, Lincoln leveled his rifle at Van Sant. "You and Merrick put Gray and me through hell the last four days. We made it this far only by our sheer will to survive."

"Blue, I need your help. I need you to watch my back while I disarm the bomb and destroy it."

"What makes you think I'd help you?"

Van Sant nodded towards Gray. "You didn't know Gray here, but you saved him from certain death several times. And—"

Van Sant paused, and Lincoln and Gray waited for him to finish his sentence.

"—any man who protects kids is okay with me."

Lincoln gazed down at the supply ship through the loading platform's metal grates. Escape from this nightmare beckoned him from just a few yards away. To ignore Van Sant, commandeer the ship, and return to Saipan would be easy. He turned to the others, torn by his need to get away and by Van Sant's new information.

Gray patted Lincoln on the shoulder. "My boy, you've done

some astonishing things in the last four days and saved many lives. Nobody would think less of you if you left this island now and never returned."

Lincoln saw the desperation in Van Sant's eyes. Van Sant was right, that his nature was to help others. He understood that he had to help him disarm the bomb. "I'll meet all of you down at the dock," he said, lowering his rifle.

"Maybe I should stay and help, too," Gray offered.

"Thanks, old man, but you'll just get in the way—no offense," Van Sant added.

"None taken."

"See you soon," Lincoln called to the crew as he and Van Sant made their way across the hotel grounds toward the concrete ramp to the cavern.

Watching Lincoln and Van Sant disappear, Gray pondered his next move.

CHAPTER 50

As HIS EMPIRE crumbled, Merrick's thoughts fixated on the two men heading for the dock. Van Sant's betrayal infuriated him as he watched him and Lincoln cross the hotel grounds and head toward the cavern. How could his loyal employee, whom he had trusted to protect his wife and property, side with a contestant—and not just any contestant, but a contestant who had been the bane of his life since the games began? The bile of resentment rose as Merrick found this treachery inexcusable. Keeping to the shadows of the hotel's exterior, Merrick darted toward the loading ramp, rage carved in his features.

The first bullet tore into his shoulder. The impact spun him around before he fell to the soft lawn, pain coursing through his upper torso. As he clutched the wound, blood seeped between his fingers. The sun's glare disappeared as a shadow moved over him. Merrick squinted to focus on the figure standing over him: an islander with an AK-47 pointed at his chest. Edging his hand toward the hidden pistol tucked within his coat, Merrick waited for the islander to make his move.

Leo's father scowled, his contorted face fixed with hatred on the man lying at his feet. "You take our island's men and use them as cheap labor to build your hotel."

"You had nothing before I came here," Merrick said. "Your people were scratching away at dust, living in hovels. Ferdinand Magellan, the Portuguese explorer, was right. You people are savages."

"So, you know our history. This is true: he did call the Chamorro people savages living on the Island of Thieves. What he and you do not know is that the Chamorro people have a rich history of bartering, something that Magellan failed to recognize. He was ignorant of our ways, just as you are. And, like you, he got what he deserved on the island of Mactan in the Philippines—a poisoned arrow sealed his fate."

"Great men will always be demonized by lesser men."

"You pay my people next to nothing," Leo's father continued, ignoring Merrick, "then threaten them and their families if they talk about this place."

"I gave you all an income, a way out of poverty. I gave you a chance to make something of yourselves. And what did you do? You squandered it on rotted fishing trawlers and clung to your ancestral ways. I was trying to do your people a favor."

"A *favor*?" Leo's father couldn't believe the sheer arrogance of the words coming from Merrick's mouth. He shook his head with disgust and brought his worn boot down hard on Merrick's chest, who responded with a groan. "Are you even joking?"

Merrick replied with a supercilious gaze. "I'm dragging you and your people out of the past and into the twenty-first century whether you like it or not."

"We, the Chamorro people, have something you will never have, Merrick—pride."

"Pride will kill all of you. Talk about the old ways is cheap, and it doesn't put food on the table. I do."

"When my people did talk, you had them killed so that your hotel, your"—he searched for the right word—"your dream, would be kept secret from the world."

"A secret that would have benefited everybody involved, including *your* people."

"Blood money!"

"Blood money? If your people didn't get drunk every other night and run their mouths off at every third-rate bar in the Marianas, then maybe they would still be alive."

"You are a murderer, Tom Merrick."

"I'm a visionary. It's a gift those with *little* minds like yourself will never understand."

"I understand. I understand all too well," Leo's father asserted with a scowl. "I know the type of man you are. You need self-glorification at the expense of the innocent."

"No, you don't understand. You never will. You celebrate mediocrity," Merrick sneered. "I despise it."

"And now you kidnap children."

Merrick shrugged.

"You kidnapped *my boy*."

Merrick thrust out his chin with his nose in the air. "A means to an end."

Leo's father raised the rifle to Merrick's face.

Knowing there was nothing he could say or do to appease the father's rage, Merrick did what had to be done. Appearing as if he was still clutching the bullet wound with his hand and moaning from the pain, Merrick slipped his bloodied fingers around the pistol grip and fired through his jacket.

Leo's father staggered backward, blood erupting from his chest. Merrick winced from the recoil but fired again. The second explosion sprayed blood across his face as the boy's father fell face down onto the lawn. Merrick dragged himself beside the dying man, his face close to the islander's. "I did what I had to do, and I'll do it again."

The last thing Leo's father saw was Merrick's cold blue eyes sneering at him from his blood-covered face. As the life ebbed from his body, he felt comfort in knowing that his son was safe. "My fellow islanders… will never again… be under your evil." He never felt the gun barrel's cold steel placed against his head, and never heard the crack of gunfire.

CHAPTER 51

LEO'S LONG-TIME FRIEND and fellow fisherman Cadassi bolted up the hotel stairs toward the penthouse. With determination and his trusty AK-47 at the ready, he resolved to find the people responsible for Leo's kidnapping and exact justice the only way the islanders knew. He reached the top of the stairs and edged along the hallway. Finding the entrance to the penthouse, he swung the rifle into position and carefully turned the door's handle.

He checked the living room for signs of life, then carefully made his way toward the bedroom and edged the door ajar. A woman in skimpy black lingerie was hurriedly packing a suitcase. An evening dress lay on the bed, unusual for this time of the day, and he realized she must be Merrick's wife. As such, she was known to be complicit with Merrick, if not the mastermind of his heartless actions. Nevertheless, Cadassi hesitated at killing an unarmed woman.

He had come for the man who was responsible for Leo's abduction—a man who was somewhere in this hotel. Noticing the open slider leading to the balcony, Cadassi crept to the glass door, gun raised, ready to confront the man who had caused his family and friends so much pain and suffering—ready to kill the man who thought nothing of murdering a child. The time for retribution was now.

The balcony was empty.

"Where are you?" he whispered.

Cadassi retreated to the living room where, to his surprise, Merrick's wife was poised with a gun in her hand. A hail of 9mm bullets tore him to shreds. Samantha Merrick watched as the islander performed the macabre dance of death and fell backward onto the glass coffee table, shattering the custom-designed glass. With her smoking pistol in hand, Samantha moved to the balcony, clad in a La Perla lace thong and bra. She glanced at the body lying on her coffee table and lowered the Ruger LC9. "Such as waste," she murmured. "And I had that table hand-crafted, too." Rather than sympathy for the dead man or empathy for his family, a bolt of sexual desire surged through her body. She gasped at the pleasure the sensation brought her. She inhaled slowly to calm her desire and to allow her to quench her unnatural thirst for the death of another human being.

The Chinook pilot and his co-pilot had had enough. Merrick had lost his mind—of that they were sure. With crew dead from the sinkhole incident and with crazed islanders firing at them, the aviators were happy to see the back of the island.

The chopper hovered above Merrick's cabin cruiser. Three canvas slings connected the craft to the chopper. A rigger on the cruiser checked the slings one last time and tapped his helmet. "Ready to go," he shouted into his earpiece as the dual turbines roared overhead. The pilot needed no encouragement as armed men in tattered clothing were gathering on the lawn beside the river.

"About damn time!" The pilot pulled back on the collective, and the chopper lifted into the sky. The slings went taut as the distance between the crafts widened. The chopper lurched from the weight of the cabin cruiser but held in a steady hover.

The windscreen spider-webbed as a shower of bullets ripped into the tempered glass. The co-pilot jerked as the bullets tore into his body. Held in place by the safety harness, the co-pilot's body hung forward, his blood dripping across the gauges and shattered windscreen. Another volley of rounds peppered the cockpit, killing the pilot instantly. He slumped over the controls, driving the helicopter into a tailspin. Unprepared for the sudden direction change, the second rigger in the helicopter lost his grip on the handle above the doorway and fell from the open cabin, screaming on the way down. The Chinook, with the cabin cruiser attached, swept uncontrollably through the sky and over the lawns toward the hotel complex.

The islanders below scattered to safety, their work done.

Still recovering from the sexual surge from killing a man, Samantha Merrick looked on in disbelief as the helicopter thundered toward her. She knew her life was over, destroyed by Tom Merrick and *his* dreams. She sighed with contempt. *Screw you, Tom.*

The helicopter slammed into the penthouse suite and disappeared in a flash of intense heat. The penthouse walls and roof exploded from the impact, blasting a shower of flaming metal and fragmented masonry over the hotel grounds, creating a deadly deluge of wreckage and spot fires.

As the Chinook evaporated, two of the canvas slings supporting the dangling cabin cruiser snapped from the tension. Appearing like a pendulum on its last swing, the cabin cruiser arced through the air.

Klaus and Wolfgang were hurrying across the foyer, desperate to escape the death and destruction, when Wolfgang dropped one of his custom leather bags, spilling the contents across the floor. He dropped to his knees and scooped up the dozens of six by nines he had taken of Leo and stuffed them back into his private folder.

"Forget them!" Klaus demanded. No amount of money could compensate for his boss's behavior and sick lifestyle. When they got off this island hellhole, he would resign his position as Wolfgang's assistant and interpreter.

"Nein, nein!" Wolfgang screamed back, gathering the pictures from the floor.

"Hurry up, you fool!"

Wolfgang ignored his assistant's insubordination. He would reprimand him later. He slipped the last of the images back into the folder and dropped the folder into his bag.

They looked up in terror as the cabin cruiser crashed through the atrium's remaining metal framework, casting a deathly shadow over them. The craft smashed bow first into the foyer and crumpled on impact, splintering the hull and deck into a thousand pieces across the polished marble floor.

A chunk of burning metal crashed down onto the hotel's fuel supply, demolishing the only petrol bowser on the island. The fifty-thousand-gallon tank buried below the bowser and adjacent to the plateau's elevator shuddered from the impact while above, the fire raged out of control.

The final stressor for Simon was the explosion outside his beloved control room. Merrick paid well, but not well enough for this mayhem and death. The feed from the cameras mounted around the hotel had been cut, and a sea of white noise filled his monitors.

Simon scooped up his meager belongings—a hard drive, a handful of USB drives, and a pistol given to him by Van Sant. He shoved them into his backpack and headed for the nearest emergency exit. The end of the hallway opened to the atrium. He gasped at the sight before him. The remains of Merrick's cabin cruiser lay in the center of the foyer. "Shit. Mr. Merrick is gonna be *sooooo* pissed." Among the wreckage, Simon spotted a bloodied lifeless hand clutching—his eyes narrowed—*a strudel?* He shivered at the thought of the Germans' horrible deaths. A muffled boom snapped him back to reality. *Better them than me.*

Simon charged through the hotel's rear emergency exit, setting off the alarm. The klaxon's high-pitched whine hurt his ears, but he didn't care. Nobody cared now. Staccato gunfire reverberated through the hotel grounds. *If I get out of this, I'm going back to Detroit where it's safe!* With his heart pounding in his chest and the adrenaline racing through his veins, Simon sprinted across the manicured lawns and continued into the green wall of jungle bordering the hotel.

The remaining islanders stood at the rainforest's edge looking back at the destruction. With the hotel in ruins, their job was done. Many had died in the onslaught. Leo's father, who coordinated the attack, had disappeared and was presumed dead. Their quick search for him had been fruitless, so they would mourn him back in the safety of their island home. His wish was to rescue his son and destroy the hotel. In this they had succeeded. After one final glance at the smoking remains, they vanished into the jungle shadows.

Merrick watched with dead eyes, his mind void of sensation, as the raging inferno guttered what was left of the penthouse suite. The concrete floor buckled from the intense heat and cracked. The hotel's upper level succumbed to the forces of nature and collapsed onto the lower level in a cloud of black smoke and dust.

With his wife dead and his empire in ruins, Merrick slumped to the ground. He kept his emotions in check and shook away the dreaded thought of his bleak future. "Not like this," he told himself, "not like this." He collected his thoughts, and his rage at the recent events returned to the forefront of his mind. Wiping away the dust and grime from his dinner jacket and brushing his hair back as if preparing for an elegant gala with his beautiful wife, he turned to the loading ramp. With his bloodied hand, he withdrew his pistol, his face etched with grim retribution. *Blue!*

CHAPTER 52

LINCOLN STOOD GUARD as Van Sant punched the code into the keypad at the base of the ramp leading into the cavern. The doors opened to reveal Merrick's cache of arms. Van Sant slung his rifle over his shoulder and hurried to the thirty-foot GBU-43 bomb resting at the rear of the stockpile. Lincoln followed and gazed with dread at the Massive Ordinance Air Blast bomb. "Is that what I think it is?"

"Close," Van Sant replied, flipping open a small cover to reveal an LED display and keypad. He reached into his pocket and pulled out the business-sized card from the hotel safe with a dozen hand-written numbers scrawled across it. "High yield. All the destruction of a nuclear blast without the radiation."

Lincoln let out a deep breath. "Shit."

"Shit all right. And Merrick was selling the bomb to the high-est bidder."

"You seem like you have a shred of decency."

"Thanks," Van Sant replied with a touch of sarcasm.

"What I mean is, you're not like the rest of the goons on this island."

Van Sant continued tapping the keypad in silence.

"Why?" Lincoln pressed.

"Why what?"

"Why are you here?"

Van Sant wiped the sweat from his brow and continued punching keys.

"You have a Rangers tattoo on your arm," Lincoln persisted.

"So?"

"Did you leave your honor and integrity back in the US Army?"

With an icy stare, Van Sant glared at Lincoln, backed down, and returned to the keypad.

"What's a Southern boy—with that twang I figure Alabama—doing working for an English douchebag like Merrick?"

Van Sant took a deep breath before answering. "Listen, Blue—"

"Lincoln."

"Fine. Lincoln…" his voice trailed off as he considered his next words. "When you leave the forces, they don't tell you about the shitty pension plan. And I mean shitty. And they don't tell you that some employers don't hire ex-special forces because they don't want a highly-trained killer on the premises in case you go nuts with an assault rifle. And they don't tell you that you have to live with your brother because you can't pay the rent. To top it all off, they don't tell you about the sleep terrors every night. Got the picture?"

"Got it."

"I've done a lot of shitty things in my life that I'm not proud of, but I don't kill kids, and I don't kill innocent Americans." He turned back to the keypad.

"So you work for ruthless assholes."

"Ruthless assholes pay well. They have to because no one wants to work for a ruthless asshole."

The sharp pop of gunfire echoed throughout the cavern. Van Sant's back arched, his eyes wide with disbelief, as the bullet pierced his abdomen. Lincoln ducked behind the crates as bullets whizzed overhead. Van Sant passed the card to Lincoln and collapsed over the bomb.

"Yes, that's right. I might be an asshole, but I'm a rich asshole now." Merrick's voice sounded from the open doorway. One hand clutched a bloody shoulder, the other held a pistol. He staggered into the cavern, his expression one of merciless desperation mixed with hatred, his mind set on one goal. Merrick sighed at the sight of Van Sant slumped over the bomb and shook his head. "I trusted you, Van Sant. I trusted you with my business and my wife. You were part of my family." He winced and coughed up blood. "And this is how you repay me?"

Van Sant moaned. His eyes heavy, he sensed the cold of death descending over his body. "Money... only pays... for so much."

"True," Merrick said with an air of defeat. He fired again at Van Sant's hapless body. "So much for loyalty."

Van Sant groaned as the bullet tore into his chest. He managed a feeble grin at Lincoln huddled beside the crate. Lincoln followed Van Sant's line of vision to the LED display. Van Sant had managed to enter the disarmament code. With the codes locked in place, the bomb was now useless.

Cold blackness enveloped Van Sant. As his eyes closed for the last time, he felt the emotional turmoil of his actions for the last six months wash away. Relief flooded his body. The sensation of what awaited on the other side brought happiness to his conflicted convictions.

Lincoln returned fire as another volley tore above his head. Merrick dragged himself behind a crate and fell, the pain from his wounds coursing throughout his body. Lincoln fired again, shattering the rock wall above Merrick's head. Merrick roared in agony as sharp stones shredded his tanned face, disfiguring his once handsome appearance.

"It's over Merrick," Lincoln called. "The codes have been entered. The bomb's useless. Give it up."

Merrick pulled a small device from his pocket and tapped the keypad. "My wife is dead, and my business no longer exists. All because of you. Do you really think I'm just going to *give it up?*" He wiped the blood to keep it from seeping into his eyes.

Lincoln crawled around the stacked crates until he had Merrick's form in his line of sight. Merrick failed to see Lincoln until it was too late. With the cold steel of Lincoln's rifle pressed hard against his forehead, Merrick managed a laugh and slipped the device unseen into his pocket. "Do you wanna know what's really funny, Blue?"

Lincoln stood over the injured Merrick and kept the barrel against his head. Unflinching, he focused on the man who had caused him and his crew so much suffering. He ignored Merrick's question and contemplated pulling the trigger. To kill this man right here, right now would be so easy. No one would know. No one would care. Lincoln's finger tightened on the trigger as Merrick stared up at him, a smile across his bloodied face. Lincoln hesitated.

He couldn't kill a man in cold blood.

A deep boom reverberated throughout the cavern. Streams of dust and dirt trickled from the ceiling. Distracted for a moment, Lincoln looked toward the entrance where an avalanche of rocks fell beyond the open doorway.

Merrick sensed the hesitancy in Lincoln's resolve and took advantage of the distraction. "It's never over," he announced. With the last of his strength, Merrick grabbed the rifle and pulled Lincoln toward him. Taken by surprise, Lincoln stumbled forward. Merrick reached out and slammed him to the ground. Lincoln's head swirled with pain as Merrick's swift uppercut connected with his jaw. Lincoln seized Merrick by the collar and thrust him to the ground. Merrick scrambled for the rifle. As he grasped the weapon, his head snapped back from a punch to the face that sent him reeling backwards. Merrick staggered but regained his balance.

With the rifle in hand and a smug grin, Merrick leveled the barrel at Lincoln's chest. "I'm a busy man. Let's get this over with," he announced. "You've been a pain in the ass from the beginning.

I'm looking forward to killing you, Blue." Merrick's cold stare locked on Lincoln's tired and weary eyes.

The last four days have been hell, and this is how it's all going to end? "If this is it, then a dying man gets one last request, doesn't he?"

"You really are something, you know that?"

"Wouldn't by chance have a cigarette, would you?"

Merrick managed a short chuckle between the pain surges. "I don't smoke. Those things will kill you."

"I know," Lincoln said, glancing at the barrel aimed at his chest. "So they keep telling me."

Merrick considered the man standing before him—tough, resilient, a fast thinker. If only the situation were different. He could have used a man like Blue. "I'd ask you to join me in my venture, but I guess I know what the answer will be."

"You got that right," Lincoln answered with dead certainty.

Merrick took aim at Lincoln. "So be it."

"Tom Merrick," came a soft voice hidden in the shadows.

Startled, Merrick spun around to face the familiar voice. As the shot reverberated in the cavern, his chest exploded in a shower of blood, and he fell backward across the open crates. Gray emerged from the darkness beside the doorway. He joined Lincoln and sneered at Merrick, lying at his feet. "That's for my good friend Lockwood," he whispered.

Lincoln scooped up Merrick's gun and turned to Gray. "Are you ever a sight for sore eyes." Sighing, he gave the man an affectionate hug of gratitude. "Didn't expect to see you."

"As they say—one good turn deserves another." Lucius twirled the gun like a gunslinger from the Old West. "Honing my new-found skills."

CHAPTER 53

TOM MERRICK LAY among the rubble and broken pine crates. He laughed despite coughing up blood and feeling the life within him drifting away. Blood oozed between his fingers as he moved his hand over the multiple gunshot wounds. Soon he would be in a better place, comforted by his wife at his side. But not before playing his final hand.

Lincoln and Gray towered over Merrick, watching the man who had caused so much death and destruction slowly die. "It's over, Merrick. You and your evil plans are destroyed, and by the looks of those islanders, they'll make sure this doesn't happen again."

Merrick grimaced from the pain but managed a faint smile. "Always one up," he whispered before his head fell to the side. His dead eyes stared vacantly toward the darkened ceiling as the remote trigger dropped from his hand.

"What's this?" Gray picked up the small device.

A cold chill ran down Lincoln's spine. "Oh, no."

"That doesn't sound good."

"It's not. That's a remote trigger."

Gray dreaded the answer but asked, "For what?"

Lincoln didn't need to search the crates. He knew the type of man Merrick was, flamboyant and arrogant, and which armament a man with nothing to lose would choose to destroy his own empire.

He scrambled to the deadly device below Van Sant's body. The descending countdown displayed on the LED: 9.59—9.58—9.57...

Lincoln quickly re-entered Van Sant's codes and pressed enter. He sighed in the knowledge that the bomb was now disarmed. "That was close," he grinned at Gray, wiping the sweat from his face. He paused at Gray's uneasy stare and followed his gaze to the LED timer. The countdown continued.

"Give me a bloody break," Lincoln groaned.

"What?"

"Merrick's overridden the codes. The bomb's non-nuclear, but, without a bottle of sunblock fifteen million plus, we're gonna have a really bad day. Gotta go—fast!" Lincoln grabbed Gray's arm and led him to the doorway as another boom shook the cavern. This time the ground beneath their feet shuddered. The two men stumbled as a larger explosion rocked the ceiling and an avalanche of rock crashed onto the concrete ramp beyond the doors, filling the cavern with a cloud of choking dust. They watched in horror as more boulders tumbled into view, blocking the doorway with an impenetrable wall of rock and rubble.

"Sounds like the hotel's tearing itself apart." Lincoln clawed at the rubble only to have more loose rocks take its place. "Damn it," he groaned. "This is hopeless."

Gray assisted with the clean-up but to no avail. He barely managed to avoid the rocks as more boulders tumbled from the ceiling.

Dog-tired from the last four days, Lincoln stared at the obstructed escape route that sealed their fate. He rested, using the rifle as support, as the energy drained from his fatigued body. "Give me a break," he whispered to himself, wiping the sweat from his face.

For the first time since escaping Neptune Island, Lincoln felt consumed with fatigue. Barely staying alive through four torturous days of non-stop, adrenaline-fueled, life-and-death situations, Lincoln had finally reached his limit. He knew that with only minutes to live and no way out of the cavern, his time on Earth would soon be at an end. He slumped down next to Van Sant's inert body, reached into the dead man's jacket, and pulled out a pack of Lucky Strikes. Gray declined the offer, so Lincoln lit up and inhaled deeply, allowing the nicotine to take hold one last time.

"Don't give up," Gray pleaded, desperately searching for a way out. "What about the tunnel leading to the sinkhole? Maybe we can climb our way up to the surface."

"Doc, that ledge is about two stories below the hotel level, and the rock face is slippery as hell. I don't know about you, but I don't fancy falling to my death. If I have to die, I can't think of a better way than sitting on a nuclear bomb, can you?" Gray sighed and conceded that maybe it was time to leave this Earth. Lincoln managed a half smile at the recollection of Slim Pickens in Stanley Kubrick's *Dr. Strangelove* riding the atomic bomb down to his spectacular death.

Gray sat beside Lincoln and looked around the darkened cave at what would become his final resting place. With pine crates strewn across the floor and the faint echo of dripping water reaching their ears, the two men faced each other, resigned. Lincoln took another drag of the cigarette and shot a look around. "Doc, I'm glad you came to rescue me. I wish I could return the favor."

Gray smile feebly and wrapped his arm around Lincoln's shoulder. "My boy, I may have to leave this world, but I wish I could go out with a bang rather than a whimper."

"Oh, we're definitely going out with a bang. I figure the explosion will take half the plateau with it"—Lincoln glanced at the timer—"in eight minutes and fifteen seconds."

"Well, if I have only eight minutes to live, then screw it. I think I will have one of those cigarettes."

Lincoln lit Gray's cigarette and the doctor promptly coughed on the smoke. Lincoln chuckled. "Maybe you shouldn't, Doc?"

"I don't care," he replied with an air of self-assurance, spluttering from another drag.

Lincoln nodded to the cigarette in his hand. "At least I can say these things didn't kill me."

As Gray became accustomed to inhaling and exhaling, the coughing stopped, but he still looked green around the gills. "You're right, you know."

"About what?"

"The slippery sinkhole walls. Very dangerous. I should know."

"What makes you say that?"

"One of Merrick's men slipped over the sinkhole's edge. Being the island's chief medical doctor, I was given the task of retrieving the body from the bottom of the sinkhole."

"What's it like down there?" Lincoln asked with genuine curiosity.

"What's it like to dredge a broken body from ten feet of water while a deafening roar from a waterfall drowns out any contact with another human being? I'd say it was one shitty place to be and a job I'd rather not do again."

"Waterfall? You mean the one running beside the hotel?"

Gray nodded. "Like I said, caverns and tunnels are all through the plateau. A tunnel at the bottom of the sinkhole must lead directly to the base of the waterfall."

A nagging memory gnawed at Lincoln's brain. "That's it!" He threw the cigarette away and bolted upright with a new lease on life. He scrambled over the crates, lifting lids and tossing them aside.

Gray watched Lincoln's erratic behavior until he had to indulge his curiosity. "My boy, what are you doing?"

Lincoln's search was over. He'd found the crate he was looking for and flung open the lid. Relieved at the sight before him, Lincoln's ear-to-ear grin was the biggest smile Gray had ever seen. "What is it?"

Lincoln pulled the bag from the crate and held it up for Gray to see.

"A backpack?" Gray asked, incredulously.

Lincoln opened the backpack and allowed the pack tray to fall out. "Not just any backpack."

Gray's eyes widened at the realization of what Lincoln was attempting.

"We don't go up to get out of here, Doc. We go down."

CHAPTER 54

BULLETS THUDDED INTO the dock's wood paneling as Mich assisted Christina from the elevator, with Enheim and Katya close behind. Joined by Rousseau, Becca, and Roland, they hastily took shelter against the rock face, out of sight of the sniper above.

Roland ducked his head out of the shadows and peered skyward. "Vhere is Lincoln and the Doctor?"

"Linc said he would meet us here," Enheim said, his arm firmly around Katya's shoulder, "but the old man disappeared."

Positioned high above at the cliff's edge, one of Merrick's men had a clear line of sight to the jetty. Before Roland could enquire further into Gray's whereabouts, Merrick's man fired again. Wood splinters shot across the quay as Roland hid from the gunman's view.

Enheim cocked his head toward the tramp steamer sitting idle beside the dock. "Why aren't we on the ship yet?"

"The captain won't allow us to board," Mich answered.

"We've got guns. Why didn't you *convince* him?"

"He has more guns."

Enheim slapped the nearest docking post with anger. "Just our luck!"

Another round of bullets thudded into the wooden slats at their feet. Roland turned to the others. "Ideas, anyone?"

Mich calculated the distance from the dock to the cliff's

precipice—too far for an accurate shot. He raised the M4 he'd taken from a dead guard. "I could try, but…"

Doubled over from a cracked rib, Christina gasped from pain as she withdrew an arrow from the quiver strapped to her back. She was slipping the arrow into the flight slot in the barrel when Katya lowered her hand onto the weapon and gently edged it back to Christina's side, indicating that she would take care of the current danger.

The time for Katya to make a stand, to show the world she could have been a gold medal winner, was now. All those long hours of training for the Olympic biathlon, which should have accumulated to the pinnacle of her sporting career, would not be for naught. She stepped forward and swapped her pistol for Roland's M4 assault rifle saying, "I can do this." She checked that the magazine was still loaded, crept out of the crawlspace, and sidled up to one of the jetty's support posts, her frame hidden from the gunman but still commanding a clear line of sight. She knelt, took deliberate aim so as not to rush the shot, lined up the sights on the barrel, and gently squeezed the trigger.

The single crack of a gunshot echoed across the lagoon. The gunman's head snapped back while he dropped to his knees and fell from the plateau's edge. His body somersaulted down the cliff face and crashed with a sickening thud through the jetty's rotted wood and into the lagoon. The group greeted her with big smiles and patted her on the back. "Good shot, Sis," Roland said, kissing her on the cheek.

"That's my girl." Enheim beamed with pride while giving her a big hug. "I don't give a shit what those friggin' Olympic assholes say. You're better than a gold medal winner in our eyes."

Napoleon contributed to the celebration with a congratulatory *woof.*

The hotel's fuel tank ignited, obliterating the elevator's top level. A thunderclap echoed through the air followed by a deep rumbling that shook the plateau. The water beneath the jetty surged from the booming vibration. A flock of birds scattered over the jungle canopy as a billowing ball of flame erupted from the plateau's edge and rocketed upward.

The crew peered skyward.

Roland and Mich glanced at one another as the still air enveloped them in silence. "We are safe, you know," Roland said with a half grin to instill a sense of calm in the others while hiding the fear rising within himself.

Mich squinted at the cliff's rock face beside the explosion. A small avalanche of rock and dust was rolling down the cliff. He wasn't certain, but he could have sworn he saw the elevator sway. *Could it have been a trick of the afternoon sun?* The anxiety of the unknown washed over him. "Did anybody see that?" he asked quietly, not wanting to trigger another avalanche with his voice.

Becca's eyes widened in disbelief, and Rousseau stepped back, a sense of dread washing over his hulking frame. Roland wiped the sweat from his face and paused, still unsure of what he thought he'd seen.

The steel mounts and support girders locking the elevator in place against the cliff face groaned under the outside forces of stressed steel and burning metal.

"This is not good," Mich whispered.

The elevator broke away from the cliff face and arced across the sky in a downward fall. In a cacophony of screeching metal, the lift smashed through the jetty and across the supply ship's top deck. Sparks from the elevator's framework struck the ship igniting used oil drums that littered the forward section, and causing spot fires to flare across the battered deck.

Nervously licking his lips from their narrow escape, Rousseau closed his eyes and made the sign of the cross.

Becca shook her head in disbelief. With eyes frozen open from nearly being crushed to death, she stared at the wreckage less than a dozen yards away.

"Ain't karma a bitch!" Enheim called with grin of satisfaction to the captain still on the bridge wing.

With a clenched jaw and icy stare, Sayoc glared at Enheim, then quickly refocused his attention on the fire sweeping across the upper deck. At the base of the superstructure, deckhands with Uzis replaced their weapons with fire extinguishers and scurried about the deck, spraying safety foam over the raging inferno.

In an attempt to encourage the others, Roland said, "We could be lying under that mess. It looks like our luck has turned for the better, you know." After all they had experienced since crash-landing on the island, the others met his upbeat response with looks of skepticism.

"How will darlink Lincoln get down here now?" Katya lamented, expressing what the others were thinking.

Mich looked over the elevator ruins lying across the shattered jetty, and then peered up the sheer precipice to the plateau. "Monk's a resourceful sonofabitch. He'll find a way. He always does," he assured the group, but behind his back he crossed his fingers.

Rousseau surveyed the carnage before them and dipped his hand into his pocket to rub Maurice the unicorn for comfort. "Mr. Pom?"

"Rousseau, we have been through several life-threatening circumstances in the last week. Please, call me Roland."

Rousseau decided he was right. Perhaps it was time to be less formal toward his boss and treat him as a friend—a good friend. "Roland?"

"Yes Rousseau."

"I'm just thinking, when this is all over, if we get back to civilization, maybe we could leave the Mariana islands and start a new business in France. Sure, the unions will break your back, but it would be...a less hazardous work environment. You understand?"

"Yes, I understand." Roland pushed his glasses up to the bridge of his nose and considered the venture. "Not a bad idea," he answered, dusting his turtleneck.

Following an almighty crack, a deep boom reverberated down to the lagoon. A chunk of rock the size of a house split from the cliff. The boulder dropped through the cloud of dust clinging to the cliff face and hurtled toward the crew.

Exhausted and supported by Enheim and Katya, Christina shook her head. "Just our luck."

Mich groaned. He grabbed the shocked Becca and leaped into the lagoon followed by the others.

The giant boulder bounced off an outcrop of rock halfway down the cliff, tumbled away from the granite wall and crashed through the supply ship's upper deck and elevator wreckage, splitting the vessel in half. The rock's mass punched through the hull, cracked the ship's back, and lifted the bow and stern from the water. A geyser spouted high into the air from the ship's midsection as the boulder sank to the bottom of the lagoon. Captain Sayoc and his crew didn't stand a chance as the diesel engine exploded, blasting apart what remained of the stricken vessel.

"Oh, come on!" Mich whined at their misfortune and at the surge of water heading their way. He and the team braced themselves as a wave washed their hapless bodies toward the base of the falls.

"Give us a break," Mich whispered, his thought cut short as the pounding water drove their bodies under the cascading veil of water and deep below the lagoon's surface.

CHAPTER 55

THE WATERFALL'S DEAFENING roar hurt Becca's ears as she surfaced behind the curtain of water. She gulped mouthfuls of air as the others emerged from the choppy water with Enheim close behind holding Napoleon high above his head.

Just above water level, a narrow ledge a yard wide spanned the width of the bedrock, offering a lifeline to their predicament. They climbed the wet rock and huddled together on the ledge, trying to hear their own thoughts over the thundering crash of water reverberating off the rock face. They sighed as floating wreckage from the supply ship drifted under the curtain of water and surfaced beside them, a grim reminder of their last hope of getting off the island.

Roland studied the glistening rock face and spotted the entrance to a cave at the far end of the ledge. "Cavern," he shouted to the others above the roar of the falls.

With water from above flowing down his face and body, Enheim glanced at the hole in the rock wall. "That's great. If we ever get out of here, we can all go spelunking. Maybe have a picnic lunch while we're there." His tone dripped with sarcasm.

Roland reluctantly agreed. In their quandary, apart from keeping them dry, the cavern would serve no useful purpose. "It doesn't happen very often, but... you're right, you know. Lincoln von't see us behind the waterfall." He reached into his pocket and pulled out his Gitanes. He flipped open the cover and sighed as a stream of water poured from the packet. Placing the wet packet back into his pocket, he caught a glimpse of a familiar form through the veil of water. The tell-tale shape of the C-47's tail and rear cabin protruded above the lagoon's surface directly under the falls, a watery resting place for the plane he and Rousseau had spent hundreds of hours repairing and restoring over the last few years. Roland grinned. "People, ve just got lucky, you know."

While Roland searched the flooded plane, Rousseau braced himself in waist high water in the C-47's hatchway with a torrent of water crushing down from above. Rousseau was wiping the water from his eyes when Roland emerged from the cargo compartment with a plastic valise. He gave Rousseau a thumbs up and dragged the grey bag through the water to the hatch. Roland marveled at the big Frenchman's brute strength as he reached for the seventy-pound bag and lifted it through the doorway.

The crew helped Roland from the churning water, with Rousseau surfacing behind him. As they all huddled on the ledge, Roland studied the instructions on the package containing the self-inflating life raft. Complete with neoprene skin, self-erecting canopy, twin buoyancy tubes, bellows, and a host of other features, the Roaring Forties Aviation Life Raft was state-of-the–art in every way. "Simple enough, you know," Roland shouted over the thundering falls.

Still in shock from the exploding ship and collapsing cliff face, Becca pulled her wet hair back from her face and looked over the fine print. "The instructions say to use only in an emergency."

"Maybe one will come up," Mich said, rolling his eyes, his expression deadpan.

Becca glared at Mich, then realized what she had said. Overwhelmed by the events of the last few days, she couldn't help but chuckle at her own comment. They laughed together in a reflex response to their grim situation.

"Ve can't inflate the raft here," Roland said after calculating the time needed to go under the falls and break the surface on the lagoon side. "Ve'll never get it through the vater," he explained, indicating the cascade beside them. "So ve need to inflate the raft in the lagoon. This means I need everyone's help, you know. The only way to do this is to go back under the vater, under the falls, and surface on the other side. Can we do this?"

They understood that going under the falls meant churning water forcing their bodies down, pushing them toward the bottom of the lagoon, with oxygen running low. None of them wanted to die this way.

"No problem, Mr. Pom." Rousseau shrugged nervously, playing with the unicorn in his pocket.

With a worried look, Enheim turned to Katya and indicated Napoleon. The little dog was licking the moist air from his face and panting. Katya cupped Napoleon's head in her hands and rubbed her face against his in a heartfelt sign of compassion. "My baby," she fretted, knowing the dog would panic from being under water for any length of time.

Enheim wrapped his arm around Katya and held the three of them together. "We can do this," he announced with confidence. "Who are we?" he repeated the phrase he had said a dozen times before when the situation had turned bad.

"We are the Enheims," Katya whispered.

"I didn't hear you," Enheim said with a smile, attempting to cheer up his wife and distract her from the thought of losing their Napums.

"We are the Enheims," she answered louder, breaking a faint smile.

"That's right. And Enheims can do anything they put their mind to." He kissed Katya on the cheek and rubbed the fur under Napoleon's chin.

"What about Lincoln and Dr. Gray?" Christina asked while

tightening the crossbow's wrist strap to try to hide her concern for Lincoln's whereabouts.

"They'll find us. Monk is good like that," Mich assured her.

"Ve take a few minutes to get our breath, and then ve go. Okay?"

With misgivings, they nodded.

CHAPTER 56

MAKING THEIR WAY as fast as they could over the uneven ground and jutting rocks, Lincoln and Gray raced through the tunnel that connected to the sinkhole. They found themselves perched on the narrow ledge overlooking the sinkhole. Lincoln secured the safety harness around his torso and fastened the last strap as tightly as possible. One hundred and eighty feet below, at the base of the sinkhole, a pool of water glistened from a shaft of light penetrating from above and reflecting across the wet granite wall.

Lincoln took a deep breath and thought of the consequences if his last-minute plan failed. Hitting the water at this height would be akin to hitting concrete, a thought he pushed to the back of his mind. He understood that the chute wouldn't deploy fast enough at this low height, but he hoped it would slow their descent. Many of the life and death situations on Neptune Island had involved heights—his Kryptonite. Lincoln dealt with issues the only way he knew how—head on. While he had to an extent overcome his fears, he preferred not to be standing on a narrow ledge overlooking a black abyss, knowing that in the next few seconds he would have to leap into the unknown, possibly to his death.

Gray sensed Lincoln's reluctance as he watched the young man beside him stare into the blackness. He had been a passenger for the last four days, a burden on this young man who had saved his life many times. It was his turn to offer support and motivation. "My boy, you've kept us both alive until now. For that I owe you my gratitude and my life. I trust your instincts. You should, too."

Lincoln caught Gray's trusting eyes and understood that the old man was right. *Trust your instincts. Don't let your fear take control.* He nodded to Gray and glanced at his watch—4:16... 4:15... 4:14— and tightened the harness one more time like a tandem jump but with both skydivers facing one another. Gray grinned and secured his arm through the harness straps attached to Lincoln's torso. "Let's do this."

Lincoln peered down at the gaping abyss. "Why not?" He stepped off the ledge and yanked the ripcord. The pilot chute deployed, pulling the sleeve and canopy from the pack tray. The canopy pulled away from the sleeve and inflated, first the top and then the skirts.

The shining rock wall passed in a blur. Locked together, Lincoln and Gray plummeted down the shaft at thirty feet per second toward the pool below. The chute caught air and mushroomed out slowing their descent, but not fast enough. The glistening water below grew larger by the second. Lincoln and Gray hit the water hard—not hard enough to kill, but with enough speed to knock the wind out of the two exhausted men.

The cool water was reassuring. Gray unhooked his arm from Lincoln's chest harness and swam toward the surface. Emerging from the pool, he took in a big gulp of oxygen as Lincoln broke the surface beside him.

"Did you know that some people do this for an adrenaline rush?" Gray laughed, spluttering water, happy to be alive.

"Good luck to them," was all Lincoln could reply, sucking in a deep breath and exhaling with relief. He gazed at the wall of the surrounding sinkhole towering above them. Twenty feet from the surface he could distinguish the ledge jutting away from the granite wall, the ledge he and Gray had leaped off. *What a rush.* He freed himself from the parachute harness and was glancing about when he spotted his Neptune cap floating nearby. "My lucky day," he exclaimed, plucking the cap from the water.

Gray was right. Eroded over time by high moisture level and softer rock within the strata, a gap opened into sinkhole's rock wall. The thundering roar of a waterfall echoed down the channel toward them, enveloping the two men. Lincoln estimated the tunnel's length to be no more than fifty feet. "Some people are just damned crazy," he said, making his way through the water toward the passageway. He glanced at his watch: 2:34—2:33.

"You got that right," Gray returned, following Lincoln closely.

Deafened by the roar of falls, Lincoln and Gray emerged from the tunnel's end at the base of the plateau. Water thundered down and crashed into the lagoon, blocking their escape route. Both men had a hard time seeing anything through the cloud of water vapor obfuscating the tunnel's exit. Gray gestured that they go under the falls. "Looks like we're going for a swim," he shouted above the din.

Lincoln was about to agree when, just inside the falls, he spotted the tip of the Dakota's tail protruding from the water. Swallowed by the lagoon, the fuselage and wings had met a watery grave and had disappeared into the deeper water, but the broken tail section remained just above the water's surface, less than a few yards away. A recent event flashed through his mind, a recollection from a few days past of Roland's fastidiousness and compulsion for preparedness. Lincoln had an idea—a crazy idea that just might save their lives. *Shit. We might just make it. Come on, Lady Luck. Don't fail me now.* "Wait here," he called to Gray, and dove into the churning water.

"Okay," Gray whispered nervously. He peered around the rock ledge at the cascading water thundering before him. "But for what?"

CHAPTER 57

THE JET SKI shot through the cascade's curtain of white water and bounced along the lagoon's surface away from the plateau. Riding tandem, Gray looked back at the plateau's towering rock face. "Looks like we finally got away from Merrick," he shouted to Lincoln over the droning engine. Lincoln checked his watch: 0.05—0.04—0.03. They were still in the plateau's shadow, so he opened the jet ski's throttle and headed straight for a tributary on the other side of the lagoon. "Not yet," he yelled.

The plateau disappeared in a flash of blinding white light. Gray shielded his eyes as a deep rumble echoed around them, shattering the tranquil setting, and scattering a flock of birds into the sky. Silence filled the air, followed by a ground-shaking thunderclap that coursed over the terrain.

The pressure-wave slammed into the hotel grounds, obliterating everything in its deadly path and hurling the debris of Merrick's dream across the island. What remained of the hotel swayed as the earth beneath shifted with the splintered bedrock. The landscape bulged upward then collapsed on itself, sending a plume of dust high into the air. A chunk of earth slid from the plateau's edge, dragging the hotel grounds and the waterfall's crest to a cataclysmic end.

Gray held on tight as Lincoln steered the jet ski away from the plateau and down the waterway.

Lincoln looked back as a wall of black churning dust and rock swept over the treetops and along the river toward them. He opened the throttle all the way and managed to extend the gap between the small watercraft and the collapsing plateau. The jet ski skimmed across the water, its engine whining in protest.

Simon, his legs aching and his lungs screaming for oxygen, rested in a small clearing watching in horror as the giant fireball less than a mile away billowed into the sky. He sucked in a lungful of air. *I'm not getting paid enough for this shit.* He leaned on his haunches and took in his surroundings.

His blood ran cold at the sight of the alpha rat poised on a boulder on the other side of the clearing, its fierce red eyes staring back at him, blood dripping from its jaws. Simon's eyes widened in terror as more giant rats waited patiently behind the alpha. Frozen with fear, Simon felt warm urine trickle down his leg as the hoard faced him with salivating jaws, ready for a feed.

The alpha's nose twitched, sniffing the air. Seconds later the other rodents turned away from Simon and did the same. Simon felt a shred of hope as the hoard ignored him. Regaining an ounce of courage, he fumbled in his backpack, pulled out the pistol and leveled the barrel at the alpha.

The rats glared at Simon, then sniffed the air and looked above his head. Simon couldn't comprehend why the rodents were behaving this way. He quickly glanced behind, not wanting to take his eyes off the rats for long.

Simon screamed as a giant claw cut into his midriff and lifted him high into the air. The ground shook beneath them followed by a thunderous clap in the sky. The giant decapod and the rodents turned in the direction of the disturbance. Through his pain, Simon caught sight of the oncoming holocaust in his peripheral vision. "Just my luck," he uttered in defeat.

Like an unstoppable juggernaut, the pressure wave raced through the jungle consuming everything in its path. Super-heated gases boiled the trees instantly, their trunks exploding from the extreme heat. The ground beneath the rain forest churned from the vacuum blast, creating a cloud of fiery foliage and debris at the forefront of the wave.

The alpha looked toward the approaching wall of fire with lips taut, fangs bared. A sea of destruction reflected in the creature's hate-filled eyes as the blast's wave tore across the clearing, vaporizing everything in its path.

The wave expanded outward across the southern face of the island. Like a blossoming wall of fiery death, the surge rolled over the jungle terrain and expanded over the landscape, leaving a wake of smoking ruin and scorched earth before burning itself out.

Mich and the crew forgot about the rotted branch snagging the life raft to the shoreline and gazed skyward toward the plateau, transfixed by the cloud of mushrooming fire and the boom of thunder rolling above them.

Enheim nervously stroked Napoleon under the chin. "Someone please tell me that's not what I think it is."

"Holy shit-balls," Mich whispered.

"I hope Lincoln is all right, you know," Roland said, shielding his eyes from the blast.

Mich stared back at the plateau with concern. *Come on Monk. Where the hell are you?*

As if reading his mind, Becca steadied herself beside Mich in the raft and held his hand in understanding and true friendship.

Rolling with the Pacific swell, the fleet of dilapidated fishing boats chugged away from the island. Leo stood, holding back his tears, at the stern of the trailing craft, gazing back toward the mushroom cloud rising high in the sky above the island. He understood that his father was dead, that he had given his life to save him. Leo's uncle approached and rested his arm around the boy's shoulder.

Lincoln banked hard around the river bend. The life raft came into view just a few yards ahead, a yellow donut-shaped craft that without warning materialized across his path. Lincoln braked and swerved, losing forward control as the front of the jet ski nosedived into the water. Gray lost his grip and fell as Lincoln tumbled over the handlebars and landed among the floating branches. The jet ski disappeared below the waves. Moments later, Gray surfaced, coughing water. Lincoln failed to appear.

Mich dove into the water first, followed by Roland and Enheim. Rousseau was about to jump in when Katya gripped his arm. "You're a brave man, but enough people are in the water."

The big Frenchman nodded. He eased back into the raft but kept an eye on the proceedings. Gray's arms flailed about as he struggled to keep his head above water. Rousseau, Christina, and Katya reached over the side and lifted him into the raft.

Gray coughed up water while giving them a thumbs up. Napoleon responded with a soft bark from Katya's arms where she held him close to her chest.

The saltwater stung his eyes as Mich probed the murky tributary for Lincoln. Enheim and Roland searched beside him. Seconds ticked into a minute. Mich's lungs craved oxygen. Just when he thought he had to come up for air, through the clouds of silt and churning water a lifeless form appeared. Mich paddled as hard as he could to Lincoln's inert body. Lincoln's head slumped to the side as Mich wrapped his arm around his torso. With his remaining strength, he pushed upward toward the surface. "He's got him!" Enheim shouted. Rousseau and Gray lifted Lincoln into the raft.

CHAPTER 58

KNOWING NOTHING ABOUT resuscitation, Enheim felt helpless. "What do we do?" he asked, his voice betraying his anxiety at seeing Lincoln lying motionless.

Mich felt for a pulse. With gentle force he pressed down three times on Lincoln's ribcage.

"I know mouth-to-mouth," Becca offered. She started toward Lincoln, but Christina blocked her path. Still nursing sore ribs, Christina clambered to Lincoln's side and without hesitation, gave him mouth-to-mouth resuscitation. Timing the thrusts, Mich continued to push down on Lincoln's ribcage, massaging the chest and revitalizing his heartbeat. Katya hugged Enheim and Napoleon as they watched Christina breathe oxygen into Lincoln's lungs while Mich pounded his chest. Rousseau held Roland's hand for comfort, his other hand firmly clasped around Maurice. Silently Rousseau made the sign of the cross and prayed for Lincoln's recovery.

Lincoln's chest expanded as he took a deep breath and coughed up water. Christina moved aside to give Lincoln space, as did Mich. Slowly Lincoln opened his heavy eyes to the joy and cheers of everyone on the raft.

"Just rest," Christina's voice was firm but gentle.

Lincoln didn't need to be told twice. He adjusted his head against the soft neoprene lining. A throbbing headache coursed through his brain, and his muscles ached from days of physical exertion, but he was happy to be alive. After a few minutes Lincoln managed a weak smile.

Mich leaned over Lincoln with a deadpan expression. "To bring you back from the dead, we had to perform mouth-to-mouth resuscitation."

Concerned, Lincoln indicated for Mich to come closer. When Mich was within inches, Lincoln whispered, "You didn't... you know... kiss me in front of everyone, did you?"

"Oh, yeah. I had to," he teased. "I gave you a big, open-mouthed kiss, and everybody saw it." Lincoln's eyes widened with angst.

"It's my turn next," Roland said playfully, then added, "A gay man can hope, you know."

Lincoln was unsure how to react. His brow furrowed as he tried to determine what had taken place while he was unconscious. Mich laughed. "Relax, you big baby! You can thank her"—he nodded toward Christina—"for bringing you back to life." Reaching behind Roland, he produced Lincoln's black baseball cap from Neptune Island. He slipped it over Lincoln's head and grinned. "I did have the pleasure of pounding your chest with my fists, though." In jest he pulled the brim down over Lincoln's face.

Lincoln turned his attention to Christina who flashed him an indifferent smile. Despite his aching head and drained physical strength, he gave her a cheeky wink. "Our first date."

Christina rolled her eyes struggling not to smile and looked away. She tried to focus on more important matters, such as survival, but she couldn't resist Lincoln's boyish charm. With her back to the group, she gazed toward the thinning jungle along the riverbanks and imagined Lincoln and herself on a real date.

Enheim glanced at the cloud of dust slowly dissipating across the basin's green canopy. "Monk, I hate to bring this up now, but that blast. Was it a nu—"

"No," Gray interjected, giving Lincoln time to recover and rest. "Non-nuclear. No radiation. Just a big explosion."

Relieved sighs echoed on the life raft. "That's good to hear," Enheim said. "I was dreading taking a leak in a couple of weeks and having bits fall off."

"I don't understand," Becca said, frowning.

"Don't understand what?" Lincoln asked quietly, trying to keep his throbbing headache to a minimum.

"We contacted the rescue services on Saipan hours ago. They should have been here by now."

"How did you do that?"

"Rousseau had a phone, and my now-dead cameraman had a working satellite sleeve. Mich put two and two together"—she gave him an admiring glance—"and we called them."

"Where's the phone now?"

"Those goons at the hotel confiscated it."

Lincoln tried to rub away the pain coursing through his head. "Well, it's my guess that Merrick must have paid off the right people on Saipan." Everyone nodded.

In a futile attempt at retribution, Becca slapped the life raft's rubber side. "Sonofabitch."

The life raft emerged from the dust cloud. The jungle had tapered away to small vegetation along the riverbanks, and soon the ocean's crashing waves echoed around them. Drifting through the basin and over breaking waves rolling along the shoreline, the raft without warning became caught in a riptide that pulled the tiny seafaring vessel out to the open ocean.

Lincoln managed to sit upright and rest against the raft's soft curve to the soothing, gentle thud of lapping water against the side of the raft. A seagull circled above, its soft squawking a welcome comfort from the last four days of man-made mayhem. Lincoln breathed in the cool salt air and tasted the sweet smell of freedom.

With her crossbow by her side, Christina slept opposite Lincoln, her back resting against Katya. Katya huddled beside the snoring Enheim with Napoleon between them, safe and sound. Roland and Rousseau sat on Lincoln's right, also resting, while Gray and Becca took in some light reading and studied the life raft's user manual. Mich sat beside Lincoln, staring out across the water. He pulled his hair back in a ponytail and got comfortable against the inflated tubing.

A thought nagged at Lincoln, an itch he couldn't scratch. The memory concerned Merrick's final event—the arena. He recalled the Chinook helicopter with the creatures flying in from an unknown destination from the north, also the source of the tributary leading to the ocean. The life raft was drifting with the current—north. It could be nothing—a coincidence, or a figment of his fatigued imagination—but then again…

He considered telling the others of the new potential danger, but one look at the exhausted people in the raft reminded him that they, too, had been through hell over the last four days, and a few hours reprieve was just what the doctor ordered. He decided against telling them—for now.

At the moment, they were safe.

Mich peered around at the multi-colored jumpsuits worn by Lincoln, Christina, and Gray. "I forgot to ask earlier. What's with the outfits? Auditioning for henchmen rolls in the next Bond film?"

"It's a long story." Lincoln closed his eyes, enjoying the sounds of nature.

Mich glanced at the endless ocean surrounding them. "I think we've got time."

As the sun dipped over the horizon, the warmth of the day's heat began fading fast. The red sky darkened, and soon night would wash over the seascape.

The lifeboat bobbed like a yellow cork on an undulating sheet of blue silk. Rolling over the swells and drawn by the local currents, the raft drifted toward the ominous island perched on the northern horizon. Behind the small craft, a growing band of fog stretched from one end of the horizon to the other, billowing across the ocean and consuming the skyline with a veil of gray uncertainty.

"Mamma Mia, here I go again…" Lincoln murmured. He drew the assault rifle closer.

AUTHOR'S NOTES

In this novel you will find instances where truth is stranger than fiction.

For example, if you find yourself being crushed by a giant boa constrictor, biting it on the back—preferably near the head or tail—is one way to get the snake to release you. However, most experts agree that the best way to stop the snake from crushing you is to avoid the snake in the first place. Unfortunately, our hero Lincoln didn't have that choice.

The GBU-43/B Massive Ordinance Air Blast (MOAB), affectionately known by the military as "the mother of all bombs," is real. This bomb *does* have the destructive yield of eleven tons of TNT and the blast radius of one mile. The GBU has the power of a nuclear detonation but none of the after-effects of conventional nuclear weapons. Scary stuff.

As an avid reader and self-proclaimed film junky, my imagination and inspiration turned to certain actors for help in bringing the characters in *Jungle Games* to life:

- Chris Pratt *(Guardians of the Galaxy; Jurassic World)* was in mind for Lincoln Monk;
- Gerard Butler's rugged yet handsome appearance *(300, Olympus Has Fallen)* was perfect for Tom Merrick;
- Matthew McConaughey *(Interstellar, Sahara)* was the inspiration for Peter Van Sant;
- Jason Statham *(The Expendables, The Meg)* was always Marcus Enheim;
- David Hyde Pierce (Niles Crane on TV's *Frasier*) was a natural for Roland Pom;
- John Cho (Mr. Sulu on *Star Trek*) was Michio Lee;
- Maggie Q *(Nikita* the series, *Die Hard 4)* was Christina;
- Olga Kurylenko *(Quantum of Solace, Hitman)* was ideal for Katya Enheim;
- Audrey Hepburn *(Breakfast at Tiffany's)* was in mind for Samantha Merrick;
- Ben Kingsley*(Gandhi, Iron Man 3)* was Lucius Gray;
- A young Jean Reno *(Godzilla* [1998], *Leon)* was perfect for Rousseau;
- Kristin Scott Thomas's presence and sophistication *(The English Patient)* was ideal for Joanna;
- Christopher Barrie *(Red Dwarf, Lara Croft: Tomb Raider* [2001]) was in mind for Baxter.

Thank you for reading *Jungle Games*. I hope you've had as much fun reading the novel as I had writing it. I love feedback, so please leave a review—and if you wish to contact me: TonyReedAuthor@gmail.com

Made in the USA
Las Vegas, NV
19 November 2020